The Good Counselor

THE GOOD COUNSELOR

A NOVEL BY
RACHEL ALEXANDER

Content Warning

The following book is meant for an adult audience and contains explicit sexual content, graphic language, drug use, and violence. Readers of this book should be 18 years of age or have reached adulthood as defined by the laws of their respective locale. Please store this book in a place where it cannot be accessed by minors or those offended by explicit content.

Be forewarned that this book deals with miscarriage, pregnancy, childbirth, and related themes. I have made every effort to handle these themes and situations with as much consideration as possible, but you are your own best guide for determining the boundaries and limits for what you are able to read. This book might not be for everyone.

For further content warnings for THE GOOD COUNSELOR, please visit my website.

for Robert, my muse

Prologue

"H E WON'T BE LONG," SHE SAID, PAUSING AT THE DOOR. Persephone grasped the handle and the aged hinges creaked when she opened it. Warmth and incense, the scents of mint and parsley, flooded from the other side. She stood in the door frame, and many pairs of tear-streaked eyes met hers.

"My lady," a frail voice said from the bed that dominated the center of the room.

"Hello, old friend," she smiled.

"Gods, it's good to see you again."

"And you as well."

"To think... I am only a child compared to you, Soteira... yet I grow old while you stay evergreen, no?" He chuckled around the rattle in his throat and managed a smile for her.

"You mean more to me than you give yourself credit."

The venerable priest squinted at her, and his forehead wrinkled with worry. "My lady, it is two days past. Shouldn't you be with your honored husband by now?"

"He understands, Eumolpus," she said, shutting the door and walking to the bed. His students and family cleared a path for her and Persephone sat beside him, stroking thin wisps of white hair away from his liver-spotted forehead. "This time you're coming home with us."

"I will only be another shade in Asphodel…"

"No," she soothed. "You're going to Elysion."

"I do not deserve it, my lady."

"Of course you do. With how good you are, with all you've done…"

"I served you for seventy years and more. But my youth was not so piously spent. No, not so." He frowned, every breath harder to draw. "I whipped my servants," he blurted. "When I was seventeen, I plied a reluctant girl with drink until she lay with me, I forgot sacrifices to the gods and—"

"We are, all of us, the sum of our parts, good and bad," a baritone voice said from the back corner of the room. Hades removed his helm, becoming visible to all within. Twenty pairs of eyes widened, then swiftly averted. The dark-robed mortals knelt and bowed to him, some trembling in fear. Eumolpus's eyes widened and he stretched a knobby hand out to his lord.

"Eubouleus," he whispered, using one of Aidoneus's many epithets.

"Be unafraid," Persephone said to the cowering Eleusinians. "Plouton is here as a friend."

They knew Persephone well, many since birth, but even members of her priesthood were wary of the Unseen One. They gave him a wide berth, crowding to the far side of the bed when he strode across the room to join his wife. Aidoneus managed a thin smile. "My queen speaks the truth. Do you suppose anyone who goes to the Elysian Fields is as pure as snow?"

He smiled and coughed again. "Of course not, my lord."

"Then you know I would welcome a mortal who has done more in his short life for my wife, and all of Chthonia, than anyone who has yet lived."

A smile spread across the old priest's face and his breathing gentled.

"We have a question for you, Eumolpus," Persephone said, blotting sweat from his forehead with the corner of her shawl.

"I might have an answer," he smiled. Though his eyes were dulled by cataracts, Persephone saw the same sparkle in them from long ago.

She looked to Aidon, who carefully removed a gold foil scroll from his robes. Persephone took it from him, unrolled it, and held it out for Eumolpus. "Charon has been finding these in the mouths of the dead. Do you know who would do such a thing?"

The dying man nodded, squinting at the text. Eumolpus turned to his youngest son. "Keryx, will you read this for me?"

A gray-haired man took the scroll and unrolled it. "It's written in Thracian."

Eumolpus closed his eyes and shook his head.

"...But on the other side, from the lake of Mnemosyne, you will find water flowing fresh. Say: 'I am the son of Earth and starry Heaven, but my parentage is heavenly: know this you too. I am dry with thirst and dying. Give me quickly then water from that which flows fresh from the lake of Mnemosyne'." Keryx looked at his father, confused.

The old priest merely nodded. "I know who writes these. He was my student several years back, practically a boy. Rumor is that Apollon is his father. Came to Eleusis intrigued by the idea of rebirth, then left for the temple on Samothrace. He had *his own ideas* about what greets those who journey across the Styx."

"Should we be concerned?" Aidon asked.

Eumolpus shook his head and coughed violently. "No... no. His heart is in the right place. But I believe you should seek him out."

"Why?" Persephone asked.

Eumolpus breathed in again, the rattle in his throat growing louder. He waved toward the door. "All of you out," he commanded, then raised his palm before anyone could protest. "Every soul in this room knows as well as I that death is not the end. I will see each of you again in Elysion. Keryx, you stay."

They filed out quickly, his eldest granddaughter weeping as others ushered her from the chamber. The door shut behind them.

"My lady," he said with a smile. "I know you have long desired a child."

Persephone leaned in. "Yes…"

"The one who wrote that… he is gifted. With his lineage, his intelligence… it's quite possible. There are rites that his order oversees—"

"Eumolpus," Aidoneus stopped him quietly. "My wife and I have tried… many methods already. Spells, rituals, traveling throughout the known world…"

"Aidon…"

"Persephone, no. Sweet one, we suffer through this once a decade, to no avail. I won't let your hopes be crushed yet again."

"My lord, please," Eumolpus strained. "It is a fertility rite, yes, but the Samothracians invoke one who is not yet born. An heir to the earth and heavens— a god of life, death, and rebirth."

Hades and Persephone exchanged a long glance.

"It requires sacrifice. A king and his barren queen have already—"

A fit of coughing cut him off so violently it bowed his back. His breathing became labored. Persephone looked up at her husband, her eyes pleading.

Aidoneus sighed. "What sort of sacrifice?"

"I know not. But it must encompass…" He took one gasping breath, feeling lighter, euphoric. "…what you are… your most heartfelt desire…"

"What is the man's name?"

Eumolpus saw the lamplight around him glow more brightly, the incense thicker, like fog, obscuring his last vision. He could feel warmth, like sunlight, and heard the laughter of childhood friends. He closed his eyes, exhaling his last word.

"…Orpheus."

1.

T HE WATER WAS CALM, CLEAR, AND INFUSED WITH
the scent of ash. He knelt and washed his arms, his legs,
and torso. It was cold and purifying. He rubbed olive oil
across his skin, banishing all *miasma* from his person.

Orpheus scraped the excess oil off with a metal *strigil* and
dried himself in the sunlight, tussling his brown hair to shake
out the water. He donned his tunic and himation, both una-
dorned and undyed.

He closed his eyes, escaping distraction, listening. A thrush
in the oak tree warbled and he hummed its song. A hymn to
the Seasons had followed him for days, but the heart of the
hymn eluded him. He had no instrument to produce harmony— none, at least, that could do the immortals justice. He
borrowed the bird's notes, slowing them to match the words.
"At play you are companions," he sang softly.

He repeated the line a few times, smoothing out the melody while he paced. Orpheus stopped and sang it again, a little
more boldly, then raised it by five tonic notes, "of holy Persephone, when the Fates—"

He stopped, a shiver rushing over his skin. Had he called
upon Karpophoros disrespectfully? *No,* he thought. Ancient

Eumolpus had assured him she was not offended by that name. And the priest knew her: he had walked beside her in his youth, founded the Lower Mysteries. *Persephone's* rites. Orpheus shrugged off the superstition.

He wondered after the old man, whether he was well. It had been years.

"And the Graces in circling dances, come forth to the light—"

He was being watched. Orpheus turned to where he felt the presence of… *something*… a wild aurochs, a man? It was more than mortal, but satyrs and nymphs were rarely seen on Samothrace.

Cold seeped into his skin and a weight gathered in his chest. For all that he was attuned to his surroundings, it was unlike anything he'd ever known. He wasn't being watched but *looked through*. Every creature in the woods had gone silent, still, and Orpheus wondered… He'd banished *miasma*. He'd called upon *her* with his song. She was here; she must be. He felt cold, a sense of dread, the fleeting thought of asphodel flowers… Orpheus dropped to one knee and bowed his head. "Lady of Spring, Mistress of the Lands Beneath the Earth… If it is you… I am your humble servant."

"It is not her."

He raised his head, his breath shallow. The voice was calm, measured, and male— its owner invisible. "I beg your forgiveness."

"No need. I know her well. Is she the one you serve, hymnist?"

He swallowed. "I serve all the gods, my lord."

"That's quite a task… To curry favor with *all* the gods."

"I don't seek *favor*. They are the highest expression of *phanes*, the light of life. I honor them with song."

"Our numbers are too great. A song for each of the gods cannot be sung in a mortal lifetime."

"I may be reborn and sing again. But if I displease them, I might find myself barred from Elysion."

"Ah," said the voice. "You have completed the Greater and Lesser Rites, no?"

"I have."

"Who instructed you?"

"The great priest, Eumolpus."

"I knew him," said the voice, the tone changing.

"Knew?"

"He passed from this earth just before winter. I was there when his family took him to his mausoleum."

"If I may ask," he said, fearing the answer, "who are you, my lord?"

"One who would not yet be known to you."

He swallowed. The owner of this voice knew the Goddess of Spring. He had attended funeral rites… It couldn't be him. Orpheus rose cautiously, his knee damp from the mossy earth. "What shall I call you, my lord?"

The presence remained silent but palpable. He was thinking. Sandals paced the ground, and if Orpheus listened closely enough, he could hear the rhythmic tap of a staff hitting the earth. "The God of Nysa."

"Nysa…"

"You know of it?"

He could only test what he knew, not say it outright. "Only in legend. The hidden grove of the gods. The place where the Receiver of Many took Demeter's Daughter from the sunlit world to be his Queen."

"Indeed."

Orpheus kept his eyes to the ground. "Then, God of Nysa, why, if I may, did you seek *me* out?"

"I've heard stories of a ceremony that takes place here. One that invokes a god that is not yet born."

He nodded. "It… It hasn't been performed in years."

"A rare thing, then. When in the year?"

"When the first seeds sprout from the earth, midway between Spring and the Solstice. Few are truly prepared to give what it requires. And not just wealth. That is given to Samothrace. Equal shares from the least to the greatest."

"None for yourself, then."

Orpheus looked down at his humble clothes. His threadbare himation, a collection of scrolls, and a colorful *zeira* from his mother's people were his only real possessions. "No."

"And what of the rites themselves? What is asked of those who participate?"

"Something that represents what you are and will be."

He stopped, seeming to mull over Orpheus's words. "Would anything I could offer aid you now? Perhaps something only one of my kind can procure for you…"

"There is only one thing I would ever want, but I live by *ananke*. My desires are irrelevant."

Orpheus heard his voice shift at this. "*Ananke*. You are the son of Apollo, but you are not immortal, *hemitheoi*. Curious that you would abide by laws which govern the deathless ones."

His chest swelled, and he willed his words to come from the heart. "Aren't we all, as manifestations of *phanes*, from the eldest Protogenoi to the lowest mortal, bound by the will of the Fates?" Orpheus swore he could sense the god smiling. He held his breath, unsure of what to make of the long pause.

"Perhaps."

Orpheus stood still, and felt himself being gazed upon, a pull at his chest and behind his eyes, as though his thoughts and his heart were being weighed and measured. He heard light footfalls and the rhythmic staff.

"My asking comes with a heavy price— you must not reveal that the ones who participate are deathless," the voice said. Orpheus felt the same heavy pull, his very thoughts sifted and gleaned. "I can see your heart. You despise lying."

"I do. Hundreds of the most faithful will be there. To hide that knowledge from all, when they will be participating in a ritual so extraordinary, so momentous…" His words faded away. Deathless ones— gods attending a rite to birth a god. His heart sang a warning in his chest.

"I would not ask you to bend your *ethos* if it were less important. But in return for what I most desire, I will give you what *you* most desire."

"A silver lyre." The words slipped from his lips.

"Yes," the voice said. "For the gift of a silver lyre, crafted by the gods— to bring forth your songs from your heart. Because for now, they are trapped within you."

"Why seek me out? Is what I have to offer unique?"

"The one you call upon— who is not yet born…" Orpheus could feel the full weight of the god's gaze upon him. "Name him."

"The Unborn One's name is only uttered in absolute secrecy and sanctity. My order does not sully it with human speech."

"*Name him,*" repeated the voice in a hoarse whisper.

His heart beat out of his chest. "Zagreus."

The god was silent again and Orpheus wondered if he had angered him. But beneath the enveloping coldness, he could feel a brief flicker of relief. Hope, even. Through the wash of emotion, the voice remained staid. "What if I told you that your Zagreus could be conceived by these rites if she and I were allowed to attend… unfettered by human fears and superstitions?"

"I would have no choice but to believe you, my lord."

"Then you understand the reason for my surreptitiousness."

He shuddered. Now he knew for certain who spoke to him. "Can I think on it?"

"Of course. You have until the first moon of winter. I will return then."

"How will I know if I don't even know your true name?"

"Because at that time, I will reveal *how* I know you, and when I do so, you will know precisely who I am."

The presence lifted. As Orpheus puzzled over the god's words, the birds started to sing again, the beetles hummed in the humid air. Everywhere he turned, narcissus bloomed in the shade of the trees.

✻   ✻   ✻

Thesprotia was warm, even in the early evening. But that warmth didn't penetrate the caves near the river. Here the chill of winter still clung to the rocks like moss.

Persephone held an herb in the palm of her hand, rooted in loose soil. Her other traced the cool stones and damp roots of the cave. She followed the echo of a single drum's steady tattoo joined by a lone piper's melody. Light flickered from the entrance of a great hall, and the smells of pitch and venison wafted from within. Neither masked the stink of sex and sour wine. The titter of dryads and naiads mixed with the braying laughter of satyrs, pervasive chatter punctuated now and again by loud moans. The court was smaller than it once had been, so many years ago when mortal men and women had made the mistake of trusting its king— when Minthe had made the mistake of trusting her own father.

When she reached the doorway, the drum stopped. The pipes faltered a moment later. Whispers, then silence, then the shifting and uncoupling of half-clothed bodies, and knees dropping to the floor. Persephone didn't look at the many bowed heads. Her gaze fixed on the dais at the rear of the hall. Her bare feet padded against the tile. "Kokytos."

The king descended the dais and bowed low to her before resuming his place on his throne. "What an unexpected pleas-

17

ure, Queen Persephone. When I heard you'd been seen about Thesprotia I'd hoped our paths might cross. Delightful to finally—"

"Leave us," Persephone said.

With the barest murmur, the entire court gathered their instruments, their clothes, and cups. Most shuffled out of the hall; some disappeared in flashes of green— high order nymphs vanishing into the ether— until only the river god and the Queen of the Underworld remained.

Kokytos spied the green sprig in her hand. "So, it's true what Minthe did?"

"Though not all of what they say."

"You can't believe everything gods and humans say. Gossips, to the last. Everyone worth knowing knows Aidoneus is faithful to a fault. And my sympathies for what befell you both at her hand."

"I was expecting something more akin to an apology."

Kokytos scoffed. "I had no part in it. She brought her schemes with her, whispered in her ear by your illustrious mother, obviously."

"Did she?"

"I took Minthe in. That was all."

"You let the men of your court violate her. They warped her, twisted her mind."

He held up his hands. "Nothing she didn't agree to. She knew the price of staying."

"Your own daughter…"

Kokytos rolled his eyes. "One of many."

Persephone shook her head. "I know all souls, living and dead, just as my husband does."

He shifted in his chair.

"You have much to answer for."

Kokytos threw up his hands. "So I whored my daughter! What of it? Are you going to condemn the father of every *hetera* along with me?"

"No," Persephone said, with a soft smile. "She is the reason we are unfortunately acquainted, but Minthe is not why I'm here."

"Then *what?*"

"There were human guests in your hall nearly four score winters ago…"

Kokytos paled.

"During the Great Famine. Do you remember them?"

"H-how could I possibly recall? Decades have passed. And so have they, most likely."

"To the last soul." She took a step forward. "You murdered them. You dined on their flesh. Your servants and guests feasted on them at your behest."

He choked out a laugh. "What nonsense… who in the world would tell you such a story?"

"The men and women you killed, Kokytos."

His face fell.

"It took all these years for me to find them. At first, they were just rumors between nymphs that reached my ears. I, too, doubted their awful tales. But the dead cannot lie."

"My Queen, you know better than anyone that food was dwindling. They would have died anyway. Once my stores ran out… My court—" Kokytos coughed and pulled at his mouth. He withdrew a mint leaf.

"Kokytos, son of Okeanos…"

"I am one of the ageless! Mortals are *livestock*. Only *they* need to live by those petty laws. I am your husband's vassal! You cannot cond—" He spat out another mint leaf.

Kokytos choked around a sprig of mint clawing at his throat. He yanked it free, then stared at his hands, mint blooming from under his fingernails, the roots twisting through his veins. He stood with a shriek, his throne tipping backward. Kokytos beat at his arms as though they were aflame, tearing leaves and buds from his skin, but the more he raked from his flesh the more grew in its place.

"Abandon all hope, Kokytos." He fell and tumbled down the stairs of his dais, his cries choked and muffled, and crashed to the floor of the cavern. Kokytos flailed as clumps of mint sprung from his mouth, his nostrils, his eyes. "For murdering your guests and consuming mortal flesh you are condemned—not to Tartarus, but oblivion."

A wellspring of green muffled his screams and twisted features. Mint burst through the fabric of his robes, the still limbs beneath a tangle of roots and soil. They wound about his fallen crown. "So say I, Persephone Praxidike Chthonios, Queen of the Underworld, Carrier of Curses cast on those who live, by the dead whom they harmed in life."

Only a sprawling patch of mint remained, pungent leaves overpowering the lingering headiness of the orgy that had raged in the hall minutes before. Mint crept between the mosaic tiles as Persephone left the chamber, the single sprout still resting in her left hand. Persephone curled the fingers of her right into a fist as she left the tunnel. Rocks tumbled from the ceiling and dust billowed behind her.

She declined to travel through the ether. She owed Minthe the walk to the poplar grove where her mother's tree stood. Mud caked her bare heels. Her green peplos swished in the breeze and she sheltered the sprig in her hand.

"I forgive you," she whispered to it. "I hope that you can forgive me, wherever you are."

The grove loomed ahead, and she slowed, listening to songbirds and crows. She reached a tree at its center, with great branches towering overhead. This tree had been here far longer than the others, and it didn't sway like the rest.

"Leuce?" She called up to it. "I come to return your daughter, and to atone."

Persephone knelt and scooped aside some of the loam near a broad root, and dug into the earth. She gently planted the cupped handful of soil and mint next to the outstretched base of the poplar. The tiny sprig leaned against the tree in a spot of sunlight. As she stood, she spoke to the outstretched boughs. "Forgive me. Forgive my husband, my mother, and Hecate. That's all I ask."

✼ ✼ ✼

Hera sprawled inelegantly on Hestia's divan, fingers plaited under her chin. "Why must I entertain that sea witch *again*?"

Hestia shook her head and ladled boiling water from the cast iron pot on the hearth, carefully swishing it until it stopped bubbling. "Come, now. She isn't all bad."

"Oh? All she talks about is the strumpets she drags to her marriage bed. If I have to hear her extol their *bedsharing* again—" Hera's face had grown flushed. "Fates preserve me. She's worse than Aphrodite."

"Surely not," Hestia laughed, then emptied the ladle over a mix of ambrosia, sideritis, sage, and a bit of hemp flower. "Here. Calm yourself."

Hera held the clay cup to her face and inhaled deeply. She closed her malachite dusted eyelids and every thought of Amphitrite evaporated. There was only the hearth, the shadows dancing on the many alabastron jars arranged carefully on the shelves, and her white-veiled sister tending to the flames. She took a sip of the tisane, and gone was the fury that still brewed over Zeus's latest conquest, a dark-eyed Theban princess. Here, that harlot didn't exist. Olympus itself could crumble to its foundations, and she wouldn't care a whit. "How do you always know the best remedy for my mood?"

"Aeons of practice." Hestia smiled warmly.

Hera sipped. "This doesn't get dull? Tending to the fire day after day?"

"I prefer it," Hestia said, pouring herself a cup. "The mortals offer me the first and last herb and drink of every meal, I take what I like, and can roam without a man's permission." She sipped from her cup, her gaze resting on a jar containing her latest acquisition— a sweet spice from beyond the Indus that curled up like a scroll and didn't resemble any leaf or seed known.

"You could have been a queen, Hestia."

"Yes, but intrigue and theatrics are not for me. And living at the bottom of the sea would be intolerable. Better Poseidon has that *sea witch*, as you call her, by his side."

Hera nodded. She'd always been drawn to warmth. The ocean would have chilled and rotted everything that made Hestia content. She wondered what life might have been like had she too had become a perpetual virgin. A visit from Zeus, disguised as an injured bird, had ended that...

"Why is Zeus summoning Poseidon?" Hestia asked idly.

"Another needless report on Ilion's wall; what else? Fates have mercy, it's been *aeons* and *still* he cannot let bygones be bygones."

"You know how he loves to stay on top," Hestia replied.

Hera looked over her cup and cocked an eyebrow. "Of course he does. It feels strange to even say this, but sometimes I wish Zeus and Poseidon could be more like Hades."

Hestia sputtered, nearly choking on her tea. "What?"

"He stays where he ought, performs his duties with all the steadfast dullness we've come to expect, no scheming, no power games... He never showed his face until he came to claim his bride. He's been so..." Hera scrunched her face thoughtfully, "perfectly reasonable."

"Reasonable? Hera, he plunged the world into famine and darkness over a girl. Courtly intrigues are tiresome, but never so disastrous as *that.*" She spoke low, as though the words themselves were a grave curse. "This flame nearly went out."

Hera scoffed. "That was Demeter. If she acted as a proper mother, not a stalk of wheat would have withered. The Stygian betrothal had been in place since the war. It was *her* folly not allowing Persephone to marry the husband chosen for her. A *king* no less..."

"If she'd considered what a fine queen her daughter would make, and how faithful her husband is..." Hestia set down her cup, her eyes sparkling. "You should send a summons."

"Invite *Hades?*"

"Not him; Zeus would feel upstaged. I meant Persephone."

Hera ground her teeth. "Demeter's bastard."

"Did you hear about what she did to that girl who tried to—"

"Yes," Hera said. "*I know.* She scared my poor Hephaestus with her theatrics. Never mind the spectacle she made of herself in Ephyra!"

Hestia winced.

Too sharp, she scolded herself. She set down her cup and meandered through Hestia's kitchen, eyeing the various herb-filled *pithoi* as she went, enjoying each heady scent. She found a familiar jar, then glanced at Hestia contritely. She was Queen of Heaven, but this was her sister's domain.

Hestia nodded and Hera pulled an alabastron of rosewater from the shelf, flecking some into her tea, then rubbing the rest on her wrists.

"Inviting her might make your afternoon less of a chore."

"Tomorrow? Here? She's not one of us."

"Perhaps not, but neither is Amphitrite. Persephone, though, is Queen of the Underworld, and equal to her in rank." Hestia smiled wistfully. "A meeting of queens..."

Hera narrowed her eyes thoughtfully. "All I ever heard after the Pomegranate Agreement was Persephone, Persephone,

Persephone. Most of them falsehoods. What do you know of her?"

"A little. You might have more in common with her than you realize. Learn more of her; ask her about this Elysion she and her husband created. Perhaps you could even strengthen the bonds between the Lands Below and the Heavens."

Hestia had struck upon something, Hera realized. The rulers of the dead had only grown in influence since their marriage. With Persephone as her friend, the two queens could easily overrule Amphitrite. And if Hera proved her worth in forming a powerful alliance with them, what would Zeus say then? "If I took her in, it would only strengthen us. And prove to *him* once and for all that I *can* make peace with his baseborn spawn."

"You remember how he welcomed you back after… that ill-gotten plot with Apollo and Poseidon? It was a long time before he strayed again."

"Six score years." Hera allowed herself a smile of grim satisfaction. "The longest he'd been faithful since we were newly wed."

"Less time you have to spend chasing a wandering husband, perhaps." Hestia ladled another cup of water over her herbs.

"Ha! I should be so lucky," Hera said. "If all goes accordingly, Zeus won't be able to resist competing with Hades to embody a proper marriage."

"And we do know how he likes to be on top." This time, Hestia smirked.

"I know him. He'd try to best his brother at the game of fidelity… He'd lose, of course, but that would make him far less brazen about his exploits. Cowed, even. And who knows? Perhaps chasing flesh would lose its luster one fine day." The Queen of Heaven set down her cup and stared at the flames.

She laughed softly to herself as the solutions to Amphitrite, that Theban harlot and any whores to follow fell into her lap.

Hestia shrugged. "I leave the marital intrigue to you, dear sister. It will be a royal event. The first meeting of the Queens of all three realms."

"My lord won't like being upstaged."

"Oh, don't hold it in the symposium. Invite them to your villa. If Zeus protests, just remind him that your hospitality is long overdue." Hestia's serene face cracked into a sly smile. "Your home is *your* domain. You have the last word."

"I'd hardly need his permission. In his mind, *nothing* would humiliate Poseidon more than coming second to a meeting of goddess queens." Hera wrinkled her brow and grew solemn. "What if Persephone is more trouble than Amphitrite?"

"I shouldn't think so. They say she is closer to your temperament. She's a quiet but strong ruler. I'm sure she has just as low an opinion of Demeter as you. And she's a paragon of wifely virtue."

"So I win her over, and the feared Praxidike becomes my loyal pet. Is that what you're saying?"

"Perish the thought. Finish your tea, then send her an invitation."

✻   ✻   ✻

The ether briefly twisted around her in silver and crimson and she emerged in the great atrium of her villa in Thesprotia. It had been abandoned for generations when Persephone had found it and was said to be filled with the ghosts of the extinguished House of Aeolus.

Persephone knew better. She had sentenced three of their ranks to Tartarus, Sisyphus chief among them. If any ghosts remained, she would have already wrenched them from this world.

25

Willows overhung the house, shielding it from the main road that led to the sea. It was modest, a short way from the city of Cichyrus. A copse of bedraggled cypresses marked the path to the entrance, and thistles grew thick around the outer door. To passing eyes, this place was as uninhabited as it was foreboding.

Inside, it was paradise. Roses climbed atrium garden walls and crocus blanketed the floor, growing through every crack in its deteriorating mosaic. A pomegranate tree— planted by Aidoneus on his first visit to their home in the world above— grew in the very center, shading a large oak stump beneath it. It was here that she found him scoring the skin of a heavy fruit and splitting it in half. It hadn't come from this tree— it was only starting to blossom. This pomegranate came from their sacred grove at the entrance to Elysion. He set it down and stood.

Persephone picked up her skirts and rushed to him. He gripped her waist and she felt her feet tilt off the ground as he lifted her level with his face. Their lips met, and she sighed, melting into him. His joy and eagerness flooded into her, mellowed by tenderness, spiked with lust, warmed with relief.

And a metallic chord of trepidation.

She eased back. "Is something troubling you?"

"No. Not yet," he said, setting her down. "Did you take care of it?"

"He's gone. His court is destroyed, and Minthe is with her mother." He scowled at the mention of her name. Planting Minthe's remains by her mother's grave had been Persephone's idea. Hades had been less forgiving when they'd discussed it. "How is everything back home?"

"Empty as ever when you aren't there, sweet one. How was this year's planting?"

"The same as ever." She hooked her arm into his and leaned in as they walked the walled garden paths. She quivered at the contact. It had been two months since her fingers had been upon his skin. She could feel his pulse and the warmth of his flesh. He smelled of raw earth, of cypress, and cool waters— everything she missed about Chthonia. The Underworld. Her true home. Persephone glanced up and caught him chewing the inside of his lip. His mind was distant, but she knew he would eventually reveal where. She let him ruminate while she spoke. "A bit less grain to sow this year, though. She was so anxious about the last harvest, it affected everything."

"Your mother needs to stop worrying after her paramour."

"I've told her as much. But can you even call Triptolemus that anymore? They share the Telesterion, but more as friends than lovers. They've barely shared a bed since—"

"I regret mentioning it," he muttered hastily.

"Ah." She fidgeted. "Hermes may have picked up Minoan."

"What?"

"Unless *you* told him Bellerophon was granted a place in Elysion."

Aidoneus gritted his teeth. "Damn him…"

"I knew it! I knew he was lying. He denied reading your last letter to me, but how else would he know?"

"I'll have a word with him."

"What if that's not the extent of it? What if he tells them about this place?"

"He won't. I made him swear on the Styx."

Persephone turned to him. "If the mortals know that we spend time here, it will be misery. They'll stop sowing crops, or build a gaudy temple. And the favors and quests of the rustic gods and *hemitheoi*—"

"They'll do no such thing because Hermes will keep his mouth shut. He takes Stygian oaths seriously."

"How will we send messages now?" A shiver rolled through her as he cupped her face with his hand.

"Perhaps I should hand-deliver them." Aidon leaned over and gave her the slowest of kisses. His dark eyes locked onto hers. "Though there's something else I'm intent on giving you presently."

Heat rushed to her cheeks. She threw her arms around his neck and collided with him, kissing him gracelessly in return, their teeth clicking together before he tilted his head and thrust and rolled his tongue along hers, a prelude for all they desired. He chuckled low and traced her spine with his fingertips.

"I'm glad you're *just* as eager to see me."

"First," Persephone whispered, "let me show you what I've been up to."

✻   ✻   ✻

Aidoneus picked up half of a pomegranate and followed her up the stairs. "A full season of sowing and still you found the time?"

"I left just after Thesmophoria, and I think Mother is starting to suspect—"

Aidon kissed away the name. The last person he wanted to think about right now was Demeter. He inhaled Persephone's scent of rose and irises. "This is my time with *you*. And no one else. Not Hermes, not your mother..."

Not Orpheus? Her voice rang through his head.

Aidon stopped. Did she know where he had been? That he had spoken to the hymnist?

"His name was in your mind. Is it about what Eumolpus said?"

"I don't want you to be disappointed again, sweet one," he interrupted sharply. "I can't bear it. Not after last time."

She nodded.

He needed to distract her, or his visit to Samothrace would pour out unbidden. Going further down that road would only raise her hopes fruitlessly. Especially if she knew he was motivated enough to speak to Orpheus himself. "I practiced a flower while I waited for you."

Persephone smiled. "You did?"

They discovered that their *hieros gamos* had not only created Elysion, but— to their mutual delight— had conferred upon each other some of their unique talents. Persephone had even called up iron from the earth seven winters ago. "Watch."

Aidoneus concentrated on the ground and felt beating warm life rush through him, from his feet upward. Each time he tried it he marveled. This must be what she had felt each time she created a new living thing. At first, he'd worried that he would taint life itself— that his efforts would result in a blight simply because of who he was. But they were the Gods of the Earth, he remembered, one and the same, infinitely bound. He closed his eyes, feeling the telltale pulse in first his abdomen and rising through his chest as a bulb grew, opened, and split the ground. The stalk shot upright, bursting at the tip into a purple iris. He heard clapping and opened his eyes. Persephone exhaled softly. "My favorite part," she said, "is feeling *it* move through you."

"'It'..."

"The earth, everything I have ever called up... it's hard to give it a name. But it moves so... differently within you."

"And you can sense every bit of *it*."

Of course I can, her voice rang, stronger this time. She turned and strolled through the palace, showing him a centuries-old tapestry she'd found in the collapsed storage room, the vibrant ochres and deep blues sealed away from the ravages of sun and wind. She picked up her skirts and climbed the stairs to the gynaikeion, giving him a glimpse of her ankles and mud-stained feet. Aidon followed, listening to her describe how

she'd made it into a place fit for them to sleep, to make love…
"Aidon?"

He smiled. "I was distracted. Forgive me."

She bit coyly at her lip. "It's just a single room. I thought black fleeces would work, but they're hard to find in the world above. Used for sacrifices too often to…"

"To me."

"They seldom sell them to anyone but priests. It took me some searching, but I eventually found what I needed at an *agora* in Locri. They were hesitant, especially since I'm a woman. But no one asked questions after the gold came out. I suppose it helps when your husband is the richest being in the cosmos," she said.

Aidon laughed. He looked up, and instead of the familiar dome patterned with stars, this flat ceiling was covered with tiny jasmine blooms— their growth carefully trained and arranged to reflect the summer sky. One vine wound toward the center, marking the tail of the Scorpion, and another the bow of the Lyre.

The Lyre… had she chosen that grouping of stars for a reason? He pushed it from his wandering mind. Aidon wanted to peel her clothes off and press skin to skin, to seat himself as deep within her as he could. But he also wanted to give her due respect as she showed him the work she'd done since they last met here.

This, he realized, was why he was creating these nervous distractions. But her breath was hitching, and he could feel her skin warming and prickling every time she glanced at him, could feel the flutter in her abdomen as though it were his own, and hear the slight tremble in her voice. His wife was being coy. She wanted him to make the first move, the first touch. He would torture her a moment longer.

As Persephone drew closer to the fleece-covered divan, his gaze rested on her hips, the pins that held her peplos taut over her skin, and the ornate girdle he had timidly left as a gift in her chamber on the fifth day he'd known her. Her back was turned. He plucked a seed from the pomegranate and held it under his tongue. He was as impatient for her touch as she was for his.

Aidoneus flicked his wrist, and *fibulae* scattered to all corners of the room. The girdle fell muffled in the heap of fabric, and Persephone gave a startled gasp. He chuckled, ambling toward her as the peplum slinked from her breasts, her only adornment the flowery crown she wore in the spring and summer. Her blue-grey eyes were wide with shock and her hands instinctively covered her breasts and mons.

"It is good to know," he said, stepping free of his clothes, "that after all these years I can still surprise you."

"I-I…" The blush creeping up her neck told him all he needed to know.

One piece of cloth remained, the only one not held by pins. Aidon reached behind and untied his loincloth by hand and let it drop to the floor. He gripped the half pomegranate in one hand and lifted the crown from her head with the other, then casually tossed the woven flowers aside. Aidon could feel the heat of her through half a pace between them. Her heels and chin lifted so she was level with him, her eyes were lidded and her lips neared his. She relished in his guttural groan as she brushed her hand up his hip, his stomach, and chest. "You'll have to put that down."

"Will I." He smiled and lifted the ripe fruit between them.

"What else do you plan to do with it?" She took a step back.

"Kiss me, wife, and find out."

The half-smile he had missed so very much these last two months appeared on Persephone's face and she closed the distance between them. Aidon sighed as his phallus pressed against her belly, as her breasts fit against his chest. He pulled her with his forearm at the small of her back and snaked the free fingers of his other hand through her hair. Her lips quivered against his before he flicked his tongue against them, bidding them to open. When they did, he pushed the ripe pomegranate seed he'd hidden away past her lips, onto her tongue, and broke the kiss to watch her.

Persephone locked her eyes with his and rolled the seed around in her mouth until it burst. Her soft moan sent a jolt straight to his groin. She kissed him again and he could taste the juice on her tongue. She pulled at his lip and nipped at his jaw. "You'll have to drop it at some point, husband."

"Oh, I will. One seed at a time, sweet one." He followed as she backed toward the divan. His cock pulsed hot between them, and her breath shuddered. He caught the scent of lilac. Her knee bumped the edge and with a light push, he sent her sprawling back onto the fleece, her hair a tangle underneath her. Aidon knelt beside her, drawing her auburn locks over the arm of the divan.

It's sweet that you do that, her voice echoed in his mind.

It's largely self-interest, he responded, giving her a wolfish grin. *It's made us stop before... at inopportune moments, and you know how I hate being interrupted.* He whispered in her ear. "And it gives me something to grasp when I want to see your face..."

She writhed. "Aidon, come."

"Not yet," he said with a light kiss. "Not for a long spell, either."

"It's been too long; stop teasing me."

"I won't leave you unsatisfied..."

He knew what she meant. He wanted that connection as badly as she... the slow sinking of flesh into flesh, the movement and rapture of lovemaking, the afterglow in which they could hold each other, feel their racing hearts slow in unison, and just *be.* But watching her twist with desire for him was intoxicating. Watching her lose herself, more so. He could wait.

He plucked another seed and held it high above her with two fingers, then crushed it, sending a spray of dark juice across her pale breast and neck. Persephone let out a delighted squeal. Aidon traced its path with his tongue, rasping at her nipple as he went. He burst another seed. And another, collecting every drop and sharing it with her in a kiss. Her amusement was quickly replaced with want, edging toward frustration. "Aidon…"

The sound of his name on her lips, and the breathy tone he'd heard only in dreams for aeons until he'd come to her, destroyed his resolve.

He grasped the rough skin of the pomegranate and crushed it to a pulp in his fist, then tossed the spent fruit aside. Juice trickled across her belly, pooling in her navel, running in rivulets across her waist and into the nest of curls between her thighs. It dripped from her skin onto the divan and the floor. He drank it from her flesh, too slowly to keep all of it from escaping. But that would just mean exploring more of her with his tongue.

It looked so beautiful, struck such a contrast, that he drew his fingers through it and painted swirls across her hips, tendrils along the insides of her thighs, spirals of translucent red up the peaks of her breasts. He drew another finger through dark pomegranate and traced the symbol of their realm— a circle where her ribs met, cushioned and held aloft above the concave of a crescent over her stomach, and a descending cross… the juncture at her navel and the tip of which he trailed between her thighs, her crease already warm and wet. He cupped his hand over her labia, resting a long finger along her seam. She closed her eyes, letting out a gasp. Aidon tasted Persephone's parted lips, their tongues rolling together, her teeth tugging lightly when they ended their kiss. Her thighs squeezed around his hand, and he drew a fingertip up to her bud, then quaked it against her. She grasped at his shoulder and moaned, her hand pawing haphazardly at his skin.

Aidoneus examined his handiwork, admiring Persephone and the juices he'd painted her with. The summer air made it shimmer as it dried and congealed. In his mind's eye, it started to look too much like blood. Dark memories began to rise from the deep— memories that had no place when he knelt here with her.

He gripped her thighs firmly, her smooth flesh rooting him in the moment. Aidoneus traced each swirl with his tongue, erasing every trail. He drew a languorous circle with his thumb around her clitoris and occupied his lips with her breasts and her stomach. She jumped with a slight giggle when he slurped that last pool of pomegranate juice from her navel. He smirked, then brushed his lips along her skin and nipped at the gentle curve of her womb, before replacing fingertips with tongue and listening to her delighted cry, muffled once her thighs closed against his ears.

One knee rested on his shoulder, his forearm pinioning her to the fleece. His other hand gripped her slender ankle to keep her from rolling off the divan. Persephone's fingers raked through his hair— pulling him closer, pushing him back, he could hardly tell or care— as he sampled juices headier than anything a pomegranate could offer. In her, he found sunlight and warmth, the fields of flowers, the sting of iron, and Phleg-ethon flames. She smelled— tasted— different when they were above ground.

She moved differently, came differently around him in the sunlit world. They had explored that on their first summer visit, when he'd taken her to Nysa, making love in the field where he'd snatched her from the earth. Aidon hissed at the memory and let go of her ankle to quickly squeeze the head of his cock. He sighed, the tension temporarily abated.

Her mewling, her writhing, all her sounds and scent and skin begged for him to fill her at last. Instead, he quenched her empty ache with two long fingers, searching softly for the spot he knew would transport her.

Persephone clenched hard against them and sat upright, her nails digging into his scalp for purchase as she crested, her voice ringing his name in his ears. When she came back to earth, Persephone spoke, her words thick. "The fleece…"

"Easily cleansed…" Aidoneus looked up at her and caught a drop of pomegranate juice on his tongue as it rolled over her hip bone, its sweetness mingling with her taste. "You're right, though," he whispered against her skin. He slid one hand under her shoulders and the other under her knees. "Best not get anything *else* on it."

She smiled weakly, still reeling. He didn't take his eyes off her, not as he carried her to their bed, not as he settled her in the middle and lay astride her. Two months was too long. The period following her return to the world above was always fraught with duty and separation for both of them— hers as the humans planted their new crops, and his when he harvested those who had passed during winter. Their palace, and especially their bed, was an empty shell without her. Persephone splayed her palms on his shoulder blades. "I love you."

"And I you, sweet one," he whispered, settling against her. He aligned himself to her, and with a long thrust, was finally home.

✻   ✻   ✻

Hermes waited in the courtyard, trying desperately to ignore the sounds from the gynaikeion upstairs. He shook the bronze cup in his hand, slammed the *kyveia* down onto the bench, and counted them up.

Seventeen. A loss.

No wonder Hades and Persephone sought the privacy of this villa, he mused. They made enough noise to wake the dead. He gathered up the six bones and shook them again.

Thirty-one with five on five. A resounding win.

Not that lucky rolls mattered in a solitaire game, but it was enough to distract his mind from the noise and deter accompanying visuals. Like his ignominious introduction to Hades's bride in the sapphire grotto of the palace when he had accidentally— No, no; he wasn't going to think about it. At all. He shook the cup.

Eleven. No pairs. Abysmal...

The rattling bones would also hopefully be enough to draw one of them out once they were finished. "Bag of bones..." Hermes chuckled to himself. Wasn't that what Alekto jokingly called Aidoneus half the time? He heard a shout from upstairs. Not so much a shout as a roar of male satisfaction.

He guffawed quietly. Oh, to tell Apollo— or *anyone*— about this secret place! But he'd sworn it on the Styx to Aidoneus that no one would know but him. Silence filled the courtyard, punctuated by the buzz of grasshoppers and crickets. It would be quiet enough to hear the rattle of *kyveia* from the rooms above. Then, an awkward conversation, and he could be on his way.

Hermes pointedly shook the bronze cup and slammed it onto the stone. He heard a female yelp and a male curse, then the sounds of them fumbling about. Down the stairs came heavy footfalls.

"Heh. Thirty-six!" A shadow fell across Hermes's perfect roll.

Hades loomed large, hair hanging loose and bedraggled over pale folded arms, his black himation wound around his waist and slung over his shoulder. He said nothing. Hermes swallowed and stood up, then bowed. He fumbled with the scroll, pulling it from its casing.

"Ah… I bear an urgent message for Persephone, Queen of the Underworld, from—"

The Lord of the Dead swiped the scroll from Hermes's hands. Papyrus crinkled in his tightening fist.

"Before you tear it up or set it on fire, it's from Hera."

"I'll see that she gets it," he spun around and marched toward the staircase. Without a backward glance, Aidoneus spoke in perfect Minoan. *"Stop reading my wife's letters."*

2.

"$\mathbf{S}$HE DID THIS ON PURPOSE," ATHENA SAID. "ON THE very day that *beast* will be there…"

"You could avoid Poseidon, you know." Persephone's gateway through the ether twisted in a winding gyre of Phlegethon flame, the marble columns of Olympus gleaming on the other side. "You don't *have* to accompany me."

"I know," said Athena. "And I hope you don't think that my ill temper is because of you. But she told *me* to bring you and what the Queen wants, the Queen gets. Father is *always* insisting we play nice with her. Much good it does any of us."

They stepped through. Persephone's first impression of Olympus had held true over the years. The perfectly manicured trees, bright halls, and sumptuous garden spoke of divine perfection. But behind it lay the stink of fruit rotting on the limb, food uneaten and spoiled, and spilled wine. Around every elegant bend was another intrigue, in each secluded bower more emotionless fornication. Deferential nymphs peered at her over cups of wine, and deathless ones were swarmed by their retinues. Many pairs of eyes found excuses to gawk at the Queen of the Underworld.

Persephone had returned only twice since her first visit: once at her husband's side to announce the creation of Elysion to Zeus and the *Dodekatheon*, and again as a guest of Aphrodite. She'd grasped for any excuse to avoid Olympus, but everyone knew the sowing season had passed, and no one turned down an invitation from the Queen of Heaven.

"You don't have to go in," Persephone said.

"Father wants me to."

"Why?"

"Strategy. He was lenient after I aided Poseidon and Apollo in their scheme. I was new to Olympus, then. He wants to make sure that his brother and I hate each other and never conspire again."

Persephone laughed ruefully. "Considering your history with Poseidon, I don't see what he's worried about."

"He has been meting out his punishment slowly, inflicting that *animal* on me for aeons now." Athena transfigured her scowl into a smile as they passed through the hall, and straightened her shoulders.

Poseidon stood before the throne, tattooed arms folded across his chest beneath a silver-streaked auburn beard. He turned and spread his hands wide when he saw Persephone, inked horses and waves rippling on his arms, aquamarine eyes alight. "Well, this is a surprise!"

She'd only seen Poseidon once at the court of the *Dodekatheon*. Persephone started to bow to them both.

"We'll have none of that!" Zeus descended the step of the dais. "You're Hades's queen, not my vassal. Hera's looking forward to meeting you."

Poseidon cocked an eyebrow. "I was under the impression Hera would be meeting with Amphitrite alone."

"I am no tyrant over my wife's hearth. She invites who she likes. That makes this a special occasion: the first meeting of all our queens. A momentous thing," he said, slapping Poseidon's back. "Don't you think, brother?"

Poseidon folded his arms again, his shoulders tense. "Indeed."

"Is Amphitrite here, your excellency?" Persephone said.

"No need to call me that, my dear," Poseidon said with a smirk. "And no, she's… hunting."

"Little untried quarry remains for *either* of you, uncle," Athena said, crowding toward Persephone. "If memory serves."

"Some remains, I imagine. I could always send Amphitrite to *your* temple." Poseidon bared his teeth in a wide smile. Persephone could feel the heat rising from Athena's skin. "If memory serves, it hosts the sweetest prey of all."

"Let's not start this in front of our guest," Zeus said. "I want her to have a *good* impression of you both."

"Perhaps we should kiss and make up," Poseidon said, stepping toward Athena.

"*That's*—" Athena said, raising her voice. She took a breath. "—quite unnecessary, uncle. Let that be the last of the jokes among family."

Persephone stayed quiet. Athena curtsied quickly and strode from the room, hounded by Poseidon's chuckles echoing through the marble hall. From the corner of the room came a glow of red and yellow, shifting into indigo and green.

A woman, kneeling low, shimmered as the light settled. She rose and faced Zeus. "Your grace, your illustrious wife sent me to escort her majesty Queen Persephone to her home."

"Yes, thank you, Iris," Zeus said, waving his hand. He turned to Persephone. "Well, I'm sure you'll have a wonderful time. Sadly, I don't think I will be free when you are finished. There's much business to attend to."

"Fates, I hope not…" Poseidon muttered. He gave Persephone a kind smile and nodded to her.

She acknowledged each in turn, then followed Iris from the symposium. Persephone had only seen her from a distance as a child. The goddess-in-waiting to Hera had hair like a raven's wing, tinged with every color of the rainbow, and her gown shifted between hues as she guided Persephone through shadow and light along the path to the Palace of Hera.

The walk felt long, and Persephone considered how odd it was that Hera kept a separate home and a separate bed from her husband, situated below his dwelling at the peak of Olympus. Just as her throne was pointedly below that of the King of the Gods. Hades's home was Persephone's, and her bed was Hades's, her throne alongside his. Olympus again proved itself a world apart.

Like the other private palaces of the *Dodekatheon*, Hera's villa was newer than the citadel of Olympus itself— the original home of Gaia and Ouranos. An orchard and villa hugged the hillside, and painted marble statues of women supporting a heavy balustrade and peaked roof with their uplifted arms. One of them looked a bit like Demeter.

"If you think that's impressive," a voice beside her whispered, "you should see ours beneath the waves. Saffron is a good color for you. The daughters of the sea rarely wear it. A pity."

Persephone snapped from her reverie. Beside her walked a curvaceous woman with rich umber skin and blue coral and cowry shells woven through her tightly braided hair. A diadem of spiraled conches sat above thin eyebrows. Her clothes reminded Persephone of the old paintings of priestess queens on Crete— a flounced skirt, and a tight blouse made of embroidered linen as diaphanous as sea foam. "Am— are you Amphitrite?"

"The same. Poseidon's queen— though not so grand a queen as our host. *One* seat to share instead of a pretty chair three steps below the throne. And *one* bed, which keeps him from straying too far, since I'm there waiting every night. And sitting thigh to thigh keeps his eyes from wandering too far by day…"

Persephone blanched, wondering how much Hera's lady in waiting could hear.

"You're an earth goddess… wouldn't you agree that the best way to keep a man from sowing his wild oats is to make sure that his grain silo is always empty?"

"I haven't heard *that* proverb before…" Persephone tittered awkwardly.

"You sit on your *own* throne in Chthonia, but Fates— don't tell me *you* sleep apart from Hades," Amphitrite said, louder than was necessary for Persephone to hear her.

"No, our room is… we definitely— I suppose, for six months of the year…"

The sea goddess threw her arm around Persephone. "Don't be so nervous. They'll eat you alive. And *she* will think you're as much of a prig as she is."

Persephone's jaw fell slack and she stared at Amphitrite.

"I don't care what the rainbow girl hears."

Iris's long peplos shifted from sky blue to a stormy gray-green and she spun about. Her face was tight. She straightened her back, her dress lightening until it returned to a tranquil hue. She spoke to Persephone. "I shall introduce the consort of Poseidon first. You, as our *most* honored guest, shall be introduced last."

The golden gate, a filigree of swirling clouds and the eyes of peacock feathers, swung wide. Iris strode through.

Amphitrite turned her head. *You, as our most honored guest, shall be introduced last,* she mouthed. She ended her impression with a spin and a courtly bow. Persephone stifled a laugh.

They passed between the tall statues. A peahen shrieked and ran across their path, pursued by a peacock. Iris led them through a grand hall, similar to the great symposium, but cast in watery light dimmed by blue veils and green drapes. Interior columns were enormous and carved with stylized lotuses. Soft divans stood in clumps here and there, covered in fleeces and rolled wool pillows. Frescos and tapestries featuring lionesses with their young, pomegranates, and the ubiquitous peacock feathers plastered the walls. Shafts of light penetrated here and there, giving the strange feeling of being submerged. The softness was welcoming after the stark symposium. A jeweled throne dominated the center of the room, empty.

"Majestic Hera, most treasured daughter of Rhea, She of the Heights, Protector of Men, wife of Zeus Aegiduchos Cronides, and Queen of Heaven," Iris said to the empty throne, "may I present Amphitrite Halocydne Nereida, Lady of the Sea, Goddess of the Encircling Third, consort of Poseidon; and may I introduce Persephone Karpophoros Chthonios, Goddess of Spring, Exacter of Justice, consort of Aidoneus, and Queen of the Underworld."

As her titles were uttered, Persephone knelt to one knee, her head bowed. She pressed her right palm to the floor, just as Aidon did when formally in the presence of Zeus. The throne before her was empty. Still, she kept her head lowered.

Amphitrite had given a customary nod and curtsy but stood tall.

"We are all equals here. Please. Stand."

Persephone rose and looked for the source of the voice. Beyond the throne, a blue veiled woman sat at a loom, her back to them as she wove a fine woolen thread through the taut strands. Iris bowed low once, backed toward the door, curtsied, and departed.

Hera stood and pushed her veil off her head. Beneath were dark locks held up by a simple green filet. Her features were sharp, yet warm, large brown eyes that reminded Persephone of Aidoneus, and a thin, serene smile. Malachite hung heavy on her lids, and kohl-rimmed the edges, making them appear even larger. "I thought tea might be in order. I know wine is not preferred in the lands below, so we shall abstain."

Persephone felt the tension leave her shoulders. "Tea would be fine, thank you."

"It might be tepid. They took it off Hestia's hearth several minutes ago."

Was she late? *No, three hours past midday was the appointed time,* she thought. *Hestia...* Persephone tried to remember. The second Child of Kronos possessed a vast collection of herbs and spices curated from all the plants of the world, some varieties lost for ages. She tended the hearth that warmed Olympus. And her fiery gateway through the ether matched Persephone's. "Will she be joining us?"

"No."

She balked at Hera's abruptness. But then the Goddess Queen smiled broadly, exposing perfectly white, if slightly large teeth. "I thought it should just be us today. The three of us have never really met."

"Strange you haven't invited her here," Amphitrite said, "since she has been Hades's queen for nearly fourscore years. We thought you'd go one hundred before holding court with her."

Hera demurred. "Alas, we've been… preoccupied. Much has transpired in that time, nay? But my dear Amphitrite, tell me about the last time you received Persephone beneath the waves."

Persephone felt like a country peasant. Should she have requested an audience with Hera? Had her oversight endangered the alliance between the Earth and the Heavens? Despite Hera's friendliness, Persephone knew that every word could be perilous.

"Speaking of, Persephone, I must apologize to you." Hera moved closer to her, her eyes cast to the ground.

"For what?"

"Your first winter… when I sent that pomegranate nectar…" She grasped Persephone's hands, her fingers warm, and looked with pleading eyes. "I never intended for my wedding gift to cause so much trouble."

"There's nothing to forgive. I assure you."

"I understand you dealt with that wretch and your mother's base behavior succinctly."

Don't ever show them weakness, Demeter had told her. *Let them believe what they must*, her husband had said. Persephone straightened her back. "I did."

"Ooh, there's an idea, Hera." Amphitrite giggled. "What would Zeus do if you made his next dalliance burst into flames mid-stroke?"

"My ways are more subtle than that," Hera shot back at her. "Thanks to her resourcefulness, Aidoneus was unharmed. And, if anything *had* transpired, he wasn't himself. He'd been poisoned by that whore."

"With ergot," Persephone said guardedly.

"As I said." Hera again cast her eyes to the ground. "I cannot express my sorrow that you had to endure that."

"In the grand scheme of things, nothing happened."

Hera clapped once, and three lady's maids dressed in sky blue peplum floated into the room, each bearing a steaming *kantharos*. Hera took her place on a divan, and Persephone and Amphitrite flanked her on couches of their own. Persephone didn't get a chance to look at the servant bearing the golden tray and her tea: she was silently retreating before Persephone's cup left the platter. The tisane was pink and smelled sweet and pungent. Persephone realized that it was rose and jasmine— a nod to her role as the Goddess of Spring. She inhaled and smiled.

"Now, Hera punishes those women's sons and daughters, also," Amphitrite said, "but *you*... Is it true what I heard from Anauros of Thessaly about what you did to Kokytos, Minthe's father?"

"It was an unrelated matter. He violated the laws of our realm, and the dead cast many curses upon him for his wrongdoings. It was my duty to carry them out."

"You sound like Aidoneus." Amphitrite laughed. "He's certainly well wormed his way into you, hasn't he?"

Persephone blushed and looked away, sipping her tea. A burst of sweetness revealed that it was full of ambrosia.

"There's no need to embarrass her," Hera said under her breath.

"Please... we're all wives, here. And they had a *hieros gamos* so impassioned it created Elysion. I think that there's little left to blush about."

"Let *her* be the arbiter of that," Hera said, an edge creeping into her voice. She forced a smile. "I've not seen Elysion yet. Though I hear from Zeus that it's incomparably beautiful."

"I think it is," Persephone said. After they had told Olympus of its existence, Zeus had made a rare descent into Chthonia to see it himself. He had been nearly silent at the time and had looked nervous.

"Tell us about it," Amphitrite said. Both she and Hera leaned forward.

"The entrance is a grove of intertwined pomegranate trees within the palace garden. Well, it *was* within our garden. We removed part of a wall and a path was laid to guide the worthy souls to their new home. Within, Elysion appears... expansive. There are many trees, of all varieties, some from lands that we've only heard about, and beyond that a sea, with green, hilly islands dotting the water."

"How large is Elysion?" Hera knit her brow.

"We haven't found its end yet."

Hera quickly schooled her expression and took another sip. "How do you determine who enters?"

Persephone bit at her lip. "Aidoneus and I spent every year since the Famine combing Asphodel for the worthy shades. With some difficulty, we let them revisit their lost memories long enough to speak with us, then sent them back to the peaceful Fields or rewarded them with Paradise."

"Sounds exhausting," said Amphitrite.

"Do you find these souls together during the winter, or does Aidoneus take it up when you are... with your mother?" Hera wrinkled her nose.

"I wouldn't delay any of... *his* subjects on my behalf. Aidoneus has ruled Chth— the Underworld for aeons, and can search out worthy shades without me."

"You've made a great change in him, I think. I didn't take him for someone quite so compassionate. What of the recently departed?" Hera asked. "What must they do to gain entrance to Elysion?"

"Their soul must be prepared. Nothing more."

"Your *Eleusinian Mysteries*," Hera said, leaving off. She exhaled. "Any news from beneath the waves, Amphitrite?"

Her wide smile exposed brilliant white teeth. "Yes. I am expecting another child."

"Oh, by Poseidon?" Hera said over the rim of her cup.

"Of course," Amphitrite hissed at her. "Allow me to share every exquisite detail of how he—"

"Congratulations to you," Persephone interrupted. She hadn't come here for this. She could very well be with Aidon right now in the comfort of their villa in Thesprotia.

"Why thank you." Amphitrite smiled at her and then winked. She knew Persephone was trying to keep the peace but readied her arrows for Hera anyway. "Poseidon was... very eager for another son."

"You know that it's a boy?" Persephone said, putting her cup down.

"Why yes," Amphitrite said. "*You* know how these things are known."

"I..."

"Your modesty is quite refreshing here, Persephone," Hera chimed in.

"I beg pardon," Persephone cast her eyes to her cup. "I cannot claim modesty when I honestly do not know what either of you is talking about."

Hera put down her cup and canted her head. "Oh dear, I'm sorry, I had completely forgotten you have no children. How careless of me."

"Good! I'll explain it to her." Amphitrite stirred her tea. "After the deathless ones create a child, they can both ...

learn about it together. Its sex, what it might look like, sometimes its sigil for the ether…"

"How?"

"The simple touch of both, upon the womb," Hera said.

"Poseidon likes to find out from inside—"

"Persephone is too much of a *lady* to listen to any more of that."

"And what sort of lady? The kind that sits beneath her lover like a concubine?"

"The sort who doesn't speak like a concubine."

"At least *she* too is *her* husband's equal."

"That is not the order of things," Hera said quietly. "No matter how crookedly you've wound Poseidon around your finger."

"Did I say *equal*? I was being generous… to Aidoneus." Amphitrite turned to her. "I know how Chthonia sees you. You can tell her, Persephone. Maybe she'll learn something and finally bring that insufferable man to heel."

Amphitrite was correct, but there wasn't any way Persephone was going to say so. She didn't know how to play this game.

Hera swallowed a polite sip. "Odd to hear you speak that way about your sworn king, my husband, while Poseidon's eye wanders afield. And debasing yourself so shamelessly for his benefit has done you little good."

"No, plenty of good, I assure you. It was during a very enjoyable 'debasement' that we conceived little Eurypylus." She stroked her belly for effect. "Our bedmate Astypalaia was all too happy to participate."

Hera sighed and set her tea aside. She dropped her head into her hand and squeezed her temples. Persephone didn't move.

"Poseidon *desperately* wanted that innocent princess but knew I was between the tides. He caressed her and lowered his lips to hers, and Astypalaia was so enrapt she didn't realize I was in the room until I replaced Poseidon's tongue with mine. She was not as innocent as Poseidon imagined. To men, certainly, but not to women. The sight and sound of us drained him of his seed rather quickly."

Persephone felt the color seep from her face, and looked from Hera to Amphitrite and back.

Amphitrite snickered, then doubled over. Her laugh echoed through the hall. "Alright, you win, Hera. I'll stop embarrassing her. Gods… you refuse to let me have *any* fun."

Persephone relaxed, relieved but exhausted. Hera exhaled and rolled her eyes. "Well since that's done…"

"I'm done, I'm done. I promise." She leaned forward. "One last thing though…"

Hera looked skyward. "Amphitrite…"

"Tell me, Persephone… have you considered inviting one of those delicate winged nymphs from the Styx into your chamber? I would be fascinated to find out what they are like."

"I have not."

"Surely after all these decades, you'd want to liven things up for the King of the Dead?"

"Neither Aidoneus nor I have any interest but for each other. And it will remain so."

Hera and Amphitrite looked at one another. Hera lowered her eyes to the floor, but Amphitrite smiled and held her belly, feeling her son turn. "It's only been seventy-five years, Persephone. You have an eternity to learn the limits of your marriage. And likewise, an eternity to try for children."

Persephone scoffed. "Despite Zeus's oath, I doubt a child will be forthcoming."

"Oath? What do you mean?" Hera said, her eyes trained on her tea.

"The Stygian oath he swore to us at the Pomegranate Agreement."

"Don't let him get to you," Amphitrite said. "Hermes told us everything. Cruel and selfish to taunt your husband that way. Zeus only said it to bring Aidoneus to heel. He does that to Poseidon constantly. Not by promising that our child will inherit the heavens, mind you, but he has other ways."

"Thank you. It's of nothing and bears little consequence. We could be content if it never happens at all."

Amphitrite was silent a moment, then squeezed Persephone's hand within hers and gave her a reassuring smile. "Only the Fates know what the future will bring."

Hera stared into her cup, her serene smile set in stone.

✻   ✻   ✻

Her chest heaved, her throat burned. She refused to let tears fall. Hera wondered yet again, as she had so often in her long life if this was how mortals felt when their hearts ceased to beat and they passed from the living world.

Whores were one thing. That impulse came not from his heart, but from that part between his legs that relentlessly craved new flesh. It happened, it ended, and she had deadened herself to that hurt long ago. Love was different. After their *hieros gamos*, Hera had been blessed and cursed by their inextricable link. She could feel when he loved another like a pit in her heart— a hollow, like the well of the cup she gripped in her hand. The clay turned warm against her angry palm.

Tears fell onto its unvarnished surface.

This was a betrayal more potent than any other— even more than the early days when he had deeply loved and begat the twins on Leto. She'd been furious, their marriage still new and fragile, his duplicity and denial so deep.

It hardly compared.

Everyone knew but her. Demeter; Hermes, who had told Poseidon, and likely others; and of course Apollo, with his foresight. How many had been laughing at her all this time?

Zeus had promised Aidoneus and Persephone the only thing that should never, *could* never, be given away: their children's birthright. All this time, one untouchable truth set her apart from all others— that her children were legitimate, and the rest of his spawn were bastards.

By giving them that, he was going back on his word *to her*, and passing the line of succession through *Demeter's* child. Even if a fertile union was impossible, it was the gravity of such a thing. A Stygian oath made by the King of the Gods! Unbreakable, beyond egregious, tempting the Fates into the unimaginable…

She could feel Zeus drawing closer to the room. Her hands tensed around the cup, nearly cracking it. His sandals slapped the marble floors. As his shadow appeared around the corner, she cocked her arm.

The cup exploded against the wall and Zeus ducked beyond the doorway.

"What in Tartarus was that for?!"

"How could you?"

"How could I…" He peered in, then entered the room once he saw that her hands were empty. Hera balled her fists, her shoulders tight. She trembled but didn't move. He scratched the back of his neck and chuckled at her. "Woman, if you want to spend an evening with me, there are better ways to get my attention. You needn't—"

"I have half a mind to never lie with you again!"

"Be serious."

"I am!"

"You've caught me on a night where I'm *alone* for once; I've not *said* a word, I've done *nothing* to cause this, so I'll ask you again. What *daimones* possessed you to throw that at me?"

"Persephone!"

"She never seemed fiendish to me. From what I heard, you had a pleasant time with her and Amphitrite. You invited her, for fatessake." He sighed and folded his arms. "You didn't let that sea witch get under your skin again, did you?"

"Amphitrite is nothing! I *know* what you *swore* to Aidoneus!"

Zeus scowled, then it dawned on him. He lowered his arms to his sides and took a step back. Hera watched him grit his teeth. He was painfully easy to read. That was the expression he'd made when she confronted him about Europa. And Danae.

"How could you make that promise?!"

"You trouble yourself over nothing, woman," Zeus said, pacing about his room. "It will come to nothing. *They* know that. *You* know that. So why pester me?"

"You have no respect for me. It's not enough that you fornicate with everything that crosses your path? Now you give away our son's birthright?"

Zeus laughed. "What?"

"To Persephone's first child!"

"Ha!" He scoffed, loud enough to make her flinch. "This is why I cannot take your mood to heart and you shouldn't dwell on it. I might as well have sworn to Poseidon that the seas would boil. Hades and Persephone will have no children."

"Not Aidoneus, no, but—"

"Persephone sealed her fate when she ate those damned pomegranate seeds."

"You don't know that! She's the Goddess of *Spring*."

"She's part of the Land of the Dead. As much a *Chthonios* as her husband, no matter how much time she spends above. And as barren as their kingdom."

"Her fertility might overpower it." She leveled an accusing finger. "And I think you *know* that."

Zeus rolled his eyes. "What's that supposed to mean?"

"That you'll try to beget on her as you did on her mother."

He blinked hard, then looked nauseous, and Hera froze. She'd only seen him this unsettled one other time and beamed at mustering a reaction stronger than lying or vague dismissal. She pressed on.

"Considering your recent depravity, I wouldn't even put lying with your own daughter beneath you."

"*Enough!*" He advanced, trapping her between his body and the bed. His eyes narrowed. "Even if she were *not* my daughter, she has Rhea's likeness. Honestly, Hera. You wound me. Say what you will about the lovers I've taken, but for fatessake, my own *children*... For shame, Hera."

He backed away, his lip curled in disgust. She seethed. He was blaming *her*. How many times had he always turned it back on her? "It didn't stop you from bedding Alcmene."

He rolled his eyes. "Not this… I told you, it's *over*. Her new husband was rutting in her well-worn passage the night I rose from her bed."

She stamped away. It was too dangerous to stay there. He'd cornered her during an argument and 'soothed' her out of her protests too many times before. This was different. He had dishonored their *children*. "I cannot believe it falls to *me* to know more about your harlots than you do."

"What are you muttering about?"

"Alcmene is the daughter of Electryon, daughter of Perseus. Who was *your own son!*"

"Perseus…" He chewed his lip.

"Fates save me for having such a forgetful husband!"

"If *you* let these pass, as I do, instead of tending your hate for *generations* you might be happier, Hera."

"He slew the sea monster Cetus. Took that Ethiopian girl, Andromeda, to wife."

He cocked his head to the side and smirked in the unnerving way he always would when he found her anger amusing. She wanted to cry, or flail her fists against his chest. If she did it would allow him to comfort her. Or draw her close. All roads led to his polluted bed. She stood her ground.

"His mother was Danae. Who you… appeared to… as a golden rain?"

"Ah, I remember!" His voice lightened, taunting her. "Her miserable father locked her away to defy the Oracle, fearing that her offspring would kill him. And as luck would have it, Perseus did! Accidentally, mind you, but…" He guffawed.

"And so you sleep with your great-granddaughter."

"Please…"

"She has your blood running through her!"

"So does nearly every noble family in Hellas," he chided. "And I've bedded half of *them*."

"So does Persephone. Will you bed her too?!"

He lunged and she tried to twist away. Hera shrieked. He caught her wrists and pinned her against his chest. "Let me go!"

His breath teased the stray hairs on her forehead. "Listen to me."

"No!"

"Hera," he said, his voice soothing. "Hera, they cannot have children. Look at me."

She kept her gaze firmly on his chest, not wanting him to see her crying.

"Wife, *gynaika mou*, look at me."

She sniffled and raised her deep brown eyes to meet his sky blue. He released a wrist and brushed a tear from her face.

"I would *never* betray you like that. Hades cannot have children. I said it to taunt him because of all the destruction his selfish infatuation with her had caused. It was meant to drive a wedge between them."

"What..." she tried to keep from leaning into the fingers stroking her cheek. Her voice wavered. "What if they do conceive?"

"They won't. I hear they've tried nearly everything. So, my empty oath to him did all it was supposed to do. It put Hades in his place. It will eventually drive them apart because Persephone would never have eaten those seeds if she'd known it would condemn her to a barren marriage bed. In that way, he *did* trick her, as the mortals say. Even if there were a way they could, even if they found some dark sorcery that could give them a child, I would never usurp ours. *Never.* If such a creature were even possible, it would be rooted to the Underworld like its dismal parents."

"You promise?"

"I promise, Hera." He kissed her cheek.

"Why didn't you tell me back then?"

"Because I thought it of no consequence. Just as it's of no consequence now."

She dipped her head.

"You see? Nothing to worry yourself over."

She tensed. This was becoming too easy for him. "What about Alcmene?"

"I told you, it's over."

"Her sons— twins, Zeus…"

"It's doubtful they're even mine. She slept with Amphitryon before the sun went down on the day I left her."

"Their blood will be that much stronger if divine lineage is on *both* sides."

"They won't. They'd be mortal *hemitheoi* at best. To amount to anything more, they'd need ambrosia. And that won't happen either."

She nodded.

"Now," he said, kissing her neck, "how best should I apologize?"

She closed her eyes and leaned in. "Apologize?"

"Of course," he said, his lips lingering on the juncture of her shoulder and neck. "I should have told you right away what I'd sworn. Would you have been as distressed today if I had?"

"No," she whispered back, feeling heat against her thigh through his himation and loincloth.

"You could have laughed her off, just as I mock her husband." Zeus teased his fingers along the small of her back and grazed her jaw with his beard.

"Amphitrite knew."

"Amphitrite is a gossip." He kissed her lips quickly. "And a hastily promoted nymph." He kissed her earlobe. "And a shameless whore."

Hera sucked in a breath as his tongue danced across the shell of her ear.

"And you are the queen." He stole a fibula from her peplos, the fabric cascading from her shoulder. He breathed against the skin he had freed. "You are *my* queen."

She touched his chest, inhaling his scent of warm oak and petrichor, then stared up at him, blinking. He loved her eyes; she knew he did. It was why she emphasized them so heavily with kohl and malachite. She also knew that her paint would be smeared before the night was over because he loved that too.

His head dipped and his tongue lashed against her nipple. Hera lost her footing, pressing against him as he squeezed her rump. He slid the other pin away and her arms flew around his neck, then pushed his himation off his shoulder.

Why was she always so helpless against him? She knew the moment she walked through that door that it would end this way. Hera puzzled over that for a moment, then felt her girdle unclasp and slink down her falling skirts to the floor, its precious jewels and gold lost in the linen at her feet. She bucked against his hand.

"Eager, are we?"

"Don't push your luck," Hera said before nipping his neck. She felt his large hand grip the back of her neck and pull her to face him.

"I'll push whatever I want, *gynaika mou.*" He hitched up one of her legs and threaded his fingers through the folds of her vulva, fingers on either side of her bud, and Hera trembled and braced herself, anticipating, like so many times before, what he would do next.

Her skin prickled from the bottoms of her feet to the hairs on her neck. A current set off every vital nerve with relentless perfection. She arched her back, and the world around her disappeared as she came.

Tears leaked from her eyes and she cried out, feeling him close in on her as he caressed her through the exquisite waves. His fingers settled there again. He had become so adept at this. Zeus used the very energy that coursed through the sky, the gift he'd received during the war, to turn her into a mewling pet. The same jolt sent her over the edge again, and again, wrenching her pleasure from her body until she quivered.

"Zeus… mercy…" Malachite trickled down her temples and into her loosened hair. His eyes darted across her face and neck, triumphant at the quivering mess he'd made of her.

"Is this not merciful enough?" He rubbed his engorged phallus against her thigh. "That you should be thrice satisfied while you leave me painfully aching for you?" Zeus growled into her ear and ground against her thigh.

"Please… please…" The dry words stuck in her throat. She was delirious. Her head was craned back and she felt a pillow cushion her neck, replacing his hand. Her legs canted upward in anticipation, but she felt his hands on her hips and he turned her over so she lay prone. He pulled up her hips and with a single thrust, buried himself to the hilt. Hera sighed in relief. No matter how practiced he was with that touch, it left her vacant, clenching around emptiness. He knew this. He would draw it out of her until she could stand no more, then fill her with hardness and heat.

Zeus gripped her hips so hard she thought they would bruise, crashing into her, and when she tried to lift herself onto her elbows, his heavy palm pressed her to the bed again. He leaned over her to keep her pinned down.

"Why," she said, catching her breath, "can you not love me as a good husband ought?"

"It's not what you need."

"What if I *wanted* it?" She squealed as he circled his thumb around her anus.

"You hate it," he growled. "You always did. *This* is what pleases you."

"So you disrespect—" she lost her words, gasping as he pushed his thick thumb inward, lighting every nerve that clenched around it. He snapped his hips, stretching her, and she mewled his name, her eyes closing, her fingers clawing the sheets.

"You were saying?" He rasped into her ear. He grabbed a fistful of her hair and turned her head so he could kiss her. She bit at his lip to break their kiss and he removed his invading digit and pulled her upright, holding her taut against his body.

"You're a brute," she cried out through clenched teeth. He increased his tempo savagely and she leaned in to take him deeper, their voices blending, animalistic.

Zeus raced toward his climax, his cock thickening within her, then returned his fingers to the apex of her mound, ensuring that she would lose herself the moment that he did. Hera shook with dread and anticipation, and then in the throes of ecstasy as he came within her.

Her very self disappeared— as though she were an extension of his body. He shook with her, their breath falling into unison. Ever so slowly— gently, even— he released her, stroking her rump, then crashed down onto the sheets on his back. She fell forward, her heartbeat thrumming in her ears, the pillow already smeared with kohl and malachite from her eyelids. She wanted to slap him. He would only take it as an invitation for more if she did.

Every time she sought him out, he did this to her. But she knew that he was right— that the proper way, the way that wives were supposed to be, supine, serene, and patient as they received the gift of their husband's seed, wasn't what she desired. They had tried that many times over their long lives, and it left her restless and irritated. She needed a measure of pain in her pleasure. And he took pleasure in her, and the more he took from her was what left him sated… for a time.

Why could she not be a proper wife? Why did she always want to make love to him like his whores surely did? Hera wondered for the thousand thousandth time if this was the reason why he constantly strayed— that she was impure, defective, that he sought out others because she couldn't even abide by the example she was supposed to set for those who worshiped her. She rolled onto her side and sighed, her breath finally returning to normal. Zeus nestled in behind her. "Better?"

"I ought to shave off your beard while you sleep."

"Mmhmm… Glad you enjoyed yourself, wife." He was already slumberous. "Come. Rest with me for a bit. You can stay the night if you wish."

Hera didn't respond except to tuck herself under his muscular arm and surrender to exhaustion.

✻　　✻　　✻

She rose quietly by a sliver of moonlight, confident that Zeus wouldn't wake up. After they lay together, she rarely

61

stayed. It was better that way. They weren't newlyweds. Languishing in his arms would only spell heartache later. She was his queen, above those childish wiles. Their love ran deeper than his affairs, and letting him pull her heartstrings would only weaken her. She gathered her strewn clothes and pulled her peplos around her. In a flash of iridescent peacock blue and green, she walked the ether back to her private chambers.

She felt immodest every time she left his room this way. But once alone, she cast her peplos to the floor and walked barefoot across the marble, feeling rejuvenated and free in her private sanctuary. Not even Iris was allowed in here.

Hestia was right. Hestia was *always* right. Perhaps Persephone and her husband *would* set a good example for Zeus. Their relationship was a perversion of the natural order, but it was certainly better than betrayal after betrayal, base lust, and defilement. Persephone had left mirroring Hera's curtness after she'd revealed Zeus's arrogant oath. Hera had been so angry she had barely said goodbye.

It would be best to make amends. Persephone was a *new* queen, one that still needed to be taught— wrought and shaped into a *true* ruler. The Queen of the Underworld could be a powerful ally, especially with Elysion still new and unknown. She could use allies. And more still, a friend and equal. Hera could tell from Zeus's reaction that she would never tempt her ever-wandering husband. Moreover, Persephone was not to be trifled with, even for one such as Zeus.

Now there was another matter to resolve.

Hera picked up the green fillet from her hair and stretched it out across the floor. Finding the center, she ripped the fabric into two pieces, equal in length, and held them tightly in each hand.

With eyes shut, she breathed steadily. The fabric thickened and writhed, and frayed strands flicked out in small forked tongues. She opened her eyes and let go. Two vipers twisted to the floor, their scale patterns reminiscent of the embroidery on her fillet.

They stared up at her, waiting.

"Go to Thebes," she whispered to them. "Find any son of Zeus that sprung from the desecration of Alcmene's marriage bed. Send them to Hades quickly and mercifully."

The vipers turned and gracefully slithered out of her room, down the slopes of Olympus, bound for the infant twins Alcides and Iphicles.

3.

"WHAT I'M TRYING TO SAY," DEMETER SHOUTED after Persephone, "is that he's behaved quite differently since Eumolpus died. Usually, he's here more often." She quickened her pace and muttered under her breath. "Too often..."

Persephone stalked ahead of her mother through the ripened field, saying nothing. The autumn sundown winds whipped past them, rising off the sea and threatening a late-season rain that could ruin the barley.

Demeter sighed in exasperation. Any talk about Hades rankled Persephone, no matter how helpful her intentions. Sometimes it seemed as if her daughter was searching for any reason to find fault with her. She only wanted her to be happy, even if it meant happiness with the Lord of the Dead.

"You should at least ask him if he even looked into that matter about Orpheus."

"Before we created Elysion..." Persephone spun about. "We opened ourselves to each other, completely. We can each tell if the other is holding something back."

Demeter rolled her eyes. "Yes, I know. That's what the hieros gamos does, for fatessake. Do you think that Zeus and I didn't share that same sacred connection? He can still hide things from you." She worried for Persephone. Her marriage was new, less than a century old, and she acted as if she and Hades had been together as long as Gaia and Ouranos.

"Just because he didn't visit doesn't mean he's hiding things from me. Fates help me if we describe every detail of our separate lives."

"This isn't trivial, Persephone. Not after that… adventure you had in Alikarnassos at that *harlot's* suggestion—"

"Stop calling her that! Aphrodite was trying to help. Do you want grandchildren or not?!"

"Of all the Olympians you could have befriended— and you shouldn't seek their companionship— it still baffles me why she holds such a thrall over you."

"She is kind to me. Isn't that what *you* taught me to value?"

"When it's served on the back of hidden demands, it's not kindness. And if that's your measure, why do you shrink from meeting with Hera?"

"If you'd been there, you'd understand. They lobbed me back and forth like an *episkyros* ball. It was disgusting! And she didn't seem pleased by my company when I left. She grew… cold."

"Yet she's summoned you to return. Twice." Demeter bristled. Why she was defending that horrible cow of a sister was beyond her. Never mind she'd just been pleading for Persephone to seek out Hades! To hear herself, she'd think she was completely mad.

"I'm not going back."

"A wise decision."

"And not on your advice! I have nothing to say to anyone there."

"Except that Eastern whore."

"Enough, mother," Persephone said, raising asphodel from the earth.

"Instead of visiting her barbaric cults, maybe you should demand Aidon—"

"I said enough!"

Demeter staggered back as a great ring of fire swirled behind her daughter. Persephone stormed through and was gone. In her wake, brambles and blackberries snagged and stained the edges of Demeter's skirts. "So dramatic…"

She walked back to the Telesterion, head held high, refusing to draw any more attention from the mortals. She knew Persephone had been disappearing to secret places over the years, and though she swore upon the Styx that she'd never done it, Demeter suspected she would slip away to her husband's palace. She wouldn't be so rash in the middle of the harvest, though. Persephone had doubtless retreated to the Plutonion, already piling up with pomegranates, dates, and olive oil.

Fine, she thought. *Let her sulk there.* It did nothing to change the facts. Aidoneus was being furtive. He usually visited Eleusis before harvest, and when he had run into Demeter he had been curt but cordial, with enough respect to carry out… marital relations… away from the Telesterion. She still choked on bile at the very idea.

Keryx stood at the Telesterion, his grayed head bowed as he swung the doors wide for Demeter to enter. She stopped. Something smelled of irises and an undercurrent of sour milk. A woman cloaked in a fine weave of saffron-colored linen stood at the foot of Metaneira and Celeus's sepulcher. Mortal petitioners across the room glanced between them, then scurried away.

The woman turned, her eyes darkly lined, her lids dusted a bright turquoise. She pulled back her veil. "Good day to you, sister."

✻   ✻   ✻

"That color looks horrible on you."

"I agree." Hera smiled. A wave of blue swirled across her himation and overtook the yellow of her veil and peplos. "But it would have been vulgar to arrive with a train of peacocks in my wake, nay? Even if that means covering myself in the colors of your glorified pasture grass…"

Demeter bared her teeth. "What in Tartarus are you doing here?"

The door banged open and Persephone burst through, bare feet caked with mud. "Mother, I need you to listen to—"

Persephone's eyes widened and she swallowed. She bowed her head and curtsied. "Your grace."

Hera smiled at her. "Oh come, this is your temple. If anyone should bow it is I."

Persephone cocked an eyebrow.

"I'm sorry for surprising you." Hera passed by Demeter without a sideways glance. "Is there anywhere we can speak alone?"

"Don't trouble yourselves on my account," Demeter gritted out, then disappeared through parted rows of conjured wheat sheaves into the ether.

Hera was silent for a moment, then turned again to Persephone. "Oh. I wasn't interrupting anything, was I?"

"Nothing that can't be sorted out later," Persephone huffed. "May I ask what brings you to Eleusis?"

The girl before her was muddy almost up to her knees, her hair wind-whipped like a mortal peasant, yet she still had all the bearing of a queen. Demeter's influence could never spoil that. "I hadn't heard from you, even after sending two messages with Hermes."

"Apologies," Persephone said. "I have little time to spare between midsummer and harvest. I must ensure the mortals survive winter."

"Of course." Hera cast her eyes to the ground. "I only hoped you might have spared a minute for me." Hera raised her hand to quiet any protest. "And then I thought, it's no wonder you didn't want to visit me, after how abominably I treated you."

She gave Persephone a sidelong glance that often worked to great effect on Zeus. The Goddess of Spring softened. "Your grace—"

"Hera."

"Hera, I… don't know what to say. The ways of Olympus are not my ways, nor my husband's. It wasn't any offense that kept me away, but realizing that I don't belong in that company."

"But that's exactly why I need you. I went about it poorly. It would have been better to meet with you alone instead, since Amphitrite is sure to bring out my worst."

"Why *me*, though? There are many goddesses in your retinue, you have countless allies…"

"I have all the servants I could want. Endless sycophants. But none among them are my equal. No one I can speak with in confidence, and no one willing to listen."

She scowled. "I do not wish to be your pet. Nor do I believe that you'd find anything I have or do to be of interest."

Hera pulled her shoulders back. The girl was smarter than she gave her credit for. In this world of men, she knew the dangers of that all too well. "I disagree. There is *much* I could stand to learn from you, in truth."

Persephone sighed. "I can't imagine what. You have been Queen of all the Gods for aeons—"

"Please. We both know how it goes in this world," Hera said, speaking lower. "That I am *nothing* but for that I wed Zeus and bear his children."

"No," Persephone replied, frowning. "That's not true."

"Isn't it? Perhaps Amphitrite is right about me."

"You are different women. It was... *uncomfortable* watching that play out."

"I fought so hard against her words because in my heart of hearts, I know she's right. Perhaps I should learn from you about reining in my husband."

Persephone's eyebrows rose. Hera thought for a moment that she had chosen the wrong words. Zeus was Persephone's *father*, after all. And she had displaced Persephone's own mother in his heart.

The young goddess spoke. "If... you think that... Aidoneus could set an example for Zeus, then I'm sorry. I cannot help you."

Hera smiled. "I don't expect to *ever* keep Zeus from his... wanderings. The Fates never had that in store for us. But... I would like to reclaim some standing with him."

"I'm not sure—"

"Please," she said, kneeling. She picked a stray peacock feather from the floor. "As it is, I sit three steps below him. Amphitrite mocks me for it, and you..." She stood back up and wove the feather into her hair. "If anything in this world of men is to change, it must start with me, the Goddess of Marriage."

Persephone tilted her head to the side and relaxed her stance, saying nothing.

"What you and Aidoneus have done..." Hera looked around them, her palms upturned.

"This is my mother's temple," she said just above a whisper.

"Is it? No matter how tall her statues are, mortals come here for the new crop after the fallow. The promise of life after death. Through your and your husband's partnership, you achieved something greater than any of us who took part in a *hieros gamos*. Possibly since Gaia herself."

"That remains to be seen."

"But it's evident. You've given them hope. How many offerings lay in the Plutonion?"

Persephone looked away and spoke low. "Too many to count."

"This world deserves to be better than what it is. I want that to come to pass above, by the same example you and your husband set below."

The wheels turned in Persephone's head. She stood a bit taller and nodded. "We should talk about this further. This season has run its course, though. The autumn harvest is tomorrow, and after—"

"Naturally." Hera smiled graciously. "I won't burden you. But in the springtime, join me on Olympus when you are able, without Amphitrite, without servants or other wayward ears, and… perhaps then we can discuss this again."

✣　　✣　　✣

After her first disastrous homecoming, Persephone's return to Aidoneus's side was always a joyful yet sober affair.

They'd cloister themselves in their rooms until the next full moon, then host a quiet feast on their anniversary. Hecate joined them without exception, as did Hypnos and Thanatos. Nyx would make an occasional appearance, as would Askalaphos and Menoetes. The Erinyes, a few Stygian nymphs, and Lampades often rounded out the feasting company. Charon was a rare sight in the hall, which made his arrival that evening so surprising.

The doors opened loudly, silencing the idle chatter between Hypnos and Persephone. Askalaphos straightened, turning away from Nychtopula, who grasped his arm and peered around him. Aidoneus sat upon his divan, then stood in mild astonishment. Charon leaned against his oar, his thin frame even frailer against the backdrop of the great hall, then moved to kneel.

"Charon, rise." Aidoneus stretched out his arms. "Come in, friend; it's good to see you."

"And you, my king." He turned to Persephone. "Aristi."

Persephone smiled and returned a slight nod.

Charon swayed, the motions of the Styx deep in his bones. "I have something for you, Aidon. A gift, of sorts. More, a curiosity I found eight days ago. Or rather, did it find *me*?"

Aidoneus glanced back at Persephone and shrugged. When he turned back, his eyes widened at the perfectly cut ruby Charon produced from the folds of his robes.

"This fell in my boat. Nearly hit a poor shade on the head."

Hypnos fought back laughter. Hecate brought her fingertips to her lips and exchanged a glance with Thanatos. Persephone's bewilderment was palpable.

"We have the whole earth above us, so pebbles and such fall all the time," Charon turned it over in his hands, letting the light from the braziers shimmer through it. "But this stone was just... so finely cut..."

Aidoneus felt heat creeping up his neck, reddening his ears. *He* knew how it fell into Charon's possession. Every autumn he would wait within the Plutonion for Persephone, her mother's priests droning as they prepared for her departure and the barren winter ahead. He would reach from the shadows, and take her hand, not daring so much as a squeeze of affection. None knew it was him. It would sully all of Persephone's work if the mortals knew that the feared Lord of the Dead stood in the shadows.

Once the door closed, they would retreat through the caverns in silence. He would hoist her into his chariot and they'd be off, emerging in the dark reaches of Erebus. Only then would he kiss her with all the uncaged fervor of six months spent without her in his bed. Normally, Aidon would visit before harvest to avoid ever-present Demeter. By the time they were finally alone, it was often two months since their last encounter. This year the wait was worsened by Aidon forgoing their usual visit.

"…and so auspicious," Charon continued, snapping his attention back to the room, "since this jewel fell into my boat on the very day our queen came back from the corporeal world…"

He'd been hasty with her. And she with him, he recalled, deepening his blush further. Her fingernails had gouged his neck and flanks as she had struggled to remove his himation and pull down his loincloth. His garments had fallen in a heap on the chariot's podium. As he was wrapping the reins around one hand and tugging at her dress with the other, he'd grown impatient, and with a growl he'd yanked her jeweled girdle off her hips, the gold-set stones clattering in the cart. Neither had noticed. By then, he was pressed deeply into her, a rhythm growing between them, his senses flooded by the warmth and sound and scent of her surrounding him…

Afterward, in the waxing light of the Styx, she'd fished for her clothes and righted his, only to discover a large jewel missing from its setting. Persephone fretted about it, but it was no matter to Aidoneus. He was the master of earth and all the precious things therein. A replacement would be easy. Amidst the following days, he had forgotten all about it.

Until now. And of all the damnable places for it to turn up…

"I thought to myself," Charon smiled, "I could keep this, perhaps with all the coin I've received over the aeons, but no, that wouldn't do…"

Hecate snickered as Aidon sheepishly extended his hand.

"Such a marvelous trinket should be given to you, so you could gift it to your dear wife." He held it aloft then dropped it into Aidoneus's open palm. "On your anniversary. In front of all of your gathered friends."

One of Hypnos's silver wings arched forward to shield his face. Tisiphone didn't bother masking her harsh cackle, her body doubling over, one hand on Persephone's shoulder. Nychtopula whispered in Askalaphos's ear and his eyes grew wide.

"Which of them put you up to this, Charon?" Aidoneus asked, his lip twitching into a smile.

"It wasn't me." Hypnos cried and gulped air. "I swear!"

Thanatos parted his hands and raised one finger. Aidoneus looked at him in surprise, and Persephone smiled, her cheeks a rosy blend of embarrassment and laughter. Aidon returned to his seat and handed her the ruby. They exchanged a quick kiss and the laughter ended in a quiet applause.

Charon smiled. "Now all's right with the world."

Thanatos would have been the likely culprit a century ago, but Sisyphus had changed him forever. He was more somber; Aidon had heard no complaints from Hecate, no boasts or rumors about him chasing after the Lampades— or *any* woman or man, for that matter. Aidon was relieved that this prank had been his idea.

"Won't you stay, Charon?"

"Perhaps. You know the first days of winter can be busy—"

"Oh, please," Persephone said. "Anyone newly arrived can wait a short hour. Come share the nectar that was sent to us."

"Nectar." Charon's jaw tightened.

"Courtesy of Hera," Aidon said.

"Do you recall the last time she sent us a… *gift?*" He looked pointedly at Aidoneus.

"It's in good faith. Persephone got on with her, and Hermes delivered it earlier for our anniversary." Aidoneus sipped from his cup. He had quietly vowed to have only one. Everyone was eager to lay the blame at Minthe's, or Demeter's, or even Hera's feet— anyone but him. But Aidon knew the truth:

if he hadn't downed the entire glass, and many before it, he wouldn't have been so gravely affected by the ergot. "It won't dull your senses, I assure you."

Charon's shoulders dropped and he sighed. "It had better not. If I forget to collect a *single* obol tomorrow, I'm laying the blame squarely on you, Aidon."

Hypnos poured him a glass and they feasted into the evening, trading tales from above and below. Orphne and Clymena brought a *cithara* and a tambourine, and with some prodding from Tisiphone, Persephone danced, showing them an *epilinios* she had learned on Crete. Aidon's gaze was fixed on her the whole time, relishing her ease and happiness at being home again. On each spin, her potent glances in his direction edged him closer toward dismissing their guests so he could have her to himself.

But he could also feel her many questions for him lingering. She knew that he was withholding something. And he needed to tell her.

✳   ✳   ✳

Warmth suffused and enveloped her. Warmth from his hands wrapped around the small of her back, from each gasping breath where she leaned against his shoulder, and radiating from where they were joined. The gentle breeze around them, his scent, and the sheen of sweat on Persephone's skin provided a cool counterpoint that made the aftereffects of her peak all the more sublime. Aidon pulled her down hard and threw his head back, his fingers digging into her hips, and a final burst of heat made her shiver.

He leaned back into the grass and pulled her with him, then uncrossed his legs. She carefully uncoupled from him and rolled away, unfolding her limbs to fall in a heap at his side. They stared up at the stars of Elysion, breathing in time, their fingers lacing together.

74

"Happy anniversary."

"Indeed." She kissed him on the cheek and lazily raised a finger, tracing the winter constellation of The Hunter. Decades ago, they had stopped wondering why the sky in Elysion was filled with stars, why the moon shone at night and the sun during the day. Instead, they decided to enjoy the world they had created. "They look like this above, right now."

"Yes. I remember."

She rolled over and propped herself up on an elbow, her eyes trained on him.

He winced, then smiled at her. "You have questions for me. You've had them since we descended."

"I *wanted* to wait. I wasn't worried they'd be anything shocking. It was more my mother hounding me about it before the harvest."

He tensed again. "I had seen to something early in the season, sweet one, and needed to think it over before I said anything. So I avoided you. I hope you can forgive me."

"Can you tell me now?"

He took a deep breath and let it out slowly. "Yes."

"Don't worry, husband," she folded her arms and propped herself on his chest with a smile. "It's just me."

"After Eumolpus died, I spent months contemplating what he said. I didn't want you to be hurt again. Not after the last time."

Aphrodite had suggested her temple far to the east, and they had participated in the fertility rites there. Persephone had cloistered herself on the temple grounds, eschewing her responsibilities, heedless of the fact that it would mean a difficult winter. When her cycle was late, she was overjoyed and told Aidoneus to hurry. By the time he arrived, she was spotting, though she was told by the attending priestess that it could be a good sign. But the next evening Aidon awoke to find her collapsed in a heap, sobbing, blood streaking her thighs.

Persephone let out a long sigh. "I understand."

"I didn't want to give you false hope. Not if it was just pageantry and nonsense. But this…"

"You met this Orpheus?"

"Right before I saw you at the villa. I couldn't tell you then. And I couldn't continue to lie by omission until we'd spoken about it."

"Is that the reason you didn't visit midsummer?"

He nodded.

Persephone laid her head in the crook of his arm. "How will this be different?"

"Remember when Eumolpus mentioned their unborn god?"

"Every fertility cult from Iberia to the Euphrates honors some unborn god or goddess."

"Which is why I did not appear to Orpheus directly, nor did I tell him who I was. Though I'm sure he suspected."

"We've done this. Masking our identities, appearing mortal—"

"We did, sweet one. Which is why I *commanded* him to name the one yet to be born." She rose and looked him in the eye, and he nodded. Persephone's skin prickled and she leaned back on her haunches. Aidoneus sat up with her. "Zagreus. Zagreus, Persephone, the name we want to give our son. Who have you told besides me?"

"Hecate knows, but no one else. When I spoke with Eumolpus, I used *brimo*— 'the strong one'— an epithet given irrespective of sex."

"How could Orpheus have known?"

What if this were another stone thrown down a bottomless well? She couldn't abandon her responsibilities ever again, or endure such deep disappointment. "It may be a coincidence."

"Or he could have heard the name elsewhere, or divined it, though I don't know how." He looked off into the distance. "Or something more sinister is at play. But Orpheus seemed more earnest than anything else…"

She was afraid to hope, but his half-hearted excuses told her all she needed to know. He believed. Decades had passed since he had dared to believe anything would come of their attempts, and yet here he sat, apprehension barely masking exuberance, waiting for her reply. She smiled and her eyes stung. "Let's try."

"I don't want you to be hurt again."

"Wouldn't all our past pain be worth it if it gave us our child?"

He let out a long sigh and leaned his forehead onto hers. "Yes."

"What must we do? I can't miss the growing season. Hundreds died last time."

"It's one day and one night, as the first shoots rise from the earth. No more."

"What does it require of us?"

"That was less clear."

"Eumolpus mentioned it would be who we are… our most heartfelt desires."

"Orpheus said the same thing and no more. But he abides by the will of the Fates. I am confident we can leave this to *ananke*. No one will know that we're attending. As far as they're concerned, we will be a mortal king and his queen." He gazed at the shallow sea beyond and cleared his throat. "There is one potential… issue."

"What's that?"

"Obtaining the boon I promised for his discretion."

✱   ✱   ✱

Wind battered the walls and guttered the torches. Winter had started in earnest. The Thracians blamed a surfeit of sacrifices to Zeus at the Spring of Midas, Arcadians feared that Poseidon had whipped up the seas in anger, and Athenians debated whether they had sent enough propitiations to Eleusis.

But summer had been kind, and bountiful stores of grain were safe in every village and citadel. Orpheus gazed at the pool that dominated the center of the atrium. The oculus above and slender clerestory windows had been sealed shut with tar-thatched reeds and hempen rope. The temple was warm enough for any who sought sanctuary. He stoked the twelfth brazier with an iron poker, the close heat stifling beneath his woolen himation.

"Where did you hear the name Zagreus, hymnist?"

Every hair on his neck stood up. Orpheus froze in the empty hall, the poker clanking to the ground.

"Tell me."

Though he was sweating, ice-filled his stomach. Orpheus fell to his knees, eyes fixed on the ground. "Is… the God of Nysa. I-it's you?"

"After the first moon of winter, as promised," the voice said. "Stand, Orpheus. I come asking *you* for favors. Who gave you the name Zagreus?"

"The name…" The visitor grew silent. He was holding his breath. Orpheus swallowed. "It came in a vision. On my way from Eleusis, I composed a hymn to the Moirai and the lands below. The night I arrived, this temple held a rite, and all within partook of a ceremonial draught left by a nymph-born woman who lives in the forest. Our order had consumed it before— but no one before me saw… visions. Sigils, epithets… and when I slept that night, I dreamed of the Mnemosyne and the waters that restore the memories of those who go to Elysion. I dreamed of a god not yet born. A babe cried out, born in a flash of flame and light. I heard his name, then. At that moment I *knew* that he would be the one to tend Paradise through the ages, who would reveal its true purpose, one who could unite tribes… nations…"

There was a rustling, then the faint outline of a tall man with jet black hair. He lowered a polished gold helm to his side and stared at Orpheus with eyes that had seen the rise and fall of civilizations. "And in your vision, the name of this un-born god was given…"

"Zagreus Sabazios Eubouleus. As clear as if I were awake. What's more, I wasn't the only one who had the same dream that night."

"There are other mystics here?"

"I wouldn't go so far as to call us that."

"If the mantle fits…"

"I merely listen. But yes, they heard it too. Saw what I saw."

The man— the god, rather— straightened. A smile teased the corner of his mouth. "Eubouleus. The Good Counselor. That epithet belongs to another."

"I know, my lord."

"You know who I am, then."

Orpheus paused. He knew it in his bones. If he were wrong, he might be struck dead. But he had trusted this god so far. Still, he closed his eyes when he answered. "You are Axiokersos. The Unseen One. The Receiver of Many."

"You are permitted to use my name, Orpheus."

"You'll forgive me if I do not?"

The Unseen One nodded at him, then shifted and paced the room, glancing at the empty niches, noting the absence of any divine statuary. "I know your reasons. You likewise under-stand why *no one* must learn our true identities if this is to succeed."

"I do."

"Have you thought about my offer?"

"It is all I *have* thought about these many months. Especially since time grows short."

"What do you mean?"

"We hold these rites once every three years, on the third full moon after the first crocus blooms. This is the year."

"I want you to know this," Aidoneus crossed the room to stand before him. "If you say 'no' to me, there will be *no* repercussions for you or yours. I, Hades Aidoneus Chthonios, firstborn son of Kronos, swear it to you on the Styx. You will not have displeased me, you will not have displeased my wife, nor any other god or creature who dwells on or below the earth. And when you pass from this world and journey to mine, your choice here will have no bearing on the hereafter."

"And what of the gods above?"

He waved his hand dismissively. "They would care little about this."

"Why would you come to me— a mortal— for something like this? We are so small and fragile compared to the Deathless Ones."

"I am not an Olympian, *hemitheoi*. I don't hold myself above your kind. The gods of the earth, whose lives are intertwined with your immortal souls, cannot afford such… vanities. And your kind has a wisdom that comes *from* being fragile— having but one lifetime to accomplish what you can. It is a powerful thing. More than you, or the gods above truly realize."

"But death is not the end. Eumolpus taught me that. In Elysion we remember what we were," Orpheus said, his voice growing earnest. "We grow and learn even after death, once we drink from the Mnemosyne."

Aidoneus shook his head and sighed. "The words written on your scrolls, the ones you place in the mouths of the dead… are a fiction. A pleasant one, to be sure, but all who reside in my realm must drink from the Lethe. For *their* sakes."

Cold crept over him. The rites for the dead he'd performed for countless adherents… Were they all for nothing? "The visions I had, though, they said that you would let those who are worthy drink from the Pool of Memory, that they—"

"I do not know whence those *visions* came. But while Elysion is new, the laws that govern Chthonia remain unchanged."

"But, the memories and lives of those who are reborn—"

"And with good reason."

His voice faintly reverberated through the hall. Orpheus swallowed. His words came out thin and reedy. "I only know I saw it as clearly as the child you believe will come from our rites. But if I say no, and deny *you*, why would you spare me?"

"Because it's not your decision alone. It is *ananke*. If our child cannot be conceived by these means, I accept that. As does my wife."

Orpheus let out a sigh, feeling a great weight lift from his shoulders. "I'll do it."

"For the gift of a lyre?"

"It is a more than generous gift. Moreover, because I know I can trust you, and that my decision wasn't compelled."

"My wife will be very pleased by this." Aidoneus folded his hands behind his back and turned away from Orpheus, observing the walls of the stark temple. Orpheus leaned against the column. The Unseen One's voice had hitched. He was moved and didn't want to betray his emotions. "The god revealed to you… Zagreus. My wife and I chose that same name when we first knew we wanted a child of our own. We never told anyone. You gave me much reason to hope."

"My lord, I have hope as well, but… I can promise nothing."

"Of course."

"Our visions were clear. All saw the same thing, and we all saw that the Unborn One will come into this world from the womb of a mortal woman."

"*Your* visions also told you that mortals' memories are restored in Elysion. When we dream, we see first what we know and believe. None in your order would imagine the rites being attended by gods."

"Certainly not."

"But only gods beget gods." The Receiver of Many hesitated. "Orpheus, tell me... Eumolpus spoke of it before he passed, and you said the same this spring: that the sacrifice we'd make would be profound and beyond our understanding... My wife and I have much to lose, so you can see how that might give me pause."

"It wouldn't—" Orpheus shut his eyes momentarily, trying to find the right words. "It would not throw the spheres into chaos. A farmer's crops would not wither, a king would not lose his crown, nor would a priest be cast from his temple. It would be something personal. Not a sacrifice for the Lord of the Underworld, but a sacrifice for... Aidoneus, the man." Orpheus shuddered involuntarily, and his gaze fell to the floor.

"You can't be any more specific?"

"I am sorry, my lord. I cannot," Orpheus said. "It is not known by me, nor would it manifest immediately. The sacrifice will unfold over time, and by the hand of the Fates alone."

✻   ✻   ✻

Hermes knew better than to visit in early winter, and his first memory of them was enough of a reminder. Even if a message from Olympus meant for Hades was urgent, he would always beg it off until the snow was deep. And in the dead of winter, the Underworld was more temperate than above, almost making it a welcome respite. Almost.

82

He sat in Charon's boat, smoothing the golden feathers of his winged sandals, and trying to avoid eye contact with the cloaked shade of a glowering crone.

"My husband sacrificed a ram to you," she said suddenly.

Hermes started, then remembered that she hadn't drunk from the Lethe. Though a shade, she wasn't yet part of Asphodel. He could hear her. "What, to me?"

"He wanted to sell sheep across the water to the Arcadians. I told him not to go into business, but no... did Stavros listen to me? No!"

"What happened?"

"You don't know?!"

"Uh..."

"I knew it! I told Stavros you wouldn't listen to his prayers! 'I know sheep, not trade, Agathe, but I gave Hermes a *whole ram*, Agathe!' Pious fool he was..."

"That's enough," Charon hissed.

The shade cowered and fell silent, but pursed her lips and stared at Hermes until the boat scraped against the opposite shore.

"Welcome home," Charon said to her and pointed his oar beyond the ghostly reeds at the cypress-lined stone pathway. "The Trivium is that way. Go to the spring beside it and wait. You are to be judged by Rhadamanthys."

The woman flitted from the boat and disappeared up the pathway. Charon pushed off and shook his head. Hermes shrugged. "What?"

"With all your infamous wiles and trickery," the Boatman said, "you had nothing to say to her?"

"And tell her what?!"

"Anything! A storm of the ages, the evil eye, any number of Olympian excuses."

"There are too many offerings... how could I have known their circumstances?"

"*You* guide the wayward dead, Psychopompos. Speak to them and find out. Or *lie*. Lies come to you easily enough."

Hermes slouched back. The palace gates rose above tall stalks of asphodel. Charon stilled his boat and Hermes debated whether or not to have the last word.

"What is your purpose here?"

"Your King summoned me. And since it was on the way, I also have a message from our Queen to yours." Hermes sighed at Charon's sour face. "Persephone is the *only* child of Zeus she's ever been kind to, so can you please, *please* do your part to not ruin it?"

The Boatman didn't reply.

"Not for me, but her." Hermes leaped into the air, finally free. Ever since the awful day he'd come at the command of Zeus to return Persephone to Demeter, he'd abided by her edict that he wouldn't cross the Styx except by Charon's boat. It was ploddingly slow, tiresome when shades were in the boat, and worsened by Charon's unpredictable temperament.

Fresh spray from the falls beside the palace was welcoming after the stillness of the Styx and the frozen world above. He alighted outside the torchlit throne room and could hear Persephone's voice inside.

"…on the full moon exactly between the first of Spring and midsummer."

"The seeds have already burst and reached into the soil by that season. Petals have fallen and the fruits have begun to pull on the branch. The weave of this is strange—"

Hecate glared and Hermes stumbled back. "Oh! It's… you… I suppose it's the last quarter of the moon, isn't it?"

Persephone sat on her throne, hands folded in her lap as Hecate shuffled closer to the Messenger, toying with him. She extended a bony finger. "The long-toothed wolf makes the pup yelp, eh?"

"We have old gods above, too. But... well, I normally see you when you're..."

"When I have more pounce than prowl?" Hecate's thin lips peaked. "Cross the still waters more, whelp, and the boatman's call might lead you to a wiser world. But I mark that the pawns of Olympus have no heart for the splendor and shades of Chthonia."

Persephone sat up. "What brings you here, Hermes?"

Hecate slid into the shadows, the crow's feet around her eyes deepening as Hermes picked at a fingernail. He bowed to one knee and held a scroll aloft. "A letter. From the Queen of Heaven."

Persephone stood and extended her hand. Hermes stepped onto the dais and handed her the papyrus, the seal marked with the eye of a peacock feather. She broke it and unfurled the scroll. Hermes stood waiting. "My husband summoned you, no? He's below, in the courtyard."

Hermes shifted. "Of course."

No wayward gossip for you, Persephone thought. With Hermes gone, she flattened the missive on Minos's table.

Hecate hobbled closer. "Queen of Heaven. A crown of twigs laying claim to the forest of the cosmos..."

"Likely not self-applied."

"What says the consort of the sky god?"

Persephone scanned the words. They weren't Greek or Theoi, but the hieroglyphs of Aegyptus. What reason did Hera have to encrypt a letter? Persephone had only learned to write it a quarter-century ago and had yet to master the spoken tongue.

My dear sister Queen,
Your absence has produced a dreadful series of storms, blanketing Thessaly in a lovely frost, but Hellas lost several ships near Crete, or so Poseidon tells me.

"The serpent begs the sparrow to nest on the ground," Hecate rasped. "She knows well that the Pomegranate Agreement binds you to the fields when the sun soars highest."

"I'm sure it's innocent. When I mentioned the Agreement with her and Amphitrite, it seemed she hardly knew it."

Hecate frowned. "A serpent smiling through a cloak of blue feathers is still a serpent."

"I don't trust her either, but she is trying to befriend me, and the last thing we need is to make an enemy of her. Besides," Persephone said. "If she is sincere, we could effect meaningful change in the world above. Wouldn't you prefer that to your followers being stoned or exiled?"

Hecate clenched her jaw. "Serpent or worm, wolf or lapdog— be certain you know which beast you see. The Queen wore a thousand masks before you first saw your reflection."

"I'll be cautious, but I won't raise a wall between her and me." She rolled the papyrus until Hera's words disappeared, then whittled her stylus to a sharp point and dipped it in the ink.

"What words will you send to the mountaintop?"

"The truth. That I won't return to Chthonia in spring or summer, under the Agreement, and never intend to."

✵   ✵   ✵

"*Hold*," Aidoneus said in the dream tribesman's language. He stepped back and flexed his palm against the pommel of his sword. As he clenched and unclenched his fingers around it, Aidon watched the deep wound on his forearm knit back together then disappear entirely.

Icelos Phobetor, chieftain of the Oneiroi, waited. His shape drifted from shimmer to shadow as he lowered his dagger and spear.

Aidon wiped the sweat off his brow. "Enter, Psychopompos."

Hermes rose from where he knelt at the entrance to the courtyard. He glanced from Aidon to Icelos. Twice as tall as him, the shifting mass kept a roughly human figure, massive weapons suspended within hazy fists, misty limbs rippling. The color drained from Hermes's face. "What... who..."

"Icelos doesn't speak Theoi. Don't bother," Aidoneus said, replacing his helm.

"What are you doing?"

"Practicing."

"What for?!"

Aidoneus glowered at him through the eye slits. "This realm stands between your world and its former masters. Should the Titans ever escape Tartarus, I need to be ready. Stay put, Hermes." He spoke to Icelos in the hollow tongue of the Dreamworld. "*Last time. Advance.*"

Hermes winced at the unfamiliar words, then the clash of bronze. "It's been forty thousand years, Aidoneus."

"And if you want another forty thousand," he said, grasping the spear to pull Icelos forward and thrust harmlessly into his immaterial form, "I cannot afford to rest on my laurels."

87

Icelos jerked his weapon back and Aidoneus dodged aside. The heavy spearhead slid by him, a hair's width from his shoulder, and struck the cobblestones with a clang. His helm vanished and swallowed the rest of his armored form, and he silently rolled backward. Icelos lunged and hacked at the ground around him with a dagger, sparking against the stone. Hades waited. He trod silently, then leaped forward. Arm cocked, he reappeared and cleaved Icelos's spear in half with a hard blow, then stood. *"That's enough for today. Thank you for your time, friend."*

Icelos silently bowed and vanished, taking the broken spear with him.

Aidon inspected the nicked edge of his sword, then sheathed it, leaning the scabbard against the wall. He'd hone it later. His helm vanished with a flick of his wrist. Hermes shifted from foot to foot. He was always on edge whenever Aidon sparred. They'd stolen his wife for half of every year, yet each spring passed quietly. Did the Messenger still fear that he would make war on Olympus?

Let them worry, Aidoneus thought, *so they don't think they can take anything else.* His armor melted and rippled into the more familiar shape of his black tunic and himation as they walked toward the courtyard gate. He could sense Hermes's relief immediately.

"Your wife sent me here. I was willing to wait in the throne room."

"Given that you read her letters last year, can you blame her for dismissing you? Come. I have a task for you." Aidoneus loomed toward the grotto and the pool beyond. He knew Hermes wouldn't enter the room until he was under the water. He'd seen enough for one lifetime. "Wait outside."

Aidon removed his sandals and clothes, leaving them in a crisply folded pile. He pulled his hair free of its band and dove headfirst into the water, then swam to the bottom, coming to rest cross-legged. The darkness and utter silence of the water was welcoming. Aidoneus opened his eyes. It was warmer at the bottom and he let the heat seep into his bones. He'd sparred with Icelos since early that morning and would have gone most of the day to clear his head. Hermes was early and he needed to center himself. His request would not be an easy one. One misplaced word might set every tongue on Olympus wagging and cause him and Persephone, and likely Demeter, endless problems. He rolled his neck, then slowly surfaced, finally propping himself up against the ledge. With a flick of his wrist, he lit the room, the torches illuminating the sapphire and diamond inlaid ceiling above. "Enter."

Hermes poked his head in the door and scanned the dim room, empty but for Aidoneus, who was chest-deep in dark water. Hermes took stock of the room before he spoke.

"Who on Olympus would have a silver lyre?"

Hermes raised an eyebrow. "Why?"

"It is a gift for a mortal." Aidon could see the wheels turning in his head. "It is not so grand a favor, Hermes. I allowed a mortal to use *my own helm* once."

"Didn't the Stygian nymphs hand it to Perseus?"

Hades rolled his eyes, despite himself. "Of course they did. What living mortal in their right mind would cross the Styx and meet face to face with the God of the Dead?" He fell back under the water until only his head bobbed above the surface. Heat crept up his neck, soothing him. "It's beside the point. And before you ask, my reasons for this are my own."

"I know you better than to ask."

"You created the first lyre, no?"

"I lost it in a wager."

"Over what?"

"A herd of cattle."

Aidoneus stared at him, water dripping down his scalp.

"It was a prank. Look; it's a long story."

"There must be more than one on Olympus. Which Muses have one?"

"Many, but not the kind you'd want. The lyre I made is now Apollo's."

He exhaled and disappeared under the surface for a long moment then came back up. "Of all the gods…"

"He doesn't use it often, but he *does* treasure it. If I told you what Euterpe had to do to—"

"I don't want to know," he said. "Turn, would you?"

Hermes complied, facing the wall. "Who is it for?"

Aidoneus hoisted himself up out of the water and wrung out his hair, then stood and wrapped his himation around his waist. "A hymnist named Orpheus; he lives on Samo—"

"Him?!" Hermes spun back around. "The one putting the scrolls in the mouths of the dead?"

"Yes," he answered, perturbed, and threw the end of the himation across his shoulder.

"I thought you'd end his *life*, not grant him a gift!" Hermes rolled his tongue on the inside of his cheek. "Wait, isn't he Apollo's *son*?"

"He is."

Hermes laughed. "I thought you had an actual *task* for me. 'Excuse me, Apollo, I need to borrow the magical lyre *I made you*, and give it to your *son* who composes hymns about *you*. You can have it back in thirty or so years when he's dead.' *That's it?*"

"Yes."

"And you're sure you can't tell me wh—"

"No," he said firmly. "All I want is discretion. Especially with Apollo. He doesn't need to know it was at my behest."

"He takes no issue with you."

"You told me yourself he is still… resentful… of how Aphrodite humiliated him on Persephone's behalf. I doubt he's changed his mind."

Hermes nodded. "If anything he detests Aphrodite, not Persephone. Aphrodite and I— well, he has no quarrel with me, you know, and she and I…"

Aidon massaged his temples with his fingertips. His voice lowered. "Is that why Ares has been making a mess of Argolis this month?"

Hermes winced. "Possibly?"

"Your affair has created endless headaches for us. It's not just soldiers. The city was ransacked. Women, Hermes. *Children.*"

"I didn't tell Ares to start a war."

He sat down on the divan. It was always someone else's fault with the Olympians. Every question about mortal suffering was met with a chain of pointing fingers. It wasn't even worth it to lecture him.

"Anyway, Apollo's my friend. It won't be difficult."

"Just make sure."

The Messenger tilted his head. "You've never, and I mean *never* engaged in intrigue. Why now?"

He stared Hermes in the eye. "I swear it on the Styx, Hermes, this will *not* affect Olympus. It concerns our matters in Chthonia. You'll have your answer soon enough if our efforts are successful."

"Our?"

Tartarus! Aidon could have kicked himself. "I want my wife's name kept out of this."

Hermes stared at him, and Aidon knew that he was trying to divine the reason. The Trickster was wiser with emotions than he. The slightest bluff, the quickest lie, laid anyone bare. Hermes shrugged. "Think nothing of it, Aidon. I'll do it."

"You have my gratitude."

"Any messages for Zeus?"

"No. Likewise, I take it?" Hermes shook his head. "You may go. Charon should be along shortly."

"Aidon… since I'm doing you this favor, could you perhaps reverse her decree so I can come and go the way I used to?"

"You'll have to get the Queen's permission," Aidoneus smiled dryly.

Hermes moved to protest, then deflated. He bowed quickly and disappeared through the doorway.

"He will be as true as any dog to a good master." Aidoneus turned to see Hecate, standing on the surface of the pool, her aged reflection perfectly mirroring her in the still water. She spoke again. "But it's not the sole storm in my mind. You not only swim against the river, young one, but you try to force it from its banks. These are not your ways. Or mine."

"Have *our* ways given my wife a child?"

"The Fates—"

"Contradict themselves. *You* said that. They told *me* that we would be as barren as Chthonia, and told *her* we would have three children. So it's in our hands. Just as creating Elysion was in our hands."

Hecate shuffled toward the deck, then padded soundlessly across the limestone. "The river forks innumerably ahead, Aidon. But too many tributaries flow into a whirlpool. Lives will be churned. Swallowed. I see agony. Suffering."

"If we do *not* go to Samothrace, we might forever question if this was our only chance."

"And so you sail with your queen. What of the other ships that sail alongside you?"

"The rite takes place in late spring. If it upsets the balance, as it did after our last efforts, we can fix it before the first chill of winter."

Hecate's face fell. "The wheel of seasons concerns me little, Aidoneus. It is the ripple that builds until it sends all ships to the deep."

"I'm not abandoning my faith in *ananke*, Hecate. And the hymnist follows our ways. I feel, in my soul, that this is right. More so than anything we've yet tried."

Her shoulders sank as she looked up at him. "If this is your course, if you sail with clear eyes and a strong heart, who am I to stop you?"

4.

*T*HEY'LL KNOW WE DON'T BELONG HERE.

Persephone looked back at Aidon and shrugged. "We're supposed to be a king and queen from Boeotia. Of course they'll think that."

You know what I mean.

They wore simple, undyed himatia as instructed, but he was right. Their garments looked too perfect. They were taller than most Samothracians, Aidoneus in particular, and it didn't help that his back was spear straight, despite his desire to blend in.

Adherents wandered the sunny vineyard flecking the ground with goat's milk, nursing and nurturing the dark-leaved vines and their newly budded fruits. In the vineyard's midst was a barren circle, the ground thrice plowed— where it would all take place.

"You brought ambrosia?"

"Yes. He knows nothing will affect us without it." Aidon stopped in his tracks. "Persephone, the last time I was without my wits—"

"That was ergot. No *cultus* would survive if they used something so dangerous." Persephone pulled back her hood.

"But… What if we reveal who we are? Or being *what* we are, what if we accidentally harm them or the earth itself? I worry this rite will swallow us whole. Hecate was none too happy about it."

"Despite what her worshippers' practice, she distrusts induced *mania*."

Mania. Madness.

She peered across the island searching for flowers and roots that could be used tonight. Grapes, if fermented. White trumpet flowers, a cornucopia of mushrooms, though most could kill a man; poppy, lotus…

"Sweet one." He broke her reverie. "We can turn back if you wish— vanish through the ether and forget this ever happened."

Persephone gazed down the road behind them. *I don't want that.*

Nor I. He took her hand. *I want to be the father of your child and for you to be the mother of mine.*

"What names did you give?"

"Melia and Dimitris." Aidoneus returned her wide smile.

The temple entrance loomed before them, silent and cool. They crossed the threshold. The main room was bare of decoration. Only a still pool, meant to represent the Mnemosyne, dominated the center. Dark reflected light under the wide oculus of the temple reminded her of the Styx. They passed whispering petitioners, bound for the courtyard and back into the sunlight.

A silver lyre, perfectly tuned beyond mortal creation, rang out. Its notes vibrated through her and echoed in Aidon. Their bare feet padded across the warm limestone to an olive tree where a man with brown hair and a threadbare himation stood. Supplicants sat on the ground, entranced, hoods drawn over their heads.

"Come," Aidoneus covered his head and laced his fingers with hers. They sat amid the gathered crowd, listening to Orpheus's hymn to Nature and Creation itself.

Eternal, setting all in motion, you turn the swift stream and flow into all things. You alone accomplish your designs, for you rule over those who hold the scepter...

His voice was so beautiful that Persephone's skin tightened, and his next chord made her breath hitch. A lump welled in her throat. She closed her eyes and Aidon likewise relaxed, leaning into her. She was transported back to grass under her heels and flowers strewn in her wake in carefree days as Kore.

... You are life everlasting, you are all things to all for you alone, you are all, and one, and bring life to all.

The last chord reverberated from all directions. Opening her eyes, she saw the crowd kneeling in a circle surrounding them. Her face flushed. Persephone chastised herself for letting her mind wander, but no one could see her embarrassment. Their eyes were closed, a serene smile on every face, palms lifted toward Hades and Persephone. The chord buzzed through them. Each of them was humming the last notes Orpheus had played. More gathered and knelt, eyes shut, intoning the same chord.

The hymnist stopped in front of them. "Rise, brother Dimitris, and sister Melia." He plucked his lyre again, and the hum of the crowd stopped. All eyes opened as Orpheus spoke. "They have come to glorify *phanes*— the first breath of life itself— to sacrifice their life *zoe*, as man and woman, king and queen, god and goddess, father and mother to The One Who Shall Be Reborn. As we all shall be reborn."

"We are the children of Earth and starry Heaven," they recited, the words shaking Persephone, "but our parentage is heavenly: know this you too. We are dry with thirst and dying. Give us quickly then water from that which flows fresh from the Mnemosyne."

These were the words Charon had found written on gold in the mouths of the dead. Aidon had told Orpheus they were not true. Long ago Persephone had described Elysion to the real Dimitris before it even existed, so she could send his wife Melia back to the Underworld. Hope— and sometimes false hope— was necessary...

Persephone took Orpheus's proffered hand, and Aidoneus rose with them and slipped him a leather satchel containing a symbolic six coins from the heavy talent of gold three supplicants had hauled from their ship to the temple the day before. The full amount would feed and clothe all of Samothrace for a year. Among the coins was a measure of ambrosia. Orpheus wouldn't be foolish enough to try it himself— it could kill an unprepared mortal instantly.

As the poem ended, the crowd advanced on them. Aidoneus visibly tensed. He looked over at her helplessly as a young woman embraced Persephone.

"Mother of the Unborn One."

Before she could react, the woman released her, and another did the same.

"Mother of the Unborn One."

She hugged her in return and looked over at Aidon, who stood stock still as the men came up and embraced him.

"Father of the Unborn One."

He held tense. Another embraced him, then another. Aidon started returning the embraces of the men, awkwardly at first, then warmly.

"Father of the Unborn One."

Three men and three women remained. They were bent with age, eyes and teeth yellowed, their hair removed by nature and a knife.

"These are the eldest of our order," Orpheus said. "You may follow them."

✼   ✼   ✼

"You won't need that either," the old priestess Lemnia said.

Aidoneus blushed as he dutifully stripped off his loincloth. No one mentioned the deep scar across his back. He was curious if the priestess was blind, but didn't want to peer too deeply into her to find out. Mortals seemed to sense when he looked through them. A pit formed in his stomach as she carried away his clothes and he tried to calm his nerves. Persephone glanced up at him, then handed her folded chiton to the woman. Where he was self-conscious, she was serene and thought nothing of her nakedness.

Was this a mistake? Hecate's words had planted doubt in him, and now the seed grew. He shook the thoughts away. A toothless man took their hands and led them into the sunlight, bound for steep stairs descending to the rocky shore below. The elder felt along the rope with a palsied hand, leading them downward. Aidoneus reached for his shoulder to steady him.

"Brother," the old man chuckled, "you needn't worry. I have walked this path at dawn for three score years. It's *you* who should be careful."

"I shall," he muttered sheepishly.

"Well, into the water with you. We must banish all miasma first." The inlet below them was a tumult of hissing foam. Dark water rose and fell just beneath the last knot of a dangling hempen rope. "It's deep enough, brother. A *very* long way to the bottom. Submerse yourself fully, then climb up."

The frigid Pontus fed these waters. Persephone stood next to him, her arms wrapped around her breasts against the cold sea air. She grinned at him then jumped, pin-straight, over the edge.

Aidoneus waited a moment, then dove in headfirst. Water rushed past his ears, then icy silence wrapped around him. He swam upward through the dark and surfaced, sputtering. Waves crested over his head and he bobbed, then paddled with a rising swell to the ladder. Persephone was already grasping for the rope, but her fingers kept slipping and her head vanished beneath the water. He got in front of her and gripped the knot, then hauled her up by her waist with his other arm. Her skin felt slick and chilled in the breeze, and her teeth chattered. The priest took her hand, pulling her back onto the platform, and Aidon followed.

The wind bit, and the sun-warmed, drying their skin as they made their way back. There the others waited, with salt and milled barley, fire, and water. Aidoneus swallowed. Only six beings in the cosmos— he, and the other Children of Kronos, knew how to render someone immortal. Many of those same ingredients were here.

Calm, Aidon, his wife said. *The Eleusinians banish miasma this way.*

He knelt, and the three men circled him. The priestesses in turn surrounded Persephone.

"Barley," said the dusky man who reminded him of Aeacus, "to cleanse the body of disease. Hunger. And death."

Milled flour fell onto Aidon's wet head, turning his hair matte gray and his forehead white. The toothless one who took them to the shore came next.

"Salt. To cleanse the mind of impiety. Vice. Sacrilege."

Aidon blinked to keep it out of his eyes.

"Fire and water," the thin voiced one said, "To banish misfortune and the sins of your forefathers. To banish infertility. For you and all your descendants to follow."

The man thrust his torch into the basin of water and it sputtered out. He took it, ash and all, and poured it over Aidon, washing away the barley and salt.

"And oil," a familiar, clear voice said, "to anoint you as man, as King, as God, as the Father."

Orpheus poured the vial and Aidoneus opened his eyes. A priest placed a crown of grape and ivy leaves on his brow. Orpheus poured oil on Persephone's scalp. "…as woman, as Queen, as Goddess, as the Mother."

After Orpheus gave her a similar crown, Hades and Persephone rose. The priests knelt as one. "Father and Mother of Zagreus, the Unborn One."

Trees stretched their limbs, and flowers arched their stems in response. Roots plunged and twisted, intertwining beneath the dirt. A passing bird left a trail across the sky. *What was in that oil?*

Phoenician rue, Persephone answered. Her voice pulsed from the earth, and inside him, and echoed in the sky, disorienting him further.

They were cloaked in leopard pelts, Aidon fastening his around his hips, and Persephone's at the shoulder and over her breast. They looked primordial, like the Titans in their earlier days.

"Rue," Aidoneus said, distantly. "The seeds."

"What do you see?" said the hymnist.

"The trees are breathing," Persephone said.

Orpheus smiled at them as the elders departed. "You see *phanes.* Life eternal. I used the merest amount, mixed as you required." He turned to Persephone. "Go into the forest and find a woman there. She is the daughter of a Dryades nymph. A bee charmer."

"What does she look like?"

"We don't know her face, nor does she give her name. But she always finds those who seek her out."

Persephone nodded placidly. Aidoneus scoffed. The idea of wandering out into the forest to meet a complete stranger seemed to make perfect sense to her, but he felt fogged, and the more he contemplated, the less he could concentrate. He focused on the trees and breathed in time with the wavering visions, voices around him sounding watery.

"She will lead you, and together find what you'll add to the unwatered wine tonight."

"Unwatered wine?" His tone was louder and sharper than he had intended.

Orpheus flinched. "It is how we first learned of the Unborn God."

"And what of me while she's away?" Aidoneus tried to take the edge off his voice.

"You'll wait. And in the meantime, gather pine wood for… the fires." The hymnist balked, and Aidon could hear his heart racing. "M-my lord, I—"

"Your tone is necessary, no? This is how the nobility of Hellas humble themselves enough to participate." Aidon paused, waiting for Orpheus to calm. "Remember what I told you in winter: treat us as you would anyone else."

He exhaled. "Your trials will be revealed under the moonlight."

✻   ✻   ✻

Somewhere, a heart beat beneath the loam. Blood pumped through roots. Leaves exhaled, and abundant small flowers and all their vines winked at her. Persephone shook her head. She knew all the plants in Hellas, what they did, how they worked, which ones could heal or harm, but had never experienced them first hand. How could she? She was deathless— invulnerable to them.

Mother would have forbidden this. A splinter of thought, spoken in Demeter's worrying voice, cried out against it all. The rest of her peered around trees, humming songs sung by cicadas. The soft leopard hide felt like her own skin, spots and all, under the dappled sunlight.

Remember who you are.

She was she. Persephone. The Queen of the Underworld and the Goddess of Spring. But she was in the guise of mortality and needed to remain that way, otherwise, all would be lost. She was she. Melia.

"Is it today already?"

Persephone yelped and whipped around so fast she felt dizzy. Her heart thrummed in her ears, her elbow and rump hitting the ground.

"Oh! I startled you. I didn't mean to."

Persephone squinted in the glare at the silhouette, taking the offered hand. She blinked and stood up. The woman before her was short, with dark-freckled, tawny skin and curls that reminded Persephone of Merope. Her gaze flitted to the surrounding trees and across the ground. Persephone took a deep breath. "It's alright. I'm not sure what I was expecting."

"I must not look like you imagined."

She'd imagined someone with the presence of Hecate or Nyx… not a friendly woman in a woven rush chiton. "I shouldn't expect anything, really."

"That's a relief. Some are so full of ideas that we spend all our time sorting out what they are underneath everything."

Persephone puzzled through what she meant. She spoke as though Persephone would know exactly what she knew. She felt a creeping dread that this girl would find out who she was, and it would all fall to pieces. "Call me Melia."

"Melia," she said, a smile teasing the corners of her mouth. "I like that name. In Hellas, it means 'honey', yes?"

"Yes."

"I knew a Melia once. A daughter of Okeanos. But there must be many Melia's. Hmm." She paused and fidgeted. "They told you I'm nymph-born?"

"Yes."

"You don't seem frightened. Some are. Especially when they walk the path you're on…"

"Well, I've known—" Persephone felt sourness well in her throat. *Careful,* she scolded herself. "I met a nymph. Only once."

"Good! One less thing in our way. I don't say this often, but… something about you is different." She smiled and extended a hand. "Eurydice."

"Pleased to meet you."

"This way. They build it in a different place each year." Eurydice tilted her head toward the trail. Persephone heard a hum from the tree up ahead, a song, a chant with a single note. Eurydice unfolded a waxen cloth. "You have to walk beside me for this. Listen to their song and you won't be afraid."

"Whose song?"

"The bees." They walked slowly toward the humming. One grazed Persephone's ear. A sting would hurt but never harm her. For fatessake, mortals could die of bee stings.

She could get Eurydice killed.

Her chest seized. Persephone could kill every mortal on Samothrace with a misplaced thought. She cursed herself. Here she was, her yearning for a child overtaking any sense of caution, playing with plants that could poison, creatures that could kill, and hovering on the precipice of ecstasy, madness, and destruction. She thought about Hecate's warning…

"Why are you afraid?"

"I'm not."

"You are. Stop being afraid. Then they won't hurt you."

"How? What should I think about instead?"

"The baby. Isn't that why you're here?"

"That would distress me more."

"Think about how you would sing to it."

Persephone swallowed. She often thought about conceiving, that first moment when she'd know that life had taken hold in her womb. They had talked about practicalities, where she'd give birth, where they would raise Zagreus, how to feed the baby with breastmilk and ambrosia so he would be as deathless as they. But nothing so real as the *songs* she would sing to soothe him to sleep. She started humming the lullaby her mother had sung to her, taught to Demeter by the mortal man Iasion, hummed to her by Charon on her first journey across the River, and by the Fates themselves when she was called to the cave of the Moirai.

One who is twice woven, cannot remain your own...

"Keep singing," Eurydice whispered to her. Persephone started again. She imagined his hair, like her husband's, her own blue-gray eyes, his tiny hand wrapped around her finger... little feet padding through the great hall of their home... A bee landed lightly on her shoulder, another on her cheek. She swore she was in harmony with the din of the hive. Bees left trails of sunlight, weaving a sphere of golden light around them.

Eurydice stretched her hand toward the entrance and let the workers crawl up her wrist and over her arm, as though she were just another honeycomb. Withdrawing her hand, she dripped honey up to her elbow, bees scurrying away. Persephone kept singing, hearing their song, feeling the brush of their wings.

They backed away and finally, the last bee flew from Persephone's hair and rejoined its sisters in the hive. Eurydice wrapped the waxen cloth around the honeycomb. Persephone stopped, and shuddered, her mind now free to ponder the swarm and how they had miraculously emerged unharmed.

"I've done this a thousand times, and fates willing, I'll do it a thousand more. A sting might hurt, but they'd never swarm me. And I *know* bees can't affect *you.*"

She froze. "How do you know?"

"Because you are the goddess Persephone."

*　　　*　　　*

104

"Tell me," Aidon asked Orpheus. He strapped a bundle of pinewood. "When does this feeling of... strangeness pass?"

"It depends," the hymnist answered. "Are you naturally uncomfortable around others?"

Aidoneus paused, considering his answer. "Yes."

"And not just worried they might learn who you are."

"No. It's a discomfort I feel around all beings," he hoisted the load and trudged through the field. "Save my wife."

"Why her? You've been married a short time. For your kind, I mean."

"It's..." he clenched his teeth. "I'm not sure you'd understand. We have a bond that stretches beyond your sense of history. Aspects of us have been intertwined forever."

"Do you love her?"

Aidon dropped the bundle and raised his eyebrows. "I created Elysion with her— a creation act not seen in this world since the days of the Protogenoi. That would be impossible had we not loved each other wholly and completely."

"Are you not also intertwined with all she holds power over in the world above? Extend that to your whole domain. You hesitate. That is why succumbing to the rite eludes you."

He felt dizzy. Everything that lived and moved within the earth... That's what she held sway over. Aidon closed his eyes. "I hold myself back for a reason. It would be foolish to unleash everything I am capable of feeling. The consequences—"

"What are you afraid of?"

Aidoneus fell inward. Fire and destruction that had leveled so much of the earth swamped his vision. The blood of allies and enemies covered the ground as he leaped ahead of a phalanx of mortals to save the few that he could... cleaving with his sword through the entrails of a rampaging manticore. Then the wasting famine... the shores of the Styx teeming with the starved and frozen, Charon's boat overflowing, his own hands wrapped around Hermes's neck...

"Leave that place," the hymnist said, shattering the memory.

"You don't understand—"

"I don't have to. It is the past. It is death."

"Who do you think I am?!" Aidoneus hissed through clenched teeth. He realized that he was gripping Orpheus's shoulders and released him, his hands shaking. "Forgive me."

The color returned to the hymnist's face, and Aidon knew he was choosing his words carefully. "The God of the Earth," Orpheus said, "the caretaker of life itself for those who will be reborn. You are shepherd to all those who wait to return above. And beyond that, even. Look around you."

Aidoneus glanced up, their conversation going unnoticed by the other men who had been hauling bundles of wood to create a series of great pyres strung in a circle around the vineyard. The pulse of life drummed, the ground swelled and breathed.

"These same souls milling about this field were in Asphodel when the two of you first came together. They are your subjects, made flesh. Abandon your presumed control. You must *be here* in your entirety for this to work. Think of what you are capable of when you embrace who you are…"

Aidoneus closed his eyes and saw the *hieros gamos*, the pomegranate trees surrounding him and his wife, the moment that the material world disappeared and was replaced with a profound sense of All, and startling visions of the world as it was and what was to come.

"You brought forth Paradise."

"There exists a veil between myself and others. My siblings… endured the same torment I did. But they emerged differently. And what lies beyond that veil and all other creatures, who I truly am… I often worry about what I am capable of doing if it were torn asunder."

"Had you ever considered that you are on the right side of that veil, and all of them are still trapped on the other?" Aidon stared off into the distance, watching the mortals move around them. The more he ruminated, the more Orpheus smiled. "Perhaps you should let them in."

Aidoneus spoke softly. "How?"

Orpheus closed his eyes and grew silent. It was likely the effects of the oil, but Aidon felt the man tentatively reaching through his consciousness. "Just let go."

✻   ✻   ✻

Persephone sank to the forest floor, her chest hunched over her knees.

"You didn't *say* anything or give yourself away." Eurydice tried to soothe her. "No one else knows."

"Except Orpheus."

"Who?"

"The hierophant! He promised…"

"I've never met him. My spirit knows you, just as the bees know me. And my mother knew you once— she attended you long ago when you were a little girl. The song you sang to the bees only made me certain."

Persephone lay back on the loam and sighed. "Fates preserve me, did my mother ask every nymph in existence to chaperone me?!"

Eurydice giggled, then looked at the stricken queen. "I'm sorry, but that was so very… Please— no one besides me *could* know. The man at the temple? Um, Or… Or…"

"Orpheus?"

"Yes. I've wanted to meet him, but… they act as though I were the spirit of the forest, and not a woman, flesh and blood. All of Samothrace regards me so strangely. Many decades ago I left a mix of plants and herbs at the temple, one my mother taught me. I thought they might have a use for it, but

107

then they started sending women to me. I realized after a time that if someone wants a child dearly enough to venture here, then they can perform the needed labor."

"How did they never notice you?"

"Blending in isn't hard when everyone is cloaked in a white himation. I have my mother's skin, but my father was Samothracian. He was a priest at the temple, long ago, my mother said. She had a *hieros gamos* with him and then had me. My mother was taught by a red-haired goddess who appeared as a girl sometimes or a crone." Eurydice stared off into the distance, lost in thought.

Persephone's shoulders fell and she breathed again. Hecate. So all of this was descended from her teachings. The Goddess of the Crossroads had nothing to fear, and her fears were misplaced. "I cannot let anyone know who I am. It could undo *everything*."

"I'm a hermit. My ways are too queer for them." She frowned, then broke into a laugh. "They probably think I'm a witch. Come. The next part is easy."

As she shed her assumed identity, Persephone saw more clearly. Honey prints dotted her skin, not unlike the spots on her wrap. The afternoon sun shone through the veins of the leaves and they pulsed like the veins in her husband's skin when he held her.

Eurydice sniffed around, then removed a few damp leaves and moss-covered rocks, revealing a patch of thin mushrooms beside a pile of aurochs dung. "Ah. Here they are."

Persephone leaned down and plucked a few caps, looked back at Eurydice who motioned her on, then gathered a handful more and examined the underside— purple and white gills, a circle of gold around the edges.

"They're prettier underneath, aren't they? From the top, they look like nipples," she said.

"This *is* a fertility rite," Persephone sat back on her haunches, staring into the forest. "I feel like I'm assembling pieces of myself, but with herbs and living things. That sounds utterly mad, but..."

"Not to me." Eurydice guided her into a clearing around a fallen cypress. "This next one might look more like a piece of *him*."

"Aidon?"

"Well, *I* can't say the Unseen One's name..." Eurydice stopped at a long stalk with a broad cluster of purple flowers. "Come see."

She examined the individual blossoms. Dark eyes stared back at Persephone from each flower face. A torso lay beneath. Little arms and legs protruded from the body of the bloom, and hanging between them... Persephone tried to stifle a laugh. "That's supposed to represent *him?*" She sized up the flower, cocking an eyebrow. "If that were real, he'd be able to fuck me from across the room!"

Eurydice gasped, eyes widened with mirth, and nearly dropped the satchel of mushroom caps.

"Oh Fates, I shouldn't speak about my husband in such a way," she said through her laughter. "What must you think of me?"

Eurydice grinned. "You're just a woman here, not the mighty Queen of the Underworld. I'd be more alarmed if a satyrion flower *didn't* make you think of that."

Persephone's cheeks hurt and she stumbled back, landing in a soft pile of moss. "I'm in the woods, half out of my wits, collecting mushroom nipples and tiny flower men with over-sized pricks for a fertility rite!"

Eurydice blushed, a note of panic in her voice. "Oh no, oh no... I'm thinking about him naked. Whenever I pictured the god beneath the earth, he was always on a throne with a crown and dark robes, and now..." They sat in the meadow and giggled like young girls. Eurydice pushed the loam and soil away from the base. "He won't see the flowers. Only the root."

"The root... the *root!*" Persephone wheezed around laughter. "If it looks like testicles, I don't know what I'll do. I'll never make it through this!"

"You tell me." Eurydice pulled it from the ground and bit her lower lip.

"Bloody Tartarus... no..." Persephone fell over, tears leaking from her eyes. "I haven't laughed this hard in my entire life. Is this the rue oil?"

"Does it matter?"

"No!" Persephone doubled over in laughter. Eurydice tucked the satyrion root into the satchel beside the mushrooms and honey. Their reckless mirth subsided. The ground was peppered with little priapic flower men, the colors of the sky shifting toward dusk. "Fates, is it almost sunset?"

"Within the hour. Then it will be your husband's turn."

"It feels backward to perform my task in daylight. Women seem more connected to the night..."

"But how much does being a woman or a man matter? You're both dressed the same, one of you has lips and the other a tongue, and it all melds together in the act. If walking on the narrow road of what you think to be true has yielded nothing, then perhaps it's time to meander a different path."

The woman got up and started walking, and Persephone sat for a moment and pondered her words. She hitched herself from the ground and followed her newfound friend over tree roots and down into a dried-up slough.

Eurydice stared forward, dark curls framing a frown. "This part is difficult."

"What's the next ingredient?"

"The final one. Mandragora."

Everything they'd gathered could be poisonous. Her husband's ergot-dilated pupils and seizing limbs flashed through her memory. She shook it away. Eurydice crouched near green five-pointed blossoms, gathered low to the ground.

"Dig until you find it."

"What am I looking for?"

"Your baby. You will know when you touch it."

Persephone raised an eyebrow. As a young girl, she'd dug up mandragora with her mother, a little wild carrot with chubby wrinkled limbs. How would she find one that not only looked like a child but her Zagreus?

Her fingers pushed through wet earth and she swept it away from the roots, exposing a thin, long-limbed thing. The soil was hard clay beneath the surface so she piled the dirt atop it, careful of the plants she wasn't going to harvest. The next was squat, with little definition other than a frown. Another was tiny, half-formed. "What if I can't find it?"

"It's different for everyone. You will know."

I am here... come to me...

The whisper roared like Aidon's but lighter... tinged with her own voice. Quickly, she reburied the exposed roots and squatted down next to another plant. Its leaves hummed and rose under her fingers when she touched it.

Digging carefully, she revealed a round head, eyes closed in sleep. Its chin was tucked against its chest with tiny arms folded around the center, legs folded beneath. In the dim light, Persephone could almost see it yawn, rustle, turn its head in sleep, sucking on a thumb, or curling a tiny fist around her finger. Her fingers supported the stem and pulled it gently but firmly from the earth, cradling it against her chest. Her vision blurred as she held it for a moment longer, then sang again, hoping against hope that she would hold little Zagreus by late winter.

"Is it him?"

"Yes."

"Take off your wrap."

Persephone slipped her finger through the knot at her shoulder and spread the skin on the ground. Face streaked with tears, she laid the mandragora in the center. Eurydice placed the satyrion, mushrooms, and honeycomb within, surrounding and swaddling the root. The chill of evening descended, but she had no other thought for her nakedness. She wanted only to bear this hard-won collection of roots and herbs safely back to the temple grounds. "And now?"

"They will mix it all with unwatered wine— one *kantharos* for you and your husband, and a *skyphos* for the rest who've gathered."

The sky turned gold, the trees silhouetted against the gathering dark. "I'm so deep in the forest, though. The moon won't be up for another hour."

"The fires will guide you back."

✼   ✼   ✼

If he were mortal, his hands would be covered in blisters. The sun had fallen from treetops to trunks while he'd labored, and gold and pink washed across the sky. Beautiful to be sure, but Aidoneus wasn't impressed by the sunsets in the world above. They held none of the penumbral grandeur of the Styx. He rubbed a stripped branch between his palms from top to bottom, just as he had at the dawn of the war before Hestia had taught them easier ways to make fire.

The wood was damp, but slowly, slowly started to steam, then dry, then smolder. He blinked through smoke, an ember flickering to life. Aidoneus blew on it carefully, then placed the wooden pad in a tuft of loose grass. He puffed air rhythmically, each burst producing more smoke. An *aulos* heralded his small flame, reedy pipes echoing through the circular pyre.

The world vanished and for a moment he was young and on Thera, his hair hacked away, his scalp scabbed over and not yet able to heal. Hecate was nursing Demeter back to health with ambrosia. He had been free for two days— reborn from his father's imprisonment— and joyfully danced that night with his newly kindled flame, building a fire to keep them warm in the frozen wastes of his father's ill-tended domain...

Smoke fanned out and he dropped the lit tinder on the kindling. When the first flames roared to life, the *aulos* quieted, replaced by the trilling voices of women. The sun touched the horizon. As the fire spread from the smaller sticks to larger logs, the smoke and crackling sap transmuted the sun from gold to orange, to a deep red.

Like wine. Like the sky when he had pulled his wife to the Underworld.

"Our order drinks unwatered wine, eat the flesh of beasts, and engages in sexual union on this day, and this day alone," Orpheus said. "All other days, we abstain from all."

"For three years?"

"Yes. Those without bonds abstain completely. Those within matrimony are free to share in pleasure and fertility. But they too go without for a month before tonight."

"And are you married, Orpheus?"

"Someday."

"I was... I lay with my wife three months ago, but we've abstained since. And it's been nearly the age of man since I drank pure wine or ate the flesh of animals. My wife has partaken of neither in her lifetime. This is momentous for us indeed."

Orpheus smiled. "You see? Three years is not so long. It's been three days since any of these men or women have had food. Including myself. And we've had no drink, not even spring water, since sunset last night."

A naked woman sauntered to his side, and thrust a *thrysos* into the flames, carrying its crackling pinecone head like a torch. Aidoneus averted his eyes from her body instinctively and watched her touch the flaming pine cone to the tip of another thrysos. A nude man held it, who in turn lit another's. She thrust the blazing staff into a woodpile and waited, smoke shrouding the glow of embers, then, at last, bursting forth with flame. She swayed, dark hair licking the small of her back like the flames before her, then leaped and twirled.

As pine bough torches lit the fires, sputtering and popping when flames enveloped them, more men and women shrugged off their somber white robes, dancing without rhythm, mimicking the chaotic twist of the flames before them.

"Does everyone disrobe?"

Orpheus nodded. "In this form we were created. It's our natural state. Those in Attica look down on us for this part; especially our women. They call them Maenads."

"Do you plan to…?"

"No; I must be present as a guide. We each take our turn. I *volunteered* this year," he added with a pointed nod to Aidoneus. The men and women danced closer, the flame, the wood, their flesh indistinguishable in the fading light. "The veil you spoke of… lift it. When your bride returns, you will both drink what she gathered. After that, she will wait, as you have, while you track a wild bull in the dark."

In his bones, he had known it would be this way. She had gathered. He would hunt. It was the way of the primordial mortals, before copper and tin, papyrus and glass had drawn them away from the deeper rhythms of the world.

"Let it all go now. Look into the fire. Don't think. Don't suppose."

Another wave of heat washed over him. The flames leaped higher into the dusky sky. One caught his imagination. He remembered Nysa, when he stood with Persephone in the falling snow, the earth coursing through him as she created a gateway of fire through the ether. His body swayed as it had that night. The circle twisted like it had that night, and pale light echoed the movement of his hips and twisting arms, his calves and shoulders. The pelt felt heavy now, a barrier between him and the fire he had built to welcome her back.

Aidon removed the leopard skin and laid it on a rush mat the women had woven. *This is where we will conceive our son.* He buckled, light-headed, then came back to the circle, dancing flames and golden skin all about him and he spun, his arms spread, his head tilted back. He drew them all in, his subjects, his equals, his children, pulling them across the divide to join their god and goddess in this act of creation.

I am here... come to me...

It sounded like Persephone's whisper, felt like her, but the voice was deeper, its tones roaring across the loam and the vines. Aidon leaped with the flames as he did long ago on Thera before the world weighed heavy above him. He never touched the others, but felt their presence as they followed him in ecstatic dance. The heady smoke filled his eyes, his limbs slackened, he felt only the ground pounding beneath his feet and heat embracing him. He reveled in it, grinned wildly, drew it in. With eyes closed, he could see the outlines of the trees, the creatures crawling beneath them.

Echoing through the earth he felt the slow footsteps of a woman, the only woman who'd ever mattered to him, finding her way back through the thicket to his roaring fire. He twisted and bounded through the crowd, his gait reforming, as though he were flame and had walked from it. Aidon stood at the one small opening in the great ringed pyre, his hands outstretched, his palms upturned, welcoming her back...

✶   ✶   ✶

Persephone clutched the bundle to her chest and felt a pull at every part of her body, from the soles of her feet to her lips, pulling her back to him. The fires grew brighter against the darkening sky.

His arms stretched wide, waiting. She stopped in front of Aidon, naked as he was, naked as all the mortals dancing around the flames beyond him.

"I found him," she blurted breathlessly.

Aidoneus smiled at her and opened the leopard pelt satchel she had clutched to her breast. Within, the mandragora root slept in a swaddle of herbs and honey. They walked hand in hand to the chanting, ululating calls of the mortals, the precious gifts of the earth cradled in her arms.

Orpheus stood out from the crowd, clothed in white, the calm eye in a maelstrom of bodies gyrating and dancing. He cloaked his head and raised his arms. Everyone stopped abruptly, silent amid the bellowing pyres.

"*Phanes*, great and ether-tossed, born of the great egg, begetter of blessed gods and mortal man alike… I call you down to witness!"

Persephone gave a last glance at the wrapped root in her arms. Aidon touched the base of her back, encouraging her, and she held it forward. The hymnist took it gently and raised it above his head.

"Behold the seed of the Unborn One! Unforgettable, attended by many rites, ineffable, hidden, brilliant scion. I beseech you *phanes*, lift the dark mist from our eyes so we may see your pure light of life. Guide these two on their holy journey and we will return to you the sacrifice of a fertile bull!"

Two of the priestesses bore cups, one gold the other silver, and two sturdy men heaved a massive *skyphos* basin forward. Persephone stared at her reflection in the liquid. It was darker than the juice of grapes.

An elderly priestess began grinding the satyrion and honey Persephone had collected in a mortar and mixed it with a black paste of elderberry, acorns, and deep red vinegar. The toothless man who had taken them to the water's edge mashed the mandragora and mushrooms with his pestle then poured the contents into the vat of wine. An old priestess stirred it.

The men and women separated from each other and herded Aidoneus and Persephone apart as well. Women rushed from the silver cup to her and back again, fingers dripping with a black paste, chanting 'mother of the Unborn One' while they swiped paint onto her skin. She shrank away at first and looked to Aidoneus, who was similarly attended by the men. He stood stock-still, his eyes locked on her and only her. This night would end with their embrace and that thought sent a shiver down her spine. She startled when a priestess smeared a soft ointment across her vulva, the last touch to cover her in the wine-dark paint. The men had covered him from his forehead to his feet. His eyes widened when a priest quickly slicked his penis with the same ointment they'd applied to her.

They were nudged back to the center of the circle, standing on the skins and the rush mat. Orpheus stepped between them. Out of the sight of the others, he poured the thick ambrosia into the wine-filled cups. He gave the silver one to Aidoneus and the gold to Persephone.

"Drink."

Aidoneus nodded at her reassuringly. She raised the cup to her lips, gulped, and sputtered. Tears leaked down her cheeks, streaking the dark paint. He had already finished his before Persephone could take a second draught. She swirled the contents of her cup then up-ended it to the cries of the women. It poured down her throat like molten bronze. She exchanged another glance with her husband.

As suddenly as it hit her stomach her mind was swamped. Her core began to ache, and she realized the true nature of that ointment as it melded with the wine and made her itch and writhe. The tips of her breasts beaded, aching for his touch. She tried asking him for help but all it came out was a needful moan. Aidon's pupils dilated and he stared through her. The fires grew and enveloped them, filling the sky and earth and retreating to reveal a golden pulse of light in every grape and leaf of the vineyard. The others drank, not from *their* cups, but the great vat. They cupped it in their hands, dark wine trickling down their skin in bloody rivulets. Their lips and palms were as dark as the paint on hers and Aidon's skin.

Orpheus nodded to her husband. It was his turn.

Aidoneus stood caked in the dark paint, the herbs seeped into his skin with every heartbeat. The sun had set, the stars were obscured by smoke, and all his sense of an orderly world faded. All that remained were the raging fires and the tumult of human bodies toward the wine vat.

"Here." Orpheus thrust two objects into his hands.

Aidon stared at him for a moment, trying to sort his wild thoughts. The hymnist had spoken to him. He looked at what he held. "A thrysos and a bone knife."

"The heart of a wild aurochs is the last part of the sacrifice."

We will return to you the sacrifice of a fertile bull. That's what Orpheus had said. Aidon struggled against the effects of the drink, then remembered. *Let go.* He closed his eyes and saw. *Lift the veil.* The earth. The vineyard. His wife subsumed with need.

Orpheus slowly spoke his instructions. "Don't harm the beast before you return. Herd it within the circle. Its heart must still beat."

Aidon nodded. "Alone, then."

"Yes."

Persephone stared up at him, drinking in their words, her lips parted, her thighs rubbing together, trying desperately to ease the ache. He leaned down and hauled her against his body, kissing her hard, tasting the wine on her lips. She shivered as he set her on the ground. "I'll return soon."

He looked back once, then left the heat of Persephone and the light of the fires. Moonlight shone silver on the fields and the trees beyond, a full moon, reminding him of silvery Chthonia. Its peace, order, and stillness were so distant… Clouds gathered. There was too little moonlight to hunt. He closed his eyes. Senses beyond sight must prevail. Leaves rustled and worms burrowed beneath the soil…

…Hooves stamped the fertile ground. Eight of them. He furrowed his brow and listened. Two massive hearts thudded in the distance, echoing through his being. He caught a scent in the air. Musk. There was a cow in estrus nearby. He trod lightly through a copse of trees and spied a meadow. A low hum emanated from the aurochs as the male circled the female. She swished her tail.

The ointment started affecting him, not as suddenly or acutely as his wife, but still he hardened painfully, his scrotum tightening beneath him until the pulse of blood through his cock became all consuming. His jaw clenched. He was supposed to be hunting, yet all he could think about was the relief he'd feel returning to Persephone's warmth. He realized, distantly, this was the point.

Painted skin offered an advantage, especially now that thick clouds obscured the moon. He was a shadow among the trees. *The Unseen One.* Why were they not alert to his presence? Birds stopped chirping and insects ceased humming when he walked the earth. But he could hear crickets, the distant hoot of an owl, and every living thing moving about him. With the herbs coursing through him, he could *feel* them. The bull's desire for his intended mate pounded in his veins, the cow's encouragement of his advances pulsed through him.

Crouching low, Aidon held the thrysos in hand like a spear and the knife out in case they caught his scent and charged. The bull reared, its glans straining, and lunged to mount the female. She stepped away. The bull licked at her haunches and tried again, only for the cow to step aside, testing his determination, her tail swishing. Aidon knew the bull wouldn't be inclined to go anywhere once he'd finished mating.

As he circled the cow again and moved to mount her, Aidoneus leaped from the rushes with a shout, waving the thrysos over his head. The cow loped away and the bull turned and snorted, his hooves digging into the earth.

"Apologies," Aidon whispered. "You're needed elsewhere."

The beast rushed at him and Aidoneus took cover under the trees. With an enraged bellow, it crashed through the brush where Aidon had stood, shaking its horns.

"*Bólinthos!*" Aidon shouted and waved his arms. The beast snapped branches, trampled brush and saplings underfoot, gouging its hooked horns deeply into the earth. Aidoneus bounded ahead of it, dodging between trees and cut by brambles until the bull spotted him in the open clearing and gave chase.

Don't run faster than a mortal. Don't let the beast gore you. Or they'll know what you are. He sprinted for the fires. Lines of light radiated from the center, caught in the tangle of grapevines ahead of them. He heard men shouting what he had shouted.

"*Bólinthos! Bólinthos,*" they cried.

The bull tried to turn, realizing it ran headlong into a trap, but thick vineyard rows stopped any chance of retreat. It hurtled into a panicked charge. Persephone stood in the center of the great circle, her arms outstretched, ready to receive him. Closer, closer. Aidon readied his knife and whipped around. He dug his heels into the dirt, nearly pulled under and trampled, but held his ground, grabbing the aurochs by one of its horns, slowing it. It tried to shake him, its pulse thundering wildly through its neck. Aidon gripped the bone knife in his hand.

"I thank you," he whispered into the bull's ear, then plunged the blade deep into a vein, cutting through tendons and sinews with a downward stroke. Blood coated his hand

and sprayed across his chest. The beast screamed, stumbled, and collapsed to the ground.

Moving quickly, he listened for its slowing pulse, then slashed deep under the ribs, spearing his fingers inside to grasp the massive heart. He planted his feet firmly in the gore-soaked ground beneath him and pulled the heart out with a bellow. Aidon held it overhead. The cries reached a crescendo.

The spark of life in it began to wane. Aidoneus turned, drawn magnetically to Persephone as she swayed and writhed in the open air, careless of all but him. Fire blazed behind him and the others rushed to the fallen aurochs, hot chaos framing his blood-drenched face and chest, his wild eyes, and Persephone distinctly felt the heart as part of him, as part of her, still pulsing. He held it to her lips and she bit deeply into it, tearing away the raw flesh, fire and iron filling her mouth until she nearly choked. Persephone swallowed the pulp of flesh and took it from him. She wrapped her fingers around the ventricles and took another bite, then another, until she felt dizzy.

Aidon breathed hard against her forehead, the zeal of the successful hunt still racing through his veins. She could smell blood, smell him. His heart pounded, and a vein stood out on his forehead. The heat of his cock nudged against her thigh. Persephone thrust the heart into his hands and Hades tore at the flesh, his teeth and lips carmine and frightful, as she was sure hers were. He bit in again and swallowed, then gasped for air, his eyes rolling back. He pushed it to her lips with a growl.

Clouds clotted in the sky, hiding the stars, and fat droplets dotted their skin. Red ran in rivulets down their chins. Persephone bit in and swallowed with a moan and he ground harder against her thigh. The heat and weight of his cock butted against her, drawing trails of arousal with each strain. Her answering need pulsed within, walls clenching around frustrating emptiness. She cried out at the unstoppable rush of warmth drenching her. His fingers pressed against her cheek, his every touch resonated like a drumbeat, and her body prepared itself to meet him equally and fully.

Persephone slipped and Aidoneus caught her in his embrace, the blood of the aurochs rushing through her, the fires around them searing through her veins. He hastily tossed the heart's remains to the side, vaguely aware of one of the priests scooping it up and presenting it to the ecstatic shouts of those assembled. A priestess gelded the bull and carried the parts to Orpheus. He held them aloft at the first fire Aidoneus had lit.

Over the din of the masses, Orpheus called down the Unborn God to join them, to witness their sacrifice. The fire spat and leapt. They could barely hear him. The sound of a beating heart flooded their ears, turning all else to distant echoes. His hand wound into her hair, gripping the base of her skull and she met his lips as they descended on hers, their tongues moving the lifeblood aside until they tasted each other. Their bodies slicked together, and Aidon pulled back, staring into her lidded eyes.

The revelers brandished bone knives and hauled off the flesh of the aurochs, careless of where it went. Their first bites were eaten raw, and the rest of the meat seared over the fires. A man carefully bore the remains of the heart through the tangle of naked feasting bodies so that all might have a small taste and join in the rite's culmination.

Persephone laced her fingers behind Aidon's neck. The scent of blood, the scent of her body engulfed him and he lifted her thigh. Persephone hooked her knee over his hip, pulling him closer, trusting in the support of his arms. She grazed his neck with her lips, his head thrown back when her hand closed around the exposed head of his cock. She needed the life and the heat of him wending through his veins, needed to pull all of him within her. He spread her apart, and she gasped as cold air met slick lips. Her heart, her voice, her womb called to him.

With one thrust he was within her, completing the rite. Euphoria, stirred by the potion they'd created, the raw flesh they had eaten, and their desire for each other came crashing in all at once.

He recalled the night they shared the Key... when the soaring voices of Asphodel reached them both, a cry of joy for his anointing, for her coronation. Those same voices trilled at their union here in the vineyard— the very souls in their realm that had witnessed it had been reborn to the verdant earth.

I am the earth and you are the sky... when and where I am the earth, then and there you are the sky... My beloved is mine and I am his...

It was as though all had been in disarray until their joining made the madness cease. During the creation of Elysion itself, the grove had come alive with fire and they had disappeared from the world around them. But tonight was inescapable. They were the fire, the field, the relief of sated hunger and quenched thirst all around them, beyond the roar of flames and flesh and life. They were the rain hissing loudly, like a pride of *drakones*. Steam rose from the hot blood on the ground. Within the maelstrom, a calm rushed over both as they moved together.

Persephone cried out, shaking as he withdrew a fraction and then reclaimed it. She quaked, convulsing around him and he growled through his teeth next to her ear, picking up tempo until his hips slapped rhythmically into hers. She heard similar cries from other women, gasps from men, but nothing existed for her except for him. Hades balanced her in his arms, fucking her with wild abandon.

Persephone threw her head back, and he nipped at her shoulder until he could no longer restrain his voice. Her eyes rolled back and she convulsed around the unforgiving hardness, screaming. Feet planted firmly on the ground, he plunged to the hilt and shouted to the heavens, his seed charging from him so quickly he saw stars. His legs gave out and he dropped to his knees. Aidon eased them onto the grass mat and pelts and laid her down, still joined.

Gently, he brushed her hair back from her eyes. He thought the potency of the herbs would lessen, that they'd lay together in the afterglow. A single flex of his hips and her wide-eyed gasp dispelled that. Rocking slowly, they breathed together, aligned in harmony. Persephone pressed down on his flanks, holding him to her, and he snaked his hips from side to side, stirring her from within. The movement set her shaking and she squeezed around him, pleasure cresting as if it had never subsided. Her head tilted back, exposing her neck, and Aidon kissed it gently, then slid his thumb between them to stroke her flesh and prolong her ecstasy.

Her back arched underneath him and he bore down on her, thumb circling her bud, cock sliding within her below it. Her nails drew blood when they sank into his shoulders. He hissed and held her there, pinned to the earth, feeling her pulse in exquisite waves around him. Aidon cradled her shoulders and plowed deeper, rolling his hips in a rising rhythm that left her breathless. He arched, her true name on his lips.

"Persephone!"

His body fell upon hers, wrenched by another climax, his seed wrung out against the mouth of her womb. Aidoneus opened his eyes in shock. No one had heard. The couple nearest to them was similarly enrapt and ecstatic. After the man reached his peak, he kissed the woman tenderly between her breasts and lay his head there as she cradled him and stroked his hair.

Persephone steered him by the shoulders and rolled them over, still joined. She sat balanced upon him and took in their surroundings, exhausted but still craving him. All around them bodies coupled and relished in pleasure. Two women gazed at each other in the afterglow, smiling as they kissed, their hair and long legs entwined. A man knelt between the thighs of a supine woman, reverently stroking her womb before he lay astride of her, their eyes locked on each other as he sank slowly down. Another man balanced his lover on his lap, his cock slowly working past his tight barrier as he kissed his neck and stroked his phallus. Aidoneus throbbed within Persephone, iron-hard, pulsing hot. His hands gripped her hips and she swooned as he surged into her, snapping their attention solely to each other.

He held her close with a growl, guarding his wife's beauty. She giggled at that and kissed him. No one was looking at them. Aidoneus smiled against her lips. He'd held her like this on their wedding night. Here, they were crowned with grapevines and ivy instead of pomegranate and laurel and surrounded by the passion of hundreds instead of alone.

The muscles of his back were tense and so slick from rain and liniment and blood and mud that Persephone couldn't grab ahold of his skin. She wove her fingers into his hair to gain purchase, forcing them to look into each other's eyes. He felt a pull from the earth beneath him, channeling itself into her. With every heartbeat, it increased, until it poured into them from every vine and leaf— the swell of every fruit echoing the blood in their veins.

Sweet is the sleep of hand to hand... sweeter still the sleep of heart to heart...

The earth and all within it rose through him and into her, an endless wellspring, fertile and potent, opening the depths of their kingdom and everything that lived and moved about on its surface to witness. Aidoneus drew her against his chest and whispered roughly into her ear. "I love you more than anything this world has to offer."

"And I you," she said, her voice shaking. "Please Aidon; I need you... Plant our child within me!"

They shuddered in unison and collapsed at last to the spent ground.

5.

"ONE OBOL. YOU CAME HERE TOGETHER, BUT *ONE* each. And… ah…" Charon trailed off, staring at the gaping wound on the captain's neck. "You must have come from Argolis. One obol. One— My lord!"

He knelt hurriedly in the boat, grasping his long oar. The three shades copied him, trembling.

"There's no need, old friend," Aidoneus said.

He pressed his coin into the ferryman's hand and spoke gently to the dead. "We also pay. But you cannot go back whence you came. Your lives are over, and you have nothing more to fear."

"Tartarus!" blurted out the dark-haired woman, bursting into tears.

"You're not going there, Cassia of Knossos. Nor you, Meriones of Knossos. Despite what your priests say, rarely do we damn a soul to Tartarus. Not even you, Hippolytos, son of Atreus."

The soldier's lip trembled. "A-Ares in h-his glory—"

"Is not here. I am now your Host, the Receiver of Many, from this day until the day you are reborn."

"Re-reborn?" Meriones's mouth hung open, still gasping from the mill fire smoke that had ended his life.

Charon raised an eyebrow at Aidon and pushed off the shoreline. "I thought you'd have gone straight to the palace. Or from the looks of you, straight to bed."

"The ether is unpredictable," Aidoneus said, pressing his fingertips to his temples, "and I don't know what might be lingering from the wine, besides this damnable headache. I need ambrosia…"

"You speak of this in front of them?"

"They'll drink from the Lethe by day's end."

"I trust your meeting with Aristi was… productive?"

"You won't get *those* details—"

"Who do you think I am?" Charon scoffed. "My brothers?"

Aidon smiled and closed his eyes, enjoying the rocking cradle of the boat. He was so weary from last night. Drained… "I'm hopeful. We awoke this morning and bathed. A great noise went up from the temple grounds. The hymnist, especially, was delighted. But it will be a difficult harvest for them…"

"What do you mean?"

"The rites culminated in the temple vineyard. At daybreak, they found every grape on the vine either emptied of their juices or… fermented. Every fruit-bearing tree on Samothrace was likewise withered. Such a thing has never happened before."

"Immortals never participated in the rites before. So there will be no *pithoi* on Samothrace to open this year at Anthesteria?"

"With the gold I gave them, they could fill the fastest ship in Hellas with the finest wine of Nemea. They won't though. That's the one night their *cultus* revels, and only once every three years."

"And I thought they performed this monthly."

"I don't see how they could," Aidon said with a snort. He opened his lids and blinked heavily. His eyes widened and the miller couple from Crete huddled against each other, staring back at him in horror. "Charon?"

"Yes, milord?"

"Where did the soldier go?"

✻   ✻   ✻

Thanatos stalked the battlements of Argolis, unseen to mortal eyes. The wounded lay strewn among their battling fellows; were he to distribute deservedly merciful death, the final vision of dark wings and hollows in place of eyes and cheeks would be of no comfort.

He heard a man's final breath rattle from a broken throat. Ares was here somewhere; inebriated, no doubt. The God of War had drunk enough to fill the Cocytus these past few months and spent his days punishing Hermes's favored city for his affair with Aphrodite. The Messenger's temple had been gutted by fire.

What more vengeance could Ares want? Stopping him would be simple. Ever since their adventure in Ephyra, even whispering the word *keres* was enough to turn him from the God of War into a lamb. Thanatos hoped it wouldn't come to that. Now was not the time to ask the queen.

The entire Underworld waited for a sign from her, any word that the rite on Samothrace had borne fruit. And considering how fragile fertility was in their world, Death was the last being in the cosmos who should visit her now.

He scanned the field and turned just in time to be knocked to the ground. The air rushed from his chest and his assailant was wrestling his sickle away. Death gripped it tighter and twisted it toward himself. His struggles were met with feminine laughter. Thanatos concentrated, and muscles and sinew wrapped themselves around his bleached bones. Skin formed around him and he rolled over, pulling her with him and pinning her to the ground.

"Hello, lover," she said with a grin.

"Eris."

"Found that soldier from the boat yet?"

"I'm in no mood." Her fingers held fast to the sickle, no matter how he tried to jostle it free.

"Liar. You're always in the mood for me," she whispered, breath hot against his neck.

He could smell her.

"Your king must have lost his head over it. Well, Hippolytos will lose his head. Not before he opens throats…"

"If I learn you had a hand in this—"

"You'll what?" Her fingers grasped his flank, squeezing, nails digging in to press him against her. She ground her thigh against his groin. The friction was delirious. Thanatos gritted his teeth, looking away. "You'll kill me?"

"Not today."

"You'll fuck me, then?" Eris smiled and raised the sickle to her throat. Her other hand wove deftly through himation and chlamys to grasp his awakening flesh.

Thanatos exhaled hard on her forehead and lingered a moment too long in the grip of her slender fingers, then pushed her away. He stood, skin and sinew shrinking away. His wings fanned out behind his skeletal frame. "Never again."

"Someday," she said, her voice low and sultry, "on a field like this one, you'll take me. You'll do it because I will give you no other choice. And they'll *loathe* you for it."

He beat his wings and rose into the air. "If you escalate the war in Argolis, I swear on the Mother River I *will* take the path the Fates set before you and I. Don't tempt me."

"I'll be waiting," she said.

✳　　✳　　✳

129

"Let me be clear," Demeter said. Hera stood quietly in the Telesterion. "I tolerate your presence only because you have been kind to my daughter."

Hera's arms remained folded, her face serene. "Where is she?"

"Is Persephone too late for your liking? Are you unable to put on the proper mask without Iris here to announce her?"

"That is *why* I chose to meet her here," Hera said, her voice lowered. "I don't have to worry about all the eyes and ears that surround me, or guard my tongue when I speak about my husband."

Demeter bared her teeth and took a step forward. "You roped others into your last little rebellion, and Zeus punished them, then slapped you on the wrist!"

"He did far more than *that*."

"If you so much as—"

"I have no such designs, Demeter! I swear it on the Styx, I would do no such thing again! It is futility— he is all but omnipotent." Hera leaned back against Metaneira's sepulcher and squinted at the statue above. "She must have been quite a woman for you to honor her so."

"She was more of a sister to me than my own."

"Demeter, I'm not here to squabble. And I'm not playing games with Persephone. She is intelligent— you must see that— but that is a dangerous thing for women in our world, especially for one who was sheltered from Olympus for so long."

"She shouldn't have any part of *your* world. *You* fashioned your own chains, Hera," Demeter said. "Don't make her wear their weight as you do."

Soft footsteps echoed from above, and Hera and Demeter looked up the stairwell. Persephone rounded the corner and made her way to the landing. The Queen of the Underworld had slept hours past sunrise, struggling to get ready. She had suffered a splitting headache the first day after the rite, but even as the pain had subsided, her fatigue had grown. "Forgive my tardiness," she said.

"Think nothing of it," Hera said. "I was just speaking with your mother about how much I admire you."

She was glad that she had prevented their conversation from continuing any longer. Demeter would be cautious about divulging details in front of Hera, but she knew her mother's temper— and could only guess at how easily Hera would manipulate it. Persephone gave her a weary smile. "You're too kind."

"I'll stay here, if you two wish to speak privately," Demeter said, reflecting her sister's affected calm. "For all the eyes and ears you fear on Olympus, there are just as many here. You are better off in the Ploutonion."

Persephone led Hera down the narrow path beside the Telesterion, gathering up her skirts as she walked. Hera followed, a long veil trailing behind. They stood before the cave.

"So *this* is where it happened…" Hera began. "The day before Aidoneus took you from Nysa, I overheard Zeus speaking to Athena. She wasn't happy that she and Artemis were to be passive accessories to your abduction."

"Athena told me as much."

"I hear Artemis still doesn't see you. You two were… closer before."

"She has never approved of matrimony."

Persephone pulled her shawl over her shoulders. The cave loomed over the walls of the Plutonion, shielding it from the sun, and only the high clerestory windows let in any light at all. "You said last year that my mother's temple was my own."

Hera noted the piles of crocus bulbs at the feet of two statues. Within their marble hands lay a shriveled pomegranate, the last offering of the harvest eight months ago.

"This," Persephone said. She gestured and the oil lamps flared to life. "This place is truly mine. And free of eyes and ears. But as I said before, I cannot take you to our realm. Not now, at least."

"Apologies. I only thought you could because…" Hera motioned to Persephone's hands. "I assume those work like your husband's?"

"We bear the same Key. But after we announced to Olympus that we had created Elysion, Aidon and I felt it was better for our agreement and the mortals… if I stay above in spring and summer."

"You are apart for all that time?"

"No. He comes to visit me."

"When? You are both so busy with your respective duties."

"We're busiest in early spring— I raise new growth from the earth, and he tends to those who lived to see the flowers bloom one last time. But we've delegated what we can."

Hera nodded. "It is only prudent. Goodness knows what Zeus would do without the others."

Persephone paused before replying. Half of the *Dodekatheon* were Zeus's children by other women; speaking for or against them would be unwise. "We are fortunate. My mother has Triptolemus to aid her, a strong priesthood, and acolytes who teach mortals how best to plant, harvest, and store their grain for the winter. And Aidon has the judges."

"You mentioned… raising new growth from the earth."

"It is a cycle that has been in motion since— "

"But since the seasons began, *you* bear fertility itself. For the earth, but not… forgive me, children of your own."

Persephone cast her gaze to the ground. "No."

Hera took a step back and folded her hands.

"We don't know. We've… tried. To no avail."

"How would you raise a child? You would take it with you?"

"Aidon and I have spoken about it. Our child would live below. The baby would stay with me in its first year, but as for its destiny… There's so much for it— in his world and mine. We created Elysion, but there is no one to watch over it. Our child could…" She shook her head. "It's such a distant thing— so much must happen before I can truly consider it. There is no blood in Asphodel, no cycle, no way to conceive. And I sacrifice our shared fertility each spring to renew the earth, leaving little chance it will come to pass."

"Only the Fates know." Hera smiled and unfolded her hands, relaxing. "I must admit, it seems strange that your *husband* would wish to have a hand in tending children."

"It takes two to create them. I don't see why two shouldn't raise them as well."

"It's a queer notion, but do you think if mortals took equal part in rearing children, it would shift the balance on earth?"

"I could only hope."

Hera nodded and paced slowly. "I have priests on Samos I commune with. Perhaps when I next visit I can… mention something. I am called the Protector of Men, after all."

Persephone's eyes widened, and a smile broke across her face. "That would be wonderful!"

"I should caution you— I can only steer the course of mankind slowly, over centuries, without alerting Zeus. It will take time. But time is all you and I have."

✶   ✶   ✶

"Say it…"

"If it's not true," Ganymede shuddered, "why would I?"

"You know it's true. It's why you're here behind my father's back."

Apollo thrust deeper, stealing Ganymede's breath and weakening his knees. A shimmery ribbon of arousal dangled from his cock to the sheets. The God of Light reached around

133

and stroked the slickness up Ganymede's foreskin and over the head, then pumped his shaft. He squeezed his fingers in a torturous ring around the base, leaving his cockhead hungry for attention. Apollo thrust slowly, teasing him.

He wasn't as skilled as Zeus, Ganymede thought; or Hermes, for that matter. His fucking always felt performative, and Apollo always made the same face at climax. "What if I say yes?"

Apollo buried his erection to the hilt, then turned Ganymede's chin roughly, "I will take you to unimagined heights."

He filled Ganymede's mouth with his searching tongue. Ganymede doubted Apollo's promise, but the heat of his cock buried within him was too delicious to risk the god stopping.

The door banged open and Ganymede startled. Apollo threw back his head, enjoying the jerks and spasms of the cupbearer quivering in shock around him. Hermes's eyes widened.

"What?" Apollo smiled, catching his breath.

Hermes folded his arms and leaned against the door. "You summoned me. At this *exact* hour."

"I did," he pushed Ganymede's chest to the sheets and snapped his hips forward.

Ganymede cried out and rocked forward, every nerve, every muscle clenching around Apollo alight, his body singing with pleasure. Apollo's groin rhythmically slapped his rear, hard and fast. When the surprise of their visitor wore off, the God of Light slowed and entered shallowly, allowing the Cupbearer to breathe and listen.

"If he thinks Father is going to catch him, he squeezes so delectably."

"Zeus doesn't care what Ganymede does in his own time."

"Care to join in?"

Hermes worried his lip between his teeth for a second.

Ganymede silently hoped Hermes would say yes. Apollo was competent enough, but the pleasure he gave was in service of himself. Hermes was unpredictable, and he was a giving lover. The thought of tasting the Messenger, both their cocks thrusting in counterpoint, and liquifying him with pleasure nearly brought him to climax. He licked his lips.

Hermes rested his hands on his hips. "I have business to tend to. So if puckering him was the only reason you called for me—"

"That's not *why* I summoned you, merely *when*." Apollo pulled Ganymede upright, locking him against his body with a forearm across his chest. He squeezed at a flat nipple and held Ganymede's cock in his other hand as though it were his to offer, gently circling the wet crown with his thumb then fondling his scrotum— slowly and in full view of Hermes, whose face remained an enigma. "That lyre I gave you to give to Orpheus… I want it back."

"It's not that simple."

"He was lucky I let him borrow it. I need it back to amuse Euterpe. Simple enough."

Hermes took off his *petasos* and brushed back his short brown curls, pausing to choose his words. "I borrowed it as a boon from *one of us* to Orpheus."

"What does 'one of us' care if I get it back early?" Apollo furrowed his brow. "And who among them thought they could give out *my* favor? A detail, by the way, you neglected to mention before."

"I couldn't say then, I cannot tell you now, and the wrath of the one who did will be *limitless* if I say another word."

Ganymede didn't care for this one bit. Apollo still had him lewdly displayed, but had stopped pleasuring him, and all but stopped pleasuring *himself*. He was softening. Ganymede bore down on him. He delighted in Apollo's gasp and he slipped free onto the sheets. Apollo returned his hands to Ganymede's hips and entered him smoothly.

"Never mind," Apollo said breathlessly. "I can entertain her with something else."

"Oh!" Hermes said, replacing his hat. "I do have a question for you while I'm here. About your *other* mortal son."

"Asklepios? What of him?" Apollo curled his fingers around Ganymede's cock.

"Hades and Persephone told me—"

"Oh, look what you did. Their names made poor Ganymede wilt. Now what are we to do?"

"You can restore him after I leave. A soldier disappeared off a boat on the Styx three weeks ago. A soldier from Argolis, where Asklepios has been seen healing."

"Ah, I am so proud of him."

"Apollo, this could be serious."

"Only if you tell them. Feign ignorance."

"But—"

"If those dirt dwellers would go about their duties quietly, we wouldn't have to hear about it. And *you* wouldn't have been scolded for getting Aphrodite with child." He hissed, turning his attention back to his bedmate. "I'm done with this. Unless you're staying."

"Fine; I'll say nothing. Asklepios is none of my business." Hermes shrugged and turned to leave. "And by that reasoning, Orpheus's lyre is none of yours."

"But it doesn't belong to—" Hermes was already gone. "Trickster..."

Apollo's fingers tightened on Ganymede's hip, and he stroked him to the brink. Ganymede thought of Hermes, how good it felt when their chests brushed together, his soft lips, and gave a plaintive moan. Apollo grew thicker, hips slapping against Ganymede's flanks. With another deep thrust he saw stars, all else forgotten.

✻   ✻   ✻

136

She'd promised she would write but could find no words to send to Aidon. Her mind was a muddle every time she tried.

Nearly a month had passed since Samothrace, and Persephone knew that if she hoped, dared to count the days, she would be lost if her courses came. What then? Aidon had said he never wanted to see her in such pain, and this was their ninth attempt. If they'd failed, would he ever want to try again?

The air was humid for this time of year, and the first harvest *still* hadn't ripened. Persephone walked on the sand between bluffs and waves, sea mist a balm on her skin and troubled mind. *A late frost*, Demeter had said, just like the year before last. What if she was wrong? They had drained the fertility of Samothrace for their own. What if their reach had extended further than the withered, fermented vineyards?

Waves lapped quietly. One could see to the bottom on a day like this. Fishing boats trawled the shallow waters of the gulf, their nets heavy with the fruits of the sea. Women stoked fires, hanging and drying the sardines they would eat until the barley was gleaned and cured. She wavered, a sharp metallic taste at the back of her tongue. Her heart drummed.

The memory of the raw aurochs' heart, beating its last, made her gag. She could still taste the iron, feel the sinew and muscle tearing between her teeth. The scent of fish choked her. She quickened her pace to escape the smoke and turned up the path, climbing the hill. Her nausea ebbed the higher she climbed. When she reached her favorite olive tree along The Sacred Way, she sat down. Her head swam, her limbs were heavy. Persephone dropped her forehead to her knees and listened to the birds.

"Daughter?"

Demeter's face was lost in the glare of sunlight. Persephone squinted. "I'm fine."

"Hermes is at the Telesterion. What should I tell him?"

"I don't know. Tell him—" She leaned abruptly to the side, her stomach emptying into the grass. From a distance, a mortal man in the field dropped his bident and ran for help.

"Kore!" Demeter crouched and raised a hand to her forehead.

Her mind whirled. She'd never vomited before. She remembered Kyrene in the fields when she was a little girl, the scent of bile… "It can't be…"

Persephone's heart pounded in her chest. Two weeks before the rites she'd bled. The moon was waxing, full in two days… She stood slowly. A woman ran to her with a cup of cold water from the well, then backed away. Persephone swished it in her mouth and spat out the rest of the bile. The whispered words 'Karpophoros' and 'with child' buzzed around her.

With child.

"Daughter, count back."

She stared at Demeter, pale. "Five weeks since I last bled. Wait; no… six."

Her mother's eyes welled and her breath was shallow. She threw her arms around Persephone and shook.

"I can't stay out here." Persephone heard her voice distantly. "We need to go back to the Telesterion."

Silently, Demeter held Persephone, and they walked backward through sheaves of barley, vanishing into the ether.

6.

"I *swear* to you Persephone said I could! I came straight from Eleusis. She withdrew her order that I cross only in Charon's boat and said I may fly directly to the palace from now on."

"Why now?"

"I'm not sure. All she said was that you need to be there at once."

An abyss formed in Aidon's stomach. They had failed. He gazed past Hermes toward the dark expanse of the Styx. Now he must comfort her. He would have to be strong, for her sake. "Tell me everything you saw."

"Demeter was weeping, but trying to hide her tears. Persephone was as readable as stone. She never moved and stared out a league away. They wouldn't say a word to me otherwise."

"Thank you, Psychopompos. Before you go," he said, catching Hermes as he turned on his heel, "did you manage to visit Argolis?"

"I did. Asklepios is in Atreus's camp, but I saw nothing out of the ordinary. Apollo didn't tell me anything useful, either."

Aidoneus nodded. This could be settled later. "If you see anything, *hear* anything, tell me at once. It *will* happen again."

Hermes nodded, then leaped from the balcony, gone from his antechamber before Aidon could blink. *Be there at once.* His chariot would draw too much attention. Aidon closed his eyes and stretched out his hand, wisps of black smoke enveloping him. He stepped forward, his mind as tumultuous as the ether surrounded him.

This was his fault. She was trying to bury it in front of Hermes and her mother… Demeter was with her. After returning from Alikarnassos, Demeter had reproached him, and despite Persephone's protestations, he'd let her do it. Now she had cause to castigate him again.

Not only had he sought out Orpheus, but he had also put them in this position anew… Persephone swore otherwise, but if he had been honest with her from the outset, he doubted she would have eaten the pomegranate and forsaken her fertility for him. She could have had children. Not *his* children, but… He clenched his jaw.

Twisting light gave way to dark mist and smoke and he stumbled forward into the cavernous confines of the Ploutonion. Aidon drew his himation over his head, shifted its color to earthy brown, and hunched to appear shorter, disguising himself however poorly as a supplicant. He climbed the steep path to the Telesterion and pushed open the front door.

I'm here. He waited.

Upstairs. She sounded clipped and distant, a league away, as Hermes had said. Echoing sandals grew louder and a man approached him at the base of the stairs. "My son, you cannot—" Aidoneus turned quietly to him and Keryx swallowed, then called up to the guard at the landing. "Let this one pass!"

Aidon glimpsed the hoplite's greaves and sandals as he ascended. Once he was out of sight, he threw back his himation, trotting to Persephone's bedroom. Light filtered through the saffron-dyed linen curtain near her bed. The room was warm and golden like the amber walls of their bedchamber.

Persephone sat on her low pallet with Demeter, tears streaking her cheeks. Demeter rose slowly, formally, and nodded her head to him. "Aidoneus."

"Demeter," he returned, politely. She refused to meet his eyes and darted from the room. Persephone and he were alone.

"Sweet one…"

She inhaled deeply and shuddered. "I think I'm with child."

He blinked.

"Aidon, I'm pregnant."

He traversed the room as though in a dream and knelt before her. "You're…"

Another tear refreshed the trail on her cheek and she stroked his face. "Yes."

He rose and leaned his forehead against hers, almost afraid to touch her, convinced, momentarily, that this would all melt away and he would awaken. "H-how do you know?"

"Nothing for certain. But I… I haven't bled for six weeks, and I was sick on the road."

"Sick?" His brow creased.

Persephone giggled. "Husband, most women become nauseated when they're with child. Even immortal ones."

Aidoneus realized he wasn't breathing and gasped, staring at her. She was pregnant. Persephone was carrying their child. *His child.* Tears came unbidden, clouding his vision, and he lay his head on her knees and smiled.

"Are you all right?"

"I might ask *you* that. But yes. I am." He lifted his face and she beamed down at him, her thumb brushing away a drop from the bridge of his nose. Gingerly at first, then reverently, he pressed his hand to her womb, then slid onto the bed and sat beside her. "Would I be able to feel it move?"

She smiled and shook her head. "Not for a few months. I can't even feel it."

Aidoneus blushed. "I'm so ignorant of the ways of birth."

"Don't worry. I am too." Persephone held his hand there. "Amphitrite said we could learn about the baby if we placed our hands together on my womb."

The Lord of the Dead shook his head, mystified. "I wouldn't know—"

"Put your hand over hers and close your eyes," said a voice from the doorway. Aidon turned sharply to see Demeter, her arms folded, a smile threatening her staid expression. He nodded at her and awkwardly held Persephone's hand to her womb. "No— arm around her. Your right hand over her left."

Aidoneus followed Demeter's instructions. At first, all he saw was sunlight on the back of his eyelids, then impenetrable dark. He heard a rhythm, faint, too faint and too fast to be his heartbeat or hers. Then images rolled over him like a wave. Amber eyes, tendrils of twisting ivy, unruly hair like Aidon's own...

"He's there," Persephone's voice quavered. "Aidon, it's him!"

He opened his eyes and held her close. "My love... We—"

Demeter's hands were cupped over her mouth, and she shook, her eyes as wide as the moon. Aidon froze. Here and unavoidable was proof that he'd lain with her daughter— the very thing Demeter had nearly destroyed the world to prevent. All the words she'd ever said to him in anger flew through his mind. He steeled himself.

"Fates, this is miraculous!" she cried. Demeter took a step forward, then halted. "I'll go. Surely you two wish to speak privately..." Aidon exhaled in relief.

"No, Deme. You're her mother. Please stay," Aidon said. Shock and delight radiated from Persephone at his words. "There's time enough for us to be alone."

Demeter hung near the doorway, then crept slowly toward them. Aidon held Persephone's hand, helping her to her feet. He stood face to face with the Goddess of the Harvest, his friend and ally during the war, his wife's mother, his bitter enemy who robbed him and his kingdom of his queen for half of every year. The woman who had kept her part in their truce, the overjoyed mother. Demeter's eyes glistened as she stared up at him, her lips trembling.

Aidoneus threw his arms around Demeter and she leaned her head on his shoulder, sobbing. She wept, her tears soaking his himation. They parted, then both the Lord of the Underworld and the Goddess of the Harvest, husband and mother, held Persephone as she fell happily into their waiting embrace.

✻   ✻   ✻

"Hello?"

There was no answer. She banged the bronze knocker against the oak door and it lurched, hinges creaking with rust.

A toothless man pulled the door wide. Behind him, Eurydice saw the great pool in the center of the atrium, petitioners and supplicants milling about it. "Can I help you, sister?"

"Sister?" Eurydice's mind drifted momentarily. This man had seen at least eighty years. Then again, so had she. But mortals aged so quickly. Their lives passed like butterflies, her mother had said. "Are you called Orpheus?"

"No, no. My name is Perrhaebus. Orpheus is away in Thrace, visiting his family."

"Oh. Does he have a wife and children?"

"The hierophant is still unwed, despite our best efforts," he said with a reedy chuckle. He smiled at her. "Is there anything else I can do to help you?"

143

"Hierophant…" she murmured. The highest of their ranks. Orpheus must be as ancient as the man before her. "Perhaps. If you can, I need you to give him a message."

"I suppose I could."

"Tell him…" No one else knew that Persephone and Hades had been the King and Queen at the rites. The last being whose wrath she wished to incur was *her's*, no matter how friendly the spring goddess had seemed. She'd heard stories. "Tell him that… I heard the whispered words of trees, the roaring of waves. Brimo shall birth Brimos."

He knitted his brow, piecing her words together. "Exactly that? He will ask who gave me this riddle."

"Call me Eurydice… but he won't know my name. I can be found in the forest, and I'll know when he comes."

"How, sister?"

"I always find them. I am the bee charmer."

✳   ✳   ✳

"A single corn, reaped in silence."

Triptolemus split the grain from the chaff with a knife, just as he had done for the better part of a century. Keryx circled thrice around Persephone and Demeter, enthroned on the great dais, just as his father Eumolpus had before him, scattering barley sheaves as he went, his acolytes swinging censers.

Keryx's wife, Desma, knelt before Persephone with a cup of *kykeon*. The young goddess lifted it to her lips. *Fates, please don't let me be sick in front of them.*

Persephone took a sip and swallowed. Triptolemus shouted, his words hollow in her ears as she fought nausea. "The Mistress shall give birth to a Holy Boy! Brimo shall give life to Brimos! The Strong One to the Strong One!"

A roar went up from the crowd. Koudounias rattled, drums beat, and the assembled chanted in reply. "*Potnia kouron Brimou Brimon!*"

You can endure this, sweet one. Beyond the chanting, Aidon's voice calmed her. He waited upstairs, having returned from a brief visit to Chthonia to tell the Underworld their joyous news, and left Hecate and Thanatos in charge of the realm while he stayed with his wife. *It's almost over.*

Persephone lifted the cup and drank its contents. She closed her eyes and gasped, wiping a drop of *kykeon* from her lips. Mint clung to her nose and throat. As their worshippers stood in the aisle to receive a drink of *kykeon* and loaves of bread, Demeter helped Persephone up from her throne. They disappeared behind the tapestry curtain.

"You did well," she said. "You may yet be sick, but you were steady for them. That's what matters. Did he return to-night?"

"Yes," Persephone said, swaying.

Demeter nodded. "I'm visiting my temple in Thassos this evening. With Triptolemus. He's waiting for me in the *anaktoron.*"

"Together?" Persephone raised her eyebrows. "So you'll be gone until tomorrow..."

"Perhaps a few days." She chewed her lip, made sure the mortals were out of earshot, then grasped her daughter's hands. "Now Persephone, this is a delicate condition you are in."

"I know, Mother, I— "

"And when you're with him, you must be careful..."

"Wait; Mother..."

"...and Aidoneus should go gently with you. You mustn't let his penis nudge too hard against the mouth of your womb."

"Mother!" Her eyes and mouth flew open.

Her voice hitched as sheaves of barley appeared behind her. "Be cautious, Daughter."

"I will." Persephone rolled her eyes and smiled. "I love you. Oh, and leave poppies in Thassos. They love them so much."

Her mother smiled and was gone.

The back of her throat felt watery. Persephone ran up the stairs, hurtling toward her quarters, praying she would reach the basin in time. The door flew open and Aidon appeared, ready to embrace her. She stumbled back, losing the *kykeon* all down the skirts of her peplos.

"Persephone!" Aidoneus rushed to her side. He blotted her lips and chin with the edge of his himation. She coughed and bent forward again, retching nothing but air, tears leaking from her eyes. He knelt and held her gently at the waist, waiting until her breathing returned to normal. Aidoneus scooped her up by her knees and carried her into her bedroom, kicking the door shut behind him.

"My poor dress," she groaned. "The Eleusinians made it especially for tonight..."

"It's lovely."

"Not anymore."

He smiled and pulled the *fibulae* loose, then untied the braided *zone* from under her bust. Carefully, he helped her peel off the ruined peplos. He balled it up and tossed it in the corner of the room, far from the bed so the scent wouldn't sicken her again.

Aidon tipped a clay amphora, pouring sweetly scented water into a cup. She waved him off, but he placed it in her hands anyway. "It's honeyed, and I crushed sage into it to settle your stomach. Just sip, then spit. Chew on the leaves. You'll feel better."

"How do you know?" She shivered.

"I spoke at length with Nyx." He removed his himation and draped it around her. "About how I can be a good husband to you now."

"You're always a good husband to me," she murmured, smiling weakly. Persephone settled into the warmth trapped within the heavy black wool. Aidon took the cup from her and flung its contents out the window, then straightened the pillows and cushions on her narrow bed.

"I'm trying." He cradled her head and laid her down. Persephone played with a moonlit wisp of hair at his temple.

"A strand of silver already?" She giggled.

"We age and change as the world changes, and I'll be a father soon, no?" He grinned at her. "I know the *Eumolpides* are rejoicing, but how did it go with Demeter's priesthood?"

"They're all very excited." She could hear the revels outside the Telesterion, songs ringing across the *agora* while cups and bowls of freshly brewed barley beer circulated. "Mother left for Thassos. With Triptolemus."

"She did." His voice caught. Persephone wrinkled her nose. He chuckled. "What's the matter with that?"

"Just some *forward* advice about taking precautions when you are... with me."

"She's right, you know." He crouched next to her. "But she has nothing to worry about. We're not having sex until you're delivered."

"What?!"

"Persephone..." He looked at the floor and took her hands within his, enveloping them. "What we did, how Zagreus came to be... we don't know, can't *ever* really know the full truth of how he was made. And we don't know if there's a way he might be... unmade."

"Aidon, he's *our* child; as deathless as you or I."

"Sweet one, please." His forehead wrinkled in consternation. "For me. If anything happened to him and I was the cause, I could never forgive myself."

Persephone sighed. "I'm in no state to seduce you anyway."

"Nonsense."

"I still have sick on me."

"Easily remedied." He dribbled water into the small basin near the window, then soaked it up with a sponge. Aidon opened the himation and blotted her skin.

"Thank you," she muttered.

He washed her belly reverently, his touch light, and his eyes darkening further each time he looked up from his work. "You're beautiful, you know."

"I feel disgusting."

He grasped her chin and lowered his lips to hers, pulling sumptuously at each of them until they parted. His tongue massaged hers, and he pulled her closer, his thumbs at her temples, his fingers cradling her neck. "Wife, if you weren't in your sacred condition, I would pin you to this bed with my cock and never let you up."

She shivered, thighs clenching at his words. "What... *can* we do?"

"Lie back." He stripped off his tunic and looked her over, his grin predatory. Persephone did as he bade, staring at the bulge straining his loincloth. He sat at the foot of the bed, just out of reach, and she twisted with need. Slowly, Aidon brushed his fingertips over her legs. "If anything becomes too much for you, you'll tell me."

"I will."

He kissed her ankle, tickling the fine hairs of her shin with his nose, and trailed his lips upward. Aidon carefully squeezed her calves and feet, massaging in long strokes. She relaxed, the stiff formality of the day melting from her muscles. His beard grazed the back of her right knee, making her jump.

"Hold," she said. He backed away.

"If you're not feeling well enough—"

"I just had to let another wave pass," she said and smiled at him. A familiar coil started winding within— a hunger only sated when he filled her. Maybe he'd change his mind. Persephone writhed and arched at the thought, her legs squeezing together, spreading slick heat to her inner lips. She exhaled.

His eyes bored into her and he moved to kiss her again, her breasts pressing to his chest as she greedily pulled him closer. He smiled against her searching lips. "Easy…"

"You torture me," she whispered back.

"You love it." Aidon nipped at her collarbone.

"Wait."

He pulled back again and held her hand. "Tell me if you need the basin."

She shook her head, her eyes closed, head swimming. When she opened them again, she nodded, and Aidoneus returned, caging her with his arms. Her gaze followed the length of his body. His damned loincloth interrupted the sinews and lines she loved studying. Then his tongue wound around her nipple and her frustration eased. She could strip him of it later…

He kissed the underside of her breasts, mindful of his weight on her. *The shape of them now,* came his voice into her mind. *They're filling out.*

We grow and change… they'll keep swelling throughout. And when the milk comes in to feed him, they'll be enormous.

Fates… he said, his eyes rolling back. A drop of his essence seeped through his loincloth and smudged on her thigh. She swept her finger across it and pulled it into a string with her thumb, then stared at him and licked her fingers. His eyes darkened.

"However will you resist?"

He rolled away from her and sat at the edge of the bed, smirking. "I'm as immovable as a cypress, sweet one."

"And just as hard." She caressed him through the cloth with a toe. He sucked in air and grabbed her ankle, his glance a playful warning. She ignored it and brushed along the same path with the other, which he let linger longer than the first.

She gently caressed the length of him, the pad of her foot dampened by an upwelling of his arousal.

"Careful," he said with a groan. Aidon wrapped his fingers around her other ankle and smiled, belying his words. He pried her thighs apart and the cool air made her jump. With another trail of kisses, he descended to her navel, then looked up at her reverently. He gave her womb a last caress, then folded his legs and dragged her backward, gently placing her thighs over his shoulders. He stared at her over the rise of her mound, his eyes mirthful. "May I kiss you?"

"I'll go mad if you don't," Persephone said, an unexpected edge to her voice. The throb had become a clench, a hunger, a vexing grasp around nothing. And just as she felt she would scream from want, his tongue traced her opening and she moaned. It speared into her, relieving her frustration momentarily, but her need returned in measures and she wanted more— his fingers, his lips and tongue... Persephone hissed and sighed. She pushed her bottom down and ground against his face, urging him toward the apex of her mound, but was stopped by a firm hand. He would not be hurried.

He slid two fingers along her seam, parting the thatch of dark hair. She wriggled but stilled as he pulled back and calmly admired every damp pink fold and curve within. He teased her labia between his fingers to the sound of her content hums, and steadied her hips when he dipped down to follow each caress with his tongue. His fingers wandered up to the hood of her bud. He petted it gently, relishing in her delight and frustration, then traced downward to her entrance before he pushed his digits slowly inward and curled them exactly where she needed to be touched. Persephone tilted her head back on the pillows, her lips parted, soft cries carrying to the rafters of her room. She felt a cool exhale on her bud, then the heat of his tongue, his lips pulling at it until she could hardly breathe. The delicious rasping and suckling became all she could sense.

Fingertips worked in concert with his tongue and lips as they thrust and splayed and stroked within her.

"Please... don't stop!" Her back arched off the bedclothes. She squeezed her eyes shut and let go, her climax breaking over her like a wave, rocking her against his questing mouth. Persephone threw a pillow over her face to muffle her cries, lest all of Eleusis hear her husband's name shouted into the night air. After a final breathless scream, she came down and threw it aside. She pushed lightly on his forehead when the sensation became too much, then let her arm flop uselessly across her abdomen.

"How are you?" His voice was low, tinged. His fingers slowly withdrew, taking a thin strand of her wetness with them.

"How do you think? Please, Aidon... I need you inside me."

Aidoneus gritted his teeth, his control visibly shredding the longer he considered. He exhaled, shaking his head. "You know I want to. I can't."

"What about you, though?"

"I can take care of myself, sweet one."

"Let me," she said, licking her lips.

"You were nauseated earlier. That... won't end well." He smiled tenderly and reached to untie the knot of his loincloth. His phallus, pinned upright against his body as he dined on her, reared in the flickering lamplight. He sighed as it sprang forward, then caressed himself, his slick fingers stroking her wetness onto his shaft. A pearl dotted the tip, welling larger. He ran his hand over his mouth and through his beard to gather up more of her essence, then gilded the crimson head with their combined arousal. Aidon licked his lips and sighed, tasting her again.

The sight was more enticing than when his face was buried between her thighs, and she still floated, half insensate from her climax. Aidoneus pleasuring himself in front of her was rare, and seldom to completion. Not when there were so many other ways open to them…

"What can I do, then?"

He shook his head and steadied himself, gripping the rail of the kline near the foot of her bed as he eyed her hungrily. His hand worked against his flesh, slowly at first, switching between quick jerks against the lust-darkened head that made veins stand out on his brow, and longer strokes down the entire shaft that made him sigh in relief. He groaned and flexed his hips, thrusting into his waiting fist. The muscles of his arms tensed and his motions quickened, his cock a furious red.

"Husband—"

"Touch your breasts," Hades rasped, his voice set on edge and dangerous.

She shivered and complied, covering them with her hands.

"Hold them," he commanded as his hand stroked faster. "From underneath."

She did his bidding, the flesh tender, heavier in her hands.

"Open your legs. Spread yourself for me… your lips," he said, his voice strangled, close to the edge.

The corner of Persephone's mouth twitched and she opened her thighs wide and drew her fingertips slowly down her belly, delighting in the rapid movement of his hand, the rhythmic thud of his wrist against his groin as she idled and further frustrated him.

"Please, sweet one," he strained. "Now…"

She wove her fingers through her labia, her entrance still spasming from her climax, wet folds glistening in the moonlight that poured through the window. Aidon threw his head back and his eyes squeezed shut, his voice silenced, his face contorted in cold pleasure. His hand stilled at the base then jerked forward, and a rope of his seed jetted toward her and landed on the floor next to her bed. He moaned and stroked himself again, the next round carrying half the distance, then the third and last coating his hand and dripping onto his thigh as he bent forward, gasping.

Aidon raised his head and let out a long sigh, picked up his discarded loincloth, cleaned first his spent cock, then mopped his seed from the stone floor. He wadded it and threw it in the pile with her dress. Persephone rolled toward the window and welcomed him into the warmth of her small bed. He nestled against her back, and held her belly gently, listening to the patter of Zagreus's heartbeat as they both fell peacefully asleep.

✻   ✻   ✻

A broken amphora, a torn curtain, threads ripped from the loom. Zeus shook his head and walked through his wife's villa. All this over nothing. Over something that would amount to nothing.

"Your grace," Iris bowed deeply then scampered after him. "Your Grace, the Queen does not wish to see anyone."

"I'm not *anyone*," Zeus growled. "I'm her husband and more importantly, her damned king. This needs to end." He entered the moonlit courtyard. No Hera. He checked the upstairs gynaikeion. Again, no Hera. At least Iris had ceased shadowing him. He couldn't stand that girl. She possessed all the joy of someone who had shoved an unripened fig up their anus.

Zeus stepped into their shared garden and picked a soft yellow apple that hung close to the door. He bit into it and spied Hera sitting on the ground beside her favorite fountain, wrapped head to toe in a thick blue himation, her knees tucked under her chin, neck, and hair veiled. She looked like a boulder.

"Ares finally saw to that mess in Argolis."

Hera sat, silent.

"A general's son died there but was mysteriously restored to life. He ripped the throats out of Hermes's priests with his

153

teeth. So both sides united to hunt him down, and the region is finally at peace again." He waited. "But to return from the Underworld? I'll have to speak to Hades. I know he won't come to the midsummer gathering, but—"

"Your disrespect for me knows no bounds."

"Hera…"

"You *promised* me."

"Persephone's pregnancy will come to nothing!"

"How did it happen?"

He chuckled. "The same way it always happens, I'd wager."

"You know what I mean!"

"Nobody knows, and you'll be happier if you forget about it. This could work in our favor. You said yourself that it would do well for us to strengthen the bonds between our worlds. I hear it's to be a boy, and perhaps in a few decades or centuries, if Eileithyia or Pasithea still need a hus—"

"If you even *dare*…"

Zeus settled on his haunches in front of her and roughly pulled the himation back from her dark hair. Hera turned her face away from him. "Look at me."

She didn't move.

"*Hera*," he raised his voice. Tears dripped in malachite rivulets down her cheeks. "Nothing has changed. You are turning our marriage into Tartarus, and this child will come to nothing. Fates… nobody knows if the baby can even survive."

"What do you mean?"

"Nothing," he said, waving her off.

"What do you mean, Zeus?! Of course it will. It's deathless, as are we all." She calmed, her voice small. "Isn't it?"

"It's not born yet. Who knows what could happen? And who knows if it's even immortal? There was obviously some sorcery involved."

"You must demand an explanation from Hades! He is your vassal."

"And have him press the advantage of my oath in front of all? I think not. Talk to Persephone, get the truth from her. You'll find it much easier."

"It was *your* oath. This is *your* mess." Hera stood up. "I've had enough. I'm going to Samos."

"At this hour?" Zeus came up behind her and held her shoulders. He rubbed her bare arms, trying to calm her. "Wife, *gynaika mou*, I'm worried about you. This isn't—"

"When have you ever cared about how I feel?" Hera said, shaking him loose. "Go find something to amuse yourself." The ether drew open like a curtain in front of her, a shimmer of cyan and blue northern lights. "It's what you're good at."

Zeus stood alone, the night still and quiet. "Fine."

He glanced up at the moon, the stars beyond. The sky seemed so vast, one of the reasons mortals gave him so much honor. But it wasn't infinite. It stopped somewhere, higher than even he had dared to go, replaced only by cold, dark, and airless reaches. The infinite extent of his domain was a fiction that Zeus was all too happy to perpetuate.

No one, save Hecate and Demeter, knew that the *hieros gamos* on Olympus had secured his rulership of the skies before the lots were even drawn... as well as the taunting, ever-present voices of Clotho, Lachesis, and Atropos ringing in his ears day and night. Were they the reason Kronos went mad?

He wondered briefly what would have happened if Poseidon had been right about the lots— if his eldest brother had received the heavens instead, and if *he* had claimed the earth. Zeus rolled his eyes. Hades would be obsessing over and lamenting his duties, just the same. And his preoccupation with justice over keeping the peace would have led to tyranny. He'd proven *that* with his unwillingness to send Persephone back, even as the earth swiftly died.

Was returning her fair to Hades? Certainly not. But it was the right thing to do. Zeus had been outraged— at Hades for holding the world hostage over a girl, at Persephone for think-ing she could upend the order of the cosmos. They'd nearly destroyed the world and extinguished the fire of Olympus for the sake of fleeting romantic love. And now they could dangle his brash oath over his head until aeon's end.

But Hades hadn't taken his pregnant bride to Olympus the moment they'd learned of it. He hadn't demanded anything. Hera would just have to make her peace with it. And if she didn't... he drew in a breath. If it came to that...

Zeus needed to be free of all of them, even for a moment. He gazed out over Thessaly and kicked off his sandals. His himation dropped to the ground, left behind in a heap. Let her find them there— she'd told him to go out and amuse himself. Zeus padded barefoot through Hera's garden, then vaulted forward, sprinting for the garden's edge.

Before he ran out of ground he was in the air. An updraft caught feathers and lifted him lightly on the breeze. He spread golden eagle wings, curled his feet beneath him, and scanned the countryside with sharp eyes. Thessaly? No. Thassos? De-meter was there with... his talons curled. Attica? Certainly not. Aidoneus would be in Eleusis, doting on his wife. Thebes... worse still. If Hera found him there, he'd never hear the end of it. He turned south, enjoying the breeze in his feathers. The wind buoyed him as it cooled along the coast. Argolis was at peace again. Tiryns. Didn't they trade a princess from Thebes for Alcmene? One from Kadmos's line, locked away in the palace to preserve her virtue until her betrothed came of age...

He circled the palace, high on the cliffside, and landed at the top of an oak tree that hung over the outer walls. Talons shifted to toes, feathers molted back into his tunic, and he scaled the branches, alighting quietly on the flat roof. He walked silently, invisibly past a hoplite, then hoisted himself onto the balcony of the gynaikeion. A woman, dark-haired and petite, relaxed alone in a deep bath. Steam rose around her, and she trailed a sponge up one tan arm, over the top of her breasts, and down the other. Her eyes opened and locked with his. He could sense the quickening of her breath, the electric frissons that coursed through her core, her thighs… knowing innately who had come for her. The only being who could or would dare.

She stepped out of the bath. Water sheeted from her skin to the tile as she took delicate steps across the room, leaving a stream behind her that glistened in the lamplight. She stopped at the doorway in front of Zeus, smelling of rosewater. He smiled down at her.

"Semele."

7.

"**F**ATES BELOW, I'D RATHER BE ANYWHERE ELSE..."

"I can go without you," Persephone said. "I'll be fine."

"No, all three of us agreed." Demeter arranged a lock of hair by lamplight. "You shouldn't travel in your condition without either myself or Aidoneus at your side."

"Mother, despite your mis—" She paused, then flew to the basin, leaning over. Nothing landed in the clay vessel, but the noise she made was ghastly, and the taste of bile only made her want to retch again. She felt her mother's warm hand on her back, stroking gently. Persephone composed herself. "Was it this bad for you?"

"Worse." Demeter chuckled. Persephone sat in the dark while Demeter motioned to a young girl for a cup of *kykeon*. "Drink this. It will calm your stomach."

"I don't want it to come up while I'm there."

Demeter sighed. "At least breathe it in."

Persephone closed her eyes and inhaled barley and sharp mint, the fragrance replacing the empty smell of sickness. Her head stopped swimming. "Did you put nectar in it?"

"No. Just the good earth."

"Would it help?"

"I didn't have nectar when I carried you. You could ask Hera since she's so taken with you."

Persephone rolled her neck. Daeira, who usually attended to her mother, had sewn a coronet of braids tight to her scalp, tresses wound upward. It was fashionable, but Persephone thought she looked like a cornucopia. She opened the ebony box Aidoneus had carved for her some years ago, and lifted her crown. Persephone draped a saffron veil of soft-spun linen over it, the edges embroidered with white asphodel. "Ready?"

"Are you?" Demeter looked at her pointedly. "The only talk on Olympus is of your child."

"It's *his* too. And we meet with the *Dodekatheon* soon. If I can reduce the distraction…"

"He'll *never* face this kind of scrutiny. You will be mobbed— every word pulled apart." Demeter watched Persephone idly spin her rings. "Do you truly wish to go?"

"I'd rather go to bed. But I promised Aphrodite I'd see her, Athena is expecting me, and—"

"Fine," Demeter said, gruffly. "Chart our path and show no weakness. Let them see you step through the fire with nary a foot set in the ether."

Asphodel grew at Persephone's feet and a gyre of flame spun from it, illuminating their faces. Her other hand beckoned their destination and Olympus swelled into view. Persephone drew back her shoulders and gracefully stepped through, then held her hand out for her mother, who lifted the edge of her skirts and ducked under the arc of winding flame.

Drinks lowered, heads bowed, and Persephone curtsied to the assembled gods and nymphs. She recognized a handful of faces. Eurynome, mother of the Kharites. Aristaios, Kyrene's son by Apollo, spoke with a river god whose name escaped her. A few of her husband's vassals, rustic gods of springs and caves, that she racked her brain trying to recall. It had been easier mere weeks ago. Her mind was fogged.

"Persephone!"

Athena wove through the crowd as Demeter glowered at her. Her mother scanned the room, and a group of rustic gods from Crete playing with a red serpent caught Demeter's eye. "Daughter, if you're well enough..."

"I am, and you have business to attend to." Persephone smiled. Demeter returned Athena's nod, her features pinched.

The Goddess of Wisdom spoke low. "So it *is* true..."

Persephone placed a hand instinctively on her belly and nodded.

"I don't traffic in rumors, but it's hard to avoid news of *that* magnitude. When it reached me, though, I said nothing to anyone else."

Persephone beamed. Maybe Demeter was wrong. Hera had come to her a month ago yearning for a better world for women, and Athena was forgoing the Olympian appetite for gossip. Perhaps she and Aidoneus could influence them after all...

"Your husband is coming, yes?"

"Not tonight," she said, wavering.

"But you have so much to celebrate!" Athena folded her arms. "It isn't right for you to bear the brunt of *them* alone."

"I'll be fine," Persephone said hastily. "There are more pressing matters than suffering bawdy congratulations from the men here."

Athena guffawed. "Ares would be the worst. His tongue's been loosened of late..." She chuckled. "Fates know I tried to reach out to your husband... I championed a hero over a decade before your marriage, named Perseus. The only way to fulfill his quest was with your husband's Helm. You have *no idea* the lengths I went to to get it. Hades wouldn't even receive me! He was so adamant about..."

"The pact with my mother."

"Yes! The Helm had to be delivered by a Stygian nymph. I think her name was Kylea... Cleyera..."

"Clymena." Persephone led Athena away from the bustle of the symposium. "Her son is the herdsman in our realm."

"I stood at the Styx, Cerberus growling the entire time, with that frightened *hemitheos* for half a day! I haven't been back since." She tittered, then grew silent and leaned against a column. "Persephone, there's something I've wanted to do for a while, but I want your permission."

Persephone raised an eyebrow. "Whatever for?"

"For the last half-century, all of Athens has made the annual pilgrimage to Eleusis. The people of my city laid the stones of The Sacred Way. I've never attended the procession..." Athena trailed off wistfully. "I wouldn't *dream* of making a spectacle of myself; I'd assume the guise of a mortal traveler! That is if you don't mind."

Persephone grinned broadly. "I would love it if you came to see me off!"

"How far along will you be?" Athena gazed across the valley, lifting a hand to her bare shoulder.

"Gods above, almost halfway. I should be showing by that time."

"Are you..." Athena leaned in. "Are you sure it's wise to journey to the Realm of the Dead when you are with child?"

She looked down, her voice as low as Athena's. "I worry about it. Aidon more so. But how could bringing Zagreus home harm him?"

"I truly hope you're right."

Persephone grinned. "Come with me and see for yourself."

"Journey to the Other Side? Again?"

"As my guest. Not lingering at the Styx but the *palace*."

"Your husband wouldn't mind? I don't think he's fond of me."

"What gave you that idea? Aidon would be delighted to have you there! And we can show you Elysion."

"Truly? Father said—" Athena stopped and narrowed her eyes. "Oh, what does he want now?"

Persephone followed Athena's icy gaze to the garden entrance. Poseidon stalked toward them, arm in arm with Amphitrite, who held a swaddled baby to her chest.

"I'll not subject you to my disgust with him. If I don't see you again tonight, then in Eleusis soon."

Amphitrite and Poseidon hurried down the hall and turned her way. The Queen of the Sea winked at her, while Poseidon's lip curled and he strode after Athena. On Amphitrite's heels was Hera, with a tanned white-veiled woman at her side. Persephone stood alone, awkwardly waiting for the Queen. Hera's golden *kantharos* twirled in her hand and she took a delicate sip.

"Just as well," Hera said, her gaze trailing after Athena. They heard Poseidon laughing.

"You must be Persephone." Hestia drew back her diaphanous veil. "Hera has told me all about you."

"Twice tonight my guests have abandoned you. Outrageous! Your mother cannot abide Athena, and then that girl scurries away like a mouse as soon as Poseidon shows his face. And that tempestuous nymph… I have an important matter to discuss with her husband, but Amphitrite makes it impossible for me to see him alone."

"You were watching me?"

"Of course. You are my responsibility while you're here. And honored more so *now* than any of my other guests."

"A shame Hades keeps to the Underworld," Hestia said, "Even now when you're—"

"He has no patience for frivolity, you know that." Hera waved her hand and Hestia sipped her nectar quietly. "You are such a good wife to him, Persephone. You know how he hates these things. I cannot imagine how difficult it is for you, especially in these early days, to face all of us at once."

Persephone's shoulders relaxed. "It's... it's not as bad as I feared. Let alone as bad as my mother warned."

Hestia rolled her eyes. "I thought Demeter would be clinging to you like pollen to a bee's ass."

Persephone tittered, holding her stomach. Suddenly dizzy, she leaned against a column, breathing slowly, her eyes closed. Hera shielded her from onlookers. "Should I fetch your mother?"

"No; it's passing."

"Have you had any nectar tonight?"

"I didn't think it wise..."

"Nonsense. I drank it with each of my children. It prevents nausea."

"And I have ginger root at my hearth, if need be," Hestia chimed in. "It mixes well with nectar."

"What's ginger root?"

"I discovered it on a journey east. Women use it before the baby quickens. Wonderful taste, too. Cool and warm all at once, and harmless, unlike willowbark."

Persephone lit up. "How far have you traveled?"

"I return to the fire here each night, so only as far as I can in a day. I'm welcome anywhere a fire honors the Goddess of the Hearth... even if it's not *my* name being used. And you?"

"Just to the shores of the Mesogeios."

"Come visit me sometime. I want to know how all these herbs grow. I only know them once they've been dried and cured."

"I'd happily show you if you'll share your tales of what lies beyond our small corner of this world."

"Thanks to Demeter, you have but half a life to explore it," Hera chimed in. "But... if your present condition is any indication, thank the Fates that the Pomegranate Agreement doesn't preclude your husband from visiting you above. Surely you two don't meet in Eleusis under your mother's watchful eye."

"No." Persephone blushed faintly. "We have our places."

"You should live on Olympus," Hestia said. "Poseidon resides here part of the time. So shouldn't *your* husband? Hera, there must be a villa for them."

"There's one free on the western side if you don't mind the wind."

The thought tempted her. Persephone imagined awakening beside Aidoneus in all seasons, just as they had planned before winter and a pomegranate changed everything. "I don't think I could convince him."

"And bless him for it," Hera said. "Olympus is ripe with temptation."

"I can visit more often, though I'll have to wait until…"

"Of course." Hera smiled warmly. "Oh, revisiting all those living herbs Hestia asked about— there are some I hear that aid in fertility, nay? Did you… find the right ones?"

"We were very fortunate. Blessed, really."

"But you don't know how it happened."

Persephone tensed under the scrutiny. "This was as much a surprise to us as to anyone. I plan to speak with Aphrodite while I'm here."

"Careful what you reveal to her," Hestia said.

"I'm careful in what I reveal to anyone here."

Hera thinned her lips. "Wise of you."

"What would that slattern have to reveal?" Hestia shook her head. "Just because she's sampled most of the men and half the women here doesn't make her an authority on fertility."

"It is her domain. And she is *also* with child."

"Licentiousness isn't a domain. The goddess of lying on her back…" Hera demurred. "Forgive me. I admire your… neutrality."

"She means you make the rest of us look bad," Hestia laughed.

"No…" Persephone paled. "Fates, I hope you don't think I hold myself above—"

Hera shook her head. "Ignore her. Hestia loves to tease. I promise you, it's admirable."

"Even if you cavort with the Goddess of Whores," a deep voice said.

Persephone turned around to find Ares swaying behind her. She craned her head upward, and immediately regretted it. His breath stank of wine. She gagged and backed away.

"Oh, and congratulations, by the way," Ares said. He chuckled. "I didn't know Hades had it in him."

"Ares!"

"*What*, mother?"

"How *dare* you shame me like this!" Hera hissed at him.

"Oh, do I need a spanking?" Ares upended his cup, the last trickle of wine staining his unshaven face. He turned to Persephone and stuck out his lower lip before snickering. "I'm sorry. I'm drunk."

"I noticed."

"I have a message for your ah… honored husband," he slurred. "About Hippolytos."

"He's been returned to Asphodel."

"Not to Tartarus? How magnam… magnanimous of him. But I *know*…" he said, leaning in and stabbing a finger into Persephone's sternum, "I know… that *you two know*… it happened again. And again. Others are disappearing… it's a trail that follows that *hemitheos* wherever he goes…"

Persephone took a healthy step back. "What should I tell my husband, Ares?"

"That I like it less than he likes it, I'd wager, and I'll stand witness at the next meeting."

"He'll be glad to hear it."

"Don't look," Hestia said, "but we'll have a quorum of the *Dodekatheon* right here if we stay longer."

"Ares, it's your paramour," Hera said over the brim of her cup.

Aphrodite walked carefully from the garden entrance, a hand resting on her heavy belly. Her dress was diaphanous and golden, pin-folded bands and embroidered roses her only real covering. She smiled at Ares. His eyes smoldered, and his shoulders squared back as she approached.

"Hello, lover…" His voice was as warm as the wine in his veins. Aphrodite beamed in surprise and took a step closer to him. Ares brought a hand up to frame her face but drew it back as Aphrodite went to lean her cheek into his palm.

Hera snickered into her cup. Aphrodite's face twisted and Hestia averted her eyes, suppressing a smirk. Persephone glowered at Ares.

He laughed and raised his voice for all to hear. "You want affection from me, *laikas*?! I wager some other man is… is dripping out of your cunt right now!"

Hera nearly spat her wine. "Ares, please. Don't be vulgar."

"*I'm* vulgar? Look at her! Big with Hermes's spawn." He whipped around to Aphrodite and growled. "I'll not come to your filthy bed."

"You've said that to me before." Aphrodite held her head high.

"Not wearing a cuckold's horns, I won't…"

Persephone lifted her chin. "You'd only wear a cuckold's horns if you were her lawful husband, Ares, which you are *not*."

"You don't know her as I do. She knows what she *really* is." He sneered at Aphrodite. "Little girl, still lost in the desert. And you'd go back there, but you *can't*."

The Goddess of Love backed away, eyes filling with tears, then turned, walking as fast as her pregnant belly would allow.

"If you'll excuse me…" Persephone muttered to Hera without meeting her gaze.

"Go after her," Ares taunted, his voice growing fainter. "It'll do *you* just as much good as it ever did me!"

Persephone's bare feet padded through the grass. "Aphrodite…"

Faint starlight lit their way. Dew soaked the hem of Persephone's dress as she trudged after her friend to the billowing tent of Aphrodite's garden pavilion.

"I'm so sorry. I can only imagine—"

"Think nothing of it. It's not the first time they've insulted me. I grow used to it in these lands." Aphrodite said. She blotted away tears, preserving the kohl that rimmed her dark eyes. "The people of the Two Rivers were never like this. A woman's fertility was sacred and respected. My priestesses coupled with men who proved themselves worthy. They would swell with life and be glorified. It was blasphemy to ask who was from whom. They were all children of Inanna."

She ascended the steps of her pavilion. Genetyllis, her midwife, was ready with a cup of honeyed water and rose petals, and Chrysothemis with palm oil for her feet. Aphrodite allowed them to attend to her in silence, then sighed impatiently. She snapped her fingers, and her servants retreated into the darkness. Persephone settled next to her and Aphrodite smiled over the rim of her cup.

"Your child also sprang from a fertile valley, no? On Samothrace. Among the vines."

She balked. The Goddess of Love had always been able to read her, had playfully teased her with details of her intimacy with Aidon more than once. Her mouth went dry. "W-what do you mean?"

"I felt the earth pour its vitality into your womb," Aphrodite said nonchalantly. She stretched and held her lower back. "I feel every release of seed into this world. Your pandemonium and passion... every drop of life drained from the soil up-on which you lay... There was a hum in the air that night, and I swear all the cosmos could feel it."

"You haven't said anything to anyone, have you?"

She set down her cup and laughed. "Nothing suffered at your hands but an aurochs, Persephone. And why would any-one here care about a fertility rite?"

"Because this was impossible," Persephone whispered, her skin pale. "Everything has been so precarious since we created Elysion. They will think we forced *ananke*... that our child is illegitimate..."

"Worry not, dear sister. No one is interested in what I have to say. Hermes and Ares escaped all blame for Argolis, but I remain a pariah. All is as expected."

Persephone's face fell. "Aphrodite, I'm sorry."

"Why? I knew what would come of it. Though I didn't know Ares would make a catastrophe of himself." Aphrodite lay on her side, pillowing her head in the crook of her arm. "So what is the little one's name to be?"

"Zagreus."

"In the east it means hunter. After your favorite stars, I im-agine?"

"That is one reason," she said with a smile. "In the west it means rebirth. The end and a new beginning."

"Fitting, since every drop of Samothrace was reborn into you from Aidoneus. Which herbs did they use?"

"I couldn't say," she lied. "I was already... affected."

"You *must* grant a favor to the mortal who made this pos-sible."

"Aidon already gave him a *great* gift."

"That was from *him*. Not you. You said it yourself— this was a miracle. Honor Orpheus for his success!" Aphrodite sat up wide-eyed, grinning at Persephone, "Let's find him a mate."

"He's already enraptured by his devotion and music."

"We will inspire him all the more. What better way for a mortal to cleave to the divine than to find it in another? Just as he brought so much joy to you. There's that bee charmer who resides nearby…"

"I'll consider it." Persephone sighed. "I wonder… I won't be able to visit you once Zagreus is born. Perhaps you could be *my* guest."

"What?" Aphrodite stilled.

"Visit my realm below."

Aphrodite flinched. Her breath grew shallow and she backed into the divan, holding her womb like a cornered animal. "Do not ask that of me…"

"Aphrodite, I mean no—"

"Curse your land of death!" Aphrodite hid her face in her hands and shook.

Persephone reached for her shoulder.

"Don't touch me!" She inched back to the far end of the divan. Aphrodite's sobs rose and she gulped air. Persephone stared at the Goddess of Love, dumbstruck. Aphrodite raised her eyes, her cheeks stained with kohl-darkened tears. "I'm sorry; I'm *so* sorry, Persephone. Forgive me."

"I… don't understand. What did I do?" Persephone whispered.

"I cannot go down there." She swayed, arms wrapped around her chest. "Please… please…"

Persephone inched closer, alarmed. "I would never have suggested it if I knew it would upset you."

"You… you forgive…"

"Of course I do. I'm worried for you, now."

Aphrodite sobbed. "You alone, sister. Why are you so kind to me when you have no cause to be?"

Aphrodite's head rested on her shoulder, and Persephone glanced around, confused. She covered the goddess's hand with hers, trying to comfort her. "Tell me what I did and I will *never* do it again. I swear."

"You know I appear different to all." Aphrodite inhaled and shuddered. "I journeyed to the Land of No Return. I left my entire being, my true self there to regain my love, Dumuzi. That's what Ares mocked me for. She—"

Persephone felt her tense.

"Your words were the very same ones Ereshkigal spoke. She *promised* me. I surrendered all that I was to have him again. But I was betrayed, and *he* is gone forever. Please, please do not *ever* ask me to come to Chthonia. I can't... I cannot make a journey like that again. It would end me."

"I swear it. I'll never mention it again."

"Forgive me, sister. You tried to be kind," she cried. "To invite me to see you with your little one so new. An honor, only to have me spit at you like an animal."

Persephone held her. "No, you shouldn't apologize. I should have known better."

"What happened to me... this is why Eros and I join those together who would not otherwise find one another. Because I know his father will never return to me. Instead, we grow that love from the smallest seed for those most deserving."

Persephone stroked her dark hair and felt the Goddess of Love's tears soak through the shoulder of her peplos. "Is there anything I can do? He might be in Chthonia right now... wandering the fields of Asphodel. Maybe I can ask Aidon—"

"No! I cannot ask that of your consort. Not now," she sniffed and held her swollen belly. "They all hate me for this. Your husband too. For those who died, and the aberrations that followed— the dead returning. But believe me when I say that this child is worth all of that."

Persephone too had undone the natural order to conceive her child— and not just this time, but so many times before.

How many lives had *she* ended when she forsook her duties to go to Alikarnassos?

Aphrodite cradled her belly protectively. "I meant what I said. I endure their scorn willingly. This child isn't ill-begotten, but something more. A being whole and complete, unbound by the yearning that drives the rest of this cosmos mad, that stripped and buried me under the Land of the Two Rivers. And you… Wouldn't you do anything and everything for your child?"

"Yes," she said after a long pause. "Aphrodite, you know better than I would. Does Orpheus truly desire a mate?"

"Desire and need are different things. He yearns quietly. With the fibers of who he is." Aphrodite's brow knit. "It's hard to explain. But he too would comb the depths of the earth for the one he loved. If you could only feel what I feel… know what I know. The same spark that exists between Dumuzi and me, between Aidoneus and you… Orpheus is capable of that, and he and his lover will inspire each other. Will you let me?" Aphrodite's voice was hollow but hopeful. "Please?"

Persephone gave Aphrodite a cautious hug. "I won't stop you."

✳   ✳   ✳

"*Za'e alaku wu'uru,*" she said in Sumerian, "*For your mother.*"

Eros lounged on the divan, a wing trailing along the ground, the other draped over the top. He ground his teeth, debating whether he should answer in kind. He sat up and spoke in Theoi instead. "Why? The mortal who helped them has already gained a favor. Persephone said so herself."

"Apollo's lyre was a gift from *him*. This would be on *her* behalf. And an alliance with her means everything to me."

He idly played with an arrow. "So you can get your lover back?"

171

Aphrodite advanced across the room, eyes blazing. "That is your father you speak of."

"And now he's dust."

The back of her hand struck like a snake, stunning him. He stared at her. Tears welled in her eyes. "*Na nis ilim zakaru Dumuzi!*"

She was so easily provoked. Eros rubbed his stinging cheek. "You nearly destroyed yourself trying to get him back the first time! And for what? That land, those people... they're gone. And with it, who you were. *Amaru'ba Ur rata.* Think about what that will one day mean for *all* gods..."

"Among them, only I remain. Does that not mean something?" She stood tall, but Eros knew she was a pillar of sand.

"You were never one of them to begin with. We were spared *only* because we fled. Hellas is not the world we left. Hades is not Nergal. Hermes isn't Enki. *Tartaros na kima Erset la Tari.* It's more complicated." Eros sat beside her and gingerly placed a hand on her shoulder. "They're gone. And with them, Father is *also* gone."

"Persephone's realm isn't *Erset la Tari.* It's timeless. You know what they created." Aphrodite whispered low. "Your father dwells in Asphodel, my child, I can *feel* it. I knew as soon as I saw her on Olympus that she walked the same lands as he. And Persephone and her husband are not bound to the mortals the way the rest of the gods are."

Eros raised a skeptical eyebrow.

"In Hellas, he can return— be reborn. And once he is, I can convince her to give him to us forever."

"Persephone cannot render him deathless; only the Children of Kronos can do that."

"Hades is one of the six. He loves nothing more in this cosmos than his wife; he will do as she bids. And, given time, she will do what I ask."

"But why this? Why Orpheus and Eurydice?"

"Because *this* will come from *us*. From me. This is but a small step, Eros. A small favor for my sister."

"A strange family you're creating…"

Aphrodite looked away. "We could be. She sees my true self more than any who look upon me. I cannot lose her friendship."

"I don't think you know what that word means, Mother." Eros shook his head and slung his quiver over his shoulder. "I'll do this for you. But it won't bring him back."

"No. But it brings us closer, *dumu*."

✳   ✳   ✳

"You nurture fruits, you haunt meadows…"

Eurydice looked up from the beehive, slowly withdrawing her arm. The liquid notes of a lyre poured through the trees. A minor chord rose, lifting, and she swore the bees themselves were humming along, that the trees swayed and fluttered like a tambourine. But it was the voice that drew her up on the balls of her feet. It was too beautiful to be human.

"…Oh sprightly and pure, traveler of the winding roads…"

This was no instrument made by mortal hands. Only a silver lyre, *the* silver lyre of Olympus could evoke this response from the trees. If it were Apollo, she wouldn't have a chance to run. If it were Hermes… perhaps she could reason with him. Eurydice moved carefully: the bees would sense her fear. She could be killed if the hive turned on her. Eurydice slowly crouched; the song of the lyre nearly drowned by their buzzing.

Eurydice peeked out, and saw a man, plainly clad in a coarse white linen tunic, a Thracian *zeira* cast from his shoulders and piled at his feet. He sat on a stump, plucking the strings with care, his short brown hair wet and curling.

"…Swift and sure, and clothed in drops of dew…"

173

It was him! She had expected the Hierophant's voice to sound like gravel, or reeds whistling in the wind. Instead, it was warm and alive, like the honey dripping off her arm. She drew closer. Her body acted on its own, and all she heard was the crunch of leaves under her feet, and the fading hum of a bee as it flew from her hair.

"…through deep ravines amongst flowers, you shout and— *gods!*" He yelped and nearly fell backward, brown eyes wide as the moon.

"Oh! I'm sorry!"

"Pay no mind, I was…" He brushed himself off, then stood, transfixed. "Who are you?"

"Eurydice," she said, extending her hand. He merely stared at her. "The bee charmer?"

Orpheus's mouth was agape. "*You* are the bee charmer? But… you've been out here for decades…"

"Did the priest not describe me?"

"Perrhaebus is blind; he has been since childhood. He only told me what you *said*, which sounded like the riddle of a wise old woman."

Orpheus looked at her extended hand reaching toward him, greeting him as a man would. Damnation; she should have curtsied, she remembered, and demurred to him. Men and women from his world were so particular about their differences.

Before she could draw her hand back, he clasped her arm, then nodded his head respectfully. "I should introduce myself. My name is Orpheus."

"A wise old woman…" she tittered, then mockingly frowned. "You know, I thought you'd look older than Tithonus. You— you're the *hierophant* of their order!"

"The youngest ever at Samothrace," he said, a proud smile on his face.

"You haven't seen thirty winters yet, have you?"

"Next year."

"I suppose I *am* the ancient one, then."

"Dare I ask?"

"Four score years." He stared at her in wonderment. Eurydice tittered. "My mother was a nymph. I'm not ageless, as she once was. I have many years ahead of me, gods willing. But..." She swallowed. "Your mother was Calliope, I heard."

"Yes, how did you—"

"So you might *still* outlive me," she puzzled to herself. "The son of a Muse—"

Orpheus threw his head back and laughed. "Oh, not *that* Calliope. My mother was named *after* the Muse. She was the princess of Thrace. Until she conceived me..."

"I'm so sorry."

"I'm not. My fate would've been courtly ignorance and decadence and I'm too peaceful for my people. I would have met my end with a knife to the throat. Better to grow up a bastard *hemitheoi*. It was freeing, in many ways."

"So you *are* the son of Apollo..."

"Yes."

"You are the child of earth and starry heaven..." Eurydice said absently. She looked at Orpheus, whose eyebrows were raised. Eurydice shook her head. "I can't hear your thoughts. It's just been repeated countless times by your followers."

"Ah," he said and rubbed his fingers together. Eurydice suddenly realized they were covered in honey.

"Oh gods, I'm sorry, I was—"

"Charming bees?"

"I suppose," she replied, shyly returning his smile. Eurydice poured water from the skin bladder hanging at her side onto a cloth and took Orpheus's hand. "Just collecting honey when I heard your lyre."

"Sorry I disturbed you," Orpheus said, amusement playing on his face as she blotted the honey from his skin.

"I don't mind," she said. Eurydice averted her eyes, afraid to meet his. His fingers were so warm. "When I... when I heard a silver lyre, I feared that an Olympian had descended to seduce me."

"No, just me." Orpheus grinned, then his face fell. "N-not, I mean, to *seduce* you, but..."

Eurydice laughed.

"Forgive me."

"For what? It's well known that my kind are the Olympians' playthings. It's been a while since I *was* seduced, so I wouldn't know if you were trying just now or not," she said, her face reddening.

It was Orpheus's turn to laugh. "I know what you mean. I haven't—" He cut himself off and cleared his throat. "Er, the message you gave to Perrhaebus— you said that Brimo had birthed Brimos."

"Yes! I was told by a cousin— a daughter of the Kabieroi— one who grew up looking after *her*."

"That's remarkable! He will be born then..."

"Zagreus," she whispered.

"You *knew* she was there."

"My mother was Persephone's companion in Nysa. The women your order sends into the woods before the rite... I have them sing, so they won't be afraid. Fear will make the bees swarm and kill you. Sometimes I ask them to sing a lullaby. And the one she sang was the same her mother had sung to her as a child, and that my mother sang to me sometimes."

"Does singing to bees work?"

"Your petitioners come back unharmed, don't they? Does anyone else know *they* were here?"

"No. I shudder to think what my brothers and sisters would say. To have helped usher in the God of the Reborn? It would turn Samothrace into a mere hero cult."

"Sons of earth and starry heaven..." she trailed off. "What does that mean?"

"That we are all of the same blood. You, me, every creature upon the earth from the smallest flea to the King of the Gods. It is a... *hope* that we will remember each other in Elysion. That we will be allowed to drink from the Mnemosyne. For those who pass through our mysteries, our order attends to the funerary rites, inscribes those words on gold leaf, and places them on the tongues of the dead."

"That's how they learned of you..."

"Yes."

"Is it true? That we remember each other in Elysion?"

"No." Orpheus's face fell. "Axiokersos— that's our epithet for the Lord of the Dead— told me it isn't so. Said that all drink from the Lethe when they die. Without exception."

"That's unfortunate. I hope you didn't tell anyone."

"No; just—" he paused and his eyes rested heavily on her. "Just you."

"I won't say anything. It's a pleasant idea..."

"But just an idea."

"You shy away from falsehood, but that hope is necessary, isn't it?" She brightened. "When did she first come to you?"

"Not she, but *he*." Orpheus paused when her eyes widened. "Axiokersos is... not what you'd think. He was humble. He isn't the selfish god of so many tales, who stole away the Maiden for half the year. I think he's just very much in love with his wife." Orpheus tilted his head. "What did you think of her? I only saw her at the beginning and end of the rite."

"Kind. Not to be trifled with. She was taken with one particular herb that we gathered. It had us both giggling like children."

"Oh?"

"I'll show you. Come!" He threw his *zeira* around his shoulders and strung the silver lyre across his back. Together they skirted around dense tangles of trees, careful to keep the lyre unblemished. Not until she stumbled over a root did she realize he was holding her fingers. Orpheus reached out to break her fall, but Eurydice recovered on her own. Instead of letting go, she squeezed his hand and led him deeper through the moss. Leaves crunched underfoot until they reached a clearing.

She remembered Persephone's unrestrained laughter echoing through the grove, and saw the shriveled remains of the plant they'd unearthed. She spied white flowers and dragged Orpheus to them. He leaned down and squinted. "What are they?"

"Satyrion. Not the name I would choose."

"It seems fitting." He chuckled. "It has little priapic men all over it!"

"But satyrs are just so…" Eurydice stuck out her tongue and wrinkled her nose.

Orpheus laughed.

"These are what made her let down her guard, finally."

"Is that why you ask them to gather the herbs?"

"If they can't relax and open their hearts, they'll pick the wrong thing and be struck dead. The women you send me are so strict about how they should be. I'm sure when you counsel the men, you must demolish the armor they've forged around themselves."

Orpheus nodded and smiled gently. He inched closer to her, his gaze flicking from her hair to her cheeks, her lips, her eyes.

Eurydice didn't back away. She felt warm, comforted almost, by his presence. His hair was soft and his cheekbones high. His nose was a bit beakish, but it suited him. "What… what were you singing when I interrupted you?"

"Nothing…" He rubbed his hand along the back of his neck. "I mean, I hope it becomes… something. I spend most of my time listening. Hoping for the right words, the right melody."

"What do you listen for?"

"The voice of the divine."

Eurydice smiled. "I find that voice in the hum of the bees."

"Or birds..."

"The ocean waves."

"Yes," he sighed. His whisper made her skin tighten, each hair standing on end.

"May I..." Eurydice blushed. "May I listen to what you were singing?"

"If you'd like," he said. Orpheus spread out his *zeira* and sat down, then carefully rested one side of the silver lyre against his shoulder, and the shell between his knees. He plucked an octave.

Eurydice hadn't noticed until that moment how lithe his fingers were, how they moved gracefully from string to string, one above, one below, curving and caressing to find the notes. His head lifted, his eyes closed. He didn't move the strings, she thought. They moved *him*. Branches above rustled as they had when she'd first heard him.

Then he sang, and his voice put his fingers to shame.

"You nurture fruits, you haunt meadows..." He played on, then stopped abruptly when he lost track of the verse. "You see? It's not anything yet."

Eurydice shook her head. "You can't hear what comes next?"

"Not yet."

"Listen!"

"For what?" he asked, knitting his brows.

"Spring is your joy..." she whispered. "It was in the leaves."

Orpheus stared at her, then blinked. "That's brilliant."

He sang the new verse and stopped again. Eurydice opened her eyes. "Listen… just listen."

He lowered his eyelids.

"No; open your eyes, Orpheus."

Leaves above trembled against branches and he moved his hands in kind. He struck another chord and the hum of insects whispered to them both. "Come with a joyful heart…"

"…pour forth streams of pure rain," she whispered as he sang the same. He stopped, and she swallowed nervously.

Orpheus set down the lyre and stood slowly, silently, inches from her. "How did you know?"

"I didn't," Eurydice said, her voice shuddering. "I listened. To you, to everything. The words just came."

Orpheus peered deep into her eyes, so close she could feel the air between them, electric and warm. He tentatively reached up and brushed a curling spring of her hair from her forehead, tucking it behind another. Her heart beat faster, thrumming in her ears, the verse they had sung focusing, becoming visceral as they beheld each other.

The edge of his linen tunic brushed against her legs, and a pure scent of olive oil and salted honey filled the space between them. Eurydice leaned up, then tilted her head to the side and closed her eyes.

His lips were soft on hers. He hesitated, she realized. How unlike most men, who when confronted with such an opportunity, knowing their seduction had been successful, would have borne her to the ground already. Perhaps he didn't truly desire her.

Her fears dispersed when his hand rose to frame her face, his calloused thumb brushing along her cheek as he deepened their kiss. He pulled away, eyes lidded. His face was inscrutable and she worried.

"Was I wrong to—"

"No," he said, firmly enough to stop her. He leaned down, cupped her face in his hands, and kissed her again, more insistently.

How long had it been? Decades since her last paramour, and that had been fleeting... pleasant friction and little more. The hymnist's kiss grew stronger, pushing thoughts from Eurydice's mind until there was only him. She met him equally, then darted her tongue across his lips.

Orpheus sucked in a breath and drew Eurydice closer, a hand at the center of her back. Eurydice fell into him, frissons traveling through her hands and legs, her back, all the parts of her that he touched. *Give in, he's yours, you're his, give in,* her body sang. She shivered and pulled back.

"I don't know you."

"You do," Orpheus whispered.

She kissed him again and stumbled. He knelt, taking her with him, each easing the other to the ground. Eurydice pressed into him as his hand traveled to her hip. When his fingertips met her bare skin, she pulled back from his kiss. "Wait..."

Orpheus flinched.

"I... you Greeks—"

"I'm Thracian."

"Y-you know what I mean. I... I've been with others before."

"So have I. What of it?"

"You don't th-think I'm lesser for it?"

Orpheus laughed. "Considering the rites I oversee, I would be the greatest hypocrite alive."

"But you don't couple with *all* those women." Eurydice blushed at her implication. They had only kissed. Fervently, passionately, but only a kiss.

"I don't. But I lie with a different woman each time, once every three years."

"I'm not bound by the rules you follow."

"I wouldn't expect you to be. If you worry that I think you're somehow impure, let me dispel that…"

He kissed her again and she melted back into him, her fears dissolving with every pass of his hands. She sighed and arched when his fingers brushed gingerly across her breast. As she melded into him, she felt an unmistakable heat and hardness under his tunic. Eurydice's eyes opened, dilated dark, and met his heavy gaze.

"I'm a priest," he said, "not a eunuch."

"That much is certain…" She touched him and he exhaled sharply, shifting away from her grasp. Eurydice leaned back into his supporting hands around her back and neck, then the cold loam of the grove. He kissed her again, one hand under her head, the other roaming the hills and valleys of her body. His enclosing arms prevented her hands from exploring, so she instead wove her fingers through the brown waves of his hair, feeling the tension in his arms and shoulders when his hands mapped the curve of her hips. She brushed her fingers over his lips when he pulled back to look into her eyes. Orpheus raised her chiton to her waist.

When the breeze met her open thighs, she sighed. He stared into her eyes, then deeper still. The gentle brush and strum of his fingers grew more insistent, and her voice filled the air. She smiled, remembering those same fingers on the strings of the lyre, now playing her just as sweetly. He circled, he released and stroked, circled again. She gripped his arm and kissed him until her mouth fell away and she gasped for air. Her spine rose from the earth and every muscle in her body stiffened, then suffused with warmth, radiating from within her through his touch. Her cry was swallowed by his lips, silenced by his searching tongue, and she held fast to him until finally, sublimely, she came back to the earth. Eurydice stared up at him through half-lidded eyes, his head haloed by the afternoon sunlight. She reached for him, eager to return the pleasure, but he smiled and backed away from her searching fingers.

"That's all we should dare for now," he said breathlessly. "Believe me, I want to."

Eurydice sat up. "Oh gods… your vows!"

"Only if I did more than that. Don't worry."

She stared at him. "What if I *want* more?"

"Then you would marry me."

She leaned back, her lips parted.

"Of course you'd be wary. Anyone with sense would. I am. But what exists between us is boundless."

"Orpheus…"

"If you didn't feel that… union from the moment we touched, saw how hard we fought it from the first, tell me now. But…" Orpheus grew serious. "I *know* you, Eurydice. I am certain of it, and I know that you are as certain as I am, but afraid to trust it. You *feel,* as I do, that our attraction is greater than this moment, this lifetime… and deeper than the earth itself."

"No." Her eyes brimmed and she shook her head and watched his face fall, but went on. "We are too different, Orpheus. Your life is saddled with ceremony and duty, while I live in a wild forest alongside all the plants and creatures within it. If you and I are to be together, it must be as we are—and not forsaking who we are to love each other. And I don't think that's possible."

His eyes lifted. "I would never ask you to be anything but who you are. But we were linked before we ever met. In what we do, in what we've brought about… Imagine all that we could do together beyond that."

Eurydice stared at him, his face earnest, his presence enveloping her. He wasn't another half to make her whole. She was already whole. But with him as her counterpart… in that there was completion. The sky was whole, though it was bound to the earth. Her eyes watered and she nodded ever so slightly.

"You will?"

"Yes. But if we do, let's wed in the final days of summer. Then we can have a whole season to learn about each other. While destiny and lust are... intoxicating, befriending each other would make for a better start, wouldn't you say?"

Eros kept to the shade so the glint of polished gold wouldn't give him away. The arrow was still nocked, and he brushed his thumb along the glistening fletching, pondering. It would be such an easy thing. One shot— *Fates*, he thought, *one scratch*— and they would complete their union in this clearing, possibly many times over before the fires died down. Eros slowly relaxed his drawn arm and set his bow on the ground. He returned the golden arrow to his quiver.

Mother might be angry. Then again, Orpheus and Eurydice had fallen in love almost immediately. Why wouldn't she attribute that to her influence?

Best to leave them to it, he thought. The God of Love smiled. His will wasn't needed here.

8.

"Asklepios must die."

"You have *no right*—"

"But I do." Aidoneus rose from his seat, gripping his raven-crested staff. He squinted in the glare of the symposium. *Artless intimidation,* he thought. Most faltered when petitioning the *Dodekatheon* as they drowned in the blinding light of the heavens.

He ruled over a third of all existence; the *Dodekatheon* did not. Zeus had treated Aidoneus as his honored guest, and Persephone sat beside him in familiar colors and crown as his queen. Demeter had maintained their feigned enmity, loudly protesting her daughter's somber appearance.

Aidoneus kept his hand on Persephone's shoulder, feeling another wave of nausea roll through her. When they had dealt with Sisyphus, they'd done so alone. He couldn't put that burden on her now— not in her condition. Ending Asklepios, a *hemitheoi,* required the consent of Olympus. And Apollo's screams would sway no one once Aidon said his piece. "He has been interfering with the dead."

"By healing mortals?" Apollo stood so fast his divan lurched back. "You hear that, Father Zeus? Hades would kill *my son*, by Coronis whom I *loved*, because he heals mankind and staves off death!"

"He is taking souls that already belong—"

"To you? So the *mortals* belong to Hades, a god who isn't even one of us! He wants more to die to enrich his—"

"I want nothing of the sort!" Aidoneus shouted. The whole of the *Dodekatheon*, even Zeus, tensed. Persephone placed a wary hand on his. He calmed and continued. "Learn your history, young one. The mortals were created from the dust of the earth, the blood of the Golden Men, and from souls that hitherto eternally dwelt in *my* realm."

Apollo sat, chastened.

"As for your other accusation, I thought it a good thing that Asklepios healed. He halted the plague in Athens ten years ago. Throughout his life, his skills were vital, and he removed from us a considerable burden. In particular, he preserved the lives of many young mothers after childbirth."

Artemis perked up and smiled. Mothers prayed to her for deliverance during childbirth; each answered prayer strengthened her worship. Aidoneus nodded to her, his expression subtly softened when he did. At least this pompous whelp's twin sister might be swayed.

Apollo ground his teeth, noting their silent exchange. "For this, you would sentence him to death?"

"No. But he delved into an art that could throw the cosmos out of balance."

"He merely calls them back from the shore of the Styx—"

"Which is not permitted."

"Aidoneus," Zeus interjected, "enlighten us. Where is the line drawn?"

He carefully considered his words. "After the last breath— when sense of self and forethought cease, and an hour passes like a thousand years. *That* is death. Once they cross that threshold, they cannot return."

Apollo lifted his chin. "When the sense of self is lost—who knows that but the soul? Who can say that those Asklepios rescued *truly* died?"

"I considered bringing Thanatos to explain, but the *Dodekatheon* does not tolerate his presence," he said. The room buzzed with his Minister's name. The truth would rob Apollo of any arrows he might have left in his accusatory quiver. "Therefore, I call on one of your own, Ares Enyalios Olympios, to speak of what *he* witnessed."

The room turned to the God of War, slouched on his divan, cup upended. At the sound of his full name, he sputtered around the last drops of wine. Ares cleared his throat and straightened his back, but before he could speak, Apollo unleashed. "If you wish to treat this gathering like your own dead court, then let's! Your witness has been deep in his cups of late because *someone* is carrying a child not sired by him. Look at the state he's in! Ares wouldn't know an arrow from his own—"

"Oh, I would," Ares slurred. "I do." He serpented a finger in Apollo's direction. "An' you... You think this... *water* is enough to level me? Maybe *you*, nymph-chaser..."

"Tell them what you saw, Ares." Aidoneus tried to keep calm.

"I know what I'm saying. I know what I saw. An' it wasn' just me," he gestured broadly at Hermes. "He was there, for a part of it."

Aidoneus glared at Hermes, who winced and avoided eye contact. The Psychopompos had shrugged off his questions about the missing dead. He would have been a more reliable witness but chose to shield Apollo.

"For what *I* saw... There was a soldier... Hippolytos." He nodded to himself. "An' *his* father Atreus was a general. A *rich* general. And Hippolytos? He was dead," Ares chuckled. "The hon-honorable death of a soldier. My worshiper. *Mine*. They put an arrow right through his throat…here, at the vein. A quick death. An' his father was crying… and cursing *me*," he leveled a finger at the dais where Zeus sat. "Oh, and… *you*, too. An' he begs As… Asklepios to bring back his son. The healer said he could *not*, but then a *mina* of gold came out, and he rooted out some tablet with…" He pointed at Aphrodite. "…*her* speech on it or somesuch—"

"Other healers lived long before Asklepios. I *myself* first taught men—"

"Oh, *cousin*…" Ares's guttural laugh withered Apollo's protests. "You never taught *this*. Not… returning like *that*." Ares summoned Ganymede to pour him another cup.

Zeus shifted in his seat. "Give us the rest."

"He came back shambling." Ares took a long draught and exhaled. "Out for blood."

"You lie!" Apollo yelled over the din of whispering voices. "How would you even know?"

"He didn't come back right, is all I know. And his father knew it. Coward, though… Didn't stop Hippolytos until he'd tore… torn open a *few* throats. But after that Atreus took off his own son's head." Ares cut the air savagely with his flat hand. "Finished him good; sent him back *down*."

Persephone wavered, nausea seizing her, and Aidon stroked her shoulder. He spoke to the assembled gods. "We received him, and he is in Asphodel. In good conscience, I cannot punish anyone stolen against their will, no matter their crimes as the restless dead. But Asklepios learned from his mistakes with Hippolytos, and not in the wiser way. He perfected his new art. Those awaiting the Boatman started disappearing from the shores of the Styx. And then shades were plucked from Asphodel itself."

All in the room collectively gasped and muttered among themselves. Apollo paled. The gods started condemning him one by one: first Poseidon, then Athena raising her voice over the King of the Sea. Aphrodite heaved herself out of her seat to hiss her disapproval, her round belly protruding from under her girdle. Hermes and Hephaestus spoke to defend him from the others, professing Apollo's ignorance of his son's wrongdoing.

"Enough; all of you!" Zeus boomed. Quickly, the assembled gods drew quiet. "Is there no remedy but his death, Aidoneus?"

"If he lives, he will persist in this abomination and teach it to others. That *cannot* be allowed. He has not called forth the damned out of Tartarus, *yet*, but suppose he did… and consider who *else* might be unleashed."

Hestia covered her mouth with both hands, shaking.

"Zeus, I've heard enough!" Poseidon shouted, trident shimmering blue in his hand. The ground trembled. "And if you don't end his life, I will!"

"W-We could send Asklepios a vision," Apollo said. "Or just enough misfortune to—"

"That would give no assurance," Aidon said calmly. "Were his misdeeds less dire, I would not ask for his life. But this threatens us all. The way Sisyphus threatened us all, and worse still if you ignore this as you did *him*."

"He is *not* Sisyphus! He doesn't think himself above the gods."

"Undoing the will of the Fates means precisely that," Athena countered.

"It doesn't mean my son should die! Hades doesn't want justice, he wants retribution against *me*."

"Don't be absurd!" Demeter shouted at him over the din. "Whatever for?"

"Because I nearly compromised your daughter, his queen, when she first visited Olympus. He's been waiting for an opportunity ever since."

Persephone hid her laugh with an exaggerated cough.

"We all know how that *really* went," Aphrodite smiled. "Or shall I regale everyone *with* your pathetic failings again?"

Apollo turned red with anger and scattered snickers fluttered through the hall.

Aidoneus smirked. "That tale is irrelevant. My only concern is that the threads that Atropos cut *remain* cut."

"But he—"

"Dies. Tomorrow."

"You will cast him into Tartarus!"

"He had a choice in life. If my judges condemn him to the Pit, he sends himself there." Aidoneus sat, his staff pounding the floor as he settled.

"As we have a quorum, we shall put it to vote," Zeus said. "Those who believe Asklepios must die?"

Every god, save Apollo, raised their hand.

"The ayes have it."

"A thunderbolt oughta do," Ares said between sips of wine. "Send a message to anyone else who—"

"I did not ask for your advice. Is there any other business?"

Ares scowled at his father, then staggered to stand. "I have business... with these two."

Persephone looked up, his finger leveled at her. "What would that be, Ares?"

"You have this... this *Elysion* now. And with all *you...* seem to have *now*, you'll let in *mine*. All that died *honorably* in battle."

Aidoneus placed his hand on Persephone's. Here on Olympus, she was considered merely his consort. Only the Lord of the Underworld could speak for them in this hall. "Those who complete the Lower and Greater Rites in Eleusis may gain entrance to Elysion. If your worshippers—"

"Ha!" Ares barked his laugh straight at Apollo. "*You* think killing *yours* is a play for power... *nothing* compared to this!"

Aidoneus ignored him. "My kingdom isn't moved by the whims of men. Even children know that. Nonetheless, souls must be prepared before they enter Paradise, to shrug off falsehood and know that death is not the end."

"And those who perish at sea?" Poseidon chimed in. "The bravest sailors are worthy of the richest rewards."

"Or children?" Artemis said. "Surely children are innocent and deserving."

"It's not a matter of innocence."

"Then tell us, Aidoneus, how *do* you determine who goes there?" Zeus leaned forward on his throne.

He narrowed his eyes. Elysion belonged to Persephone and him. None of the gods, least of all Zeus, should dare interfere in his kingdom. They'd certainly never shown interest before. Persephone squeezed his hand. His jaw unclenched and he relaxed. "It's a matter of the worthiness of the soul."

"So you wan' me to… shut my mouth and watch *my* honors go to you—"

"All souls come to me, Ares. What else would you expect? Do you covet the burden of ruling over the dead and all that comes with it? Are you eager to ensure Kronos and his ilk remain imprisoned where they ought?"

Ares swallowed, then composed himself. "So… we're jus' supposed to… what do I tell them?"

"Tell them what you will. But my judgments are my own. Just as they always have been since the casting of lots," he said, looking pointedly at Poseidon and then Zeus.

"You owe me, you know," Ares muttered into his cup.

"For *what?*" How could he possibly owe Ares *anything* after that wine-soaked testimony?

"First for Aphrodite… finding that pretty girl for Apollo's other *hemitheos-s* spawn—"

"That is not our business or concern. Whatever transpired with Orpheus is between my consort and Aphrodite. And you have no claim over her favors since she is Hephaestus's bride. Consider her present condition in case you'd forgotten."

That was uncalled for, Aidon. Persephone said. He stroked the back of her hand in apology. Despite his misgivings about the Goddess of Love, she had always been kind to Persephone.

"Fine. Did *not* want to *say* it, but… fine. I am owed by *you*, given what you're due to receive, oh Receiver of Many," Ares said with an exaggerated bow. "Right after *you* nearly ended us all over a girl, Zeus swore that if your *consort* managed to get—"

"Silence!" Zeus stood and slammed his eagle crested staff onto the marble dais. The roll of thunder was deafening.

Whispers filled the symposium as Ares sullenly returned to his place. Apollo stayed quiet, gripping the edge of his divan, his eyes fixed on Hera, who sat still as stone, unreadable under her veil.

✲   ✲   ✲

From across the room, Aidoneus heard Persephone laughing with Aphrodite. The names of Eurydice and Orpheus floated through their conversion; the match was harmless, Persephone assured him, since the two were so naturally well suited. Aphrodite proudly claimed credit, saying her son's arrow wasn't even needed. *Fortunate them*, Aidon thought, recalling *his* brush with it.

After Zeus closed the assembly, the gods dispersed to the gardens and halls with their retinues. Apollo had slunk away quickly, and Hera and Zeus were nowhere to be seen. Aidon needed a private word with the King of the Gods, to set straight Ares's drunken assertions, and to reassure him that Zagreus's destiny was not for the heavens but instead below, as the God of Elysion.

"I thought you'd have ended Apollo's whelp yourself instead of coming here. You're always avoiding us by whining about leaving the Underworld unguarded. Some excuse about Titans using your absence as an opportunity." Aidoneus turned to see Poseidon grinning at him. "Good to know everything you say is rubbish."

He clasped Aidon's right arm and drew him in for an embrace before he could react.

"It is good to see you, brother!"

"And you, Poseidon." He glanced over his brother's shoulder to a woman nursing a baby, her hair wound up under a spiked crown of tibia shells. "Amphitrite?"

"Aidon! It's been too long!" Amphitrite sauntered up to him and grasped his hand briefly, her other arm cradling the baby.

"It has," he said. His shoulders sank. "All these aeons, I should have visited you two under the waves."

"Ha!" Poseidon clapped him on the back. "That would have put you too close to Demeter."

"Perhaps."

"Although I did sense you and your lovely wife entering our kingdom near Samothrace," Amphitrite said with a smirk. "Briefly, of course. The timing is… interesting…"

"*Potini-ja qpa-jo*, don't tease him…"

Aidon swallowed.

"What teasing? Everyone knows he comes above to visit her. How else would she be only three months along?"

"Amphitrite…" Poseidon said low, gently warning her.

"At least we know you didn't do the deed at Eleusis, thank Gaia. So — these secret places you two meet… Samothrace? Or was that just the one…?" Amphitrite winced as the baby unlatched from her breast.

Aidon politely averted his eyes, grateful for this distraction. He wondered for the thousandth time why his marriage held the gods above in thrall. They'd been trading tales about it since the day he'd taken her below.

The baby stared up at Aidon with dark eyes.

"This is Eurypylus. You can hold him."

"I-I shouldn't," he said.

"You'd better get used to it!" Amphitrite nodded her head in Persephone's direction. "Here. It will give me a moment to fetch the ambrosia." With practiced maternal grace, she thrust the child into Aidon's hands. "Hand under his head. Fair warning, he squirms."

Aidon cradled the baby like he was made of glass. His face scrunched up and a yawn revealed tiny new teeth jutting up from his gums. Without warning, Eurypylus cooed and kicked off his chest, then twisted. Aidon's eyes widened and he shift- ed the baby up onto his shoulder, terrified of dropping it. Eurypylus promptly yanked at his hair, tilting his crown of golden poplar to the side.

"She warned you," Poseidon laughed. "So are you raising yours above or below? Surely he cannot go back and forth all his life."

"We have yet to decide," Aidoneus said, carefully handing Eurypylus back to Amphitrite and righting his crown. Out of the corner of his eye, he caught Persephone gazing at him, grinning broadly, and could feel soft warmth radiating from her. "He will be with her for the first year, certainly, but much will depend on who Zagreus becomes."

"Looks like your son is already putting gray in your hair. Just wait until you're the patriarch of an entire family," he said, pointedly stroking his beard, shot through with silver strands.

"Well… we shall have to see about more. This one—"

"If it worked once, she'll welcome another babe soon enough. And just think… not too long from now, grandchil- dren, Aidon! Of course, by that time you'll be so gray in the hair and beard that you'll look like…" Poseidon trailed off and his face sank. Amphitrite shot him a cold glare.

Kronos, Aidon thought. It was meant in jest, but Poseidon was as still as the grave, worried he'd offended his elder brother. Aidon gave a low chuckle and the King of the Seas relaxed. "That is a long time off."

"Not so long these days. Since the start of the seasons, all our little ones are growing up so much faster thanks to—" Poseidon looked over Aidoneus's shoulder. "Shit and Charybdis…"

"Poseidon! Not in front of the baby." Amphitrite followed his glance and her eyes narrowed. Persephone ambled toward them, the Goddess of Love at her side. "I hope your wife isn't offended if I make myself scarce. I cannot tolerate her companion."

"Persephone makes her own choices in who she befriends," Aidoneus said quietly. "Would that I could dissuade her."

"Your wife has a talent for attracting the most dangerous women in the cosmos. Athena, Aphrodite… Hera. Most especially her." Amphitrite pulled Eurypylus to her shoulder and leaned in close to his ear. "Careful she does not drink in the queen's bitterness."

✳ ✳ ✳

"The audacity!" Hera followed Zeus toward his apartments. "Sitting in our court, begging you to strike down a mortal. While *they* dictate who goes to Elysion! I ought to poison the waters of Eleusis just as I punished Aegina for—"

He grasped her arms and slammed her against a column. "You'll do nothing of the sort!"

"*No one* will sacrifice to us now! Mortals will just walk through Eleusis to Paradise without favor or thought given to us. Our priests are as gelded as you are!"

"You think I haven't tried a thousand ways to undermine them?!" He released her. "What Demeter forced on us, and what *those two* wrought… what it means for our future…" Zeus glared at Hera. "But I cannot. The Fates—"

"Oh, the Fates dealt you a sorry lot, indeed. Poor, sad *Aegiduchos*, who rules us all."

"Do you think this is easy? I've spent every day since the war keeping you fools from destroying each other, or the entire race of men! *Kakodaimonos*, Hera, every time a new moon approaches, I'm practically guaranteed... poison the wells of Eleusis..." He chuckled and pivoted to walk toward his bedroom. "Not a month after you and Hestia invited them to *live* up here! I should've checked its phase this afternoon."

She ran at him, fists raining down on his back. "You did this! Tempting the Fates; making that oath!"

Zeus spun around and grabbed her wrists. "Hera..."

"You don't have the stones to fix it!" She struggled in his grasp. "It's not enough to have every finger pointed at my back, but to be publicly shamed by our own son!"

"The oath is toothless."

"Tell that to Ares!" She breathed hard, then quieted, staring up at him. "You're hurting me."

"Good." He tightened his grip, his gaze flicking to her collarbone, exposed when a fibula came loose during their struggle. His voice rumbled in the pit of her stomach. "I need say nothing. If he wanted the oath fulfilled, he would have pressed it *today* in open court. I ought to have Ares scourged for giving Hades the opportunity," he snarled. "But he didn't take it because the Underworld softened him. You talk about gelding, look at what all those *women* below did to him. He was the most bloodthirsty warrior among us, and they turned him into a eunuch. Just as you plot with *her* to castrate me."

She paled. "Persephone—"

"I see all, wife. I know you've written to her... visited her. Asked her to take you to Elysion. What seeds are you sowing?"

"You wanted a stronger alliance with them." She lowered his lids. "I was only doing as you bid."

"Bullshit." He crowded her, pulling her arms to her sides, his chest rising against hers. She quivered against him and he pressed flush against her at the contact.

"The truth?" A tear rolled down her cheek unbidden. She cursed herself. "Is it so bad to want what she has? You saw them together. He only wants *her*. Don't you think I wanted that with you?"

Zeus sighed and released her hands. "Fidelity was never in my nature. You knew that."

"You never gave me the choice to reject it!"

"You could have *moved on* after I seduced you, Hera. As Themis did. Binding us in matrimony was *your* idea."

"To live disgraced and sullied forever, or marry *you*. That was my choice!"

"More pity for you, then."

She wiped the tears from her face. "What do you want me to do, Zeus?"

"Stop obsessing over this… I'm tired," he said, softly squeezing her arms. "I want peace with you."

"You'll have peace once you've undone—"

"There's nothing to undo. Hades could have struck Asklepios dead himself, but he petitioned Olympus because he's my vassal and respects order." He framed her face with one hand. "They aren't a threat to you, *gynaika mou*."

"Please, husband." Her fingers danced across his collar and over the shoulder of his tunic, tracing a pin. "Take back the oath. Censure them for the Eleusinian Mysteries. A public statement. That's all I ask."

"No." He held her hand in place. His pulse raced.

"Please," Hera whispered. One shoulder hung by a single remaining fibula. She let it slip further. "Zeus…"

"What are you playing at?" He loomed over her, his body eclipsing hers.

"I'm not," she whispered, her breasts flattened again at his chest. "I'm not toying with you."

"Aren't you now…" Zeus trapped her against the wall, but her thigh brushed insistently between his.

"No." She breathed onto his neck, her hands on his chest, her finger following the edge of his himation, then hooking under the collar of his tunic. "But… anything you wish of me…"

"Anything?"

He unbound her *zone* so fast the beaded tassels lashed her back. Hera's eyes went wide as he pulled her wrists together and looped her belt around them, knotting it in the center. He slapped the unlit torch out of the sconce above and she jumped as it clattered on marble. Hoisting her arms overhead, he slung the rope over the metal post. Her toes barely touched the floor. Hera had hung like this for a year in the cold sky, with only coiling aurorae to keep her company, until Zeus was finally satisfied enough to release her.

His breath was hot on her cheek. "With nothing in return."

"Nothing, I swear," she said, accepting his kiss. His hands wound their way up the open sides of her peplos, fingers tracing her ribs and the sides of her breasts. She twisted under the sconce, seeking the touch he withheld.

"We'll see, *gynaika mou.*"

Her dress ripped in his hands along the embroidered edge and she gasped, crying out when a fibula raked her arm. Zeus kissed the scratch as it healed, and the fabric slithered to the floor. Cold stone shocked her back, and her skin prickled. He stepped away, studying her.

"Wh-what are you doing?"

"Hush," he stared at her, his jaw set. Hera glanced about, fearful he would leave her this way, that someone would enter his atrium and see her dangling, helpless and exposed. He snorted. "Don't worry about interruptions, my love. They're all crowding around *them* right now. Seeking *their* favor and company."

How easily he gave himself away. His eldest brother's growing influence, first with the mortals and now in their own court, boiled under his skin. He was angry. Hera could work with that. He wanted her. She could work with that too. Zeus pushed off his himation and kicked it behind him, advancing on her.

He drew out his belt, the tip snapping, and made ready to toss it aside. Hera mewled and stared at it. He froze, eyes locked to hers. His voice rumbled. "So. This again, then…"

Hera hung still, but her very heartbeat betrayed her. She swallowed heavily and her thighs squeezed, a steady thrum starting within, grew louder, more insistent. He prowled, regarding her from every side, then threw his tunic into the center of the hall and wrapped the leather thrice around his hand until less than a *pechys* length remained. She squeezed her eyes shut, trying to will away her fervor and failing utterly.

"Hera," he said softly and pulled closer to her, fingers warm, caressing her skin. She opened her eyes. His face was almost vulnerable, begging for the trust he didn't deserve. "I won't… I would never unless you tell me."

"You honestly expect me to beg for…" She sighed when his fingertips brushed her vulva, gentle at first, then firmly when they found a wet rill of desire. She moaned.

"You already are." His breath fanned her neck, her whispered name entreating as her mind rioted against his soft voice. The leather brushed against her neck and over her collarbone, bringing his words into sharp relief. "We could play this game more often… if you could just tell me what you want."

That would require her to trust him; she did not. Her body cried out for him all the same. Tears spilled from her eyes. He brushed one away with his thumb.

"This is ours alone. I would never share this with anyone but you. I could give you all you need if you would just let me…"

She arched against him and he backed away until the air hummed between them. The looped belt caressed her hip, her waist. "I can't… I shouldn't want…"

"The first time, when you hung above the clouds… I intended to punish you. I couldn't have anticipated what came of it." After he'd taken her down from the sky, Zeus had been faithful for over a century, with scarcely a wandering eye.

The thrice wound strap grazed the undersides of her breasts. Her eyes locked to his. "Neither of us did."

"You gave me leave over you, but all I want is your openness, my love." Zeus stroked her cheek and dragged the loop of his belt slowly against her crease. "So tell me… do you yearn for that again?"

His hand shook. He wanted her. She needed… She fought to suppress it, fought against the glorious friction against her sex as he goaded her on, but desire rose faster than pretense, dry words crackling from her throat. "Yes."

Silence hung between them for a long moment, then Zeus spun her around, her wrists and toes a tortured axis. Her breath clouded the polished wall, his reflection loomed behind her… an eternity passed. The first blow snapped against her thigh. She yelped. His voice ground out. "For what shall I punish you this time? For months of your insolence?"

The strap stung her again in the same spot and blue light crackled behind her eyes. "Yes!"

"For your foul temper?" His body trapped her against the wall and she jumped. Cold marble nipped her breasts and stomach, and her bottom squirmed against the stone-hard erection beneath his loincloth. He grazed his palm and then the warm leather over angry welts, abrading them, refusing to let them cool even as her skin swiftly healed. The fingers of his other hand stroked along her crease, snaking toward the apex of her mound. She recoiled from his touch at first, but when she finally leaned into it, he backed away. "Do you need more?"

She nodded but he stayed still and silent, letting her shiver in the absence of heat.

"Tell me."

"Please!" Her agony was a perfect counterpoint to the throb within, empty and unfulfilled. The next blow struck her other thigh and she shrieked. Another, then another, one side, the next. Heat rose from her skin and at last Hera felt *him*, just as she had in those few centuries after her *hieros gamos* with Zeus, when every touch echoed between them, when she could sense his every thought, knew where he was… and he could hear her. Feel her, now.

He landed a last strike against both cheeks at once, the leather landing so hard she felt the blow reverberate to her tensed jaw. Then the lashes ceased. Her knees shook and her thighs squeezed around slick, traitorous heat. As if distantly, she heard the belt drop quietly to the floor beside him. She could feel his every step across the marble.

Hera pulled against the *zone* trapping her wrists, her back arched as she struggled to stay on the tips of her toes. Zeus panted against her shoulder and traced thick fingers over his fiery handiwork, making her cry out. His touch was gentle, and she calmed as he brushed his palm over her hip bone, caressing supple skin, then across her thatch of hair, until his hand gripped her mound, a solitary finger revolving around her clitoris. She held her breath, waiting for the sudden spark he'd send through her.

"That's not what you need this time, is it?" He whispered hard, gleaning her thoughts, savoring the eternal bond they'd momentarily rekindled.

"No," she exhaled. He pulled away completely and Hera sobbed, breathing hard and following his reflection in stone, her heart racing. Zeus discarded his loincloth and spun her quickly to face him. She heard the restraint tear above her, felt frigid marble rioting against the lashes on her flanks. Hera kicked out to regain her balance and he immediately caught her ankle in one hand.

Zeus hauled up her other leg, hooked her knees in the crooks of his elbows, and looked her in the eye. He thrust to the hilt, suddenly, completely, her pubic bone grinding against his groin. She cried out in pain and relief, pleasure searing through her, rolling in waves over the unforgiving width of him. She arched her back and screamed her completion. His hand clamped over her mouth.

"Quiet," he ground out.

She nodded desperately, still spasming, choking back her mewling voice under his hand. Hera leaned into him to relieve her wrists, forcing herself into the support of his arms and further down onto his cock, focusing, deepening her climax. The last braid of her *zone* finally wore through and snapped, and her arms fell to her sides, useless and limp. He pushed deep into her, his hands gripping her lashed thighs, her back braced to the wall, and growled against her throat. Zeus withdrew, then nipped at her collarbone and planted a trail of rose blotches across her neck when he reclaimed her.

She bore down on him and he gasped, leaning into her, cursing against her skin. When Hera squeezed again, his voice broke and he bit at her shoulder. She yelped.

"Be silent, *gynaika mou*," he rasped. Zeus tongued her broken skin until it healed, then kissed the tears that leaked from her eyes.

He cradled her and stepped away from the wall, still intimately joined, and dropped to his knees. Hera spilled from his arms, splayed before him on her back. Zeus rolled her over and pulled her hips back, mounting her against the cold floor. His dark reflection rose and fell behind her, eyes burning, teeth set on edge. Cold seeped into her cheek and breasts as he drove her into the unforgiving stone.

At last, she felt him seize, shuddering above her. He collapsed onto her, crushing her, his heart pounding against her back. Slowly, he slid to the side, petting her hair. She leaned into his gentle caress and shut her eyes, drifting. Hera was insensate, drawn into him, the air humming between them. He stopped suddenly and exhaled hard, recoiling.

Still breathing heavily, Zeus stood and wiped away his seed with half of her shredded *zone*. Hera tried to sit up but collapsed back to the floor with a sigh. She had been undone. But so had he, satisfied in a way she knew he wouldn't be for a long time.

"Husband…"

"No." Zeus casually wound his loincloth back and tied it, then stretched his arms and neck.

She gawked at him, gathering her torn peplos to her, every limb lividly marked. "What do you mean 'no'?"

He pulled his tunic on and shrugged into it, smoothing the folds before belting the waist. "I mean no, Hera, I'm not going to reinforce our son's position, especially with the state he's in right now. No, I'm not going to rebuke Hades in any way, either regarding the oath I made, or his grip on the mortals. It will sort itself out."

Tears sprung into her eyes, and words turned to ash, choking her. "But we… What I…"

He smirked pointedly. "And also, no, I will not be staying longer than it takes me to dress. You got what you wanted from me."

Her body ached from her toes to her throat. And in the haze of their damnable connection, she knew. Red descended over her vision. "Whose bed are you off to now?"

"I'm doing as *you* bid," he mocked. Zeus wound his himation inelegantly around his waist and threw it over his left shoulder. "After your last tantrum over Persephone, you told me to find solace elsewhere."

"Another whore, Zeus. Another?!"

"*You* abandoned *me* to run off to your island, and you're in no position to say anything about her. Better we're honest with each other, yes?"

"What is her name?"

"You suppose me an idiot?" Zeus scoffed and straightened the folds of his robes. "I'm not giving you her name; especially after what you did to Alcmene's children."

Hera's mouth opened and shut dryly.

"You honestly think word of that escaped me..." He planted his foot next to her shoulder, staring down at her. "Did you hear? You might like this— you loosed two serpents a year ago to murder her twins in their crib."

"Zeus, I never—"

"Lying doesn't suit you. But through it, we learned that one of the twins belongs to her husband, while the other is mine. *My* son strangled both of your cursed snakes. One in each hand. But it gave Alcmene such a fright that she renamed the child Herakles... to honor and appease *you*."

Hera stared at him dumbfounded.

"Isn't that funny? One of my windblown seeds bearing *your* name. The Glory of Hera. I'm eager to see how he turns out..."

"To Tartarus with Alcmene's bastard. But mark me. When your seed takes hold in your new conquest, I'll—"

Zeus laughed. "I enjoy her too much to beget on her." He leaned in close to Hera's face. "She doesn't play the harlot when she wants something from me."

"How... after you... after we..."

"It's refreshing. She wants *nothing* from me but my company. I intend to keep her warm this winter, so consider this our last meeting for a time. At least until our yearly night together at Gamelia."

The floor stretched cold beneath her. Its marble polish reflected her twisting features and the folds of his himation as he stood over her triumphant, inverted and shadowed, his image speckled with her tears.

"Go tend to yourself, Hera. Fates knows what Eileithyia would think if she saw you like this. Or Pasithea, heaven forbid. Don't subject our daughters to your depravity."

The room flashed with brilliant white and blue, blinding her as he disappeared into the ether, a crack of thunder echoing through the villa. Hera was alone, a whine in her ears and the sound of her whimper her only company.

She pulled at the tattered embroidered edge of her gown and ripped it loose with a shout. Her shoulder pained her below the healed skin. She belted the strap of fabric around her to close her peplos. She would go to Nauplia, she thought, rejuvenate in the springs at Kanathos and rid her body of his touch, put this out of her mind. Put *him* out of her mind. Each step across the garden stung her skin and shifted her insides, reminding her of him, of his mastery of her.

She knelt next to her tree and stared out at Thessaly. All the pent-up rage, the fresh anger, the pain after he had mercilessly fucked her… She clutched her dress tighter and let her voice ring out in the open air, screaming obscenities into the sunset, hoping that Zeus could hear her, wherever he was, that his penis would shrivel, or his lover would be raped by jackals.

Hera cried until her chest ached and her eyes swelled shut. She dropped her head into her hands. "Why…" she heaved. "I should have listened to Tethys… I should have wed Poseidon, or said the vows… before… before…"

Hera heard footsteps. *Zeus?* She thought she felt an iota of remorse coursing through him as he left. Had he come to beg forgiveness? When she looked up, she clutched at the front of her dress, holding the worst rip shut. Hera snarled. "How *dare* you come into my presence!"

Apollo only smirked. "A bad time, dear queen?"

"There is *never* a good time for you," she hissed. "Away from here. If you come seeking Zeus—"

"What happened to you?" His brow wrinkled, and the sneering facade that perpetually marred his face momentarily dropped. But Hera knew him too well. Even that was an act. He was just like his mother.

"It doesn't concern you. Go... or I'll summon Iris to escort you out."

"If Iris were here, you wouldn't be in this state," he said. Apollo's eyes traveled up and down her ruined dress. He took a step closer. "Was it Zeus?"

Hera blinked back tears. "Find him yourself. Go plead the life of your idiot spawn to—"

"I would never go to him for this. I came to find you."

"I cast my vote for Asklepios's death, same as all present. Excepting you."

"Yes. But I know why you were sitting quietly."

"Oh... Tell me then. You always *love* to prophesy."

"You were staring *her* down."

Hera stopped cold. "I don't know what you speak of."

"You do," Apollo said. His smirk returned. "Asklepios isn't the only one of my sons who has upset the natural order of late. And while his actions *do* threaten us, this other present *problem* with your newfound friend is a threat to *you.*"

"What do you mean?"

"All I want is a balancing of the scales. A life for a life..."

9.

"SACRILEGE."

"Mortal women do it all the time."

"And they should go to Tartarus for it!"

"You'd be doing the Fates a favor." Apollo set his jaw. "Hades and Persephone bent the cosmos *to their will.*"

"Quite the accusation." Hera snorted.

"I wouldn't have made it before today. Your son, in his excess, revealed that Persephone gave Aphrodite leave to find Orpheus a mate."

"Aphrodite is laden with child and exceptionally bored. Naturally, she reeled Persephone into one of her intrigues. Persephone has been entranced by that whore ever since they embarrassed you in front of the entire court."

He smirked. "I thought, why would Hades and Persephone approve such a thing? They never meddle with individual mortals. Or so I thought…" Apollo mapped the confusion on her face. "Last winter, Hermes begged after my silver lyre, a gift for Orpheus. I thought nothing of it until I couldn't get it back. Hermes was protecting the god who stole it as a favor. I assumed it was Zeus, and let it go. But I was wrong."

Hera rose haltingly.

"Every three years, during the third moon of spring, Samo-thrace holds a fertility rite to birth an unborn god. Orpheus oversaw the rite, three months ago. My lyre was given to him as a bribe— by Hades himself. They were *there* on Samothrace. Participating in the guise of mortals, profaning the land with their bodies and sapping it of its fertility, betraying our kind… all to conceive a child that will fulfill Zeus's reckless oath."

"You're connecting stars on opposite sides of the sky to weave your story."

"I have proof, Hera. After my child was condemned to die, I went immediately to Orpheus's temple and gleaned the name of their ineffable god. The name is familiar— one you doubt-less loathe with your very essence."

Every limb felt heavier. "Zagreus."

"The beginning and the end. Appropriate, since it's Per-sephone's path back into the line of succession."

She braced herself against her apple tree.

"Hades's bright star rises high in the firmament of dawn these days, does it not? Poseidon embraces him, Hermes pro-tects him, your son, even, bends to his will. He created Elysion with that upstart slut of his and stripped us of honors. Now they spawn this child to deny you your divine role."

"Get out of my sight."

"Why?" Apollo circled her. "So you can fade away in the dusk of the evening? Queen of Heaven in name, but… what *are* you now that *her* child will inherit the Heavens?"

Hera collapsed, sitting against the roots, still tender. She wept anew. She didn't care that he saw her break. It didn't matter anymore. She curled up, shuddering, sobs bursting from her chest, tears staining her ruined dress. "Leave me alone. Just leave me be, Apollo… *please*."

He crouched next to her, saying nothing, then reached for her shoulder. She flinched, but he caressed it anyway and spoke low. "This can be averted. No one will know it was you."

Hera raised her head, looking at him warily.

"I will need your promise first. A life for a life."

Hera stared at him in the waning light. "There are only six of us who can do that."

"Which is why I came to you."

"If I render Asklepios deathless, they will know!"

"No one will look twice at you. Long-suffering Hera, who saves her wrath for her husband's lovers. Zeus, Poseidon, and Hades will be too busy pointing fingers at each other."

"And what will you do with Asklepios once he is deathless? Our fears are not idle— if he brings back the damned, your pettiness could unchain Kronos."

"My son will become the God of Medicine. He won't steal from the Underworld again. I swear it on the Styx."

"We conspired together once, Apollo. Against my better judgment, I included you. For it, you slaved with Poseidon to raise the walls of Ilion. I was chained in the sky. But for all we did, we never stooped to murder."

His affected voice faltered. "We aren't... no, i-it's not—"

"Don't trivialize this." Hera's eyes were cold and clear. "That is *precisely* what you're proposing. What will our punishment be this time? Tartarus?"

Apollo swallowed and continued. "Persephone goes below in six weeks. New life shouldn't survive the journey to a realm of death. You'd be fulfilling the will of the Fates."

"Their will... All the insight you've ever had comes from little girls sucking in fumes at Delphi." Hera grew cold.

Apollo laughed harshly. "Oh no, you see, my *father* gave me that gift." Apollo's lip curled. "Zagreus will *never* be born of Persephone. The Sparing One's words are distant and mysterious, but that much has always been clear."

"I'm greatly relieved, Apollo. Now I know nothing needs to be done by my hand. Be gone."

"You'd wager your position on that? Unless we act as their instrument, your future is… tenuous."

"You and I will be condemned for eternity."

"Olympus will mourn with them. But we all knew this was ill-fated from the start. And that Hades and Persephone have done something… unnatural."

Hera considered quietly. In the symposium, Aidoneus had hovered over his wife like she was made of glass. They were acting cautiously, with fear and uncertainty. It wouldn't be the first time their efforts to conceive had failed— this would be a great loss, but not unforeseen. "On one condition."

"Name it."

"Orpheus dies."

"No."

"Choose, Apollo!"

"Not between my sons!"

Hera stood over him. "Asklepios or Orpheus! Orpheus dies, or this will happen again three years hence. What will stop them from returning to Samothrace?"

"Kill the girl, then. Eurydice."

"Where's the sense in that? *He* oversees the rites!"

Apollo rose from his crouch. "But she is the key to their success. A child of the *Kabieroi*. They're to marry soon, but I care not; in time neither will Orpheus. Without her herbs, this never happens again. Let him live."

"You will say nothing."

"And you likewise."

They stood in the waning light, silent. Her heart thudded in her ears, her stomach churned, her fingers were numb.

He seemed unaffected. "Now for the means to seal our pact…"

Hera clutched her dress closer to her body.

"Nothing as scurrilous as that," Apollo chortled. "What do you take me for? But if one of us is discovered, what is to prevent the betrayal of the other?"

"What do you propose?"

"A kiss."

Hera's gorge rose. "As if I would debase myself with you."

"I know how jealously Zeus guards you. His wrath over daring even a kiss would be unfathomable. Think of what he did to Ixion. This would ruin both of us should one betray the other. So, my Queen, what are you willing to do to possess my knowledge?"

Hera took a step forward. Apollo's back straightened and she read all the coiled anger in the set of his jaw, the vengeance he had always wanted to exact on her for chasing his mother Leto from island to island to her destruction.

She gave no warning. Her body crashed against his, her hand a fist in his blond hair, and she pulled his mouth to hers. Eyes closed, her lips crushed against his, savoring his fear and surprise and warmth. Her teeth pierced his lip and he hissed when she pulled away just as violently. Apollo tongued blood and stared at her, reeling, breathing hard.

His practiced, self-assured mask returned and he smirked. "Go to Hestia. There is an herb from one of my cities in her collection…"

✲   ✲   ✲

The iron rasp glinted in the firelight. Hestia ground the rough bark off the nut, a recent treasure from distant islands where the sun shone brighter and familiar stars sat low in the sky at dawn. The people there fascinated her, their intimate communities on the outskirts of the great empires of the Indus. She dabbed the orange powder with her finger and tasted it. "Merciful Fates!" she sputtered.

When a long drink of honeyed water didn't soothe her tongue, she quenched the lingering burn with nectar. *There must be more to it*, she thought. The taste she sought was sweet but strong, and she *swore* it came from this seed. Hestia carefully sawed it in half. She sat back on her haunches and smiled. Beneath the stinging hot exterior lay her prize. She scraped some off and dusted it over the fire, little white sparks flaring and dancing as they burned.

A fist rapped at her door.

"Hestia?"

What was Hera doing here at this hour? She brushed herself off and stood. "A moment."

There was only a muffled sob in response.

She knit her brow. Hestia opened the door, hinges creaking in the quiet night. "What in Tartarus happened to you?!"

"May I come in?"

"Of course," Hestia glanced about, reassuring herself that no one else had seen Hera in this state. When the door was shut, she threw her arm around her sister. Hera was shaking, embroidery ripped from her peplos, and though any wounds had healed, there was a pain in her halting steps. Hera shied away when Hestia tried to touch her shoulder.

She collapsed on the divan. In the light of the fire, Hestia could make out smudges in her makeup, trickles of kohl down her cheeks. The streams were refreshed by new tears.

"Tell me."

Hera looked up at her. "Do you even need to ask?"

She gritted her teeth. Hestia had taken the vows out of self-preservation as soon as Kronos spat her out. She'd known they would be freed— the offerings of Prometheus's creatures flowed from every fire in every cave and under every outcrop, secretly preparing them for the war to come. All the while, Hestia feared being married off to Aidoneus or Poseidon once they escaped. It had taken only that first brief meeting with Zeus to convince her to save herself.

Her sisters had not been so fortunate.

"Another affair."

Hera crouched forward and nodded. "Why do I bother? I *know* it does nothing. He just uses it as an excuse to... *unleash* on me."

"Whatever he said isn't worth a brass obol," Hestia said. She looked upward, trying to quell her rage. "I thought you'd be in Nauplia by now."

"I don't want to go."

"The spring will rejuvenate you."

"I don't want to come back with child," Hera said, her voice choking.

Hestia's face fell. "But the moon..."

"He refuses to beget on this new one so he can have her for longer. So he released in... you know how potent he is. In the early days, it wouldn't matter the phase of the moon. If I wasn't wearing a tortoiseshell, he could practically *look* at me and..."

"I take it you didn't have one in tonight."

"No."

Hestia stared at her feet.

"I cannot have another by him. Not now."

Hestia floated behind her and leaned her head on her back, careful not to touch her arms or shoulder. "I have acacia."

"It's too late for that. The way we argued, the way he... had me, it would be deformed. Monstrous. He heaps scorn on me for birthing Hephaestus; if I birth another monster, he will cast me out."

Hestia ground her teeth and broke away. "Hera..."

The Queen of the Heavens looked up at her, wide-eyed.

"What I'm about to say— please don't be angry. It has prevented so much chaos and heartache for you already.

There's one thing I have that will… start your courses immediately."

"I can't start now. I have another week. If he suspects—"

"If I am to say more, you must take the oath. The *full*
oath."

Another tear slipped down Hera's cheek. She took a
breath, then looked Hestia in the eye. "I, Hera Acraea Olym-
pia, Queen of Heaven, Most Blessed Daughter of Mother
Rhea, swear upon the Styx that I will not reveal anything said
or done within these walls." She squeezed her eyelids shut. "I
just need this… problem… dealt with."

Hestia trudged to her shelves, running her fingers along
several alabastrons on the highest shelf until she reached a
group that sat unlabeled. She opened one, then another. At the
third, she sniffed the contents, and returned with it to the divan, staring level at Hera.

"They call it silphium. Apollo's worshippers grow it in Cyrene. He procured some for me centuries ago to… start the
courses of one of the Muses."

Peering inside, Hera started back, scrunching her nose.
"The smell."

"Yes, it's pungent—"

"It's downright awful!" She stilled her anger. "He'll know."

"I will draw the resin out." Hestia lifted a segmented stalk
with short leaves at each separation and shriveled yellow flowers at the tip. She shook out a handful of seeds and stripped
the leaves. "It quickens the blood, awakens passion. Which is
exactly what you'll tell Zeus if he finds this before you use it."

Hestia set her mortar in her lap and mashed the root and
seeds with a pestle until its bitter tang filled the air. She lifted
the lid off a *pyxis* near the hearth and extracted a large bead of
crystallized honey.

"Wait." Hera looked up at her, her forehead creased, her
voice hollow.

Hestia stopped. "It's your decision. Either way, we won't speak of this after tonight. You have my word."

She quietly motioned for Hestia to continue. She crushed the sugary lump with the silphium and poured it into her ceramic ladle, melting it over the fire until it boiled and turned dark amber. *Askos* in hand, she quenched it. Hera jumped when it sputtered.

"Grain spirits." Hestia rapidly stirred the mixture. "Just enough to distill it."

"At least the smell is lessened."

"Its potency remains." Hestia set it aside and stared at Hera. Her sister's eyes were deadened, her face set in stone. They sat in silence, waiting for it to solidify. Hestia tipped the dark mound into her mortar and ground it rhythmically.

"What if he sees me take it?"

"It won't matter. Ambrosia will delay it by two days. Then your courses will start, likely in the night, and appear natural." She poured the fine powder into an alabastron and corked the top.

Hera took it gingerly, turning it over in her hands. She barely breathed. "How much?"

Hestia thinned her lips. "Enough so you'll never need to ask me again."

Hera nodded.

"In nectar; with an extra measure of ambrosia."

"What will I feel?"

"Nothing, at first; some nausea later. Bear it as best you can when your courses start. It will feel like the first pangs of childbirth."

Hera shivered and almost dropped the alabastron. "And if... he drinks from it?"

"His heart will race, he'll think it's desire, and within the hour I imagine you'll make sure he's forgotten all about it." Hestia purified her tools with fire, glancing back at Hera.

Hera stood, eyes averted, silent. She stiffly curtsied, and held the alabastron to her chest, pulling her dress closed with the same hand, and made her way to the door. Hestia worried that she'd deeply offended Hera. But before she could turn and apologize, the Queen was gone.

✻   ✻   ✻

"Push; push!" Eileithyia gripped a leg with one hand while reaching with the other to supply Persephone with a fresh bladder of hot water. Persephone held it in place against Aphrodite's side.

Tears trickled from Aphrodite's eyes as she bore down silently, digging her nails into Persephone's hand.

"If you do not cry out, you might hurt the baby," the dark-haired girl said, her brow furrowed.

When the contraction ended, Aphrodite gasped then turned to Eileithyia, eyes burning. "I have birthed five children, girl! I know what I'm doing!"

Eileithyia rolled her eyes. Persephone looked across to Hera, who dabbed Aphrodite's forehead with a rag. Hera had invited Persephone to the birthing room— a great honor, for which Aphrodite leaped to take credit. When any of the Olympians gave birth, the two set aside their ancient rivalry to usher new life into their ranks.

"Now breathe," Eileithyia said quietly. "Fates, Pasithea! Make yourself useful for once! Get the basin; her water…"

The blonde girl, another of Hera's daughters, nodded and awkwardly placed a bronze bowl under the birthing chair. Pale and grimacing, she backed toward the door.

"Let me up," Aphrodite said, breathing hard, stumbling out of the chair.

"You need to lie back on the—"

"I need the ground! The baby turned."

216

"I *know* the baby turned," Eileithyia said, her voice brittle. "A birthing chair is the proper—"

"Don't tell me what's proper!" Aphrodite snarled. "Persephone, help me to the floor. These foolish women of the west... I am alive; not marble on display!"

"What shall I do?"

"I must... touch the earth. Hands and knees." She gritted her teeth while Persephone stroked her back. "Please..."

Persephone pulled Aphrodite's arm over her shoulder and helped her kneel. Aphrodite planted her palms to the ground and rocked, her distended belly swaying gently beneath her. She sighed through the pain.

"*Kouritsi mou!*" The fist hammered against the door for the third time that hour. "Let me in!"

"Damn you, Ares, this is a time for women!" Hera shouted in response. "Have some respect and stay outside!"

Aphrodite took long, focused breaths, moaning around another contraction. Eileithyia shook her head and dropped to one knee beside Aphrodite. "Please, the chair will ease the birth."

Aphrodite's eyes squeezed shut and she shook her head. She sobbed again, the pain relentless.

"You bloodless *kakodaimones!* Let me see her!"

"Oh, for fatessake, bar the door!" Hera yelled over the commotion. Pasithea threw the iron bolt. Ares bellowed in frustration.

"To think... in five months... this will be you." She hissed through the next contraction and glanced toward Persephone, her laugh strangled. Aphrodite stopped and sighed. "It turned... it's time."

"The baby's crowning," Eileithyia said. "Aphrodite... push. Now!"

She strained, her face red, cheeks wet, veins standing out. Her voice broke, her guttural cry filling the room. She released, falling to her elbows.

"A shoulder, it's here! It's…" Eileithyia's face fell. "It's…"

Aphrodite cradled the babe, warming it against her skin. A great shuddering breath of air filled tiny lungs, followed by a high-pitched cry. Genetyllis pushed the bowl under Aphrodite to catch the afterbirth and cleansed the sweat and blood from her lady.

Eileithyia stood stock still next to her mother, expressionless. Hera turned to her. "Well? Is it a boy or a girl?"

Aphrodite turned the child in her arms as Genetyllis cut the cord and sponged the baby clean. "It's mine."

The child's parts were unique— male and female. The cries were plaintive and helpless; and then the baby quieted, settling on its mother's breast, blinking at Persephone with exhausted eyes. Her heart skipped and her voice caught in her throat at the child's beauty.

"Get us to the bed so I can feed," Aphrodite heaved. "Genetyllis, ambrosia. Now."

Persephone and Hera bolstered her under her arms and helped her cross the small room. She sat on the bed and they lifted her legs onto the pallet as she lay on her side. Hera peered around Aphrodite, hovering over the infant. "What *is* it?"

"I told you. The baby is mine," Aphrodite said, her voice becoming a gentle warning. "Whole and perfect in every way. Atlantiades."

"Mother, I'll break down this door! I swear on the Styx!"

"Fates below… Let him in," Hera seethed.

Pasithea pulled the bolt. Ares threw the door against the wall and strode to the bed, cuirass glinting in the light of the oil lamps. Aphrodite cradled Atlantiades protectively to her chest and crowded back into the pillows.

He stood over her, breathing hard, then knelt beside her bed. "*Kouritsi mou...*"

Aphrodite smiled at him weakly. "Enyalios."

"This is the babe?"

She nodded and a tear lost its way into her hairline. Ares's face grew serious and he grabbed the waiting jar out of Genetyllis's hands. Aphrodite stared deep into his eyes and lifted a heavy breast. He dipped his finger in the jar and carefully, reverently coated her nipple with ambrosia for the baby's first meal. Aphrodite pushed the swollen tip into its waiting mouth. Atlantiades latched on, tiny eyelids closing, nourished and content.

Ares gingerly traced the baby's features. "Look... the nose, hair, all of it... so perfect. Like all our children," Ares's forehead knit and he looked from the baby to her. "And you were so brave. Through everything. Can you forgive me, *kouritsi mou*? For all I've done?"

"But have you forgiven me?"

Ares turned to her and whispered something out of earshot. Aphrodite ran her fingers down his jawline and he caught her delicate hand in his large one and nuzzled her palm. Ares leaned carefully over mother and child and kissed Aphrodite on the forehead.

Hera's jaw set sharply and she turned. Persephone followed her from the room. When the door shut, the queen shook her head and spoke. "She had told him her plans to conceive by Hermes before she even went to the Messenger's bed. Ares was devastated. That woman is his mortal wound. I thought, perhaps this time... I still cannot fathom that I raised him as I did, yet he lays down all he is for *her*. But at least when Ares is with Aphrodite, he isn't tearing himself and the world apart."

Persephone nodded and leaned against the wall. "I'd never seen them together. He isn't fond of me."

Hera raised her brows. "He's terrified of you."

Persephone chortled weakly, then slid until she sat on her haunches, leaned back against the cold wall.

"My dear, are you alright?" Hera crouched and placed a hand gently on her forearm.

"Thank you for thinking of me— bringing me here, to help and to witness this." She leaned her forehead into her hand. "This may have been too much for me."

"I should have remembered. You're only in your fourth month. Though now that you've quickened, your nausea must have lessened, at least."

Persephone's brow creased. "I haven't quickened yet. I'm *certain* he's there and well, but..."

Hera's shoulders relaxed and she bowed her head. "I'm... sure there's nothing to be concerned about."

"Above all else, I am exhausted."

"Unfortunately, that doesn't go away. Not for years," she added ruefully. Hera removed a small parcel from the fold of her peplos and offered it to Persephone. She carefully unwrapped the linen to reveal a knobby, crisp-smelling root. "A gift from Hestia. Ginger."

Persephone broke off a soft yellow finger. She bit in, surprised by its spicy flavor. "Please give her my gratitude. It's better with nectar, I take it? Mother told me to ask you. She never drank it with me."

"Ambrosia requires the water of the Styx, and we were barred from the Underworld by Iapetos. By the time he was vanquished, Demeter was too far along for it to help."

"Am I, though?"

"That was her eighth month. With you, it's still fairly early. I'll fetch Ganymede. He can send some along."

✢   ✢   ✢

"No, no, upwind of the hive."

"It's shifting," Orpheus said. "I suppose I could run circles around it."

Eurydice laughed. "Just… wait." Orpheus held the pitch torch aloft again, squinting when the smoke hit his eyes. He stayed put, and let the wind carry toward the bees.

Orpheus had spent most of his days with Eurydice. They had shared nothing beyond a kiss since that first day he met her. He was glad for it. Now there was more between them than the transcendence of their songs— each knew when the other was about to speak. Each could feel the other's joy or frustration. They would sit silently at the edge of the cliffs and watch the sun fade on the horizon. She had been a woman set among the stars. Now she was his friend, his companion. What had started as adulation had resolved into love.

"There… they're relaxing." Eurydice ambled over to him. "Next is the fun part."

"Reaching into a beehive… Delightful."

"You'll be fine. The bees are asleep for the evening. Thanks to the smoke, they ate their fill and will sleep soundly."

"And this won't harm them…?"

"No! It helps them," Eurydice said, grabbing the torch from his hand. She doused it in the creek and pulled him toward the ancient oak. "Too much honey means too great a hive. Then they overflow and swarm to make a new one. The fruits and blossoms were sapped during the rite, so there's only enough left to feed one hive this year."

Orpheus nodded, his body tense.

"No harm will come to you. I promise." Eurydice stroked his back, waited until she felt him relax, then gently pushed him forward. He reached, delved softly into the crevice, fingers coated in honey, pushing until they brushed the ridges of the comb.

He exhaled. "I feel one on me."

"That means they don't fear you," she said, her breath warm on his ear. "Grasp just a handful, and draw it back out."

He breathed in time with her and removed his arm slowly. His hand clenched around the heavy comb and the sleepy bee returned to its sisters.

"Well done," Eurydice said aloud. She fished the linen wrap from between her breasts and folded the honeycomb inside it as they walked away. The sun peeked out under wind-whipped purples and orange clouds. A flash illuminated their faces and thunder resounded through the glade.

"I should go back," he said.

"You'll be the tallest thing on the meadow."

"What does that mean?"

"You might be struck."

"I've done nothing to incur the Loud Thunderer's wrath. Just the opposite, I hope."

"Funny how Zeus reserves so much of his wrath for the tallest trees, then," she laughed.

"You mock me," he said with a smile.

"No," she said and kissed him on the nose, "but don't cast blame on the gods for what can be explained by nature."

A fat droplet splashed on his cheek and lightning twisted through the clouds again. The thunder came quicker. Another drop fell, then a multitude. He smiled up at the sky, rain pasting his curls to his forehead as he thought about the song they'd composed that afternoon.

You tear the robe that cloaks heaven.

He looked at her wide-eyed. "Shit."

"What's wrong?"

"Shit, shit… the lyre!" He took off running, Eurydice close at his heels, bounding from the creek to the great linden tree where he'd left it. Only a few drops had fallen on it, but he hovered over it, cursing, trying to keep any more rain from falling on it.

Eurydice dropped the honey and untied her belt.

"What are you doing?"

She shot him a pointed look. "Saving your instrument." She pulled off her reed woven chiton and laid it under the tree. "Put the lyre on it!"

Orpheus blinked, drinking in her form, his stomach fluttering. Raindrops perched in the tendrils of her hair and sat on her brow like a starry crown. She put a hand on her hip. "What are you waiting for?"

"Y-you..." Her rough-hewn chiton and the bulky tools, slings, and kits had concealed her all this time. Words would not come, no matter how desperately he summoned them.

"You'll have to take yours off too if we're going to keep the lyre dry."

"I could make it back if I—"

"Don't!" she shouted. "It's too sudden a squall. You'll be struck, or..." she looked down. "I'm not losing you to a roll of the *kyveia*, Orpheus."

He nodded and removed his *zeira*, stretching the colorful hooded cloak between two branches. "This won't be enough. The wind..."

"Well, off with *that* too, and you'll have to lash it down with... something," she said, her voice catching in her throat as he pulled his tunic over his head.

"With 'something'?" He grinned at her. Eurydice blushed deeply and tried to avert her eyes.

"I-I'll tie the other side with my belt."

The corner of his mouth ticked up and he quickly pulled off his loincloth. They bound her chiton to his tunic, stuck fibulae along the windward side, and stepped back, sighing in relief. The shelter would hold.

"There! That should..." She laughed, clutching her naked belly, wandering about under the tree. "Oh, Fates below... To find ourselves in this mess."

"Indeed."

Eurydice spread her arms and smiled at the dim clouds, her eyes blinking against the downpour and flashes of lightning. "Why are you raining on us? He just wrote you a hymn! We—"

Orpheus caught an outstretched arm and spun her to him. His lips met hers, one hand framing her face, the other pressing into her soft skin, drawing her close against him. Eurydice's fingers traced the bones of his hips, the curve of his back, and settled on his rain-slicked shoulders. She arched against him, perfect brown nipples grazing his chest, and hot blood charged through his loins so suddenly he groaned. He bucked against her and the sweet friction of her skin provided little relief. Orpheus grasped her thigh and raised her leg, trying to draw her up.

"Orpheus…" Eurydice broke off from his kiss. "We can't…"

"Please, my love…" He stared at her face and his heavily lidded eyes traveled down her body, memorizing each detail, every freckle. "My vows wouldn't… You're my wife in all but name."

"You'll regret it the moment after," she whispered back. "We have all winter. Wait, marry me, and make a better memory."

He claimed her mouth again, his tongue stroking hers. Lightning crashed against the rocky hills above and she drew closer. His mind swam with images of them tangled in the sheets on his thin pallet bed, spending all winter in the shelter of each other. His body pulled inexorably toward hers. "I can't prolong this anymore. I already can't rest at night when I think about you, and now that I see you fully…"

She wiped droplets from his face and leaned her forehead against his. "After the last stalk of wheat is cut, we will lay down together and not rise until the first crocus blooms."

He sighed and nodded, clutching her for a reluctant moment before pulling away.

"But I didn't tell you to stop kissing me."

"I *assume* it's been dealt with," Aidoneus said. "Zeus assured me as much. The disappearances, at least, have ceased."

"But we haven't received him yet?" Rain poured outside. Demeter would be upset when Persephone returned from Thesprotia. This late in the season, rain meant ergot on the wheat and rye, and the mortals would have to work tirelessly to keep the barleycorns from molding. But they would address that tomorrow. For now, they were enjoying their last late summer evening together before she returned below for the winter. She lay fitted to him, both spent and satisfied, his hand resting on her womb.

"We have not, but I told Minos to be vigilant," Aidon said, rounding his hand over her belly. Fingers of lightning arced across the sky, and the interplay of light on her skin and hair reminded him of the flickers of the fire in their room at home. "If Asklepios is wandering as a ghost, Hermes will deliver him soon enough. But—"

Aidoneus stopped short, eyebrows raised. Persephone had felt it too. She held her breath.

"Sweet one… was that—"

"It's…" She turned toward him and propped herself up on her elbows. She gasped.

Another kick. Another rumble of distant thunder. Aidon splayed his palm on her belly. "Will he do it again?"

Zagreus kicked against his thumb. Persephone smiled. "Fates… I thought it would be a little thing— barely noticeable."

Aidon stared at her belly, his mouth dry, pulse drumming in elation and fear.

"He's…" Persephone burst into tears. He looked up at her, distressed as she brushed them away and tried to calm herself. "Aidon, I was so worried. Hera asked if he had quickened, and the way she looked at me when I said he hadn't—"

"He's fine." Another bump against his palm made him smile. He closed his eyes and listened. "I can hear his little heart. Do you think he can hear us?"

"I don't know. But it seems he knows where you are," she said. "You should talk to him."

Aidon looked puzzled. "Do you?"

"Only recently. He hears my voice every day, though. I want him to know yours, too."

"What should I say?" Aidon put both hands on her belly, spanning the slight protrusion of her womb. Another bolt of lightning ripped across the sky and again he felt a tap on his palm. Aidon stroked her belly. "Don't be afraid, little green one. It's only weather. You're safe."

She met his eyes and whispered. "Go on."

"Your name is Zagreus Sabazios Eubouleus Chthonios. You are my son, and your mother and I are eager to meet you," he said. His vision clouded and he wiped his eyes briskly with his fingers. Aidoneus sat back facing Persephone. "We should have him in the world above."

"What? No! We want him to be born at home."

"We can't risk…" his voice choked.

"Aidon, we've been through this. He is *our* child—"

"Conceived in the living world during a rite that nearly drove us out of our wits. Drawn from the spark that created the cosmos. What happens if…" He closed his eyes, willing away the very thought, as if thinking it would make it come to pass. "There are women here who can midwife. Your mother. Hera…"

"I don't want to give birth here in the dead of winter. Our villa could be discovered. Or his birth would be attended by suffocating mortal ceremony in the Telesterion."

"We could have him at Olympus."

"Not there. Not with all of *them*. Please," she said, "let's take him home. You've done so much in my absence... the wool basket you made for our bed—"

"It can be taken anywhere. A year above will make no difference."

"A *year*..."

"Until he has been fed ambrosia, and made fully—"

"Next you'll tell me we should stay above until he's grown, Aidon." She stroked his careworn face. "It will be alright."

"What if we took Hestia's advice? We could settle on Olympus, just while he's a baby, so we can be together as a family."

"You would hate it. Is that the world in which you wish to raise him?"

Aidon knitted his brow and looked down. "No."

"Then don't worry, my love," she said. "No ill will come to him. Not after all we've endured."

10.

IRIS SLOWED HER PACE, PAUSING AS PERSEPHONE LEANED heavily on the atrium column. "It was the same for me, your majesty. I was so fatigued with Pothos. Almost constantly."

"I didn't realize he was your son," Persephone said. "Forgive me; I thought his mother was one of the Kharites."

Iris darkened before her peplos became the color of winter fog. "He was too close with Harmonia, and constantly in Aphrodite's thrall," she said. "Zephyros said it was because I wasn't an affectionate enough mother."

Persephone frowned. "What an awful thing to say."

Her dress took on too vibrant a hue. Iris forced a smile. "He's cold, but not so terrible in the end. My affection— or lack thereof— would have changed nothing. Children seldom fulfill the destinies we imagine for them."

Persephone nodded and followed her through Hera's villa, emerging on a veranda shaded by pomegranate and quince trees, overlooking all of Thessaly. She stood entranced by the view, the plains rippling with golden wheat and the rust and amber shimmer of turning sycamore trees. Iris curtsied once and was gone.

"Demeter let you escape?"

Hera sat at a small mosaic table, her dark hair bound with a beautiful peacock green fillet. Persephone bowed. "Mother forbade me from working this season. It would pass the time better than sitting around the Telesterion, but she wouldn't hear it. Thank you for inviting me, and easing my boredom."

"I've enjoyed our time together," Hera said, "and shall miss you these next six months. But you'll be glad to be with your lord…"

Hera's gaze fixed in the distance. Zeus hadn't been seen on Olympus since the day the *Dodekatheon* convened. Rumor had it he'd already found another lover, and so soon after Alcmene. Persephone drew in a breath. "If there's anything I can do…"

Hera bit her lips and lowered her head.

"I cannot imagine what you must be feeling."

"My heartfelt hope is that you never will." Hera's eyes grew flinty for a moment. She breathed. "But surely, we can speak of something other than my wretched husband, nay? What of Eleusis? Has Demeter accepted that you'll be a mother on your return, or has she torn every golden hair from her head?"

Persephone swallowed. None of the Olympians knew her husband and mother were on better terms. "She'll come around."

"Every autumn we expect her to drag you bodily from the doors of the Plutonion, so I suppose that's the best you can hope for," she said, pouring herself some nectar.

Persephone smiled as the golden elixir sloshed into Hera's clay cup. "Thank you so much for sending that along with me last time. It was so helpful, I ran out."

"How long ago?"

"Two days past. I was… more liberal with it after I received your invitation, knowing I'd be here."

"Doubtless it's also a useful salve for hovering mothers."

Persephone snickered and pushed her cup toward Hera's offered amphoriskos. "I wouldn't complain about that effect, either."

Hera frowned when the pour filled Persephone's cup only a quarter full. "Oh."

"It's fine. My nausea's fading. And there is my good news…" Persephone smiled. "The baby quickened! He's strong and healthy."

Hera's shoulders slumped and she sat back in her chair. She glanced away, gulping in a breath. A tear crept down her cheek.

"Your grace?"

"No, I'm…" she said, her words choked. She sniffed, then roughly wiped her tears away. "I'm… relieved. Deathless children tend to quicken a month before yours, but I didn't want to…"

"To worry me."

"Look what a poor hostess I am." Hera shook her head. "Inviting you here before you descend to the Land of the Dead, and all I can do is dampen your spirits."

"Please… I'm the last thing you need to worry about. When I return, there's so much more we can do to—" She closed her eyes again, feeling lightheaded, and breathed slowly.

"Let me fetch you a full cup of nectar." Hera's chair scraped back and she stood without looking at Persephone. "Give me a moment."

"Isn't Iris about?"

"I don't want her to see me crying. Every tear I shed in this house becomes a public affair."

Hera carried the amphoriskos away and Persephone felt the familiar rustling and unfurling as Zagreus awoke, ready to somersault for the next hour. Her fatigue ebbed as he moved, and she stroked her belly. "Hush, little green one. You'll hear your father's voice again soon."

Hera reappeared in the doorway. "I spoke to Ares like that."

"Can he hear me?"

"No one knows." Hera refreshed Persephone's cup and chewed her lip. "Are you sure it's safe to travel there in your condition?"

She scoffed and took a quick drink. "Aidon was just as worried. He even suggested we live on Olympus for the baby's first year. Can you imagine?"

"I cannot," she swallowed. "But… this has never been done. It's unthinkable for one of us to go below when we are with child…"

"Except for my mother," she said, returning her kantharos to the table.

"There was no order to the cosmos then. The laws have changed."

"But we are not just journeying to Chthonia. We *are* Chthonia." Persephone smiled and took another long sip of nectar. "My child is a part of our realm just as it's a part of us. As much a miracle as when Aidoneus and I created the Elysian Fields."

Hera sat back and poured the nectar into her own cup. She drank, her face composed.

✳ ✳ ✳

"What a day we chose…"

"I like it. The eve of autumn is auspicious, considering how we met… and what we know." Orpheus stared up at her, his head pillowed by her thigh. "In the morning, before we wed, I'm going to tell everyone—"

"That they were here?"

"I wouldn't dare. But I'll announce Zagreus's coming. It's time his name is known."

"Perhaps you *still* dare too much," she tittered.

He shook his head sagely. "I don't think so. They're not capricious." Orpheus rolled away and sat opposite her. "Eurydice…"

She pushed a final stem into place and set the crown of golden leaves and pale haberlea on his head. As she drew her hands back, he caught them in his. She tilted her head. "What's wrong, Orpheus?"

"After winter, I'll take you with me across the sea. To Eleusis for the Lower Rites in spring, and then the Greater Rites in autumn."

"Orpheus…"

"We could spend the summer in Thrace. My mother would adore you and—"

"That's lovely, but why Eleusis?"

"I've been inducted into the Mysteries, Eurydice. If I live a good life, free of bloodguilt, then I'm bound for the Elysian Fields. And I want you there with me."

"Eternity in paradise, with you, my love… if only I would still know you! But Axiokersos told you himself that we lose our memory. With none of myself, or of you… what would it matter?"

"It matters," Orpheus stroked her cheek, "because I would rather spend eternity beside you not knowing who you are or why we are drawn together than to be separated from you ever again."

Eurydice stared at him and her eyes welled with tears. She leaned in and kissed him. "Even if we can't find each other?"

"I'll find you. There is no other way for us." He pulled an echinacea flower from the soil and tucked it behind her ear. "Like the earth to the sky. I *know* it, as deeply as I can know or feel anything— a certainty past living memory. We've been bound before, you and I. And I'm not untwining my soul from yours ever again."

✳   ✳   ✳

"Nothing I can say will make you reconsider?"

"Mother…"

Demeter braced herself. She had brought it up before, and her obstinate daughter's *husband* had agreed. But if Aidoneus couldn't convince Persephone to stay above for the birth, she had little hope of doing so. "It's dangerous."

"You took me to Chthonia in the womb."

"I was given no choice! Do you have any idea what Iapetos would have done to me— *to you*, if he'd caught up with us?" Demeter relented. "I know you want to be… at home when you give birth. You probably feel as vulnerable as I did."

Persephone's shoulders relaxed. "If you understand what I'm going through, then why are you pushing for this?"

"Because… I'd made my peace with not being there. Or so I thought. But I worried while he refused to quicken, and the idea of him coming to any harm…" Demeter remembered Kore's tiny pink hand wrapped around her smallest finger. "You'll understand once he's in your arms."

Persephone shook her head, her voice edged with exhaustion and irritation. "The *reason* I'm taking him to Chthonia is to protect him. Even those I trust on Olympus hover over me. And from what I saw when Atlantiades was born, I don't want any of them near me when I give birth."

"Wisely chosen, I suppose," Demeter sighed, resigned to losing this battle. She gritted her teeth, imagining Persephone in the throes of childbirth like her own delivery. The unrelenting pain as though her hips were going to break apart, gasping for a mere breath, the loneliness, dread preceding each birthing pang, and after everything: exhaustion. "You need a midwife. *Not* Hecate. A mother, who *knows* all you will endure."

233

"Lady Nyx—"

"Is Protogenoi," Demeter finished. "Childbirth is different for them. She and her husband *willed* thousands of their children into being in the depths of Tartarus. But we..." Demeter grasped her hand. "Persephone, I don't want to miss it. It's *too important*."

Persephone sat, rubbing her forehead. "Then come with me."

Her fingers felt numb and her skin prickled. "You know I cannot. You forgave me, your husband... perhaps. But I am hated in your realm." She waited for Persephone's reply, but none came. "Daughter..."

"The nausea was worse today." She breathed hard, head bowed into her folded arms, her knees tucked up to support them. "I feel as though I'm losing control..."

"Do you have more nectar?"

"I forgot the amphora Hera offered me. I shared a cup from it with her, but... Why has my mind been such a fog these past months? And why do I feel so worried all of a sudden?"

"Persephone..." Demeter shook her head and sat next to her daughter on the divan. "I'm sorry. I wish there was some way I could help you. But every woman who has ever given birth does so alone. No matter who's in the room, who wipes your sweat, who changes the linens. It's lonely. And *you* choose how it's done."

"I'm so afraid." Persephone leaned against Demeter's shoulder. "I feel I don't have the slightest idea what I'm getting into."

"No one does, Kore." Demeter smiled, then scoffed. "And if we did, no one would have children."

✻   ✻   ✻

His instrument fell silent, but the assembled voices carried his last notes— a hymn to the Goddess of Marriage. Orpheus raised his hands above the pool, his voice resounding throughout the temple. "I invoke the divinities dwelling in the sky, in the air, in the water, on earth, under the earth, and in the fiery ether."

He lowered his palms and stared across the reflecting pool, seeing the faces of his order, of initiates, and of those who had come to hear the son of a god who played Apollo's silver lyre. They watched him intently, crowding the pool, waiting for dawn, for the sky to fill with golden pinks and bright orange. The heavens were reflected in the water, and the faces of those with him were inverted and dark. His gaze fell on her again, her hair braided and wound back for their wedding, a wreath of shells, lilies, and haberlea crowning her head. Today Eurydice would become his wife. *His wife.* His heart quickened.

"We are the children of Earth and starry Heaven," they recited. Orpheus let the chorus wash over him, but he keenly felt Eurydice's gaze. The congregants dipped hands in the pool, each sipping the clear water.

"Today the Maiden descends to join her honored Lord. Axiokersos will reunite with Axiokersa." He smiled. "It is no coincidence that I chose this day to wed."

"About time," muttered Lemnia, the ancient priestess. Smiles and muted laughter rippled among the elder members of the priesthood. The acolytes and visitors glanced at each other, nervous to join in. Orpheus's cheeks reddened.

"It was through my bride Eurydice, daughter of Erymanthe, that we heard in the whispered words of trees, and from the loud roar of waves... the Unborn One shall be born this very winter!"

Those gathered murmured. The priesthood stared at Orpheus.

"For so long we've waited. Now the beginning and the end will begin again. *Phanes* has created him, and his name is a holy one. Zagreus Sabazios Eubouleus. Fear not, my brothers and sisters, the God of Elysion shall reign forever!"

✳ ✳ ✳

The sun breached the horizon, casting gentle light on the initiates' bowed heads. Walking slowly along the banks of the Eridanos in Athens, a *hiereia* of Demeter trickled cold water on their scalps, then marked each with oil after the ritual cleansing.

Athena hadn't traveled among mortals for an age. Not since that terrible night at her temple, when she was still young. She had never been a child— only green, and lacking wisdom. She imagined how it might feel if the priestess's words were true— if the sins she had committed that night could be washed away. But she knew it would never be so. She would always carry bloodguilt for Medusa.

Children had tied bright saffron ribbons to her wrists and ankles, contrasting with the stark indigo himation wrapped around her, worn by every mortal in her company. Barefoot, they walked. And walked. And walked westward in silence along the narrow stream until it vanished underground at Karameikos. *Alade! Mystai,* they called out to all. *To the sea, you initiate, to the sea.*

A bright sky opened wide beyond the willow and ash trees. Athena wondered what mortals felt as they walked on these carefully laid stones. Did their burdens weigh heavy? Were they able to let them fall? She touched an olive tree that stood sentry along the blue expanse of the gulf, decorated with fluttering strips of saffron ribbon. She remembered the morning Persephone was newly returned from the Underworld, how Athena had practically begged her to restore these trees.

236

She'd been terrified to ask, wondering if Persephone knew of her role in the abduction. She and Artemis were supposed to provide the Lord of the Underworld enough time to court and seduce Kore before the Harvest Goddess returned. No one had expected Hades's chariot to come roaring from the depths of the earth to carry her below. Athena thought Persephone would point the same accusatory finger her mother had, then sap all fertility from her favored trees as punishment.

"Come and see, you initiate!" A voice rang out ahead, and several men, each carrying a branch of white poplar, appeared over the cresting hill. The leaves had turned bright red. Athena watched as they lightly scourged the travelers ahead of her. "Come and see that all are equal here."

Her shoulders tensed instinctively, anticipating the thrash of the small branch. The leaves rattled against her back and she felt a rush of indignation. Would these mortals dare strike her if they knew who she was? Then again, the *archon basileus* of Athens himself wasn't far behind her on the road…

"You women and men! Slave. Freeborn. The richest and the poorest, the greatest to the least. While you live, you feast upon the earth— but when you die, the earth shall feast upon you."

You care very much for the people of Athens, Persephone had told her, *and this is their greatest crop.* She hadn't restored the olives for Athena, but *them.* Athena furrowed her brow. All she'd been concerned with that day was Poseidon's bid to gain favor in her city, with the problems it would cause her alone. But Persephone had thought solely of *them.* Of their pressed fruits, *their* oil, and all they would need to live.

"Abandon your pride!" The men cried out. "All are equal in death. Let your soul be nourished above! For no one, when the earth has covered him and he has gone down into the darkness, has the pleasure of hearing the lyre, or tasting wine and bread. Prepare, you weary, to meet your Host. Rejoice, you initiate, for death is not the end!"

Athena raised her ribboned wrist to her eyes and wiped away tears. The people of Athens *loved* her, yet all she offered them was continued strife. She sighed and saw the faces of women. They chanted an *emmeleia* for Persephone, a funeral dirge, a wedding song. They scattered chaff at Athena's feet. The hulls crunched under her toes. One close to her whispered in her ear. *Rejoice you initiate, for death is not the end.*

She had visited the Plutonion many times. Persephone, she knew, preferred this smaller temple to her mother's lofty one on the hillside. But Athena had never before seen it thronged so with devotees, nor piled so high with pomegranates and olive oil, figs, and *kykeon* and dates.

Amid these offerings stood Persephone. Chanting ceased. All stood quiet, solemn.

A man in saffron walked forward and carefully unfurled an aged scroll. "I sing of lovely-haired Demeter, great goddess, of her and of her slender-ankled Maiden, whom Zeus, all-seeing and loud-thundering, gave to the Receiver of Many to wed…"

Athena tried to keep her head bowed throughout the long poem, tried not to stand out among the mortals as she had promised Persephone. She fought the urge to run to her and help her pregnant cousin stand under the weight of her saffron veil and her asphodel-wreathed crown. She would have time with her soon enough. It would take days for Athena to circumvent the barriers between the verdant and chthonic realms, but then she would see Persephone again, not as the Goddess of Spring but as the Queen of the Underworld.

Eyes wandering, she caught the staid glare of Demeter, her hair concealed by breeze-tousled indigo linen. She gave the slightest of nods. Athena bowed her head respectfully, staring at the ground until the hymn ended. An indigo-shrouded man stepped forward from Demeter's side and raised his voice to the gathered initiates. "Now she descends into the earth. But from the earth, she brings the seed, and from the seed the earth bears life."

Persephone scanned the faces gathered before her. When she caught sight of Athena, she looked down, fighting a smile. Athena couldn't hide her grin, and covered her face with her hands, in keeping with the solemn masses.

"On this return, the Mistress shall bear up from the earth a holy child. Brimo shall birth Brimos! The Strong One to the Strong One! *Potnia kouron Brimou Brimon!*"

"*Potnia kouron Brimou Brimon,*" the assembled chanted. Athena's voice joined theirs.

With a loud groan, the door of the Ploutonion opened. Demeter solemnly approached Persephone and stood before her, then threw her arms around her. She held her for a moment too long, and the last man to speak placed a familiar hand on Demeter's back.

That must be Triptolemus, Athena thought. Who else would dare touch Demeter while she said her farewells to Persephone? Demeter nodded and stepped back to Triptolemus's side. A pale arm extended from the open door.

Athena exhaled with a shudder. This was no mere priest playing through the pageant of Persephone's descent, Athena realized. Mortals would never know, but the luminescence of ichor beneath his skin gave him away. This was Aidoneus himself. Persephone took the proffered hand and stepped forward. Before she disappeared beyond the door, she locked eyes with Athena and smiled.

✻   ✻   ✻

Lemnia shook out the saffron veil and draped it over Eurydice's head, carefully placing the shell and lily crown atop it. "Orpheus is from my tribe in Thrace, the Cicones. You join a proud line by marrying him."

Eurydice nodded. "My mother was a dryad daughter of the *Kabieroi*. I suppose that would be my tribe."

"Indeed," she said with a smile. "My allegiance is to this temple before my kin, of course. I'm proud to have such a talented woman join our ranks." Lemnia wrapped her tattooed arms around Eurydice, giving her a squeeze and a kiss on the cheek. The entire priesthood had welcomed her as family, showered her with love and respect. She returned the old woman's embrace.

"Will I be expected to wear those too?"

Lemnia looked at her faded ink and chuckled. "No, they reflect your father's tribe by birth. That's why your husband is unmarked… he wasn't born legitimate. Besides, you have such lovely skin. Why mar it?"

Eurydice frowned thoughtfully. "I don't know. I think the wildflowers would do well on me."

Lemnia smiled. "If you wish it."

"What do the Ciconian women do when they marry?"

"We break a loaf of bread over the head of the bride, and after the ceremony, she and her husband share a morsel with each guest. Otherwise, we're much like the rest of Thrace or Hellas."

"And before the wedding?"

"Solitude. To reflect on leaving one's family to make a new one. For though you are your own creature, you are no longer alone. You are bound to another. Forever."

Eurydice drew in a deep breath. "That may be well for me…"

"It would be wise. Usually, it is done with the door closed, in the house of your family. But your home is all of Samothrace, yes?" Lemnia smiled then paused and grew solemn. "I knew your father."

Eurydice stiffened.

"His name was Deimas. He was a hierophant when I was but a water bearer, just eleven years old. In that time before the great famine when Da Potnia drained fertility from the earth."

"I was barely walking and still at my mother's breast," Eurydice mused. "Had she weaned me before the famine, she told me, then I would not have lived."

"The winter took your father." Lemnia paused, her eyes unfocused. "He was a good man and a better leader, who respected the old ways."

"Can you tell me more about him someday?"

Lemnia lingered at the door. "Of course." She nodded to Eurydice and quietly left the room.

Eurydice gazed into the bronze mirror. Her dress was simple linen but felt like the finest lawn compared to the woven reeds she'd worn every day. She reached to her hip for her water bladder, but her fingers closed around nothing. Her effects were all stowed away, just as she would be. She swallowed.

In spring she would return, and take Orpheus with her into the wilderness, to collect honey and herbs, to tend the trees, and feel the grass under her feet. And he would take her to Eleusis. She smiled. Perhaps she would see Persephone again. The goddess she had befriended would be caring for an infant by then.

Eurydice rose from the table. All of Samothrace was her home. If she was going to spend the winter within walls of stone with her beloved, she should have one last hour in the wide-open spaces she knew so well. She opened the door, traversing the porch to reach the grass. The autumn earth was warm, the soil cushioning her feet.

Then a rustling, and she winced at something sharp against her ankle. She crouched to pull the thorn free but instead found two deep marks. The dry grass parted, and a flash of peacock green serpentined through the field. Eurydice drew a ragged breath and sat down, her head impossibly light. Her lip was wet. She touched the trickle beneath her nose through the veil, looked at her fingers. Blood. Warm on numb fingers. The edges of her vision darkened around it, and she saw no more.

⁂　　⁂　　⁂

Once the door to the Plutonion had closed, he lifted her veil from her head. Aidon whispered, knowing that all of Eleusis stood outside. "Greetings, wife."

"Hello, husband." Persephone returned his brief kiss. "Zagreus missed you too. He's been thrashing wildly since I awoke."

He led her beyond their statues at the mouth of the cave. The effigies were crowned and laden with lilies and pomegranates and surrounded with beeswax votives of infants swaddled in linen. "I thought we'd go directly. The chariot could be too rough a ride for you."

She smiled. "My nausea *was* abating, but I felt faint in the sun just now..."

"I thought nectar helped."

"It did, but I ran out," she smiled at him. "It isn't as bad as it was."

"I will have Hermes bring more if you need it."

She leaned into him and he reveled in her warmth. Every year she spent an hour under heavy veils and the relentless sun, waiting through pomp and ritual as the mortals prepared themselves for winter. Every year she arrived at his side dewy with sweat and the scent of violets.

"Let me take you." He circled his arm about her waist, a half-smile teasing the corner of his mouth. "It's rare that I get to escort you through the ether, sweet one."

When they traveled together, he usually followed her path of Phlegethon fire; Persephone could bridge the divide instantly. She bit her lip and wrapped her arms around his neck, just like the first time he had taken her through the ether— when

242

the snow fell all around them in Nysa and the Hundred Handed Ones called her by name. He leaned in and kissed her deeply, his palm splaying across her back. Smoke enveloped them, then melted into the crimson and silver threads of the ether.

The rings on their hands shone brightly as they passed through the great Void between realms. "You don't feel off balance here, do you?"

"No," she said, nestling into his embrace. She planted a kiss on his cheek, which he promptly stole. She smiled after their lips parted. "Fates, I feel… normal. For the first time since I knew I was pregnant."

"Good." He kissed her again, delight coursing through him. Aidon sighed against her lips and his voice echoed in her mind. *It was foolish of me to worry— selfish when you needed reassurance.*

I know why you did, she answered. Persephone settled his hand against her womb. "Do you feel that? He knows he's coming home and that you're here."

"He's as strong as you are." He cupped her cheek and parted her lips with his tongue, deepening their kiss. *And perhaps the… restrictions I placed upon us these past months aren't needed either.*

Only if you're sure. She shivered, meeting him equally.

"Seeing you swell with life… It's taken everything to restrain myself. Now that he's quickened, that he's safe, all I want is to break our abstinence and touch you everywhere."

She traced his jaw, her eyes lidded. "I would like that."

Aidon pulled her tight against him and readied his stance, waiting. Darkness swirled around them, then cleared. He steadied, rooting his feet at the shores of the Styx— their home.

"Not straight to our rooms?"

"My last precaution as we cross into Chthonia." He tended to her, straightening the fibulae that had slipped down her shoulder in their embrace, pushing a fallen flower back into her crown. "Besides. Charon is expecting us."

✳   ✳   ✳

Dryas shaved Orpheus's face, as was the wedding custom among his people. Of all in the priesthood, the Bithynian elder had the steadiest hand. Orpheus wore a newly woven *zeira* to match the crown of autumn leaves Eurydice had placed on his head the day before. He stood in the temple courtyard, his lyre beside him, waiting. Perrhaebus would arrive at any moment, escorting Eurydice to wed them. It would be a small ceremony— those who had made the pilgrimage this morning had already begun their journeys home before the autumn winds tossed the seas wildly.

His stomach roiled like waves. So much lay undiscovered and unseen— Eurydice had yet to see his hearth and the cloistered confines of his quarters. He'd been afraid to take her there, and of all the temptation that might follow. But after the ceremony, after they had broken bread for their guests, he would carry her to his modest home and spend the winter with her…

They hadn't even dared a kiss since a fortnight ago. She'd been right— had he given in that day under the linden tree, he would regret it now.

"About your beloved's name," Dryas said, startling him, "and what it means."

"Broad justice."

"Potent for a girl." He leaned in. "The Moirai must have known the part she'd play in welcoming the Unborn One."

Orpheus held his breath. He faintly heard a long cry, lost in the wind.

"Your beloved's patroness, the Exacter of Justice herself was here with her consort, was she not?"

"Dryas—"

244

"We knew." His temples crinkled with his smile. "The six of us, who shared your vision when you first came to Samothrace, we who beheld the rites… we knew. And we will take that ineffable knowledge to our graves."

Orpheus exhaled hard. "I was sworn to secrecy and she was the only other—"

"Perrhaebus couldn't see them, but he never forgets a voice. And he remembered hers from his boyhood… when his family journeyed from Dion to Eleusis for food during that dark winter."

Orpheus sighed. His brothers and sisters were among the wisest of mortals. How had he ever thought they wouldn't find out?

"Be at ease, Orpheus. We knew it would come to pass. Who else could birth the God of Elysion?"

"The Good Counselor himself said as much. But if anyone else knew, base superstition would hound us forever. All we've worked for would be lost."

Dryas turned toward the path, and Orpheus followed his gaze to Perrhaebus, inching along the cobblestones alone. His face was blank, with unseeing eyes rimmed with red. Orpheus tittered. "Did you forget someone, brother?"

Tears fell down the old man's cheeks and he reached for Orpheus's shoulder with his palsied hand. "You must listen to me! We found her. Lemnia and I…"

"Found who?"

"Brother!" Perrhaebus cried. "It was too late. Forgive me, it was too late! She sat against the foundation. We thought she was watching the sea in solitude."

"Where is Eurydice?"

"A viper. I felt the marks on her heel. Only a viper could have left them. Orpheus, I cannot… I am so sorry. Eurydice has journeyed below." He sobbed, holding onto Orpheus for support.

Orpheus could hear Lemnia wailing now, her tortured voice carrying across the courtyard. He stared out at the sea, colors muting. A songbird piped discordant notes in the oak tree above.

Perrhaebus shuddered, wiped his nose on the sleeve of his himation, and took a deep breath. "We must prepare Eurydice for the afterlife, brother. We must. She cannot cross without our help. It is all we can do."

A whine rose in Orpheus's ears and his voice sounded like it came from the bottom of a well. "But there are no serpents on Samothrace…"

✳   ✳   ✳

Aidon stole another kiss before the Boatman arrived. Bright torches flared around the palace, their glow dimly mirrored in the Styx. The water itself was black as night. Quiet waves lapped the shoreline, foretelling the arrival of Charon's boat, and their lips parted. Persephone closed her eyes, listening to the voices of her kingdom. *Soteira… Annessa… She has returned… Metra… Mother to many…*

"Do you think they know?"

"They will soon enough." Aidon listened too, idly rubbing her lower back. He heard their son's heart, drumming quicker.

Charon's oar dipped through the water, then ground through the silt. The prow scraped the gravel and came to a halt.

"It's good to see you again, Charon…"

He knelt. "And you, my queen." Persephone motioned for him to stand.

Before the Boatman could offer her a hand, Aidoneus swept Persephone off the ground. She squealed in surprise. He waded knee-deep into the Styx and set her gently on the center bracing of the boat, then handed Charon an obol for his passage before settling in behind her.

246

Persephone hissed and held her lower back.

"I didn't hurt you, did I?" Aidon said, alarmed.

"No," she said, "I've had small pangs since the morning. This one was worse. Mother said they were to be expected."

Charon spoke. "So soon?"

"How would you know?" Aidon scoffed as they cast off.

"It is my sad duty to—" Charon caught himself and cleared his throat. "Now isn't the time to speak of such things. Your... *esteemed* mother won't visit you this winter, I hear?"

"I invited her many times. Though considering how surly *you* are," she said with a half-smile, "can you blame her?"

"Fair enough," he chuckled.

Persephone exhaled hard.

"Sweet one, are you sure you're alright?"

"It felt like a low kick, that's all."

Aidon smiled. "I started preparing your old quarters."

"I don't want him that far from us."

"Not in the first year. But someday."

Persephone smiled and scrunched her nose. "It's a rather feminine room."

"It is. But surely you've sensed that from him as well."

"I have." She leaned back against him and nodded. "It feels different, though. More like..."

"A balance," he tilted her chin up with a finger and kissed her.

She convulsed and broke away from him, her eyes squeezing shut. Aidon felt pain coursing throughout her body. She groaned.

"Sweet one?"

Persephone doubled forward. "It's nothing... it's..."

Charon turned around. "Aristi?"

"What's wrong?!" Aidon crouched over her, both desperate and afraid to touch her.

Persephone cried out and Aidon grasped her around the waist. Her eyes went wide and she exhaled forcefully. "No…"

Mother to many…

"No, please, Fates, no…" Persephone dug furiously at her skirts. She struggled to breathe and reached between her legs, then looked at her fingers. Her hand shook in the dim light. Blood.

Mother to none…

"Persephone!" Aidon held her as she tensed again and slumped to the side. She gasped, gritting her teeth. He tried to touch her womb, to listen for their son's heart, but she batted his hand away and curled forward, her voice strangled by sobs. "No, no, sweet one… be calm. My love, you'll be fine. This isn't— this can't be—"

"Hecate!" Charon drove his oar into the water desperately. His voice echoed across the silent river. "Hecate; please! Help us! Hecate!"

11.

"T HEY WERE SPRAWLED THERE," HYPNOS SAID, "drenched in the afterglow. And who should saunter in but Melampus and me? Mind you, it took us some effort to rouse them back to their full *potential*..."

Thanatos snorted. "You went to Chios again?"

"I like their andron. It's so warm and well designed..."

"You've savored three generations of their men. I don't think it's the inside of the *andron* you find so inviting."

"They have *heated* water flowing through clay pipes *underground*, Thanatos. Like old Crete! Come next time, and see for yourself."

"No," he said with a thin smile.

Hypnos sighed. "Brother, it's been a very long time. Are you going to weep for Merope and punish yourself for Voleta until the world breaks apart?"

"I'm not punishing myself. Merope is at peace in Elysion, and I have no reason to seek her out. As for Voleta... wanton rutting lost its appeal after I watched her die for my sake."

Hypnos shook his head sadly.

"Who would I care to fuck, anyway? Hecate's latest initiates? It's... not worth it."

"It was always your salve for the duty the Fates accorded you. You understand how it worries everyone when, after Sisyphus, you turn on an obol and become as chaste as Charon."

"Oh, I understand. And I—" He stopped mid-sentence, eyes wide.

"What's the matter?"

Thanatos spread his black wings and stood, his voice clipped and quiet. "Hypnos, you must bind me in the Chains."

Hypnos stared at him incredulously as Thanatos reached for the ground to summon them from Tartarus. "What are you talking about?"

"I don't have time to explain! I can already feel the pull…" He doubled over, clutching his chest. The links wound molten from the floor, cooling as they piled on the ground before them.

"Thanatos—"

"Do it now!"

Hypnos raised his hands. Adamantine links clattered as they whipped the air and encircled his brother. Constricting coils bound his arms to his sides and crushed his wings, tangled his legs until he crashed in a leaden heap to the stone floor. Hypnos bent down, his voice raised over his brother's pained groans and the rattling chains. "Now can you tell me why?!"

"I was being pulled to… to…" The links glowed red wherever they touched his skin and Thanatos cried out, writhing.

"Do you have any idea what you're doing to the balance right now? While you thrash about, nothing in the cosmos is allowed to die!"

The door flew wide and Hecate ran into the throne room, white peplos gathered to her knees. She stopped and knelt near Thanatos. "I feared the rippling wake had not reached you in time."

"I felt it long before you did." Thanatos's eyes rolled back and he spasmed, breathing through clenched teeth.

Hecate placed her hand on his shoulder. "The pain can't be helped but—"

"Never mind me," he ground out. "Go to *them*."

✻　　✻　　✻

This was his fault.

Aidon sat against the doorframe outside Persephone's old bedroom. He should have insisted— should have *told* her that she would not make the journey until Zagreus was born and held firm. He was her protector, and he had failed her.

Now his wife lay on the other side of the door as Hecate worked to save their son. No sound came from within. The barriers Hecate had erected to protect Zagreus from the Land of the Dead were so strong he could barely feel Persephone's presence.

The Land of the Dead. His throat ached. How could he have been so foolish? To flout his intuition, *ananke* itself, such hubris against the Fates… They were being punished. And it was his fault.

When Hecate had ushered him out yesterday, he'd left without question, despite the urge to comfort Persephone through her screams and sobs. Moments after the door shut, all was silent. Aidon had sat outside, unmoving throughout the night, and over the course of the day. Now the light was fading from the Styx.

He knocked his head hard against the door frame and squeezed his eyes shut, but hot tears returned. His ribs were an empty cage. Aidon sucked in a sharp breath, hands squeezing his temples.

She was the one suffering. Her blood still stained his clothes. He didn't deserve to grieve. Aidon splayed his palm on the door, desperate for any sense of her, then drew it back

251

as if he'd touched a bronze cooking pot. If he tested Hecate's protections, it might kill their child.

He rocked forward, eyes stinging again. This was unfathomable. They were deathless. Zagreus was *deathless*. But the Fates had told him he would sire no children in Asphodel…

"Aidon." Hypnos's voice from the doorway jarred him. "Aidoneus, please. You *must* rest."

His voice was brittle. "How can I?"

"Hecate is tending to her. There's nothing more to be done."

He looked away and cleared his throat. "Is your brother in much pain?"

"That's not important right now. He'd be the first to say so."

"How could this have happened?"

"You should come away from the door—"

"No!"

Hypnos's wings lowered and he walked across the room. He dropped down and folded his legs, sitting next to Aidoneus. "This wasn't your fault."

"You don't know that."

"My mother and father conceived and birthed Thanatos and I as young Protogenoi, not much older than yourself and the queen, here— in Chthonia." Hypnos paused pensively. "And Clymena walked the whole way here pregnant. During the war, no less. Chthonia is not the cause. Something must have—"

"But we're different. We're Ouranic; we don't come from your line. I should have known." The words caught in his throat. "I shouldn't have put my own pride, my vanity above… Fates— so many mortal women cross into these lands after… after losing a babe in this very manner. We're deathless. And if this could happen to Zagreus, what if she… w-what if…"

"That *cannot*, will not happen to her, Aidon. You know that. And this could be temporary— by crossing the Styx, or traveling the ether and… Hecate might emerge with Persephone, with her and the babe whole and well, and—"

"There was so much blood."

Hypnos frowned sadly. "Aidon…"

His shoulders hunched forward and he propped his forehead against his knees. Hypnos rested his hand on his back and Aidon stiffened. He was too exhausted to wave him off or shrink away.

Hypnos sighed. "She'll need you when this is over."

Aidoneus crumpled forward, every exhale burning like acid, sobs shuddering through him. Persephone would need him. Once she learned their son was dead. He sucked in deep breaths, choked back his anguish. No sound came from within the room, but who knew what those within could hear? She couldn't know he was falling apart. "I'm not leaving this room."

"You won't have to." Hypnos stood and offered his hand. "Lay on the divan. The poppy will do the rest."

✻   ✻   ✻

"We're the children of Earth and…" Orpheus went silent. Sighing gently, Lemnia herded the others from the room, following them out so he could conduct the final rites alone.

He couldn't write the instructions to find the Mnemosyne. Not when Eurydice knew the truth. Her body had been washed afresh, no trace of blood from her nose or eyes or mouth, no remnant of that horror. She lay on a pallet surrounded by freshly cut mint, her body wrapped from foot to neck in white linen. Orpheus stroked the stubble on his unshaven face. He took the beaten gold leaf and carefully poked at it with his stylus, imprinting four simple words:

Eurydice, Beloved of Orpheus.

He carefully unwound her shroud and picked up her left hand, shuddering at its coldness, at her ashen skin, and wrapped the gold leaf tightly around her ring finger.

Would they recognize her? Would Persephone take pity and grant Eurydice a place in Elysion? They were kind but adamant. Would ushering Zagreus into existence be enough to sway the King and Queen of the Underworld? He tucked her arm back into the shroud, concealing the gold leaf that he should have placed under her tongue.

Eurydice likely wouldn't even see them. She would stand before Hades's judges, another shade in a long line of shades. But if there were a chance... He placed an obol in her mouth and carefully wound her hair with the last length of linen. He tightened the shroud around her jaw until only her face remained.

Come back. Please.

He stared unmoving, his motions mechanical. Like pulleys on a ship. He wasn't here. He hadn't been here for three days.

There are no serpents on Samothrace.

They were punishing him. They must be. A viper was a message as deeply chthonic as any that could be sent. He'd revealed too much and angered them. Broken covenant with the God of the Dead...

"Orpheus?"

He slowly turned to see Lemnia lingering in the doorway. "It's done."

✻   ✻   ✻

The ropes let out slowly and Orpheus leaned over the pit, the pallet swinging ever so slightly. He expected her to open her eyes, centers of blue with earthen brown rimming her pupils. He would reach down, take her hand, and lift her...

The pallet knocked against a stone and settled. Eurydice stopped swaying. The ropes were pulled up the sides. He had angered Hades and Persephone, and they had taken *her*. They should have taken him. Speaking their child's ineffable name aloud was *his* doing, *his* hubris.

Follow after.

He felt leaden, pulled down into the earth with her, and imagined lying beside her, letting the acolytes heap dirt over them both until cold soil blanketed his skin, seeped into his bones, filled his lungs. He pictured seasons passing eternally above them.

He barely felt Dryas's hand tap on his shoulder. When it was clear that Orpheus would neither move nor speak another word, Lemnia lowered Eurydice's waterskin, her tools and belt, the Thracian wedding dress she'd worn to take with her to the afterlife.

"Is there a song you wish to sing for her?" Perrhaebus said. "So she knows it is you sending her on her way?"

The lyre sat silently at his side. He considered casting it over to rest beside her. "No."

His elder brothers and sisters exchanged worried glances.

Morpheus, awaken me from this dream. Orpheus could see her sitting up and stretching, unwinding the shroud and shaking out the taut curls of her hair. Instead, a handful of dirt splashed across her body, jarring him from the vision. Dust floated upward, and flecks of mud marred her face. Dryas shielded his eyes and dropped another handful on her body, beseeching the Boatman to take her coin and allow her to cross into the Underworld.

Orpheus stood like a stone. He stood as they heaped dirt on her, as she disappeared beneath it, as the last of the linen shroud was obscured. He stood while the others left and acolytes from the temple filled in the grave, first with thorny brambles to keep jackals from digging too deep, then dirt. He stood watch that night as a light rain came down, then the following day as they planted asphodel roots on her mounded grave and arranged stones to mark it.

"You must come in, brother," Dryas said.

Orpheus heard him as if distantly. His *zeira* was soaked through. His crown of fallen leaves and haberlea, the one Eurydice had woven for him, still hung on his brow. "She is dead because of me."

"Merely at rest now, Orpheus."

"She should be standing here. Not I."

"Atropos cut *her* thread; not yours. You welcome the evil eye by lingering, brother. Please. Come inside and wash; eat. Rest; let *her* rest. She would have wanted—"

Orpheus walked away, toward the forest, his lyre under his arm. Dryas hobbled after him.

"Where are you going?"

"The chasm."

Dryas jogged at a limp after Orpheus, favoring his bad hip. "I know what you're thinking!" he called out. "But that is no pathway to *Domos Haidou*— you cannot even hear a stone dropped in. And if you think to throw yourself in, to murder yourself in grief, you take on bloodguilt that will separate you from—"

"Then I shall wait."

Dryas tripped and stumbled, catching his breath. "For who?"

He walked on.

"Orpheus!"

The old man's call grew distant, lost in the trees and the crunch of leaves under his feet. After an hour's walk, he stopped at a bog, water-blackened cypress roots reflected perfectly on its surface, then turned up the side of a short hill until he could hear a constant drip of water echo from deep in a cave.

Orpheus cleared wet leaves from a slab of stone and sat, his lyre in his lap. It was still in tune, despite weather and disuse. He plucked the chords in a fifth, ascending the scale until he found the three notes that rang the clearest, that echoed furthest into the heavy darkness, and used the drip of water as the measure. His voice broke at first, but he sang on and it grew clear, matching each note.

"You dwell on the road we all must take— a path of no return. Guiding us through the nether gloom. Hermes, son of Maia, I call upon you… hear me… guide me, too…"

✳   ✳   ✳

At a certain distance from the world above, the ether could no longer be called upon. Up to that point, it was simple enough to cross the boundaries between worlds. Athena would open a path marked by her sigils of twined olive branches and serpents, and travel as she did above. Then without warning, the ether would break, and Athena would lurch forward, stumbling from twisting light to solid ground. These were the great boundaries— the invisible and insurmountable walls that could keep Olympus's defeated enemies at bay. Some left tangible scars, their ancient presence deforming the rock or splitting chasms in the earth. She'd pass an underground lake or sharp abyss, then travel anew. Every subsequent summoning of her immortal pathway required more concentration but left less ground covered. The intervals became stadia, then fathoms, then no distance at all.

The last time she'd descended into the Underworld, Perseus had been at her side. She'd been preoccupied with keeping him safe and had spent little time taking in her surroundings. Now she saw how soil gave way to bare layered rock, then granite and gneiss. Here and there along the way lurked reliefs of ancient creatures or shimmering veins Hephaestus might envy. Athena felt the currents that flowed through the rocks, the still air reversing and twisting, transfiguring. Where did the Earth become the Underworld?

A shade passed beside Athena, ephemeral as smoke, then another, then a multitude, flooding onward as if they'd been held back from death. When the last one flitted past she squinted, wan light emanating up the bend. These were the outskirts of the Underworld. The ether was precarious here, but no more barriers save the great Styx itself would stand in her way. Athena set her mind on the shores of that mighty river and traveled the remaining leagues.

Her sandals touched the stony ground. Only the distant hiss of the falls beside the palace broke the silence. Athena tensed, eyes and ears alert. No torchlight flickered from there. The water was like glass. Where was Cerberus's watchful baying?

"Hello?"

And where was Charon? They would have known she'd crossed the many barriers of Chthonia by now— no immortal could travel the ether here unseen. Persephone was expecting her, knew she would arrive by this time on the fourth day.

"He's not here yet."

The voice was that of a woman— a shade— sitting on a rock in a Thracian wedding dress, a broad cuff of gold on her finger.

"Doesn't he come on the hour?" Athena asked.

"Something's wrong. There is so much grief here."

"Well… this is…" she began, haltingly. "You've passed to the Other Side, you know."

"Oh, I'm aware that I'm dead. But a terrible thing has happened here. Surely you feel it…"

Athena nodded. There was a deeper sorrow in the stillness.

"I wasn't supposed to die as I did," the shade blurted.

Athena sighed gently. The girl's thread had been cut by the indomitable will of the Fates. How on Gaia's earth could she explain, or offer comfort? Mortals simply… were. And then they weren't. And she had little to do with their coming and going. Those who had *touched* a corpse were barred from her temple until they'd been fully cleansed.

"I'm sure everyone says that." The shade looked away, abashed.

Athena shrugged. "I'm sorry."

A ripple teased the shore of the Styx. A bowsprit appeared, a dim lantern held aloft in the iron teeth of the central of three hound heads.

She smiled, snorting to break the tension. "You're late."

Charon's face was cloaked, only his mouth visible. His lip trembled.

"Oh, right…" Athena produced an obol. Charon looked at her, his eyes unfocused, and snatched the coin from her outstretched hand.

"Not you," he croaked, looking past Athena. "I'm not bound for the Trivium. You wait."

The shade retreated from the boat and returned her coin to the hollow under her tongue. Athena raised an eyebrow. Hermes had told her shades would share the boat with her— that Charon ferried them across to face the judges before moving on to the Palace. She climbed in carefully and sat at the stern bracing, her sandals wet from wading into the Styx. The Boatman cast off silently. Athena was unnerved— Persephone spoke of him fondly, Hermes less so, but Charon's talkative reputation was well known. Instead of the expected riddles, he pushed on silently, as wooden as the craft itself. She cleared her throat to gain his attention. "Charon…"

"You will know soon enough." His voice wavered.

"What do you mean?"

He stilled his oar and turned to her. The boat dragged to a halt in the middle of the river. He shook, eyes sunken and red.

"Persephone…" The quiet closed in. "Charon, you must tell me what happened."

"She was sitting as you are…" He ran the back of his hand across his eyes, then stood and plunged his oar back into the water. "I was helpless. I couldn't…"

"Couldn't what?"

"Save her! I couldn't row fast enough! The child is lost. It's…" Charon shuddered and she covered her mouth with her hand. "So little remains. So very little…"

A tear tumbled down Athena's cheek. "But… how?"

"I don't know. More urgent matters await us." Charon gave a final push against the deep and the prow scraped the rocks.

Athena clambered out, looking up into the mists at the dark escarpment of the palace. Winding halls and hollowed-out balconies twisted through the cliffs. At the entrance stood a great golden poplar. Charon pulled back his hood and turned to her.

"You, Olympian… I remember your mother fondly. We all do. I pray to the Fates that her wisdom survives in you."

Athena frowned. "I don't understand."

"Please. You must convince Persephone to let Zagreus go." Charon's eyes were wet with tears. "There is no other way."

She shook her head, overwhelmed and mystified. "How do I reach her?"

"Take the hallway…"

Athena darted through the labyrinthine palace, following Charon's careful directions. From the atrium to the entrance hall, piled high with offerings from the world above. Broad steps led upward. She stood in front of their cold chairs. The throne room was dark, braziers unlit, celebrations canceled, hopes dashed. She passed the olivine dais, lifting a tapestry to find the narrow staircase hidden behind it. At the top was a set of doors inlaid with gold and lapis and to the right a hallway.

She turned down the corridor and looked out across the wide Styx. All the torches were out. She could barely see.

A woman appeared in her path, red hair strung with selenite beads. Hecate.

"Where is she? How did this happen?"

"First we tend to the fruit, then seek what gnaws at the roots," she said. The Goddess of the Crossroads was haggard, her face drawn and weary. Blood, Persephone's blood, streaked her white peplos.

"Hecate, please!" Athena whispered sharply. "Charon let me cross when by rights he should have turned me away. Please tell me something. Anything."

Hecate leaned against the wall. "I could only save his heart. The rest is as if beset by wolves— but as no man or god has seen."

"Because she came here?"

"Chthonia would not do this wickedness. His small heart holds the truth, and it must not die."

"So he is alive!"

"Held fragile by chthonic sorceries and ethereal conjuration. But a shell is not life. And it will crack: if the moon shines full while he is still below, the light, in turn, will fade from his heart."

"Then why hesitate?" She knit her brows together, voice rising. "If he needs to go above, take him above, Hecate!"

"Persephone is as all mothers are when a child would be taken."

Athena sighed. *I pray to the Fates that her wisdom survives in you.* "Can she not break through her grief long enough to see that keeping him here is madness?"

Hecate's lips thinned. "To wrench Zagreus's heart from her breast would dig a hole for the madness to pour into. That curse swims freely in your bloodline, and above all, I fear its teeth."

Athena drew in a long breath. "Where is Persephone?"

"Ahead. In her tattered nest. Her husband watches with raven's eyes."

"How is he?"

"He has taken grief as his consort; and guilt, his solace against all wisdom."

"Let me speak with them."

"Let the wise beware to walk where they will not be known, little owl."

She placed her hand on Hecate's shoulder. "Charon told me something." She let a tear trickle down her cheek and fixed her clear grey eyes on Hecate. "I am my mother's daughter. You put yourself in Metis's hands long ago. I beg of you now, put Persephone in mine. I can speak with her. Reason with her. And if you are right, and if there was any treachery behind this, we will uncover it together."

Hecate covered Athena's hand with her own and squeezed her fingers. She nodded. "Come."

The hall was long— the queen's quarters at its end. This was intentional, Persephone had told her once. Aidoneus had built the chambers millennia ago to give her a place to grow comfortable in this world, then become his wife at a time of her choosing. But the Fates paid no heed to his plans. Not then, and not now. They entered an antechamber hewn entirely from amethyst and Hecate held up her hand to signal a halt. Aidoneus was crowded in the frame of a heavy set of doors, barefoot, unshaven, his head leaning heavily in his hand, fingers laced through a tangle of dark hair.

Athena waited quietly for him to look up at her. His eyes were bloodshot like he hadn't slept in days. She drew out her skirts and curtsied low. "Your grace."

"Forgive me." He didn't meet her gaze. His voice was thin and fragile, so different from his commanding, inexorable presence at court. "I forgot you were coming."

Athena knelt. "No, please. The Ferryman had every reason to ask me to turn back."

He was quiet for a moment. "He knew you were needed. Charon is a devoted servant of *ananke,* despite all he's endured…"

She nodded. "Perhaps the Fates had a reason for allowing my passage, then. I'm sure Hecate told you there's little time left."

"I know."

"My lord, I want your permission to speak with your wife."

"You needn't ask it," he said distantly. "But she will not speak. She hasn't since…"

Athena nodded. She clenched and unclenched her fists, trying to push the consequences of failure from her mind. She opened one side of the doors and peered around. Lamplight illuminated the walls, extending upward to a dome of opal where nymphs draped gossamer linen panels around an empty wooden crib, hewn from ebony and date palm.

On the floor she saw a tangle of dark fabric, arms and legs protruding. Athena tamped down the urge to run to her or call out. Persephone lay on her side, her body curled around a heavy box inscribed with sigils from the worlds above and below. Athena knew nothing of the esoteric, but she could still sense its potency. Within this box was Zagreus's beating heart— all that remained of Persephone's long-sought child.

Athena padded across the room, stopping at Persephone's feet. The Queen of the Underworld merely stared, unmoving. Athena knelt, then lay down across from her, cheek on the cold floor. Persephone remained still and limp, looking into nothing. Athena waited.

Persephone met her gaze, finally.

"I am so sorry," said Athena.

A tear leaked out of Persephone's eye. She drew her knees tighter around the box.

"This isn't the end," Athena said. "I was there with you in Eleusis… when they said that death is not the end."

Persephone closed her eyes and her face twisted, anguished. Athena reached for her hand, squeezing her fingers.

"Sister… Zagreus is *alive*. He is the god of rebirth. This is part of his story— another feat the mortals will sing about him when he is grown. How he overcame death before he even drew the first breath of life."

Persephone shook her head slowly, feverishly.

"He is immortal. There is no question that he will live forever despite—" She stopped herself and stroked Persephone's palm. "I must take him above to protect him. Let me go where you cannot, do what you cannot."

Persephone stared blankly for a long moment, then exhaled a whimper.

"Will you help me save him? Please."

Her lip trembled. Persephone's voice was little more than a whisper. "Zagreus…"

A tear trickled over Athena's nose and landed on the black marble. "Persephone, I swear to you on the Styx, whose waters I have newly crossed, that I will safeguard your baby to the ends of the earth. I will bring Hecate with me, and we will find a way to bring your son back to you."

Persephone uncoiled and gulped in a long breath. She placed Athena's hand on the box and her features twisted, then rolled onto her back, staring at the ceiling, tears streaming into her hairline.

Athena touched the box gingerly, then gathered it to her. She leaned over Persephone and kissed her on the forehead. "Persephone, listen to me. What I swear now is deeper than any oath on any river. As your friend, your sister, I promise you he will live."

She picked up the box and looked once more at Persephone before walking toward the door.

"Wait."

Athena froze.

"Where is Aidon?"

Athena heard him shuffle outside the doorway, and the other door creaked open. He staggered in and knelt, gathering her up in his arms. Persephone had gone silent but his muffled sobs filled the room.

She offered the box to Hecate. The Goddess of the Crossroads held up splayed palms. "He is your charge."

"Isn't he safer in your hands?"

"All roads lead to two destinations. You came here with an owl's wings and insight, even unknowing; and you must go too, swift and silent." Hecate motioned to Athena and she followed.

"The full moon is in two days! I cannot make the trip in time from here, and I have no means to travel between the realms as you do."

"The dark chariot outpaces even winged sandals. Those wheels will carry us to the corporeal world, then you shall fly for Olympus. Before the name of Zagreus echoes across that peak, I must bend the ear of Demeter."

Athena nodded and stared down at the box.

"Let no eyes nor ears but yours cast upon that heart, Daughter of Metis. He must go to the citadel of Gaia and Ouranos to survive, yet there may we also find the thorned roots of the treachery that unmade him."

12.

T RIPTOLEMUS STOKED THE HEARTH FIRE. "I KNOW you're not *that* cold."

He threw in a handful of small branches and rose from a crouch. Demeter surveyed him with hungry eyes, her skin cast in golden firelight, a saffron wool blanket drawn up, her hair spilling across the pillow. She bit the back of her finger and smiled.

He shook his head. "You got me out of bed to watch me."

"So what if I did?"

He turned to face her, tall and smiling. Flickers and shadows danced along the indent of his hip. She stretched her arms above her head and arched her back. Triptolemus vaulted the space between them, pouncing on the bed. She yelped and he peppered kisses over her shoulder and breast, then her lips, pulling at them sumptuously. "I missed this. It's good to see you happy again."

"I missed this too. Thank you," she said, sheepishly, "for everything since we returned from Thassos. This hasn't been easy, and neither am I. I know that." She traced his shoulder and arm, then took his palm in her hands, massaging his fingers. "I'll be less anxious when I know she's delivered."

He played with a curl of her hair. "Do you regret refusing to attend her?"

"I can't fathom traveling there. I'm glad I can stand to be in the same room as Aidoneus these days, but his kingdom still regards me as the enemy."

"You should go anyway."

She balked at his frankness. "She's not expecting me."

"All the more reason," he said. "My grandmother helped deliver me, and later two of my sisters. She went to the afterlife before Deme and Demophon came, and it was all my mother could talk about, not having her there. I know it's not—"

There was a knock at the door. Triptolemus leaped out of bed and wound his himation around him. He disappeared around the corner and Demeter heard hinges creak.

"Yes?"

"There's a visitor here," Keryx whispered from outside.

"Can't it wait until sunrise?"

"No. It's an emissary…" His voice wavered. "From below. For our Lady."

She held her breath, unable to discern their whispers. Triptolemus returned, frowning. "I've never seen him so ill at ease."

"Who is here?" Demeter asked.

"A woman from below. Short of stature, cryptic speech, wouldn't tell Keryx a thing."

Demeter sat bolt upright. She threw back the blanket and dressed, tied on her sandals, and wound up the mess of her hair. Triptolemus dressed for the outdoor chill and banked the fire against sparks. They walked down the stairs by brazier light, then by a four-post torch picked from the wall. Demeter opened the Telesterion door.

Hecate stood cloaked in white, her favored garb before the full moon. Her face was careworn and she looked aged beyond her maiden form.

Demeter clenched her jaw. "Why are you here?"

"Two paths lead me to one door. One, that you hear a true voice before the winds bring echoes. Two, your daughter…"

"Is she well? And the baby!?"

Hecate looked down. "She is safe, guarded by her mate. But the babe…"

Demeter's throat constricted. Frost prickled the dying flowers. "No…"

"What? What's wrong?!" Triptolemus raised his voice.

"Patience, Demeter…" Hecate's torch flickered and extinguished.

She cried out and fell against Triptolemus. A snowflake melted on her cheek and the air grew chill. More flakes clumped and settled to the icy ground. "This cannot be!" The wind began to whip through the snowfall.

"Deme!" Triptolemus held her tightly.

"On *your* watch!" Demeter roared at her. "How could you have let this happen?"

"Demeter, do not bury the mortals in your grief!" Hecate shouted over the sudden gale.

"Why not?! Let the Fates save them, just as they *protected* my child! My Kore…" Demeter screamed into the wind, fists clenched, sobbing.

"Raining death upon the mortals will flood your daughter's lands. Let them rest, that she may rest!"

Demeter shook in Triptolemus's arms. The wind calmed, the last snowflakes melting as the frost receded. She wept and collapsed. Triptolemus eased her to the ground. He looked up at Hecate. "Please, my lady, tell us what happened."

"She crossed the Styx with Aidoneus in the Ferryman's boat. They alighted on the shore having trod the ethereal path—"

"The ether? He took my pregnant daughter into the Void between realms? How could he be so reckless?!"

"Those same long footsteps likely saved—" Hecate bit back her words. "The ill winds blew *not* on Aidon's path."

"How do you know? You've always been quick to pronounce him blameless."

"Demeter…" Triptolemus helped her stand. "*O helioeida…* please. Remember what you told me— he *never* wanted her to go below. Surely he was cautious."

"What account has he given for himself?" Demeter demanded.

"Aidoneus swims in a bog of guilt and sinks into its sorrowful depths. Little escapes the prison of his lips, save the pangs that wracked her womb. But they began in the world above."

"Entirely normal for an expectant mother," Demeter said, throwing her shoulders back. "As any who've carried children would know."

Hecate pursed her lips. "Perhaps."

"So you cast blame on me, who saw her last on this earth."

"No. I am certain the strangling vine grew from Olympus. I need your help."

"How?"

"Neither owl nor crow can see it. But a mother's eyes see far and look deep. And yours have spied the serpent already…"

∗　　∗　　∗

The shades in the boat would not speak to her. She was as much a ghost to them as she would be to Orpheus in the world above. Charon moored the boat at the dock and a pathway led up from the river. A towering black marble frieze stood in the distance.

Eurydice tried not to think about Orpheus's grief— about how he'd buried her just days after they would have been married. She'd considered wandering the dark roads between the

269

worlds, but didn't know the way back, and could scarcely remember time transpiring between her last glimpse of daylight and finding herself at the Styx. She twisted the golden scroll, wrapped ring-like around her finger.

Eurydice, Beloved of Orpheus.

The queen would recognize her. If only he'd told her where to go, or etched a map on that tiny scroll, so she could plead before Persephone. But knowledge of this landscape was beyond even him.

"Welcome home," the Boatman said. "The Trivium is that way. Go to the spring beside it and wait to be called."

"Charon, is it?"

"Who doesn't know my name?"

"I beg your pardon, but I must speak with the queen."

"Oh?"

"She…" *How stupid and conceited he must think I am.* "She would know me."

He cast his eyes down. "Even if I could take you there, she will receive no one right now."

Charon cast off, and Eurydice was left standing on the dock, alone. She walked up the path and around a bend. A hulking mass lay by the side of the road, a serpentine tail wrapped around the body of a dog. Eurydice swallowed the stone in her throat. Cerberus was whining with each breath, almost too soft to hear, and while two heads seemed to be sleeping, one sat atop them staring forlornly into the distance. She had heard tales of this frightening creature, who would devour any soul who tried escaping Asphodel. All he seemed to her now was sad— enormous and terrifying, but whimpering like a pup put out for the night. She stood in front of the beast, wishing to comfort him, but before her fingers could reach to stroke his wiry fur, one of the sleeping heads growled. She sprang away. The whimpering head snorted and the great beast rolled over and curled up, face turned from the path. Two breaths later, he was crying again.

Gravel crunched under her feet. The frieze loomed, its black columns sharper. She heard a trickle in the distance and followed the sound. A few shades stood huddled around one side of a long rectangular pool enclosed with stones. Bronze cups hung on chains in a row, submerged in the water. The shades stared over the edge and Eurydice followed their gaze. The water wavered, but the pool reflected nothing— not even her face.

"Eurydice, daughter of Erymanthe."

She looked up, surprised. They had called her name, though others were waiting. Was she late? Three men sat on the raised dais of the frieze, and a painfully beautiful woman with golden wings and coiled hair stood behind the man in the center. The bald man spoke a single word.

"Asphodel."

"But…"

"Do you wish to plead otherwise?"

"There is no changing my fate, I know," she said.

"Then what have you to say?"

"My husband— well, he would have been within the hour of my death, if – he was initiated at Eleusis and will go to Elysion. I beg of you—"

"Were you initiated?"

"No."

"I'm sorry. The laws of this realm are firm. You will drink the waters of the Lethe and be at peace in Asphodel." He pointed two fingers at the broad pool in front of her.

"My husband was Orpheus," she called out. She knew she had little time. "He and I helped conduct the rites on Samothrace this spring, which gave your King and Queen their long-sought child. I guided Queen Persephone and helped her gather the needed herbs for the rite. Please, I *must* speak with her."

The judges exchanged glances and the winged woman pursed her lips. The judge sitting to the right shook his head. "It seems you have not heard."

"What?"

"Rhadamanthys, she isn't—"

"She will remember *nothing*, Minos. It may help her seek peace, so she doesn't end up waiting like *them*."

Rhadamanthys pointed, and Eurydice looked at the few shades staring at the water.

"If you choose not to drink from the Lethe, Eurydice, you will remain here— entranced by the waters and lost to your indecision. That one," Minos said, pointing at a dark-haired woman in a flounced skirt, "has been standing here unmoved since before the destruction of Akrotiri."

"Don't become as they are." Rhadamanthys nodded before continuing. "The King and Queen will not grant you an audience, I'm afraid. They mourn the loss of that same child."

Eurydice's jaw dropped. "Zagreus is dead?"

"I told you not to say anything!" Minos hissed.

The winged woman tightened her grip on the scourge, but dark tears stung her eyes.

Eurydice cried. "I felt that something terrible had happened. But…"

Rhadamanthys ignored his brother's grumbling. "As for your beloved, you may yet see him again— but not in these lands. If you know a little of the Eleusinian Mysteries then you know that death is not the end."

She wiped her nose with her sleeve. "I do."

Aeacus spoke. "I am sorry, child. Hearsay is not enough; you haven't completed the rites, so your fate is inescapable. Your life is at an end, and in time your beloved's life will also end. As we all do. Do not cling to the pain of your mortality and follow in *their* path. Choose to go on. And to one day be born to the world again."

Eurydice's eyes watered. She looked at the blank expression of the woman from old Crete, and back at the judges. She hauled up a bronze cup, hand over hand, its contents sloshing and spilling over the edge. Orpheus was lost to her. The child was lost, and with him, all hope of pleading for Elysion. All paths led here. All ends for everyone led to this pool, this moment. As she brought the cup to her lips, all the pain and loss fled her thoughts.

The water was warm.

✻   ✻   ✻

Damn you, Demeter, she thought.

Hestia bundled her himation tighter. Last night's deep frost had reached its icy fingers under the door and up the outer wall. Now she had to dry her sage leaves and hemp flowers before they started to mold. Some were already too far gone.

Hestia pulled loose a flower and coated it with ambrosia. She crushed it with a twist of her fingers, then dropped an ember from her fire into the stone mortar. Her hooded veil kept the wafting fumes in and she inhaled the smoldering flowers. She pushed the cloth away and breathed the bracing air, then muffled a cough and sat back, closing her eyes, flooded with warmth and pleasant numbness, her limbs heavy. A persistent clucking of disapproval filled her head, a voice that sounded a bit like her brother's or Apollo's. Someone rapped at the door and Hestia fell back on her elbow, then snorted. *Perfect timing.*

"Coming!" She stood and dusted herself off, then sauntered to the door and pulled it open.

"May I enter?" Demeter stood at the door, her eyes puffy.

Hestia tried to hide her shock. "Of course." She stood aside as Demeter trudged in and looked around. "It's been a while."

"I know. I'm sorry. I rarely find myself on Olympus."

"What brings you here? Usually," she coughed into her sleeve and cleared her throat, "you're in Eleusis this time of year, yes?"

"Usually." Demeter sat down on the divan. Her gaze drifted over the drying herbs.

"From the Bactrian roads," Hestia said. "Lovely flowers, this time of year."

"I'm familiar with them."

"Would you care for some?"

"Not now, and I'm sorry to have interrupted you. I'm sure you weren't expecting company. I came to speak with you and Hera before Hermes said anything. But she won't receive me."

"She's kept to herself the past fortnight. I haven't seen her either— don't take it personally."

"That's unlike her," Demeter said, her voice taking on a quiet edge.

"There was… trouble between her and Zeus. She hasn't sat there since the night he left," Hestia said, nodding to Demeter's divan.

"If you see her," Demeter said, "you could convey the news, I suppose. If Hermes or Iris doesn't…" Demeter stared at the floor. She shook, her lip quivering.

"What happened?"

"Kore— my daughter. Hestia, she…" Demeter swallowed. "Persephone lost her baby."

The cold that crept up Hestia's spine could have banked the fire of Olympus. She covered her mouth with her hands, trying to hide at least some of her reaction. Her heart drummed.

"We don't know how it happened."

Hestia's breath caught in her throat. *It couldn't… she wouldn't…* "When?"

"She was crossing the Styx with Aidoneus, and felt pangs like she was giving birth, and her courses started…"

Demeter's voice became muted, lost in the tumult between the ringing in Hestia's ears and the aftereffects of the hemp. She would be thrown into the lowest level of Tartarus. Bound in chains next to her accursed father. Tears stung her eyes. Demeter was crying, her words coming in bursts between sobs. Hestia heard something about Hecate seeing her in Eleusis last night…

"…and I couldn't stop myself, in my grief… I froze everything, all the last stalks of wheat ruined. Even the sea iced over before I could regain control."

Hestia got up and sat next to her, holding Demeter, letting her sister cry into the folds of her himation, her head bowed to her bosom. Hestia's jaw clenched. Hera had come to her broken and ravished— how could Hestia *not* believe Hera with the state she was in? And to have wagered their kinship, their aeons-long sisterhood… Hestia tried to tamp down her anger lest the hearth fire flare out of control.

Ambrosia will delay the effects by at least two days…

Hera met with Persephone exactly two days before she went below. She'd poisoned her. *Murdered* Aidoneus and Persephone's child with the very silphium Hestia had given her and timed it to coincide with Persephone's descent. And she'd secluded herself since. It was all too clear.

"Hecate says there was something darker at work."

Hestia swallowed, terrified that somehow Demeter had read her thoughts. Her alarm went unnoticed by her bawling sister. If she told Demeter what happened, what would her sister do? She almost destroyed the earth over her daughter once… "What makes her think so?"

"It's a suspicion. But my poor Kore is listless, and Aidoneus lays the blame on himself. They cannot…"

Demeter sobbed afresh. The weight of her sister's sorrow sank into her bones. If the truth were to become known, it would mean war between the realms. First Zeus and Demeter keep Aidoneus's wife from him for half the year, and now this? If he discovered Hera and, by association, Hestia had caused his child to die, he would lay waste to the earth and Olympus.

She would say nothing. She could still deny her part if they sought her out later, and would have to cling to that. But she must be silent now when vengeance would be foremost on Hades's mind. "Can you go to her? To comfort her?"

"I cannot. Hecate understands that I am not responsible for this, I believe, but Nyx's children are suspicious of me. Always. They despise me. I fear the Boatman would heave me over the side if there's even a whisper of condemnation among them."

She swallowed. "If I can help in any way…"

"There's nothing to be done now."

Hestia's voice ground dry. "No. Not yet, at least."

✻   ✻   ✻

"You may enter."

"Not unless you promise," Hermes said through the door.

Apollo laughed. "Fine. I swear I'm alone."

Hermes pushed open the door to Apollo's antechamber and was greeted by sunny warmth filtered through panes of thick quartz. Apollo sat on a divan, golden himation slung over his shoulder and around his waist, basking in the late autumn sunlight.

"Who brought that?" Hermes pointed at the wine in Apollo's hand.

"Not Ganymede, if that's what you're thinking." He took a sip and laughed. "He is searching for entertainment though, while Zeus winters elsewhere. You should go to him. He's more fond of your cock than mine, anyway."

276

"There are more urgent matters at hand, Apollo."

He lolled his head back with a dramatic sigh. "Of course there are. You seldom come to me for anything else these days."

"Who granted Asklepios immortality? Was it you?"

"How in Tartarus could I, even if I wanted to? Only the Children of Kronos can do that."

"I'm trying to help you, Apollo," Hermes said, stalking closer. "When Zeus returns, he will want answers."

"It could have been any of them. Maybe Poseidon, to gall Zeus, or Hades changed his mind. Or Zeus did it to teach Hades a lesson after he came here and made such a spectacle of himself this summer."

"I doubt it."

"You could start by asking him." Apollo swirled the wine in its cup.

"I have no idea where Zeus is," he lied, "and I'm not going to him now. He has a new lover and Hera is doubtless watching my every move."

"I don't know what to tell you. This is the first I've heard of it."

Hermes narrowed his eyes. "You of all people know I would be the last to believe that."

Apollo chortled. "Fine. I learned of it just after Zeus's bolt failed to kill him. If it's any consolation, I *will* take Asklepios in. He won't be conjuring the dead again, but we need a God of Medicine. Men are learning too much too fast to not have one, and I'm preoccupied with music these days." He glared at Hermes and raised his voice. "Speaking of…"

"Don't. My answer is the same as last time."

"Why not? Orpheus isn't using it."

Hermes cocked an eyebrow. "What?"

"It's gone silent since his woman died." He idly picked at a thread on his himation.

"When did Eurydice die?"

"A week ago, and he hasn't played since."

"And you care not?"

"Why should I? It was a season's romance. He'll get over it. But he's not playing his way out of it. And since he no longer plays my lyre, I want it back."

"No. And you know why I can't."

"I'm no idiot, Hermes." Apollo's lip curled. "I *know* who asked you for my lyre. And with the latest news from the Underworld, that promise is now as useless to him as it was to Orpheus."

Hermes stared at him, jaw slack, brow knit.

Apollo rolled his eyes. "Would it make you happier if I *feigned* sympathy?"

"They lost their child!"

"Oh, save your outrage! Everyone knows it was conceived unnaturally. The cosmos always balances itself, and it does so again."

"With the loss of *their child?!*"

"More pity them, but they should have known better. They're gods of everything that dies. If they didn't see this coming, they're fools." Apollo waved him away. "I'm sure the miscarriage will be forgotten in time."

Hermes shook his head. "You know, both you and I were conceived on the wrong side of the blanket, Apollo."

Apollo shrugged and took another sip of wine.

"But you really are an irredeemable bastard."

Apollo slammed down his cup in answer, but Hermes was already gone.

✵ ✵ ✵

Aidon held Persephone until tears ran dry. He lifted her carefully and carried her to their room, then set her down alongside their hearth and washed her with a sea sponge and warm water until she no longer smelled of blood.

Persephone said nothing.

Athena and Hecate had departed for the world above, carrying Zagreus's remains. He recalled when he'd tended to Persephone after their first journey to Tartarus after the Keres almost tore *him* to pieces and *his* blood stained their skin. He scoured himself and purified their clothing in the Phlegethon fire.

She didn't move.

Aidon picked her up again and carried her to their bed. After an hour she finally drifted off, and he allowed himself to follow. Persephone's pitched wailing woke him in the night. He jostled her into wakefulness and she fell silent again, and he held and rocked her until she closed her eyes. He couldn't fall back to sleep.

When she awoke, she stood, saying nothing. He helped her dress in silence. *She will need time*, Hecate had said. Persephone huddled at the foot of the bed, staring into the flames. Aidoneus sat quietly beside her. Light faded from the Styx, and night fell again. Aidon helped her undress for bed and fitful rest.

She woke the next morning and he asked if she wanted to go downstairs. She shook her head. He was restless: their world had contracted to only their bedroom. Aidoneus stood on the balcony that night, the full moon washing the river and Fields of Asphodel in silver.

It was their anniversary.

Persephone walked to his side and stood, her arms wrapped around her middle, staring into the gray reaches beyond the river. Aidon waited.

"It's so quiet."

It was the first she'd spoken since... His insides twisted. "I know."

"We danced last year."

"We will again," he said. Persephone leaned on his shoulder, the waterfall beside the balcony whipping the air around them into a soft breeze. "Someday."

Her silence stretched on.

"I thought, if you wish it," Aidon began, "we could walk through Elysion together."

She shook her head and trudged back into their room, curling into a ball on the bed. Aidon stared out, his hand tightening into a fist. He unclenched his hand and returned inside, fitted himself against her back, and followed her into sleep.

A knock woke them in the morning. Aidoneus twisted to pull his wrinkled himation out from under him, then kissed Persephone on her shoulder. She was motionless, but her eyes were open.

He left the bedroom and crossed their antechamber, then cracked the door. "Now isn't the time."

"Even so, the Thief must steal some from you. And his ill message may help us learn who—"

"I don't know what you see in pursuing this... wild theory, Hecate. It is clear that we are not meant—" he glanced toward the bedroom and closed the door behind him, lowering his voice. "That we aren't meant to have children. This will happen every time if we bring a babe in the womb between the worlds."

"Your certainty has strong roots?"

"Does it matter?"

"Her heart still reaches for that sunlight."

Aidoneus bristled. "Where is Hermes?"

He followed her down the stairs and moved the tapestry. The Messenger knelt before the dais, *petasos* in hand. Aidoneus skirted by and settled on his throne.

"My lord, I want to say, and I hope you'll believe me… I grieve for you. I am so sorry for your loss and when I heard, I felt it deeply. I…" He glanced up, his face drawn.

Aidoneus nodded once and took a long breath. He avoided looking Hermes in the eye.

"I've lost children before," Hermes blurted. "Mortal children, after they'd lived their lives, and I escorted them here, but—"

"Stop. Please." Aidon said just above a whisper. Hermes fiddled with the edge of his hat as Aidon descended the dais. "I thank you for your sympathy, Psychopompos."

"If there is anything I can do, you'll let me know, yes?"

"I will, and thank you," he repeated and cleared his throat. "Why do you come here?"

"I wouldn't interrupt your grieving except for an important question."

"From Zeus?"

"I hope to have an answer in hand before he asks. Would you know anything about Asklepios being made an immortal?"

Aidon drew back, shock furrowing his brow. "No."

"Then it wasn't you."

"I wanted him sent to Tartarus, not made a god!" Aidon roared. "Who is responsible for this?" Hermes cowered, and he raised an open palm in apology.

Hermes spoke low. "That is what I'm trying to discover. I suspect Apollo is involved and may have sought petty vengeance."

"For what?"

"He deduced the reason Orpheus was given his lyre."

Aidon shook his head. "I can't say I'm surprised. His objections at court to ending Asklepios were… unusual. He rarely cares for his *hemitheoi* children."

"But he can't render a mortal deathless. Unless one of the Children of Kronos instructed him."

"None of us would share that knowledge."

"So you'd never tell Persephone, despite sharing everything else?"

"Never. She knows I keep that from her, and why— why we *all* keep it. It is too much power for any of us to have. Or have ever *had*. History has borne that out."

Hermes nodded, his voice gentle. "How is she?"

Aidon sighed and sat on the edge of the dais; Hermes joined him. "She will not leave our room. Or speak. Or sleep longer than an hour or so."

"I can only hope she becomes herself again soon."

"Or at all."

"She will in time. Won't she?"

"I'm not sure of anything right now," he confessed. Aidon ran his fingers back through his hair. "Least of all, who among the six of us would aid Apollo. Zeus?"

"Doubtful. Why bother with a thunderbolt?"

"To avoid culpability. Still unlikely."

"Perhaps Demeter? She has a troublesome history with you."

Aidoneus looked down. "She does, but she would never spite her daughter."

"Poseidon has allied with Apollo before," Hermes said.

"They despise each other now. Poseidon has nothing to gain. What of Hestia or Hera?"

"What of them?" Hermes considered. "Hestia is, well, Hestia. She has less cause than anyone. And Hera has thought about nothing this year but Zeus abandoning her. First for Alcmene, and now the princess in Tiryns… Semele, I think. I also can't imagine her crossing your wife after the friendship they've developed this past year."

"You're right. Find out first if Zeus is responsible. There's little I can do if he is."

Hermes groaned. "Hera is stalking me like a lioness. I cannot go to him now."

"You *must*. There is too much he doesn't know. He must be told that one of the Six rendered Asklepios immortal. And he needs to know that… that my son is…"

He couldn't finish the sentence.

13.

*"*Y*OU HAUNT THE SACRED HOUSE OF HADES AND Persephone..."*

He was certain he heard it this time. Hermes halted mid-flight.

"You give men sleep, from which you rouse them again."

He'd know the sound of *that* lyre if he were seeking it blind and drunk. It was *his* after all— before a game of chance left it at Apollo's feet. Hermes reached a crack in the earth that led to Samothrace, and listened again.

"And they gave you leave to lead the souls forth. Hermes... hear me, guide me, grant me a good end..."

The voice haunted the lyre's melody, a perfect pitch as dry as autumn leaves, as though its owner had sung for days on end. Apollo told him Orpheus had gone silent. To his ears, perhaps— but the hymnist's voice echoed through the depths of the earth. Hermes had been drawn to Samothrace years before when Orpheus composed a very different, far cheerier hymn. He flew to a fathom below the source.

"Orpheus?"

The music ceased. Hermes willed himself to the surface, alighting on bare stone. The man's lips were cracked, his feet caked in mud, a tattered *zeira* his only shelter. He stared up at Hermes. "My lord… You're here."

"How long have you been—" He slumped to the side and Hermes caught Orpheus just before his head cracked against the rock. "Orpheus, wake up!"

Hermes laid him on his side. He was exhausted, gone too long without food or water. Should he give him ambrosia? He was a *hemitheoi*; would it kill him as it would a full-blooded mortal? He couldn't risk it. In a flash, Hermes was off to the old northward city. He gathered a bladder of water, a handful of figs, and a crust of bread from… well, he wasn't sure which tables they came from, but none of it would be greatly missed. Thanks to Hades's generosity in spring, Samothrace was flush with sundries from the mainland.

An instant later he sat beside the unconscious man and held his head up, forcing his lips to the water skin. Orpheus drank and sputtered.

"Are you awake yet?"

"Take me… they know me," his voice crackled. "Eurydice. I deserved to die. Not her."

"You're delirious." Hermes sat him up. "Drink some more water. Oh, and I brought these."

"I'm not hungry."

"You're starving."

"Just take me to the Underworld. Please."

"Oh, no, I'm not helping you end yourself. You'd be separated from her and Elysion."

"She wasn't initiated. I'd be kept from there, just as she is."

"Orpheus." Hermes crouched. "I know you're grieving. I am so sorry. But her thread was cut."

"There are no serpents on Samothrace."

"What of it?"

"I angered Axiokersos and Axiokersa. I revealed the name of their son and trespassed on their goodwill. They sent a viper to kill her."

Hermes frowned. "That doesn't sound like them. Aidoneus isn't..." He scanned the dimming horizon and picked at his fingernail. "Look, it's getting late. You'll need a fire. Wait here."

Hermes flew again, this time borrowing a bundle of wood and flint and firestone. The house already had a roaring hearth fire and a cord of wood stacked outside. It probably wouldn't be missed. Orpheus jumped when Hermes landed moments later.

"Where did this come from?"

"I... found it. It's not important. Just light a fire before we both freeze. I must consider your request."

Orpheus arranged the wood over a pile of dry leaves and struck the firestone against the flint. Hermes wound his himation around himself, his *petasos* tipped back. Soon the flames roared and danced between them.

"You've been without a fire this whole time?"

"Yes." Orpheus took a timid bite from a fig.

"There are wild dogs here. You could have been torn apart."

"Three approached me two nights ago— hungry. But they listened as I sang, and lay down."

"Ha!"

"What did you mean earlier? You said that a snake doesn't sound like... them."

"They're not petty. If you had wronged them, your punishment would be direct." Hermes paused, minding his tongue. "Presently, they have no thought for you at all, Orpheus. Her fate sounds like misfortune. Your island has seen ships recently. People here to trade, to see *you*, in particular," Hermes said with a half-grin. It melted when he saw Orpheus staring into the flames. "A serpent could have slipped into a hold."

"No. It was no common snake. They found it hours later, near where she fell. It didn't look sick or injured. It had simply… stopped."

Hermes looked at Orpheus quizzically. "What did it look like?"

"Shimmering green like a peafowl's tail, a pattern of teardrops and lines on its back, the likes of which I'd never seen."

Hermes froze. A year ago, he had brought word to Olympus from Thebes: Zeus's son by Alcmene had nearly been killed by two such snakes. Little Herakles had strangled them in the crib, saving his twin brother. Zeus was angered but told Hermes to say nothing— that he would deal with Hera when the time came. Why would Hera send a viper after Eurydice? Perhaps at Persephone's behest? That didn't sound like the Queen of the Underworld. Hermes had witnessed *her* wrath.

"Tell me how you might have displeased them."

"I am sworn to secrecy."

"They joined in your rites in spring, didn't they?" Hermes chuckled at Orpheus's alarmed expression. "I'm more clever than I look."

"I said their son's name aloud in the temple."

"They would not be so capricious. Especially now, since…" He bit back his words. Orpheus didn't need to know Zagreus was dead. He was here to offer comfort, and the man's *cultus* would tear itself to pieces if they knew. He changed the subject. "How did you put the jackals to sleep? Probably not by singing about me."

"No. I sang a hymn to Hades and Persephone, honoring their marriage; and it was a plea for Eurydice to return as if I stood before them."

"Would you sing it again for me?"

Orpheus leaned the lyre against his shoulder. He tuned up the scale, then plucked in intervals. Hermes found the tune familiar, but when Orpheus sang, he was transfixed. The harmony of instrument and voice echoed into the chambers behind him, surrounding Hermes, washing over him. Orpheus poured out his verses, describing the gods below as few knew them, and eulogizing Eurydice. Hermes pondered the unknowable wrath inflicted upon her and felt a flash of anger at Apollo's pettiness. He thought of Aidoneus, sitting despondently at the edge of the dais, unable to even speak of his lost child. Hermes wiped tears from his eyes.

Apollo's son sang of a love that Hermes had never known himself. He'd felt that rare void before— when he'd stood before the King and Queen of the Underworld, sent by Zeus to separate them forever, wondering why he'd been ordered so when they loved each other. Orpheus had loved Eurydice for only a season, yet time seemed an inadequate measure for so deep a thing. Apollo's callousness… the coveted lyre… Hera's serpent… He couldn't be the herald of such deeds, not when he only had the half of it…

The fire sputtered and sparks danced into the starry sky, and Hermes realized they had been sitting in silence. An idea dawned, half-formed and Hermes flew, searching for something he'd once seen nearby. He stopped above a rocky cliff, where a hempen rope dangled from a platform above the tumultuous water. He wound it around his arm and flew back to Orpheus.

The hymnist blinked in astonishment when Hermes landed in exactly the spot he'd disappeared from seconds before. Hermes started uncoiling the rope. The length was perfect. And there were already knots in it for footholds…

"I don't know where you found the figs or firestone," Orpheus said quietly, "but I know *exactly* where that came from. It belongs to our temple!"

"You'll bring it back." Hermes lashed it to the rocks, throwing the long end into the chasm.

Orpheus remained indignant. "Initiates won't be able to banish miasma!"

"They won't miss it for long, and *you* will need it to climb out from *there*," he said. Hermes fished through his satchel and dropped a small stone next to the rope. "And Eurydice with you. If you can put those jackals to sleep, it'll work on Cerberus— I'm sure of it."

"Wait," Orpheus stared at him. "What?"

"You were right, Orpheus. Eurydice wasn't meant to die. You need to speak to them," Hermes said. "I'm taking you to the River."

✳   ✳   ✳

"Have you lost your mind?!"

"Did you ferry her—"

"You want me to take a man," Charon bared his teeth, "a *corporeal*, flesh and blood *human*, across the Styx?!"

Hermes stood his ground. "*Did* you ferry Eurydice across, Charon?"

"Of course I did! What cause have I to leave her stranded?"

"Because she wasn't supposed to die! A serpent was *wrongly* sent after her," Hermes said, pointing at Orpheus, "and *this* flesh and blood human is the one to whom Aidoneus gave the lyre. The rites in springtime gave them Zagreus! *Eurydice* gave them Zagreus!"

"And Zagreus… is dead. So you would have me bring them Orpheus, a living memory of their sorrow? I say again, Hermes. Are you mad?" Charon said. His lip quivered but he bit it and looked at Orpheus, who stood transfixed. "And what say you, mortal? Are you aware that if the shades of Asphodel find you, with blood flowing through your veins, they

289

will tear you limb from limb to drink and remember their lives?"

Orpheus stared at Charon. "Zagreus... the God of Elysion died?"

"We lost..." Charon scowled, pulling his hood over his eyes, and climbed back into his boat. His voice wavered. "I don't have time for this. Take him back, Hermes. Get him away from here."

"Wait! Please." Hermes had been convinced with a song. Charon might not be so moved, but what recourse did he have? Hermes nodded to Orpheus, who took out his lyre and plucked an octave, letting it ring across the water. Ripples wavered across the glass surface of the Styx and the caves reverberated.

Keep your eyes open, Eurydice had told him. He could see and feel, and the lyre seemed to move his fingers... just as it had when he was with her. He sang of Charon's king and queen, of the Boatman's unrequited love for Styx herself, before she had become part of the great river. Charon sat on the bracing, his oar falling softly to his side.

Orpheus could see into the ancient ferryman. The words came, and Orpheus sang them. He tried not to notice how easily they fell from his lips— flowing from hand to heart and outward. They were the same notes that had transfixed Hermes and convinced him to bring Orpheus here. He sang of Charon guiding Eurydice across the river to the path where all must go. Orpheus ended his song and plucked the same octave.

Charon looked up, streams meandering down his hollow cheeks. "How did you know that melody?"

"Eurydice sang it."

He picked up his oar. "Come."

"I have no *obolos*."

"Neither are you dead, so get in." Charon motioned him forward. "Before I come to my senses!"

"Here," Hermes said, closing Orpheus's fingers over an oblong rock.

"A lodestone?"

"Of a sort. There is only one way down but the roads up are endless. This will guide you back to Samothrace. I placed its mate there." Hermes nodded at him once and disappeared through the passages.

Orpheus climbed into Charon's boat. The last sinew connecting him to the world of the living was severed. He was in the Underworld. *Domos Haidou.* Chthonia. The boat lurched forward and rocked gently on the water. Across the Styx, he saw three sets of white teeth glinting like knives. A low growl rumbled through the very center of him. As the boat approached the palace, Cerberus stalked and paced along the shore.

"Will he let me pass?"

"Not unless you can convince him," Charon said, rowing along the shore. "And I can't stop him from eating you if you don't."

Orpheus drew in a long breath. Either way, he would be with Eurydice. If Cerberus devoured him, if the shades tore him apart as Charon had warned, he would still be with her. But it could take *lifetimes* to find her after his memories had been washed away by the Lethe.

With his lyre against his shoulder, he sang anew, watching Cerberus. He began his song with his mother, Echidna, and the dog rumbled angrily. Orpheus quickly sang of how Hecate had given Cerberus to Hades, how he'd fallen asleep on his master's lap as a pup, to the rhythmic stroke of his fingers. He sang of the spots of his youth that gave him his name. Cerberus quieted and trotted to the palace gate. Words flowed. Orpheus sang of Persephone playing with him in the garden, and how he cried when she took her annual leave. Cerberus yowled softly and stood at the river's edge, still, all three heads whimpering a discordant harmony. The beast's massive serpentine tail smacked the ground when Orpheus sang about his faithfulness.

The boat drifted closer, and Orpheus's song came to an end. They drifted past falls that seemed to flow backward—streaming upward to the world of the living. Around the bend, Cerberus stood guard in the rushes and asphodel crowding the river.

"Was that all?" Charon muttered.

"All that came to me."

"I hope it was enough." Charon looked up at Cerberus as they approached. "He seems… calm. Quite a thing to wager your life on, though."

"I chanced as much with you," he said. "You had every right to pitch me into the river."

Charon scoffed softly, and Orpheus held his breath.

A golden poplar stood up the slope, shining against the dark cliff. There were doors. And stairs. And staring down at him, the Hound of Hades. The boat scraped across gravel. Orpheus looked up at a wide snout, a hint of teeth. The dog snorted at him. He felt his cold, wet nose nudge his entire arm, lifting him to his feet. Orpheus cautiously disembarked, glancing back just once. With a knowing smirk, Charon pushed off from the shoreline.

The center head of the great beast gently butted Orpheus forward while the right and left looked to each side and growled low. The snarl shook the column of his spine… his knees… Orpheus saw faint, fleeting faces peering from behind the asphodel and fading back between the tall stalks. He walked forward, wet gravel crunching underfoot, heart drumming in his ears. Four enormous feet padded behind him. A pale arm reached for him. The right head lunged and snapped.

Orpheus clutched the lyre to his chest, fingers numb, his erratic breathing filling the stillness.

...they will tear you limb from limb to drink and remember...

Was Cerberus protecting him from the shades? He passed under the golden boughs of the poplar tree and stood on wide stone steps leading to the great door.

Suddenly the great Hound of Hades howled and yapped with all three heads. Orpheus squeezed his eyes shut, deafened as Cerberus called for his master. At last, the beast sat back on his haunches, massive paws on either side of Orpheus, breath acrid, crimson tongues panting from three grinning mouths.

With a creak of wood and the grind of ancient hinges, the door to the palace swung open.

✳ ✳ ✳

"Sweet one." She didn't respond. Aidon knitted his brow. "I'm sorry... something requires our attention downstairs."

Persephone blinked. "I can't."

"A mortal has crossed the Styx."

She turned to him, her eyes slowly focusing. "What?"

"Forgive me, my love. I need your help; I need your counsel as Queen."

"Who would cross willingly?"

Aidoneus drew in a breath, preparing for her to curl away, to stare into nothing again at the reminder of their lost child. "Orpheus."

She watched their hearth fire for a long moment, then nodded.

"Do you need my help?" Aidoneus asked.

She nodded again. Aidoneus propped her in front of the mirror and unbound her sleep-bedraggled chignon. She winced as he loosened the tangles with his fingers, then combed her wavy locks. He braided her hair and wound it up neatly again, then placed her crown on her head.

293

She stared into the polished hematite mirror, garnet and ruby glinting back at her as Aidon fastened her armband, her necklace, her jeweled girdle over her black peplos. He held her about the waist, lifting her slowly to her feet. With a brush of his hand, his gray himation darkened to jet black, a gold meandros winding along its edges. He snapped gold bands onto his arms, adjusted a torc around his neck, and placed his crown of golden poplar on his brow.

She took a step and faltered, knees wobbling. "I..."

"Let me." Aidoneus held her under her shoulders and swept his arm under her knees, lifting her to his chest. She crumpled against him and laid her heavy head on his shoulder. He carried her from their bedroom and carefully, slowly made his way down the winding stairs.

The throne room was empty. Hecate had answered Cerberus's call, escorted the *hemitheos* through the palace, and left him outside the throne room before bringing word of the arrival of Orpheus of Samothrace to Aidoneus. No mortal had ever trespassed so deeply into his kingdom.

He set Persephone on her seat and her limbs unfurled, lethargically settling into the throne. Aidon studied her for a moment and adjusted her crown, then tucked under a wayward lock of hair that had escaped his braiding. He kissed her forehead and whispered. "There. Now we're ready."

Hades took his place on his throne beside Persephone, placing a protective hand atop hers.

"You may enter." The door opened slowly and he appeared. Aidoneus saw into him instantly and sighed. His betrothed, Eurydice, was dead. Orpheus looked from one to the other and knelt to the floor, his *zeira* pooled around him, lyre upright against his shoulder. "Stand."

"My lord, my lady, I come before you to beg—"

"I cannot reverse the will of the Fates, Orpheus."

He nodded and spoke. "I offer myself in her place."

"Do not ask me to end your life. I don't yet know the hour when you will arrive as my eternal guest, but only then will you walk with her again."

"But I won't." Orpheus took a deep breath. "We'd planned to journey to Eleusis in the spring so she could take part in the Mysteries, as they are the only path to Elysion. I was taught by Eumolpus himself. But Eurydice…"

Aidoneus closed his eyes. *Polydegmon, I am here.* Sure enough, he could hear her shade, rustling through the asphodel. "All drink from the Lethe when they arrive. You would know of her no more, were she with you in Elysion or not."

"Eurydice and I are intertwined. Since before we knew each other. You and your queen know that better than anyone, as you are likewise bound. I beseech you, let me take her to Eleusis. Then she will enter here again, and we may someday reside together in Elysion. It matters nothing that I will not remember her." Orpheus gazed at him directly. "For though both of us would drink, we would not cease to be. Some part will always remain."

Aidoneus narrowed his eyes. He had said those exact words to numberless reluctant shades. His jaw set and he listened to the hymnist go on.

"What brings us peace," Orpheus said, "what resides in our souls, stays with us forever even after we let go of the pain and suffering of our mortality."

"Eurydice…" Persephone's voice cracked. Aidon turned to her in surprise. "I knew her."

Aidoneus held his breath. She had said nothing to anyone but him since their child was lost. "Yes, honored queen. Eurydice helped you gather honey and herbs for—" he stopped. "Hermes found me at the entrance to your realm. I sang to him, and he said I must go before you. There is a thread in the Cloth of Life that binds some in this cosmos forever. Through sorrow, through death, through life. And I humbly beg to sing to you of yours, for it is the same song she sings for me."

Aidon sat back on his throne and scoffed. "Well, *he-mitheoi*... It is clear now, as it was when we first met, that your gift is in reading people— an inheritance from your father, no doubt. As is your gift for song. That was how you came across my river, no? First by entrancing Hermes, then Charon, then Cerberus. But no song will move me to break the laws of this land."

Orpheus sighed and cast his eyes to the ground. "I understand. I—"

"Play."

Sweet one, are you sure?

Persephone didn't answer. She had been listless since they lost Zagreus. The merest mention of him would send her into the abyss, and if this man sang of their sorrow and hurt her further...

"Play, Orpheus," Persephone whispered.

Orpheus nodded and plucked a note on his lyre, then shortened the string to the higher fifth. Fear welled up and words failed. Her whisper echoed in the strings.

Can't you hear what comes next? Eurydice said. *Were you listening?*

Orpheus raised his eyes and looked directly at the King and Queen and sang.

A binding oath in time of strife, betrothed upon the river
Across the fields and through the fire you cleaved to one another
That seed grew within dreams to nourish boughs and sunlit leaves
Far above the soil is stripped, the land by winter hollowed clean

Stay with me, and break the world, or you'll be lost forever

Persephone's breath hitched, the fresh words recasting a familiar melody. Aidoneus closed his eyes, fighting back his tears. All he could see was the look on Persephone's face when he'd knelt before her in this very room, begging her not to leave him, even if it meant the end of all things. He clutched her hand.

I'll find a way, I will return, six seeds in secret bound you
Walk on, my love, I'll not look back, and I'll be right behind you
You bloomed in spring and then returned in autumn, king and queen
To reunite, and so entwined conceived the sacred green

And so I seek Eurydice, who sang her songs to sprouting seeds
Whose thread lies cut, her grave above, now ever parted from me
Walk on, she said, do not look back, we will again be one
Reborn to moonlit fields and golden sun, within Elysion.

Persephone covered her mouth. A tear... the first she'd shed since Zagreus was taken above, ran down her face. She turned to Aidoneus and touched his shoulder. He startled and opened his eyes, mapping her expression— blue-grey eyes that saw him again, instead of the yawning abyss.

"Husband..."

"Sweet one?"

"Aidon, our son..." She swallowed, her voice choked by grief. "I'm sorry."

"No, Persephone..."

"I tried... I couldn't..." she broke down, her words unintelligible.

"Don't apologize, my love, please..." Tears streamed down his cheeks and she touched his face, brushing away a fresh drop. Aidoneus held her to him. In an instant, a suffocating terror dissipated. He had faced that same specter only once before: on her first day with him when she'd run into the Lethe, when he thought he'd lost her forever.

"There has to be a way. We'll bring him back." Suddenly, words spilled from her. "He cannot be lost to us, to the world." Persephone kissed him, for the first time since they stood at the Styx before their world fell apart. She looked sidelong at Orpheus. "But for them, the ones who gave him to us… Just this once. There must be something we can do for them. Just once."

Aidoneus leaned his forehead against Persephone's. Orpheus stood before them, his lyre resting at his side, not breathing, not moving.

"Hymnist…" He swallowed hard to stop his tears. Aidoneus stood from his throne and Persephone with him. He wrapped his arm around her. "My wife… I thought she was lost forever. For your words, for bringing her back to me, I will grant you this."

Orpheus exhaled, then bowed his head. "You have all my lifetimes of gratitude and fealty. I am deeply grieved for your loss. If not for me—"

"No," Persephone said and roughly wiped her tears away. "He wasn't lost because of you. And we will have him back again, won't we?"

Aidon looked down at her expectant face. "Yes. I swear to you we will."

"Is Eurydice here?"

"She is in the fields," Aidoneus said.

He descended to the table beside the dais and stood over a kylix filled with clear water that mirrored the ceiling above. Aidon produced a small golden knife from the folds of his himation and closed his fingers around it, then pulled the blade through quickly. He hissed and blood streamed into the cup from his extended fist, diffusing in the water. The carmine tinge flashed gold and disappeared.

He splayed his fingers, the wound healing. "After we creat-ed Elysion, we searched the Fields of Asphodel. Shades would drink from the Mnemosyne, much as you tell your initiates, and we would read the manner of their mortal lives. My wife and I would then give them the waters of the Lethe, to restore them to eternal peace, and welcome any deserving souls to Paradise. It was... exhausting work. The Mnemosyne will re-store Eurydice's memories; ichor will affix them to her, and return her to life."

"Your blood..."

"I have never allowed this before." He grew solemn. "Once she drinks, she will begin her journey back to the world of the living unformed. When she beholds you, her memories will be of you, of her past life. It is how she will come back as herself. As Eurydice."

"Then I beg of you... let me see her."

"I'm not finished." Aidoneus circled him. "You will not be able to hear her or touch her. She will be as immaterial as any shade in Asphodel. You *must not* look upon her. If she is beheld by mortal eyes during her metamorphosis, that form will be cast upon her forever. She would return to your world as one who is neither living nor dead. I cannot allow that. The laws of Chthonia, which have existed longer than I have ruled, will not allow that. Eurydice will be pulled back, her memories will return to the Mnemosyne, and her soul must dwell here forev-er."

"Forever?"

"At peace; I promise you. You see why I've never allowed this. A reborn soul cannot emerge twice from my realm. To do so would undo the cosmos. If you fail, Orpheus, her ability to be reborn will be forfeit." Orpheus nodded slowly. The Lord of the Underworld's gaze fell so hard upon him that he flinched. Hades enunciated every word. "You *must* tell me you understand."

"I understand, my lord. I won't look back— I swear it. I will trust that she is behind me."

"Blood is a dangerous thing in Asphodel. The shades will tear you apart for it, so Cerberus will bear you past the Lethe, where they cannot go. The rest of the journey is up to you."

14.

"I CAN DO THIS," PERSEPHONE SAID. "YOU'VE BEEN SO patient with me."

Aidoneus stood aside as she undressed in the flickering light of the hearth fire. "How could I not? You've shouldered so much pain."

She nodded as he unwound his himation. "Can we please not speak about…"

"We don't have to."

The soft rush of the falls outside was soothing— its voice fresh and alive. The hymnist's song had reawakened her senses. "Do you think they'll make it?"

They had summoned Eurydice's shade soon after Orpheus began his journey to the surface. Aidoneus had beckoned her to drink from the Mnemosyne, and she recognized Persephone the moment the cup left her lips. But before she could say a word, the ichor drew her away, across the Lethe, toward Orpheus and the living world, her immaterial form wafting like smoke.

Persephone rubbed her gooseflesh-prickled arm and climbed into bed. Aidoneus unpinned his tunic and her eyes followed the scar his father had carved across his back. He crisply folded the cloth and set it with hers.

"He'll start to hear her footfall," Aidon climbed into bed beside her, "after they cross the last barriers between our worlds. I can't fathom the temptation. I hope his resolve is as strong as his love."

He unwound Persephone's chignon and unbraided her hair, part of their evening routine before they lost… She felt hollow. Aidoneus held her close and she relaxed, her back against his chest, flattening her palm against his hip as he settled behind her and stirred to life. Persephone listened to him breathe. His body tensed and his arms wrapped tighter around her waist and under her breasts.

He whispered against her shoulder. "I was so frightened for you, Persephone."

She turned and faced him. Her thumb traced the worry lines creasing his forehead. "I know."

"Your body was here, but it felt as if the rest of you was gone." He looked down and caressed her arm. "I was unsure you'd ever emerge after…"

He swallowed any mention of Zagreus to spare her, she knew, but the memory still sat like a weight upon her. He stroked her skin, hands brushing up and down her arms, her waist. She didn't know what to say and instead leaned her head on his chest and heard his relief in the steadiness of his heartbeat.

"You have no idea how glad I am to have you with me, *truly* with me again." Aidon stroked her hair, then lifted her chin. He hadn't dared a kiss since they both wept in front of Orpheus. When his lips met hers the weight and emptiness in her chest only spread, as though it was suffocating her, stopping her voice.

She pushed past it. He wanted to love her. To reunite, to find solace after mourning alone. Persephone felt her own desire rise, but it stung her insides instead of flooding her with smooth warmth. His tongue stroked hers and she felt his answering arousal awaken against her thigh, hot and needy, seeking relief. Perhaps he could sense the gulf, the grief-filled void between them, and desperately wanted to conquer and reclaim it. Persephone broke off their kiss, overwhelmed, and gulped in air.

He'd tended to her, deferring his sorrow… she wanted to at least try. Persephone focused, listened to his breath by her ear, felt Aidon's teeth gently nip at her neck, his lips kissing her collarbone.

She willed herself to respond, to touch him, and buried her face against his skin, taking in his scent. Her fingers brushed along his erection, his body bowing. He sighed against her forehead, his hands tensing. They traveled familiar paths, ones that had delighted and inflamed her before. But every caress grated and when his long fingers stroked between her legs, finding heat and wetness, she flinched back with a hiss, rolling away on the bed and curling into fetal position.

He froze in place. She heard his harsh panting, then felt the bed shift as he lay on his back and stared at the canopy. Long moments passed. "Sweet one—"

"I'm sorry."

"No, I am." He exhaled a long breath. "It's too soon."

"I thought I could, I…" She blinked back tears. "I know how scared you were, that you grieve for him too, that *you* need comfort."

"I do. But…" he ground his teeth, searching for the words. "I wasn't the one who carried him."

"You know I love you, Aidon. You can still lay with me tonight, and I can try to—"

"I don't want to have you for the sake of having you. We can wait. I can wait until you're ready." His voice was clipped.

She swallowed, afraid to ask. "Will you still hold me?"

"Yes." He sighed, unmoving, his fingers unclenching. "Just… give me a moment for my passions to die down, wife."

*   *   *

"Did anyone see you?"

Hecate hobbled into the room. "As a sleeping man sees a bat. None would think to look."

Athena pulled her small bed back from the wall while Hecate held the oil lamp. She leaned over and carefully lifted the wooden box. Hecate softly snickered and Athena knitted her brow. "What?"

"I've seen many gods across the cosmos, but none stowed beneath a pallet."

Athena shrugged. "There was no other place for him. I've never been one to hide things away." Her fingers tensed on the lid as Hecate reached to take it from her. "Please don't tell Persephone."

Hecate nodded. "I fear this secret will be a ripple among raging waves when this matter is ended."

Athena thinned her lips. She had sworn to guard Zagreus, to find a way to bring Persephone's child back to her, but her oath felt hollow, hanging solely on the wisdom of the Goddess of Witchcraft, a Titan, and a stranger to her. "I plan to stand guard the whole time, you know. I owe her that."

Hecate inclined her head. "So bears the Aegis bearer."

The night was chill and quiet and her breath hung on a cloud. Athena pulled her cloak over her shoulders, the gold embroidered snakes glinting in the torchlight.

"Douse the flame," Hecate said quickly. Athena did so.

Her eyes adjusted as they walked in utter darkness through the citadel, among worn stones that had stood since Gaia and Ouranos ruled the earth— before mortals, before gods. Hecate approached the ancient well, a bore that dropped to the Styx itself, and stood beside it. "Now what?" Athena whispered.

"Four may know what three divine. The Moon rises in the Hunter tonight."

Four? Athena looked east. Sure enough, the great constellation of the Hunter peeked over the hills in the midnight sky, the waning moon perched on his shoulder.

A cool, shimmering light fell over the stones and Selene walked barefoot to the well, pupils pinpricks in her flashing eyes, her fine hair awash with silver and white. She cradled her swollen belly with dark arms, soothing her growing babe. Selene nodded to Athena and addressed Hecate. "It is good to see you again. Where is your niece?"

"I'm here." Athena spun around to see Artemis silently alight, dropping from the branches of the olive tree. She glared at Athena. "But why have *you* come?"

"Pallas Athena is the child's champion, young one," Selene said. "And she will speak no word of what she sees here. Will you?"

Athena shook her head.

Hecate smiled at Athena, the wrinkles near her eyes crinkling. "Only as the crone may I see what we must do for Zagreus: at once his source, his stream, and the unknown sea beyond."

Athena looked over the trio. Moon goddesses. The maiden huntress, mother of many, wise old woman. The night wanderers. Accustomed to seeing Artemis in her daylight roles, Athena had all but forgotten that she was Selene's apprentice… and a protector of young children. Hecate held the wooden box, one hand above and one beneath, over the well. Selene and Artemis bound the rest, each covering opposing sides until all six were within their grasp. They closed their eyes.

The sigils marking the wood surface began to glimmer silver and Athena felt a pulse wash through her flesh, around her bones. She stood tall, unafraid, eyes fixed on the box. The edges melted away and a glow spread outward to the three goddesses. A heart pounded softly, casting no shadow, filling the well with muted light.

"Fates," Selene said. "Could it have been something so mundane?"

Artemis squinted in the light. "Why would anyone do this?"

"Helios ran his course twice while the poison rested," Hecate said. "Taking the deep and darkening path beneath the earth did him no harm. Aidoneus was wrong."

"It came from Apollo's city." Artemis's jaw clenched. "Why would my brother do such a thing?!"

"Do not let anger break your focus," Selene said swiftly. "Keep your hands steady, your mind clear. We know only the method, not the murderer."

"He never held the sword, nor let it fall," Hecate said. "Persephone thought no distance too far from the Light Bringer. But still, the blade fell from the Mount."

"She trusts none of us, and wisely so," Artemis said. "Though she has formed an attachment with the Goddess of Love. Could it have been her?"

"Poison is not Aphrodite's weapon."

"A poison for the child and the mother's womb," Hecate said, her face falling in defeat. "Only in arms may she carry him again. He shall be as foretold, a god *twice* woven…"

Athena stared helplessly, tears welling up. Her promise was impossible. Would Persephone ever forgive her?

Selene's voice lifted. "Twice woven! So it heralds rebirth."

"But not upon her. So how?" Artemis asked.

"The Bull is rising," Hecate said. "Quick. Let the heart be hidden!"

The edges of the box glowed and then faded, and Artemis and Selene let go. Hecate opened her eyes and held the pyxis in her bony hands. Athena stepped forward and took it from her, cradling it under her arm. "What has this to do with Apollo? What did you see? You must tell me!"

"Silphium," Artemis said, then mapped the confusion on Athena's face. "It's an herb."

"It has saved the lives of countless mortal women," Selene added. "Without it, many would have perished in the throes of unnecessary childbirth."

"They could have spurned male pleasure," Artemis muttered under her breath.

"Pleasure?" Hecate hissed. "You and I are women who roam the field and sky by *our* whim and will. Mortal women walk a road paved by men, led by men, to be bred by men. From queen to peasant, all are slaves."

Athena sighed, frustrated. "What cause would Apollo have? Could this have any relation to Asklepios being made immortal?"

Artemis, Selene, and Hecate fell suddenly silent and stared at her, all three wide-eyed.

Selene breathed. "Fates…"

"At least that narrows it down…" Artemis said.

"A pact writ in blood: a life for a life. Apollo never held the sword," Hecate repeated, "but clasped the hand that took the hilt." The four goddesses exchanged haunted looks. Hecate broke the heavy silence. "And if it was her, the path of truth leads us to the precipice of war."

✻   ✻   ✻

Before him was another split, and no hint of fresh air from either tunnel. Orpheus took the lodestone from his pouch and held it tight as he approached the rightward fork. It was cold and still. He stepped in front of the left tunnel and felt a metallic pull, soft but distinct. He turned left.

Hermes had dropped the stone in his hand with nary a word of guidance. He'd taken a wrong turn early on and had

307

felt the lodestone pulling him back in the right direction. Since then, he'd known how to follow its lead.

He walked in silence. While passing a deep chasm, he'd plucked a lyre string, listening to the note reverberate downward. The emptiness of the deep earth was too much to bear; he hadn't done it again. Orpheus had sat to eat a bite of fig, take a swallow from the water bladder, and conserve his strength. He hadn't slept.

What if he awoke and she stood there? Even if he saw her by happenstance, she would be lost. If he lingered too long in one place, doubt crept into his consciousness. He feared that Hades's words were said only to cajole, to give him the peace to return home and wait for Eurydice, to wait endlessly for her to emerge until old age claimed him. What if a soul could not be sent back to earth? The Lord of the Dead had said himself he'd never done so before.

What if they sought vengeance for their son's death? Orpheus shook his head and slowly scaled another rock face. A heady scent tickled his nostrils. Peat. Loam. The warmth of decaying leaves. He hadn't smelled the living earth since he had descended with Hermes.

He took a few steps and heard rustling behind him. Orpheus halted, his skin prickling. More shuffling. It wasn't an echo; it had its own rhythm. His heart nearly stopped. Orpheus took tenuous steps forward and hummed quietly, trying to distract himself from the off-rhythm footfall. Was it real, or was he imagining what he wanted to hear? He would drown the maddening noises in the music of his lyre, but he needed his hands free for the hard climb ahead.

He could feel the air grow colder, wind whistling through the upper reaches of the caves. So close… but where were they? Perhaps Samothrace, or anywhere else in Hellas. What if they emerged in Scythia and were set upon by the Getae, the wild people of the mountains? He looked up. A shaft of light pierced through the caves. He climbed a short rock face, testing each stone before settling his weight on it, and stood at another division.

The lodestone. Orpheus fished it from his satchel and it drew him to the right, the path sloping upward and narrow. He heard rocks jostle loose behind him. Eurydice. Stones tumbled, and he began to turn, arm reaching to aid her— then stopped, clutching the lodestone in his fist. He shut his eyes, then returned the stone to his bag and looked to the rocky way ahead.

The walls of stone closed around him. He moved one rock aside, then another, and pushed his *zeira*, the lyre, and his bag through one by one, then one shoulder, then the other. Orpheus eyed the stones perched above him warily. A great chamber lay on the other side, and he threw his cloak back on, tied the lyre in place, and slung his satchel across his shoulder. More rocks clattered loose behind him, and he could hear feet and hands scramble over them. Orpheus pressed onward, then leaned around the bend. A sheer drop made him turn his face away and shut his eyes. His cheek and hands pressed against the unforgiving granite and he inched along the precarious path, barely a foot's length wide in parts. As he rounded the corner, he saw an opening and...

The rope! It was the rope Hermes had set for him— the only way to ascend the last two fathoms. A little way more and he could touch it.

"Orpheus..."

He tensed, almost slipping and falling back into the abyss. Was that her voice, or the wind? He'd heard his name, he was sure of it, sure it was her.

"It won't be long now..." he whispered to nothingness. "It won't be. I promise."

The path broadened but sloped downward and he struggled to keep his balance. The rope hung well above his head.

He reached and barely touched it and it swung away; on the return, he grasped a large knot and dangled on the end.

"Just like the water…" he whispered. Anything to steady his hands, stop his heart from drumming in his ears. "Just like every morning after you cleanse miasma…"

Orpheus climbed, hand over hand, the knots giving him purchase. He wrapped his feet around the lowest knot and exhaled in relief. He climbed faster, his legs no longer deadweight. Halfway to the surface, he felt a tug on the end of the rope that set it swinging again before it stretched as taut as a lyre string.

"Orpheus…" The whisper was louder this time, more like Eurydice's voice.

"It's not much further," he said aloud. His voice startled him and reverberated down the chasm. He could smell autumn leaves and petrichor above, and see blue, wisps of white clouds, barren aspen branches.

He reached into the sunlight. His palm smacked against the sun-warmed stone and he saw the charcoal remains of the fire. Orpheus pulled himself up.

"I'm behind you." Eurydice's voice rang clear in the enveloping dark.

"My love, we made it. It won't be long now," he said, surveying the hillside. He set down his lyre, waiting.

"Oh!"

"Are you alright?"

"The rope is harsh on my feet, is all. Wait. I—" She shrieked. "I'm slipping! Orpheus!"

"Hold on!" He reached into the shadows. He caught sight of the gold band around her finger. His fingers passed through hers, immaterial, grasping nothing. Her eyes widened and Orpheus froze. "No…"

Eurydice screamed his name soundlessly. She fell away like dust and ashes, her eyes, her mouth the last to waft into the darkness. His voice carried her name through the depths of the earth until he didn't know if it was him or the chasm wailing.

Orpheus rolled back and stared at the clouds gathering across the sun. No. No, it was his fear, a bad vision. She would be there, she *must*, hanging on. He couldn't have… not after all he'd done. This couldn't have ended this way. It couldn't. He peered in. A rope dangled in the dark. Silence.

The wind picked up, biting his skin. He stared west and saw the white smoke of offerings rising along with a short column of black. They were goldsmithing. Turning the bounty that Hades had given Samothrace into thin leaves… prayers to the Mnemosyne.

Eurydice will be pulled back, her memories will return to the Mnemosyne, and her soul must dwell here forever.

She was lost— trapped in Asphodel, never to be reborn.

You shy away from falsehood, but that hope is necessary, isn't it?

Meaningless leaves, reburied in the earth, filling dead mouths when that gold could feed multitudes. The prayer was a vain hope he could speak no more.

White smoke. It was the first day of the week. He'd walked below for four days. Everyone would be in the courtyard. Everyone who had participated in the springtime rites that created Zagreus. The Unborn One. The Deathless One who died.

Orpheus picked up his lyre and ran, retracing the path he'd taken when he had left Eurydice's grave to call Hermes up from below. The wind-tossed sea peaked with white caps as a storm approached. The ground was frozen. He slipped and skidded on his knees before picking himself up and strode on, blood soaking his sandal straps and greasing his heels, through the autumn-stripped vineyard and onward to the courtyard.

Perrhaebus stood at the altar beside the great olive tree. Orpheus's heavy footsteps pounded against the stones and a hundred faces turned to see him. The blind priest halted his recitation.

"He returned!" A voice called out from the crowd. "The hierophant returned!"

"Where was he?"

"Mourning that woman from the woods."

"The nymph?"

"Orpheus?" Lemnia pulled back her hood, her ancient brow crinkled with worry.

"He's walked the wilderness for days. Look at him!"

His lips were cracked, his skin was caked with dust, his hair tangled, and blood trickled down his legs. He panted and pulled his lyre to his shoulder. "I did not walk the wilderness, but a place far different. I journeyed below."

"Does he truly mean that?"

"No, another vision from the gods…"

"He's come back with news of the Mnemosyne!"

"I have. All of you, listen!" Orpheus stood tall, his voice strong. "I came to the very seat of Axiokersos and Axiokersa themselves!"

They gasped, then descended upon him. Faces, endless voices, grasping hands, questions.

"Hierophant! Did you see my husband?!"

"No, I—"

"You oversaw my sister's funeral rites last year. Surely she remembers me."

His shoulders fell. "I saw none of your loved ones. No one remembers. None have form. We were wrong."

They all quieted.

"Orpheus…" Lemnia shook her head. "That can't be true… the visions we saw."

"We saw what we wished to see, Lemnia."

A young girl shouted. "That's not true!"

"What about what you told us before?" Her father held her.

"There must be a mistake." Their faces were blurring. They were surrounding him. Hungry, reaching hands, clawing for any morsel of truth...

"And worse. The Unborn One..." The entire crowd fell silent, eyes wide, each glancing at another. Orpheus burst into tears. "He is no more. Zagreus is dead."

Dryas cautiously approached him. "Brother, you are... delirious. You've been out in the sun and wind for days. Come... we will put you to bed."

Doubt overwhelmed him. He'd seen others driven to *mania* by grief. Had it all been a dream? Did everything he had seen arise from lack of water, sleep, and food? He closed his hand around the lodestone. No. No, he was *there*. "I was *not* in the wilderness! I journeyed *below*. I saw *them*."

"He drank bog water," a woman's voice said from the white-clothed crowd. "That's the only source near the chasm."

"Help him! He is shaking. What if he has the fever?"

"I was covered by the earth..." Orpheus said quietly. "Hermes bore me to *Domos Haidou* to retrieve Eurydice."

"He's gone mad..."

"I crossed the wide delta of Acheron."

"Apollo cursed him with madness..."

"By his own father?"

"We don't even know that's true."

"It's his hubris! Claiming that lyre was a gift from the gods!"

"Take pity on him, please!" Lemnia put her hands up. "Can't you see he's grieving?"

"I grieve but I tell the truth! I stood before Hades and Persephone!" Several in the crowd covered their ears. One of the men spat three times, chasing back the rulers of the dead lest they take him too. "They gave me leave to bring her back, Lemnia. They allowed her to drink from the Mnemosyne."

"Of course they did. You performed the rites for her. She will dwell forever—"

"She cannot be reborn. Because of me! I almost had her but I looked behind… He told me not to look and I looked back the moment before… And they did this for me, even though *they* grieved horribly… Persephone lost her baby. Zagreus is dead!"

"You mustn't speak such things aloud," Lemnia hissed at him. "Stop this!"

"Blasphemer…" The word flew like a spark in a withered field. It caught slowly at first, flames curling up a tinder: a whisper became a murmur and a chorus and a roaring shout. "Blasphemer! Heresy! Blasphemer!"

"You've followed me this far— why won't you listen now?!" He beheld their snarling faces, jeering, jabbing fingers. Spittle landed on his face. They backed away as Orpheus jumped up to the altar and scattered a handful of gold leaves, showering the crowd below. "These are lies! Can't you understand? I spoke to Hades! No visions, no secret knowledge. The words of our mighty god himself! We are all equal in death. Rejoice! You will return and be reborn! Your suffering will be forgotten."

The mob reached for him, clawing, faces twisted in anger. They hissed and seized, shouting, spitting their fury through bared teeth and snarling lips. Cerberus could not protect him here. He whispered one last prayer as he plucked a lyre string. "Please, Aidoneus, let me forget."

"*You tear us free from the corporeal hold…*" Orpheus sang his last hymn. The tones were discordant, his voice exhausted from calling out after Eurydice, the lyre untuned after his journey. A young woman covered her ears and screamed obscenities back at him. "*Undo nature's bonds and bring the long slumber. The endless repose of the—*"

A sharp sting crossed his throat ear to ear. Cold air sputtered wet as he tried to draw a breath. He couldn't sing, couldn't speak. The lyre was torn from his fingers by a flurry of hands. Orpheus fell, eyes cast to the darkening sky. Perrhaebus stood above him, remorse written across his face, blood staining his blade and hand. Strong fingers gripped his arm, dragging Orpheus from the altar. He heard the lyre strings break, the carapace shatter, the pieces crackling in the fire. A blade pierced his side, another his heart, another, and another. He could hear nothing. Snow fell around him. His head and limbs were wrenched, ached terribly, then ached no more. The flurries shimmered ever brighter. He saw dark wings and a sickle. Then nothing.

15.

T HANATOS HOVERED IN THE DOORWAY, WONDERING IF he was looking upon the Thrones of Chthonia for the last time. A single brazier held back the encroaching dark. He spread his wings, arms folded across his chest. "I know what you're thinking."

"Do you?" piped Hecate, her childlike form belying the sternness in her voice. She hopped down from the base of the colonnade and her feet tapped across the stone floor. "Did you stand so long you sprouted roots like a tree so you could read my mind when I returned?"

"If you do this alone," he said, voice clipped, "they will never again trust any of us."

"I have to. Zagreus isn't just a mortal weft in the Cloth of Life." Hecate bunched her long skirts in her hands, peplos trailing as she paced. "If I don't, you know what fruits will fall, Thanatos. Rotten fruits."

"So war with the world above is imminent?" He scoffed. "We've been here before, Hecate. Doubtless, we'll come to this crossroads again. The world ending in fire. Or we do nothing and let it slip quietly away into the abyss."

"That is what I'm trying to prevent."

"With everything the gods above have done, with all that we *know* is yet to come, have you never considered that we might all deserve it?"

She stopped in her tracks. "What?"

"What if we all, from the oldest Protogenoi to the youngest mortal, *deserve* oblivion? Think what the Olympians proved they can do on a whim… Maybe you shouldn't reweave him. Perhaps the gods above, and you and I, and all of us should slip quietly into nothingness."

"So you earned those marks for nothing?"

He glanced at his arms. The smooth scars would fade, likely by the next moon. He could still feel the Chains of Tartarus smoldering and adamant against his skin. Stopping himself from reaping Zagreus had a price, but had he known that it would launch them into war regardless, he might well have let his death come to pass. "Paltry compared to how crookedly we've all bent the will of the Fates."

"They told *her*—"

"That he would be twice woven!" He shouted, then composed himself. "Hecate, she *clings* to that hope, has extracted a promise from Aidoneus—"

"He shouldn't have given it. Zagreus can't remain her own. The Fates told her that, too."

"And you'll do it, expecting no consequence…" Thanatos laughed ruefully and gazed up at the empty thrones. "The entire Ouranic line is mad. Yourself included."

"I can't tell her. Persephone's barely resurfaced after she lost him."

"And if you resow him, without them knowing, it will send her right back down. Or worse."

"You keep a secret in the dark too, Thanatos." She softened. "I know who you reaped two days ago."

He sighed and looked down. "Am I wrong to spare them more ill news?"

Hecate spread her small arms and stared up at him.

"If you fear for her, tell *him* the truth, then."

"That path could end in flames," Hecate said, her voice faint but clear.

"Give only what needs to be known. For now. Be gentle. And don't say a word to *her*. Aidon can tell her more softly than you ever could, and you *know it*."

Hecate nodded, her small face scrunching up. She fled the room before she could cry. Thanatos considered following but stayed rooted at the door.

✳ ✳ ✳

"Walk with me."

"Aidon…"

"I cannot speak here."

Persephone lay curled up on the bed. "What does it matter?"

He paced around their hearth fire. "Staying here is not good for you. You shouldn't isolate yourself here, Persephone."

"I know myself better than that."

"Do you?" He cocked an eyebrow and her lips parted wordlessly. "Please trust me, sweet one. I know from bitter experience what comes of cloistering oneself, nursing sorrows without end…"

"You never went through—" She stopped herself. He'd lost a child too. "Just tell me what Hecate said. You've delayed it for a week."

"Then walk with me," he repeated. "Please. We don't need to go far."

Persephone unfolded herself and followed him down the twisting stairs to the great hall and finally out to the garden. Askalaphos was halfway up a myrtle tree, meticulously clip-

318

ping small branches. He stopped dead and watched them pass, averting his eyes.

"Everyone is afraid of me," Persephone whispered.

"They don't know what to say to us." Light flooded between the six pomegranate trees encircling the entrance to Elysion, casting their shadows behind them. Aidoneus lifted a low branch for her and she ducked under.

Once through the trees, they were enveloped by their new realm. The sun shone, and songbirds warbled in a tree. The scents of apple blossoms and hyssop wafted on a calm breeze. Blessed shades picked flowers, ran through the tall grass, basked in the sunlight. They made way for their king and queen, their immaterial forms fading, scattered like windblown seeds, no memory lasting long enough to root them.

Hades and Persephone made their way down a favored path to a grassy slope with a clear view of the sapphire sea. She closed her eyes and felt cool salt air on her face, the sun on her shoulders and back. His fingers brushed her hand until she took hold of his.

"Please look at me." She turned and his dark brown eyes met hers, piercing and discomfiting, words hanging at the precipice. "Losing our son was *not* your fault, Persephone."

"Don't try to comfort me. If I had listened to you, or my mother, then he—"

"I don't patronize you. It's the truth. We didn't lose him because we carried him below." He paused. "Something from the world above was to blame."

Persephone looked up at him, wide-eyed. Her chest constricted.

"Silphium," Aidon spoke the word hesitantly.

Ice wended through her center, worming from womb to throat.

"You know of it?"

"I do. But if it was silphium…" Her brow furrowed.

"Then it means his death was deliberate."

"No." She freed herself from his grip and shook her head. Persephone spun on her heels and trudged down the path.

"Persephone..." he followed after her. "Persephone!"

"Hecate read it wrong!" She stalked off. "That *cannot* be, Aidon."

"I thought the same at first. I dismissed it outright. But—"

"Silphium doesn't grow anywhere near Hellas! It's from the far west across the Mesogeios. Apollo's herb. Whatever Hecate *thought* she saw..."

"She didn't just *see* it. She gleaned it from *our son* alongside Selene and Artemis. They invoked the moon..."

"How could they have—" Persephone stopped in her tracks as though a wall impeded her.

"What's the matter?" He caught up to her and followed her startled gaze to the pathway ahead. Aidoneus gripped Persephone's hand as a shade ambled toward them on the path, singing clear and warm, his voice unmistakable.

"Aidon..."

"How... He left our realm for the sunlit world; I felt it. I *knew* it when he left!"

"But if Orpheus is in Elysion... where is Eurydice?"

Orpheus turned and looked at them, his expression blank. Like every shade, he knew them only as king and queen; he had drunk the Lethe and remembered nothing of how they had allowed him to return to the world above with his beloved. Orpheus bowed and started to dissipate, clearing the way for them.

"Stay," the Lord of Souls commanded, extending his palm. Orpheus remained fixed in place, heels lifted off the ground. Aidoneus stared at Orpheus, preventing his shade from drifting away. "Persephone, quickly. Get the waters. I must know *exactly* what happened. Not simply *how* he died. *Everything.*"

Without a word, she reached her hands through the ether, pulling the kylix to her from the throne room. The water of the Mnemosyne settled within it and she walked carefully toward Orpheus, repeating the words they had used to find worthy souls in Asphodel. "You are the child of earth and starry heaven. Now drink. Drink and remember."

Orpheus looked confused, but beneath the oblivion of the Lethe, a ray pierced the dark.

"Yes," she nodded. "You know those words. They are why *your* golden leaves first drew our attention."

"What leaves?"

"Drink, Orpheus," Aidoneus said calmly.

The shade knit his brow, unaware of his own name, but took the cup from Persephone. She held the base firmly, prepared for what would happen. Orpheus sputtered and coughed, staggering back as the water ran down his throat. Aidon caught him, supporting him while he collapsed to the ground. Orpheus wailed, memories flooding his mind in a torrent. The joy and sadness of a lifetime mixed with pleasure and pain, all sorting themselves and birthing awareness. Huddled and sobbing, he felt the pain of his death, both fresh and distant. His immaterial shade solidified, nearly human, the Pool of Memory giving him shape and form.

Aidon covered Orpheus's eyes with his hand and he slumped into sleep in the grass. He examined him for a moment, reading him. "Orpheus looked back after he had crossed, but before Eurydice entered the light."

"Gods above…"

"He was murdered by his own people. They set upon him after he returned to Samothrace and told them about his journey. Smashed the lyre, tore him limb from limb… then burnt his remains with a coin so he wouldn't return to haunt and curse them."

She shuddered. "Why?"

"They thought he had gone mad, that he spoke blasphemies that would damn them all to Tartarus." He clenched his jaw, his voice low. "They won't go there, but they will spend *centuries* staring into the Cocytus once they become our guests."

Persephone handed Aidon the cup. "And Eurydice?"

Aidoneus looked away, combing the whole of Asphodel. "I'm trying to find her…"

"Spare him the Lethe." Persephone's eyes welled with tears. "Aidon, let them be together, after all they did for us!"

"Orpheus *begged me* with his final words to help him forget, Persephone. We *must* allow him to drink again." He ran his hand back through his hair. "I cannot reunite them. Not in a meaningful way."

"Iasion drank from the Mnemosyne. You tried to send him back to my mother."

"He was already returning to the world of the living. There are rules."

"*Asphodel* has those rules!" She wiped her face roughly, but more tears came. "This place is *ours*, and so are its principles."

"Eternal memory is a *punishment* we reserve for those in Tartarus. We promise peace to the souls, and freedom from all the pain of their lives."

"Aidon." Persephone drew in a halting breath. "If we were human and one day destined to dwell here… would you wish to forget Zagreus?"

She had been unable to hear or feel Aidon since they lost the baby. But for a brief, agonizing moment, his thoughts were laid bare. She saw the memory of her face when he'd opened the door to her room in the Telesterion, the look of cautious, disbelieving joy when she told him she was with child. The memory of lying in bed together in Thesprotia during a late summer storm, feeling their son kick. He had felt the pain rolling through her body when they crossed the Styx, her hand red with blood, her screams. And then the door shut on her.

She knew he felt it close, too. His eyes swam. "Not for anything. Not even to spare us his loss."

She interlaced her fingers with his. "The worthy souls *earned* Paradise, Aidon. Trust them. Trust that they can live with the knowledge of their lives. Oblivion isn't paradise. It's just the absence of suffering."

"We cannot break the rules for Orpheus and Eurydice alone," he said, taking her hand. "This must be for every shade in Elysion. All of them."

"Then let it be done." Persephone stared up at him, adamant. Finally, he relented and looked away from her, gazing into the fields. She squeezed his hand. "Aidon, where is she?"

He closed his eyes, seeking her out, beckoning her to them. When he opened them, his gaze was drawn to the grove at the top of the hill. A lone figure took in her new surroundings, blinking in the sunlight. She walked around the bend, staring out at the sea and smiling. She approached slowly, her skin regaining its warmth as she sloughed off the wan pallor of Asphodel and became part of Elysion. When Eurydice saw them, her face fell. He offered her the cup. "You are the child of earth and starry heaven."

Eurydice regarded Hades fearfully and shrank back.

"No, no," he said. "It won't be like the last time. I promise."

"Who is that?" Eurydice said. She looked at the man lying in the grass. Her expression softened and she circled the *omicron* of Orpheus's name on the gold ring of her left hand. "I feel as though... as though I know him."

"Here," Persephone said and sat on the ground. "It's easier if you're laying down."

Eurydice accepted her hand and settled on the ground with her head in Persephone's lap. Aidoneus leaned over them, blocking the sunlight. "Drink the Mnemosyne again, Eurydice. Drink and remember."

The cup came away from her lips and she convulsed and cried out, as Orpheus had, as Persephone had on her very first day in the Underworld after she'd run headlong into the river Lethe. Persephone held a hand to Eurydice's forehead, and Aidon knelt beside them both. Once Eurydice had ceased writhing, Aidon sent the kylix away, gently picked up the shade, and laid her alongside Orpheus.

"We should leave," Persephone said.

"Wait," Aidon whispered.

"They'll awaken soon."

He cast a glamour over them both, rendering them invisible to all the souls of Elysion, to Orpheus and Eurydice. "I need to know if this was the right thing to do."

Eurydice opened her eyes first. The breeze stirred her hair, and she sat up, the ocean wide before her, waves glittering. She heard the faint hum of bees gathering nectar in the open field. When she stood to seek them, Eurydice stumbled in shock.

"Orpheus?" He lay in the grass, the remains of the autumn crown she'd given him the day before their wedding tangled in his brown hair.

He blinked, as she knelt over him. Her smile widened.

"Eurydice." She pulled him up and he threw his arms around her. "Eurydice!"

"They heard me," she said, weeping. "I wanted to go to Persephone, but a terrible thing happened, Orpheus. The judges told me she lost Zagreus. And after that, I thought all was lost, and I didn't want to forget… I wanted to see you again, however that might be… but I couldn't stand in a stupor at the Trivium forever… I drank from the Lethe, *knowing* it would separate me from you."

"I know."

"How?"

"Because I went before them." He kissed her cheek and held her. "I came for you, across the Styx, to the Palace of Hades."

"I vaguely recall… there was a song across the River Styx. I saw their faces. I drank and was pulled away. And I felt rocks beneath my feet."

"I sang. Of you, of them, for days… Hermes brought me here, Charon rowed me across and they allowed it. I walked. Endlessly. I could hear you behind me. But after I'd climbed to the world above, you were slipping, you were going to fall back to Hades, and I reached for your hand, I looked and reached back, and…"

Aidoneus tightened his arm around Persephone. She could feel the heartache of seventy-seven years, of losing her each spring, again and again… the fear that she would be adrift forever after the loss of their son… her sense of all he felt had been muted, damaged by grief, but a tenuous thread remained. Persephone broke away and stood before Aidon, her hand resting over his heart.

"…I thought I'd lost you. How are you here with me?"

Aidoneus regarded her, his hands framing her shoulders, drawing her in, his lips warm on hers. Persephone's hands tangled in his hair as she returned his kiss, silence and relief spilling over. He pressed her closer and a frisson traveled the length of her body— one that normally would send her deeper into his embrace but instead lanced her with anguish, then guilt, then anger. She tried to bury it, but the more she resisted, the deeper it cut.

"Don't you see?" Eurydice smiled. "They had mercy on us."

Orpheus laughed nervously. "I thought they were punishing me when the snake attacked you. Hermes said they hadn't sent it, but… I'd never seen such an unnatural pattern of green and blue."

Aidoneus broke their kiss and stood still as stone, his entire body tensing, knuckles turning white. Persephone looked up at his shocked face. His eyes were unfocused.

"I was so afraid. I saw you moments before I was allowed to drink… to remember. I saw you… they were here with you— Hades and Persephone, and you were laying just as I saw you now and… I *knew* it was you. Even after forgetting, I *knew…*"

Orpheus pushed a wayward lock behind her ear and lowered his forehead to hers. "Didn't I tell you that would be so? The day before our wedding I told you. No matter what, I would find you here."

Eurydice placed her palm on his arm and her lips slanted against his, their hands traveling across cloth and skin, memories of warmth and longing drowning out all else. Orpheus coaxed her back to the earth and their hands furiously pulled at pins, they shrugged off spun wool, desperate to free themselves while their lips remained locked together, eager to enjoy in Elysion what they were denied in life.

Persephone averted her eyes from the entangled lovers and made her way up the hill alongside Aidon. His pace quickened and he surpassed her, shoulders stiff, fists clenched. The brief causeway he had opened to her was dammed up again, yet she could sense waves of barely restrained anger rolling off of him. She heard a distant cry of pleasure from Eurydice.

He wishes it was us in the field, Persephone thought. A fortnight had passed since she'd broken free of her overwhelming grief, and she had rejected his every overture. His attempts were becoming rarer and timider. Persephone hadn't dared to kiss him until today, terrified that he would think she toyed with him. Each step they took toward home drew them closer to their bedroom and inevitability.

Her eyes welled up again and she stopped under the rustling leaves of a sycamore on the edge of the broad meadow.

She wilted and sat. Aidon stood over her and she leaned her forehead into her hand, sobbing. "I can't give you what you want. I want to, but I can't. I'm sorry."

Aidoneus was silent, his fingernails digging into his palm. At last, he sat in front of her and crossed his legs. "In time, my love. That's not what weighs on me. Not by far."

"Don't lie to me! You're furious. I can barely feel you anymore, but I can sense *that*. What are you hiding?"

"My anger is *not* at you," he began. "Persephone, we *must* speak about what happened to you… and to our son."

"I can't even mourn him properly!" she cried. "Because Zagreus isn't even dead! Just waiting in a… vessel… somewhere."

"Listen to me." He took her hands in his. "I know you wish it weren't so, that what Hecate discovered was a mistake. I did too. But it is all true. The silphium—"

"It's not possible. I'm certain Apollo found out about the lyre, sought his petty vengeance by petitioning hard for Asklepios. But he didn't dare come near me. He tucked his tail and ran after we met with the *Dodekatheon*, and I've not seen him since. Silphium grows in *his* city. Who else could have?"

He bit his cheek and looked away.

"Who?" She leaned into his field of view. "Who, Aidon?"

"I couldn't bring myself to believe she could do it," he ground out, "until now when I heard Orpheus speak. I held out hope that it was someone in her household, acting as Apollo's agent. But it was Hera. She sent the serpent to murder Eurydice."

Persephone sat back, stunned. "Why?"

He turned to her, eyes narrow, jaw set. "Tell me everything about your *friendship* with her. Every detail, every *iota*, no matter how insignificant."

Persephone curled forward, staring at the ground between them. "I can't…"

"You must. Please." He picked up her chin, angry desperation written across his face. "Persephone, you cannot hide from this. Tell me about your first meeting with her."

A blue veiled woman sat at a loom, her back to them... Each memory was a shard of obsidian— darkly reflective, slicing her flesh as she recalled each meeting, each mention of Zagreus... Persephone thought about the deep chill permeating Hera's villa when Amphitrite spoke of Zeus's oath after the Pomegranate Agreement. Hera's single-minded interrogation after she'd conceived. The flash of relief on Hera's face after the birth of Atlantiades, when Persephone told her Zagreus hadn't quickened...

Her voice had grown hoarse by the time she retold the meeting on Hera's veranda. "The summons came two days before I descended."

"Two days..." He looked away.

"She cried. She said she was relieved that Zagreus had quickened... that she hadn't wanted to worry me. But... she was distraught *because* the baby was healthy, wasn't she?"

"Two days for the silphium to work."

"Hera hoped that I would miscarry before— so she'd be free from guilt. Then when that didn't come to pass, she... she thought we'd blame it on the journey to the Underworld. All her kindness... She fetched that last amphora of nectar *herself*, instead of summoning Iris..." Persephone remembered the wave of nausea that night, the pangs she felt the next day, Zagreus frantically kicking, struggling, trapped in her poisoned womb...

Sycamore leaves fell around them in clumps, cascading through newly withered branches, dead and white and stripped of bark. Persephone pushed his hands away angrily. She wobbled as she stood and shook off the dead leaves, breathing erratically, staggering over shriveled roots.

"Sweet one..."

"Why would she do this?!" Persephone snarled.

"Because she was fashioned into a weapon by—"

"Don't you dare absolve her of this!" Persephone shouted down at him. "She killed our son!"

"I'm not!" He stood and grasped her arms. "Persephone, she will pay, and pay dearly, but I don't blame the arrow for hitting its mark. Not when the man who aimed it stands ready to loose another!"

"Apollo?"

"No. *Zeus.*"

She blinked, her lungs burning. "Why would Zeus... why would *my father* want this?"

"The oath." He ground his teeth. "He meant for it to drive a wedge between us, to place his thumb upon me again after the famine. He thought it impossible for us to conceive. Everyone did. Ares called the oath down before the entire court—in front of his mother. And Zeus knows exactly how to manipulate his wife. That one act of singular cruelty would be enough to unchain her."

Bile welled in her throat. "They fought terribly that day. But they've quarreled before... to the point of nearly separating. What made this different?" Aidon looked away. "What?"

"I know only rumors," Aidon said hesitantly.

"Tell me." Her eyes were embers. "You must."

"After I sent Briareos to break the rebellion on Olympus, Zeus dealt with Hera swiftly and harshly. Chained her in the sky for what was supposed to be a decade. But he released Hera far earlier than anyone expected, and was faithful long after because, as I've heard it told, they found new pleasures in their marriage while she was bound..." He looked up at Persephone pointedly. "They are ones you and I have enjoyed in love, honoring each other's tolerances. But he twists them, uses that vulnerability against Hera to shame and debase her."

"Then he abandoned her."

"And pulled the bowstring taut. Apollo found his opportunity: he bartered our son's life for Asklepios's immortality." Persephone heard his words distantly, the stripped branches spinning. Hades ruminated on each realization. "Orpheus spoke of that serpent. That is how I knew for certain it was her. Hera sent it… the same that has sent many ill-fated women to our realm, created from the very cloth she wears— an extension of her will. She killed Eurydice so we could never conceive at Samothrace again."

Persephone remembered the peacock green filet Hera had worn that day and her skin prickled. A whine grew in her ears. The grass rippled and shimmered in the Elysian field, like the turning sycamores in Thessaly, far below Hera's veranda on Olympus. Like the world on fire.

"Sweet one?"

It wavered like the nectar after she set down her cup, like the waters of the Styx as Charon rowed madly for shore. The warm grass tilted, the Fields falling on its side.

"Persephone!"

✻　　✻　　✻

He stepped out of the ether and into their bedroom, his wife in his arms. As smoke and mist dissipated behind him, he set her down gently on the mattress.

"I'm fine."

"No, you're not."

"Aidon, I'm fine."

"You were staring off into nothing! Just as you were when—"

"Stop cosseting me!" Her eyes filled with tears. "Please."

He backed away and sat at the hearth. Persephone sobbed and curled up, holding her bare shoulders. He sighed. "I'm sorry."

"I'm tired of apologies. I'm tired of apologizing. Especially when we know. We *know* that there's nothing to apologize for. None of this is *us*; this was done *to* us."

Aidoneus said nothing. Every part of him rioted, pulling in all directions at once. He wanted to scream out across the river. He wanted quiet solitude to reveal a course of action. He wanted to split the earth and topple mountains, or drink the Lethe so they could forget the last crucial detail Orpheus had revealed. He wanted to stare up at the stars, alone, at peace. He wanted to gather up his wife, seduce and cajole away any hesitation left in her, and take her so deeply and ravenously that it banished all their emptiness and anger. He wanted to sit beside her in tranquility, just for a moment, without the shadow of loss looming over them. As if sensing his tumult, she spoke.

"There's nothing we can do."

"I will not accept that."

She breathed steadily, a line of tears drying on her face in the flickering light. "Nothing that won't end in fire."

"I pushed you too far, wife. Sought too much from you. But I can—"

"No," she said evenly. "I'm glad for it. Everything feels clearer now."

"Sweet one…"

"He's *gone*, Aidon. Trapped forever. Even if we found a way to have children, they'd never let us. And if we seek justice, it will destroy the earth."

He wanted to hold her but knew she would only shrink away. Aidon spoke softly. "I refuse to go quietly about my duties while they carry on without consequence."

"I'm tired. Tired of clinging to empty hope."

"Persephone, I swear it to you. We will have our satisfaction."

She nodded in clear disbelief, tears still dribbling down her cheek. She covered his hand with hers, intertwining their fingers, and drifted into an exhausted sleep.

Aidoneus could not. He was weary, but his mind was agitated and restless. He lay beside her until he was sure she wouldn't wake, then gently rose from the bed.

Aidon closed their doors and walked to the furthest edge of the terrace, staring into the Riverlands of Acheron. He sucked in a breath and bellowed into the enveloping silence until his throat ached and his lungs were emptied. He watched the unmoving river.

"Many true fires burned." Hecate appeared next to him, her gown white, ready to deepen to red as the moon changed. "But you did not light them all."

"How could I tell her that even if we find a way to restore Zagreus, she cannot carry him?"

"Wise to leave that unkindled."

"Was it?" Aidon scoffed. "It wasn't so long ago that I wouldn't be able to hide that even if I wanted to. Before this, we knew each other's thoughts. But that bridge is eroding every day. The connection we have through our *hieros gamos* is *fading*, Hecate. Only turmoil throws a rope across the gap. I feel as if I'm sacrificing our bond to spare *her*. It's absurd."

"It is love's sacrifice. A well-trod crossing is always rebuilt."

"I'm not so certain. She even refuses to…" He looked down. "Through other hardships, other quarrels, we could reconnect where words weren't needed, and find our lodestar in each other. But I'm lost, and Persephone more so."

"A dozen moons ago, I told you the perils of the course you charted. Now you have reached the great fork in the river."

"There is no path but one, Hecate." He raised his palms. "Persephone is right. If we attempt to have children, they will stop us, and if we make war on them, as we have *every right* to do, it will end humanity."

"The mountain is home to many allies."

He shook his head. "Not enough to hold Hera to account. Zeus knew that when he set her loose."

"Yet the Aegis-bearer stands with you. She is shield and spear for your son, steadfast as iron, silent as an owl." Hecate frowned sadly, the final truth written on her face. "But courage and arms will not slow the wheeling stars in the sky."

"What do you mean?"

"Midwinter winds come swiftly. When the walls between the realms are as the brittle leaf, so crumble the wards that give Zagreus life."

"No. I *promised her…*"

"You, and all." She placed her hand on his. "Lift the weight of this duty from her back, Aidoneus. You cannot see the manner of his weaving, but his thread shall not waste on the floor. The Weavers shall weave him anew, but on an Olympian tapestry, not a Chthonic one."

One who is twice woven cannot remain your own… He looked away, sickened. To let another bear their child, and in doing so, rob their son of his birthright…

"He was sired by those who dwell in the earth, but his lineage is heavenly. The cosmos is wide and wild; a descendant of Ouranos will need a guardian, from seed to sprout to stalk. Only one can protect him, and no other stands so greatly in your debt."

She may as well have run him through. His voice ground out, airless. "Not him. After all this, not him."

"Your child floats outside of life; he must be reborn, and soon, or he will die."

"Zeus will never agree to it."

Hecate focused her gaze on him. "You *will* show him the cold clarity of a winter pond, Aidoneus. And you will not do so alone."

"If my son dies, Hecate," he said dispassionately, eyes fixed on the river, "I will tear down that mountain stone by stone."

"Then there is no path but one before us."

16.

T HE HEARTH FIRE ROARED, BANISHING THE MIDWINTER chill in her room. Zeus sat on a leopard skin rug, garbed in a simple tunic while Semele lounged in his lap, basking in the warmth. With her, he felt like a young man again.

She kissed him, her mouth warm and sweet like honey. Her ripe berry nipple stiffened against his palm, and the low hanging southern sun defined every exquisite crinkle of aroused flesh. Her peplos was slung about her hips, the fibulae long since scattered, a sash alone holding it aloft. Zeus was in no hurry. He enjoyed Semele's eagerness and zest. Her desire was pure, untainted. No games to be played, no scores to settle. Just sweetness and sunlight.

"My lord…" she sighed against his lips.

"What is it, sweetling?"

"I want…" She paused and blushed heavily. "I want what I asked for last month."

He smiled. "You still can't have it."

"You've said that every time." Semele pouted prettily. "You've had children with others. Do you think so little of me that—"

"Of course not. Perhaps you've heard the legends of my wife's wrath falling upon those women? All true. I would spare you that. You are dear to me and I won't see you tormented, or your child tormented, all the days of your life."

"I am strong enough to withstand her."

He smiled and framed her small face with his hand. "You're not. I love you, but you're not."

"Show me you love me. I want to be deemed worthy of your child. I have only the memory of you *telling* me you love me, but spending upon my thighs and breasts."

"I do so *because* I love you. Any child I begot on you would be your undoing."

"Please… Zeus, it's almost midwinter, but I'm as fertile as a field in spring. Just think how strong he would be. I would give you a son… a great hero to venerate you, whose name would live on forever; the equal of Perseus. Please—"

The girl fell over, dead asleep. Zeus overcame his surprise just in time to catch her head before it could crack against the stone floor. He laid Semele down softly, suddenly alert to the silence, and pulled back the thatch covering the entrance to her balcony. He gazed over the sea, recently roiling with winter waves, now smooth as glass. There was no clamor from the marketplace. No calls of cranes and kestrels. Everything had gone still. Turning around, he saw a broad silver wing fold back. Hypnos crouched over Semele, poppy in hand.

"What in Fates are you doing here?" Zeus strode toward him, eyes crackling. "You could have killed her!"

"He is very skilled with the poppy, young one. He won't kill her," a voice said. "But I still could."

Thanatos lounged at the foot of Semele's bed, tracing the curve of his sickle. Death's black wings stretched and the flesh started to peel back from his face. The King of the Gods sucked in a breath and cautiously took a step back. Decay receded, restoring Thanatos's youthful visage, and he walked to Hypnos's side.

"Don't you touch her."

"I don't intend to," Thanatos said, his voice unnaturally warm.

"We are merely heralds." Hypnos smiled.

The room darkened, dim colorless light replacing the midday sun. A white corona glowed in its place, and stars pricked the sky. Shadows rippled on the floor. Nyx floated just outside on the veranda, as though swimming through the air. The shadow of her dark consort, Erebus, wound about her. Zeus backed away slowly. "Lady Nyx. What business do you and your children have here?"

"Perhaps you can guess," a deep voice intoned. Zeus knew who spoke. The Lord of the Underworld removed his helm and stepped into the room, a young woman in white by his side.

Hecate. Zeus hadn't seen her since the Pomegranate Agreement. He paled, looking from one to the other. Hades wore his full armor, dark cloak hanging from his shoulders, sword slung across his back. The last time he'd seen that armor it had been smeared with the gore of Titans and monsters. And Death was here, brandishing their father's lethal sickle...

Zeus's mouth went dry. Feigning ignorance would only incense Hades. "Hera was out of line. She shouldn't have—"

"But she did. And you unleashed her."

Zeus snorted. "I am *not* responsible for your son's death."

"Your oath drove Hera to poison my wife. A *sacred, unbreakable* oath, and a pure mockery."

"Your love affair nearly destroyed the earth. You're lucky my ridicule was the *only* consequence you suffered that day. If Persephone hadn't come up with a tidy solution—"

"You will *not* speak her name!" The Lord of the Dead's eyes grew wide and cold, and his stare chilled Zeus to his core. "My child, Zeus. My *son!* You *killed* my *son!*"

He'd never seen Hades this enraged. Not even during the war. And if he didn't bank his brother's anger quickly, there would surely be another. "Aidon—"

"Not by your hand, no. But with the *poison* you have leached into your wife for aeons. A poison that murdered my son in the womb." His fingers twitched.

Zeus swallowed. *Placate him. It's the only way this won't end in fire.* "You're… you're right." Zeus spread his arms in surrender. "I know you're right. Aidoneus, please… Cast blame on me, rend my flesh, but please absolve Hera."

"I will neither absolve nor forgive her. Nor you. And if you think I will forget this—"

"I know you won't. What happened was a tragedy. An absolute *tragedy*, Aidoneus. Everyone on Olympus mourns your loss. Do you truly think I wanted my firstborn daughter to suffer this way?" He looked down and sighed. "What is it you want of me?"

"You will make this right. And you will do it by keeping your oath," Aidoneus said. "I never thought to call it up before. But now…"

"Aidon…" Madness. A *madness* that could unravel all existence— the curse of their kind. He spoke gently. Carefully. "Brother, he's gone. Zagreus is dead."

"His heart yet beats," Hecate said. "Sheltered safely by a fruit plucked from your *own* tree."

"What do you mean?"

The ether bloomed, ringed in snakes and olive branches, and through it stepped Athena. Her eyes were piercing silver-gray: and she breathed shallowly. What had they done to her? Zeus ran to her.

"Daughter, are you well? Tell me they didn't harm you."

Athena pulled away from him with a sneer, crowding closer to Aidoneus. She clung to a cubical wooden box, polished dark and reflective, carved in adamant on all sides with the symbol of *hieros gamos* and wrapped in potent wards of protection from the worlds above and below.

"Athena… They can't threaten—"

"Why would they when I stand with them?" Athena wept, unable to hold back. Her heart was too soft for her own good. Just like her mother. "I went below to see my darling friend after she descended. My *sister*. I found her in shambles, Father. *Destroyed*."

"Daughter—"

"You *destroyed* Persephone! How could you allow this?! You knew this could— this *would* come to pass. And you *let* it happen. Like you always do. You… who have the Fates themselves whispering in your ear, and still!"

"They speak in riddles and contradictions, daughter. Aidoneus, tell her. You know better than anyone here—"

"Don't look to me for excuses," Aidoneus interrupted. "My son's future is my only concern. Zagreus will be reborn. You, Zeus Aegiduchos Cronides, will keep your oath. *You* will ensure his safety. And after you, he will inherit the heavens and the earth alike."

"And if I refuse?"

Hades Aidoneus Chthonios stared him in the eye, emotionless. "War."

Zeus dragged his hand back through his blond hair. "You realize what you ask of me."

"*Timoria*, Zeus. *Justice* for my unborn son. The line of succession will pass through Persephone— *that* is the blood price I demand for your wife's treachery. Be glad I do not ask for greater vengeance against Hera."

He looked at Athena. "And you agree with this *timoria*, daughter? Knowing what it means?"

"If you do not," Athena said, swallowing, "I will see you next on the field."

Zeus seethed. He had forgiven her the last betrayal because she had been so young, too easily swayed by Poseidon. And now she was in the thrall of his eldest brother. He balled his fists and took a step forward.

Athena was unmoved. Her arms tightened around the box and she threw back her shoulders. "If I stand with Chthonia, so will Hermes, and you know it. Demeter goes without saying. And we know what she is capable of."

"I overlooked treachery once, girl, but—"

"I'm not finished," Athena said, raising her voice. "I've considered this carefully, Father. Have you? Artemis—"

"Wouldn't dare."

"She wouldn't shield Apollo, knowing he launched this conspiracy with Hera, all because of his wounded pride over a missing lyre. Artemis let Persephone be taken to the Underworld, at my urging; she won't betray her a second time. Then there's Aphrodite."

"She hates you."

"But she *loves* Persephone. And with Aphrodite and Eros, goes Hephaestus."

"He would never take up arms against his own mother."

"No. He'll *forge* them. Hera let Hephaestus languish for ages with Thetis after you threw him from Olympus..." Athena's eyes were the color of frost. "He has had a friend, a counselor— a *father*, even— in Aidoneus. More than he ever had in you. *You've* seen to that over the years. And where Aphrodite goes, Ares follows. And without Ares's legitimacy, you have no cause to fight for."

Zeus opened his mouth to speak but stopped. His son only thought with his cock when it came to that woman.

"Who do you have left? Hestia? She won't stand with you— she never really has. That would leave your beloved conspirators— the God of Light and the Queen of Heaven. A formidable trio, to be sure. Thanks to how you've arranged this cosmos, you're practically omnipotent. You might sway Poseidon, but we both know he would be all too happy to betray you. As soon as he recognized Aidoneus's advantage, he would bring the seas crashing down upon you.

"You would have no warriors save an archer who is bested in every way by his twin sister, and a goddess whose most formidable weapons are useless on a battlefield. You'll have no forge, no herald, no stratagem, no hope of victory. Because if you ever gained an upper hand, I will set free the Titan who masterminded your father's downfall. And I don't think Prometheus has taken kindly to being chained on that mountain with an eagle forever feasting on his entrails."

Zeus stared at Athena, dumbstruck, then from one chthonic god to the next. They would go to war. And she would lead them. Her… his Aegis-bearer, the child prophesied to end him— the very reason he devoured his darling Metis. His eyes settled on Aidoneus, his brother's expression flinty, unyielding.

"Either we rend the world asunder, Zeus or Zagreus is reborn." Aidoneus pointed at the unconscious Semele. "And it shall be upon this woman. Who has already said she wishes to bear… *you* a child."

Aidoneus sallowed as he ground out the last few words. Zeus scoffed. "If I do, you fool, Zagreus won't be your—"

"You think I don't know that?!" Aidoneus bellowed, his voice filling the chamber. He loomed forward. "That I would choose this?! If it means he lives, it's a sacrifice I will make. To stand afar alongside his mother, to watch our son grow to manhood in this corrupted world, to see him live as one of your carelessly sewn bastards, because thanks to *your* wife's murderous spite, he cannot *survive* if my wife bears him."

"Passing him off as my spawn will not save him from He-ra."

"Zagreus won't be a mere *hemitheos*. He will be deathless, and when he comes of age, he will sit at court on Olympus as your heir."

"Aidoneus…"

Zeus trailed off and looked from Nyx to Hecate, to Thanatos and Hypnos, to Aidoneus, and Athena standing tall beside them. In this instant, she looked just like Metis. He blinked and saw the guiding vision of the Fates— chains wound about him in the Pit of Tartarus, just as they bound Kronos. And another— the chains slipping from their accursed father's arms and releasing him to burn and bury the remains of the earth. Compromise wasn't a choice; it was a necessity.

"I relent." Neither Hades nor Athena budged from their stance. "Damnation, I yield, Aidoneus; do you hear me? Do what must be done!"

The Lord of the Underworld nodded. "Hecate?"

Athena handed the wooden box carefully to the witch and backed away, her resolute visage twisting with grief.

"Daughter, wait…" Zeus reached for her but she flinched away. Eyes running with tears, she opened a pathway back to Olympus and was gone before Zeus could say another word.

Hecate raised her hands and the vessel floated over the sleeping girl. The sigils on every side began to glow. Louder and louder, a heartbeat thrummed through the room until it became a pounding rhythm. The box disappeared in a blinding radiance, brighter than the sun, finally incinerating its wooden confines. Zeus squinted. Hecate closed her eyes and the brilliant heart settled between her outstretched hands. She lowered it onto the girl, her body drowned in light, hands hovering above Semele's womb.

Hecate's palms crashed together and the light vanished. The girl convulsed once, and Zeus blinked as Hecate spoke. "The ground is fertile. He has taken root, already nourished. Zagreus will be reborn, but not of that name— he will be twice woven as Dimetor. He of Two Mothers."

"But..." Aidon's hands shook. "Hecate, you cannot... Persephone is—"

"...the mother who gave him life, Aidon," she finished, "and this mother will let him keep it." Hecate stood and touched his cheek. He batted away her hand and turned from all of them. Zeus lowered his eyes. He could never know Aidon's anguish, but he'd felt a flicker of it. Though all were *hemitheoi* and destined to die, he'd lost a hundred sons and daughters over the aeons, and had felt each death keenly.

"This is a simple favor, Cronides," Nyx said. "It is not enough. You may have placated our Liberator, but you owe our realm much more. You've deprived Chthonia of our queen for half the year, and now you deprive us of the God of Elysion. When this child is born, he will no longer be of our world. He will be of yours. Alive, but without the destiny given him."

"You don't rule the Underworld anymore, Nyx. My brother often forgets that, but I don't."

"But I value her counsel greatly." Aidon turned again to face him, his voice edged with anger. "She speaks the truth."

"One from your world for one of ours. You and your consort have many children, Cronides. You can spare one," Nyx said, narrowing her eyes.

Zeus eyed the assembled gods. Thanatos leaned on a column polishing his accursed sickle. Hypnos twirled the poppy that kept Semele and the city of Tiryns in a stupor. "Fine."

"Which will you offer?"

"Pasithea is unwed. We'll make a bond between her and one of your sons, Nyx. I will give her to Hypnos."

"Hypnos doesn't..." Aidon began to protest, then caught himself.

The God of Sleep paled, then stared at his mother. Nyx looked upward, listening to Erebus speak words only she could hear.

"This is amenable to us," Nyx said.

Aidon muttered words to Nyx that Zeus barely recognized— the Speech of the Protogenoi, a language that hadn't been spoken above ground since the time of his grandfather. He strained to glean a few fleeting phrases: *Not lie with woman... unjust to both...*

Hecate spoke in the same cryptic tongue, but it was clear they were all quelling Aidoneus's protests. Nyx responded in Theoi for Zeus's benefit. "She will see in time. Pasithea will live outside the cage that the Tyrant and his son have fashioned for all womankind. Far better to thrive below than as breeding stock for the spawn of Ouranos."

"It is done, then." Zeus was no fool. He knew that Hypnos enjoyed only the company of men. Now by the decree of his own mother, Zeus could wipe that arrogant smirk off the God of Sleep's face. It served him right for what he'd done to Semele.

Semele...

"Enough of this. Hades and Persephone's child will grow to manhood in the guise of my own. To save him from himself, it will be with *no knowledge* of his origin. And when he comes of age, he will be welcomed to Olympus."

"As a member of the *Dodekatheon*," Aidon declared.

"As a... Hades, you know what *dodeka-* means don't you?" Zeus said, an eyebrow raised.

"It means you have a difficult choice ahead of you," he spat back.

Hypnos was solemn, his eyes fixed on the ground. "When will... will I be married to Pasithea?"

"Two weeks after the next new moon, during Gamelia, as is tradition," Zeus said. "And it will be dreary enough that she will have something to look *forward* to when I send her below to you."

"It's settled, then," Aidon said. "Remember your part, Zeus. I would demand a Stygian oath, young one, but I know that though you hold all others to them, they are meaningless to you. So know this: break this pact and I will bring the full weight of my kingdom upon you. If you or any of yours ever move against me again, I will scourge the earth with the dead. And you will not prevail because I, not you, hold the balance of life and death, and the end of this cosmos."

Zeus's eyes flicked to his brother's left hand and the rings emblazoned on it. His voice came out far quieter than he would have wanted. "I swear it."

Aidoneus merely nodded.

"Now what?"

"Do what you do best. Rut on an innocent woman who doesn't know you the way we do."

Zeus opened his mouth to retort but nothing came out.

Aidoneus donned his Helm and walked toward the portico, speaking over his shoulder. "Do not betray me again."

As suddenly as his last words were uttered, they disappeared. Night lifted. Shadows grew constant in the waxing sunlight. Terns circled over crashing waves. Men in the market laughed, as though they hadn't felt the effects of Hypnos's poppy.

Semele moaned and stirred. "What happened?"

"Are you alright?" Zeus asked gently. "You fainted. Too close to the fire."

"I don't even remember becoming lightheaded."

"It happened so quickly."

She stared up at him and her eyes softened. "My poor lord, look at you… you're shaking. Did I worry you so much?"

He swallowed. "No, sweetling. I was merely contemplating…"

"Did you consider what I said?"

"Yes." He kissed Semele again and slipped her sash from her waist, her peplos falling away. He pulled her beneath him before the fire. "Yes, I did."

✻   ✻   ✻

The curtain opened and the bed sagged beneath his weight. Persephone lay still, eyes closed. "Where were you?"

Aidoneus lay on his back, staring up. "Tiryns. I confronted Zeus directly."

"Without me?" He said nothing. She propped herself up on one arm. "Are we at war?"

"No."

"Then…"

"I extracted from him… an accord."

Persephone rolled away from him. "What… *accord*… could possibly make right what they did?"

"One that will be meted out over time."

"Is that all you're going to say?"

"For now." He exhaled. "Get some sleep, Persephone. It's late."

"Nothing you have arranged with him could equal what she did to me."

"The first part comes due soon," he said. He felt his throat closing. "I'll tell you in the morning."

She sighed and shut her eyes. Tension clung to her even after she fell asleep. Her breath was even. The sheet spilled over her hip and trailed down her back. His hands itched to hold her, to nudge her awake and let everything he'd done come pouring out, but he knew he could not. Instead, he stared at the canopy, restless— craving solace, wanting her, having neither.

17.

T HE WATER WAS WARM IN THE KANATHOS SPRING AT Nauplia, soothing in any season. But during Gamelia the air was frigid, thanks to Demeter, her sow of a sister, and— she didn't want to think about Persephone. Not at all. Months had passed and she had finally shed the weight of what had been done. The waters were a balm, and she wouldn't let that be ruined by a chill wind.

"Wife." Zeus approached her; thumb tucked alongside the knot in his tunic's belt.

Zeus and Hera had discovered the restorative spring early in their marriage. He took particular delight in breaching her renewed maidenhead each year, and in those days, she had, in turn, relished his enthusiasm. Once, long ago, he had blurted out that he loved her above all women, that he worshiped her, his senses overcome as she rode atop him— a position he rare-ly allowed.

"Let's get this over with, shall we?" Hera pulled her shawl off her shoulders. "Then you're free to return to your whore."

With each of his numberless wanderings, Nauplia had in-creasingly become her refuge— a place to forget Olympus, forget *him*, to leave all behind her and be a free maiden again.

But at the damp end of every winter, there was Zeus, waiting to cover her in his scent and sweat and remind her that she was his property. Mortals had built her a grand temple, a place for her to be consecrated, for him to be anointed by her body every year as the ruler of Olympus. A *hieros gamos* in the way only men could perceive such a thing.

Hera unslung her girdle and pushed up her peplos, then took her place on the wide couch, thighs open. She turned her head away as he threw off his tunic, and bit her cheek when Zeus settled between her legs. Her eyes squeezed shut, denying him the satisfaction of a cry or even a wince as her hymen tore anew. He lay heavy across her, panting hard in her ear with each stroke.

"Face me," he rasped. She stiffened her neck. "Have enough regard to look at me."

She turned slowly, her eyes flitting with contempt from the sweat on his brow to the clench of his jaw, a hair in his beard that shone more silver than the others.

"Damn you," he muttered. Zeus covered her lips with his and stroked his tongue into her open mouth, faster, echoing each thrust within her. He flicked and pinched at one of her nipples and Hera couldn't silence herself anymore. She mewled into his mouth, suffocated, and broke free, smothered by the friction of him everywhere upon her and within her. He growled and bucked, gasping against the hollow of her neck.

Zeus withdrew and walked to the basin to clean off. Her passage stung, the sheet beneath them flecked with blood. Hera sat up slowly. "She's pregnant, isn't she?"

He spun around, flinging a stained rag to the floor. "You will do nothing this time. Are we clear?"

"I followed Hermes to Tiryns. So foolishly close to here, Zeus— I expected better of you. But I'm impressed you lasted as long as you did, spilling outside her. You hate doing that if memory serves. Though perhaps you didn't hold out as long as

I thought, since Semele is showing sooner than expected. Surely her benefactor, King Sthenelus, has taken notice of her harlotry."

"Stay away from her."

She smirked at him. "Amphitrite gave me such a lovely idea. Maybe I should burn your lover alive mid-stroke the way Persephone did when that whore nymph tried to seduce Aidoneu—"

She was flat on her back again, pinned underneath him, his hand tightening around her jaw.

"You will *keep their names out of your mouth!*" His eyes burned. Hera struggled, trying to wrench free. When she went slack, Zeus released her. "I know what you did."

All protestations died in her throat.

"You will never comprehend the price I had to pay for it, Hera. *Never.*" He backed away from her and donned his tunic. "Or how fortunate you are, that Hades laid all the blame at *my* feet after you murdered his child in the womb."

Her chest felt hollowed out. Everything she'd drowned in bathing, weaving, and wine flooded to the surface. "What price?" she choked out.

He mumbled unintelligibly and wound his himation around his shoulders.

"What price, Zeus?!"

"Let's just say, I hope you found some time for Pasithea this winter."

"No..." Hera lunged, clawing at him. "What have you done?!"

"I kept you out of Tartarus!" He grabbed her wrists and forced her back down. "And prevented a war. You're welcome."

"You married off *our daughter* to them! You have countless bastards to choose from!"

"They wouldn't settle for a bastard," Zeus growled. "The price was a child sired on *you*. It's too late now. We held *proaulia* at the symposium with Athena and Eileithyia yesterday. Hermes already took her below to wed Hypnos."

She sat on the bed and stared at him blankly. Hypnos. The God of Sleep...

"Best make your peace with the marriage arrangement. And be grateful I was able to keep what you did quiet among the others. Because if they knew that you nearly cost us forty thousand years of peace, they'd have me remove you from the *Dodekatheon*. And I'd be right to do it. Have a care, wife, because there is a *long* line of gods who imagine themselves worthy of a seat."

A brilliant flash blinded her, and he was gone, a deafening roll of thunder following him. Hera shook, limbs failing her when she tried to stand.

*　　*　　*

Aidoneus adjusted his crown of golden poplar and looked back at his wife. "I need to clear my head. You can still come with me, you know."

"No thank you."

"I'll be back in time."

"Why did you arrange this in the first place? A sham marriage to avenge the murder of my baby?"

"This is neither the first nor the last consequence, sweet one. I swear it."

Persephone sighed. "She's from the world above and she's going to hate it here."

"You've seemed to enjoy yourself," he said flatly.

"What's that supposed to mean?"

"Nothing." He carefully draped his himation over his shoulder. "Pasithea will know greater freedom here than she

350

ever would have above. She will be able to travel freely, unveiled, unmolested…"

"And what of Hypnos?"

"He knows his duty."

"Utterly thoughtless." Cold blue-gray eyes glared up at him. "You know he *only* prefers men!"

"Nothing will change for him, wife."

"No? And for her?"

He gritted his teeth. "I'll return before dusk."

He spun on his heel and walked downstairs to the great hall. Divans and braziers had been dragged into the room, just as they would be whenever Persephone returned. Tempting fruits gathered from Elysion lay heaped on black clay plates, but he doubted she would eat any of them. Neither Pasithea nor his wife.

He nodded curtly to Nyx and Hecate, hurrying his pace before they could speak. Aidon crossed the garden, where Menoetes and Clymena were weaving golden poplar crowns for themselves before the festivities began. He didn't return their bows, his eyes trained on his destination. He approached the sunlit grove and ducked under a branch, letting his eyes adjust to the brightness of Elysion.

One who is twice woven…

She deserved to know. Even if they could never have Zagreus back. He'd asked Hecate and Nyx about bringing the baby to the Underworld after he was born; they'd explained that if ambrosia weren't taken with his mother's milk, he couldn't survive in Chthonia, let alone become deathless. They'd watch their son die a second time. He passed the sycamore that Persephone had killed with her grief and anger—the only lifeless thing in Elysion, now an eternal marker of their mourning. Aidon paused beneath it, then turned right, heading for a small valley with a pond and a grove of linden trees.

The sun was hot on his shoulders, every ray swallowed by his heavy black himation. He climbed a high bank and stripped off his clothes, setting his poplar crown atop them in the dappled shade, then dove headfirst. The water hit him with a slap, wrapped him in ice, and he surfaced with a gasp. It prickled and tightened his skin, but he was grateful to feel something. He floated, limbs splayed, the cold seeping through skin and bone. He closed his eyes.

"Orpheus?" A bright voice called from the hillside.

"No, it's me." He submerged himself, obscuring his nakedness.

Eurydice traipsed down the path. "Oh! My lord, I'm so sorry."

"It's no trouble, Eurydice. And please, call me Aidon. I consider you and your husband my friends."

"Thank you… Aidon. I'll leave you in peace."

"No, just… turn around. I'll only be a moment." He pulled himself from the water and wrung out his hair, then dressed, leaving his himation and crown heaped on the bank. "Where is he, anyway?"

"Trying his hand at smoking out the hives."

"Going better than last time?"

"He's…" She laughed. "I'm sure he'll get the feel for it one day. He has an eternity to learn."

Aidoneus sat on a low branch and relaxed back against the tree trunk. "I am still baffled that of all the things you could do in Paradise, you choose to toil as you did in life."

She shrugged. "We'd be bored stiff if we just lay around staring at each other. I mean, the first month here together all we did was…" She looked away and blushed.

"I learned quickly to announce my presence whenever I came to visit," he said, giving her a smirk that quickly fell from his face.

Her mirth faded as swiftly as his. "How is she? Have you said anything?"

He shook his head. "It would only make things worse. I can't risk destroying her all over again."

"You need to tell her." She looked toward the woods, where Orpheus trod toward them. "It's... strange that we know, yet she does not."

"You've seen the sycamore on the hill." He looked up with a nod to Orpheus. The man sat next to his wife, having overheard the gist of their discussion. "She shows me nothing but anger, but I will take every bit of her ire if it keeps her above the darkness."

"That was nearly three months ago," Orpheus said. "Doubtless she is starved for good news. And there *is* good news. Your child will live."

"But not as *our child*, the god who was supposed to rule Elysion."

"Who's to say that the Fates would have given him that anyway?" Orpheus glanced at the crown and black himation with its gold meandros. "I'm guessing the wedding is today."

"She's none too happy about it."

"The bride or your wife?" Eurydice asked.

"Neither, I imagine."

"Do you seek my advice?" Orpheus said.

"It's among the reasons I am here."

"Tell Persephone. And tell her soon. If she finds out another way, you won't be able to forgive yourself." Orpheus frowned. "And forgiving yourself will be the least of your problems."

*　　*　　*

He'd said little on their flight from Olympus.

She was dressed for her wedding in peacock blue, her mother's color. She'd wished for one final visit with Hera before descending, but this was the way of things. Her father's word was final. Pasithea had never seen her husband. He was a monster: a Protogenoi of the ancient order, who could place mortals and gods alike in a stupor with a flick of his wrist. What would he do with her?

"You know, of all of them, he's the most like us." Hermes cleared his throat. "Except for the wings."

Pasithea shuddered, grateful for her thick saffron-dyed veil, glad they wouldn't see her face. After she had been ritually bathed, Aphrodite had attended her. She'd instructed Pasithea to think about the kohl around her eyes, that it would keep her from sobbing. It had worked so far. "Will I need a coin?"

"Not this time. We're headed straight to the palace," Hermes said as they neared the Styx. "Charon's attending the wedding feast. Hypnos is his younger brother."

She chewed her lip. The Ferryman of the Dead, the Minister of Death, the Goddess of Night, Keres, and Erinyes… her new family. What would they do if she displeased them? "There's more light here than I imagined."

"For now. Your hosts, the king and queen, wanted us to cross into their world at dusk." Even as he spoke, magnificent hues flared before them, pink and gold, then a wine-dark riot of purple and red, all calming to ink blue. Mists high overhead darkened to pitch, like a winter's night before the snow. The unexpected beauty of this realm did little to quell her fears.

The King and Queen of the Dead. She had yet to see their subjects. Or their three-headed dog. Or the Hundred-Handed Ones. Or other ghastly things dwelling in the Underworld. *Chthonia*, she reminded herself. That was their name for it. A dark palace carved into the cliffs above the river loomed ahead, its twisting halls lit brightly along the rock face. Hermes dove, landing on the terrace of a grand throne room, the walls dark and covered in tapestries, the dais glittering olivine, with braziers lighting the broad capped columns and high ceiling.

"Well," Hermes said, "I'm here as our father's proxy, but I can't eat at the feast. They know that. You should probably hold off too. Until the unveiling."

Once the marriage was sealed, she would be expected to eat the food of the dead— and be trapped here forever. Hermes loitered on the terrace, but Pasithea walked to the center of the room, lost in the new sights. Each tapestry told a story, mostly from the Titanomachy, long before she was born. She heard voices from the great hall and ducked out of sight when a woman with selenite beads strung through her hair approached.

"An Olympian marriage ceremony, here! The passing of *property*," Persephone hissed. "In *our* realm, Hecate! *How* is this *timoria*? If anything, this makes it worse."

"The sunlit world weighs far short of its debt to ours. But the Fates alone shall deliver the balance."

Pasithea had learned from Ares of Persephone's true nature. She was not the tenderhearted spring goddess everyone above remembered— she was the Carrier of Curses, who had called up the Keres to drag Sisyphus to his doom, who had incinerated Minthe, who had obliterated Kokytos, who freshly mourned her miscarried child… and she didn't want Pasithea here.

"A sham marriage," she said. "They owe us *everything* and all we received was a *marriage arrangement!* Hypnos is surely baffled, and she's probably terrified!"

"The full fruit has yet to ripen. Watch the vines and see," the Goddess of Witchcraft said. "She will see the fruit as well."

"I grow tired of waiting. Speaking of, where in Tartarus is he?"

Pasithea turned on her heel, running through the darkened portico, nearly knocking over Hermes.

"Easy, now, my lady."

"Hermes, you must take me from here," she whispered, gripping the folds of his chlamys. "This is a mistake. I shouldn't be here!"

He looked at her ruefully. "You *know* this was your father's arrangement. It can't be undone. You can make the best of it— this isn't a dreary realm. It's filled with riches, and the residents will... surprise you. I mean, Persephone has made this place her home, and now— well, there's been better times for that example, but you know what I mean."

They waited there, Pasithea's knees wobbling, for what felt like aeons. The door finally opened wide and Hades and Persephone walked arm in arm into the throne room. The queen's face was solemn. Hades nodded when Pasithea dipped into a low bow, then motioned her to stand.

"Welcome to our home," Persephone said. She managed a faint smile. "This way."

She walked behind them, Hermes at her heels. Their demeanor was so different from when she'd seen them during summer. In the presence of the *Dodekatheon*, they'd moved as one, and once the meeting broke, all could feel the pull between them, like lodestone and iron, even when they were on opposite sides of the room. Now they seemed stilted and unmoored.

In the great hall stood a tall man clad in a rich purple himation, broad silver wings folded behind him. Golden poplar leaves sat atop his silver hair. This was Hypnos, she realized: her husband to be. Flanking him were two of his brothers, both dressed in black. Thanatos, his younger twin, had wings as dark as his cloak. Morpheus, his elder brother, wore his hood low over his blinded eyes. Hypnos gave her a wide grin and she froze. He flourished and bowed to her, silvery wings outstretched. He raised his head first to meet her eyes, a soft smile lingering on his face. Pasithea's knees nearly gave out when she curtsied. He silently offered her his hand, then seated her beside him on a wide divan.

As the feast began, the proceedings magnified the strangeness of Pasithea's surroundings. Men and women sat intermingled, instead of separated as they ought to be. Pomegranates and figs, olives and dates, and foreign rarities like walnuts and oranges littered small plates between the divans. Here and there were clay cups of water. There was no music, only halting chatter, and the sparse assembly of chthonic gods seemed collectively ill at ease. Hypnos stood off with his family.

When Hermes walked past, she whispered to him. "Where is the wine?"

"They don't have any."

"A wedding with no wine?"

"There is none to be had in Chthonia," Hermes said, "and they've never hosted an Olympian wedding. Those ceremonies are *very* different here. They put on this feast especially for you." He smiled at her. "To make you more comfortable."

She ate nothing, and the guests seemed to barely touch the food. Hushed conversation echoed off the walls, and their royal hosts sat together in stony silence, observing without partaking. It felt more like *prothesis* for the dead than a wedding— and she was the corpse at the center of it.

It wasn't until Hypnos spoke and thanked the guests that she realized this was the moment of *anakalypteria*, the removal of the veil and feeding of fruit— the sign to all that she was now in her husband's care.

Her heart raced too fast to hear him. Pasithea bit her lips to keep them from quivering, and cool air washed across her face as Hypnos lifted the veil away. She prayed she wouldn't shame her old family, or offend her new one. She looked at Persephone, and as soon as their eyes met, the Queen sighed and looked away. Persephone despised her.

Pasithea's new husband cut a section of quince and held it before her. She trembled. Hypnos leaned in and whispered low. "Don't worry; it's from your world. I asked Hermes to bring it."

"The quince? But… the fruit should be provided b-by the husband."

"I'm holding it, aren't I?" He gave her a crooked smile. "Our fruits are far too binding. You won't have to unless *you* one day wish it."

Pasithea was confused, but all eyes were on her; she nibbled at the quince, savoring it even as she sealed herself to him in the eyes of the Olympians. She wasn't bound to Hypnos fully— not *yet*— and dread crawled through her, knowing what came next. The assembled gods clapped, their felicitations muted, and she wondered what she'd done wrong now.

Hypnos grasped her wrist and pulled her from the divan, leading her from the great hall and through brightly lit passages to his bedchamber. She breathed evenly, fighting the urge to cry or scream. Thanatos was waiting outside— as was Olympian tradition, lest she try to escape her wedding night— and raised an eyebrow at his brother. Hypnos swept a hand under her knees and lifted her over the threshold, then slammed the door behind them.

A single oil lamp at the bedside provided faint, warm light to the small room. While her eyes adjusted, he stood behind her, removing pins and loosening threads to pull her tight coiffure apart, until her hair relaxed into blonde waves down her back. Hypnos unsnapped her chafing armbands and set aside her bracelets, ornate necklace, and heavy girdle. Her thin peplos, held at the shoulders by simple pins and at the waist by a thin linen sash, was all that remained. The bed lay before them, black, soft, almost inviting, except for the perfectly placed white sheet of linen glaring at its center.

"Pasithea…" His wings lowered and she spun around to face him. "What is it that *you* want?"

Her mouth was dry. "Wh-what do you mean?"

"I mean… I want to know what you are expecting."

"That," her lip trembled, "you will… take me to wife."

He nodded slowly. "Is that what you want?" Hypnos sighed. "Our ways are not the ways of the world above. I swear to you, you have nothing to fear, so tell me truly… is sex something you actually desire from me?"

She crumpled and sat on the edge of the bed, shaking feverishly. A tear trickled down one cheek, then the other. How could she answer him honestly and not be punished? Was he trying to trick her? Hypnos sat next to her.

"I'll take that as a 'no'."

The dam burst and she wept, no longer caring if the kohl streaked. "It doesn't matter what I think."

"Yes, it does. A great deal. We were both pulled into this by forces far greater than us, but you and I are the only two people in this room."

The white cloth glowing in the lamplight blurred amidst her tears. "They expect it of us."

"Some do. Before you came to me, how did you imagine your wedding night?"

"I didn't. I never wanted one." She expected him to laugh at her, but he looked her in the eye and nodded, waiting. "Mother thought I was simply reluctant… being difficult… that I'd change my mind once I saw my husband, or had a child. But I never wanted to marry *or* have children. Ever."

"Then we have that in common."

She looked askance at the sheet. "They will expect *that* to be marked. Th-that my—" Pasithea faltered.

"I know." He put his hand over hers, gently as a butterfly landing. "They want me to *violently* break your maidenhead— a thing not all women have to begin with…" He chuckled, shaking his head. "I'm sorry. Their ways up above are so tiresome."

Her mouth fell open.

"We don't have to have sex tonight, Pasithea. Or *any* night. You're your own woman."

"But without you..." She looked pointedly at the sheet. "Hermes must bring back proof of the marriage," she said. "Or it will be illegitimate."

Hypnos shrugged at her, a slight smile still decorating his face. "Well, I suppose we'd better mark it. It won't take me but a minute. Just... relax. Close your eyes if you must."

Pasithea froze, then lowered her head to the pillow as he bade, shifting her body to lay on the cloth. She shook uncontrollably. A tear ran into her hairline and she lay stiff as iron until the bed shifted with his weight. She breathed through her nose. Hypnos picked up her hand, cradled it in his, and... she winced. He pinched and rolled her finger like a grape and she opened her eyes. In his other hand, he held the knife he'd used to slice open the quince, and her pricked fingertip was already healing. A last drop of blood spread through the linen sheet.

"There. It's done."

Pasithea's eyes opened wide. "Then you meant it."

"Of course I did," he said with a shrug. "No one will know the difference."

She was still a maiden. "But... what are we, Hypnos?"

"Married. By *our* measure." Hypnos grinned, then looked at her quizzically. "Are you cold, Pasithea? You look cold."

"Yes," she sighed. She'd been shivering since the veil came off, and with her fear of him snuffed out, the chill overhanging his room had settled into her. Hypnos drew a woolen blanket over her.

"Night and day will feel strange for some time in our realm, but try to sleep. Perhaps tomorrow I can introduce you to a few of the nymphs, and you can meet some souls in Elysion."

"The… the dead?"

"Yes. It's a beautiful place, home to philosophers, poets, musicians… They love to discuss their greatest memories. But that's for another day. When you're ready." He stroked her forehead and extinguished the lamp. "Rest well, wife."

18.

T HE BED JOSTLED AGAIN AND HER EYES PEELED OPEN. Persephone lay absolutely still. She felt the rustling, rhythmic pull of their bedclothes on her naked waist, heard Aidoneus breathing harder through his nose, then go silent. He wrenched forward, body seizing, a hard and soundless moan escaping as his head lifted from the pillows and crashed back down. Another tremor, then he relaxed, gasping before each breath settled, growing longer than the last. At last, Aidon sighed, swung his legs over the edge, and stood.

Persephone rolled over as he retrieved his discarded loincloth and wiped his stomach and groin. When he turned toward the hearth, he caught her gaze and froze, his expression quickly shifting from placid to wary, eyes studying her face.

"You don't have to do that."

"I don't?" There was an edge to his voice as he dragged the cloth through the fire to cleanse it.

"You could at least tell me if—"

"The answer is the same every time." He shook out his loincloth and neatly set it atop his folded tunic. "At this point, I'm simply weary of being refused."

"You know why, though. That it isn't *you*."

"Yes," he said. Aidon returned to bed and landed hard on the mattress, his arm tucked behind his head. He stared at the ceiling. "I know."

His voice betrayed nothing. She clenched her jaw until her neck ached, and turned toward the wall.

"You don't have a monopoly on grief, Persephone."

"I'm aware of that."

"Sometimes I need a release from mine. To know I can still feel *something* besides loss and anger. I'd rather be with you, but you've made it clear that's not possible. And belaboring it would betray my principles."

"Maybe, just maybe I could feel *anything* if there was real *timoria*… if Hera, Zeus, or Apollo suffered any meaningful consequences. Instead, we have a girl who's been sleeping alone in Hypnos's bedchamber for a fortnight, and…"

He sighed long and loud enough to interrupt her. Aidon closed his eyes.

"What?"

"Vengeance cannot be meted out all at once. Pasithea's wedding Hypnos was a particular— not the outcome. Broad justice is coming for them, Persephone. I promise you."

"When?"

"The seeds have been sown."

"*When*, Aidon?"

"Please… we'll speak on this again in the morning, but I'm tired. As are you."

Nothing more was said, and she felt him shift on the bed. He settled on his side, away from her, his dark hair spilling down his shoulder and across the pillow. His breath settled, soft and measured, and she waited, wishing she could join him in sleep.

She lay awake for the better part of an hour, then slunk out from under the sheet and through the great curtain around their bed. She picked up her peplos from its heap on the floor, and pinned up the shoulders, belting her sash as she walked to the terrace. She loosely bound her hair.

Zagreus would have been born by now. If she hadn't lost him, he would have been in her arms. He would have been sleeping in the wool basket between them on their bed… waking every few hours to feed, nuzzling into her, as perfect as Atlantiades had been in Aphrodite's arms. His infant demands would have kept them both awake instead of the emptiness that now robbed her of sleep. The whole Underworld would be rejoicing instead of trapped in a liminal stupor, everyone afraid to speak to her, waiting for her to forget… to let time wash over her and drown her fury.

Did they sincerely think that Hera's daughter was a reasonable exchange for their lost son? Wed to Hypnos and trapped below, but *alive*, and far freer here than above. Zagreus was all but dead— stored away in a warded pyxis on Olympus, forgotten.

Vengeance cannot be meted out all at once, he'd said.

"And why not?" Persephone whispered into the dark.

She listened. *Annessa… Thea… Aristi…* A loose cluster of shades waited on the opposite shore, and she could hear their thin voices through the Key. Persephone concentrated, and the whispers were joined by the wails of the damned in Tartarus, all screaming for mercy that none deserved.

Fresh air from the falls filled her lungs and she felt awake, finally. She was the Exacter of Justice. The Carrier of Curses. Months of sorrow had softened and weakened her, and she had relied on Aidon's slow reprisal for too long.

Their time will come.

It could be decades, *centuries* before Hera and Apollo finally reaped what they had sown. No more. Persephone closed her eyes and a flash of Phlegethon flame spiraled out of the darkness before her. With her hand, she beckoned her destination closer. Beyond the Phlegethon, beyond the Ouroboros of Kampe, to the dark recesses of Tartarus itself.

✳   ✳   ✳

"Wanakt-ja! Wanakt-ja! Praxidike!"

A few solitary Keres crawled among the overhanging stalactites. Persephone walked into Tartarus, the ever-shifting pathway set precariously above the nothingness yawning below their world. Flimsy wings flapped and soared through the dark, scattering the dull light of Ixion's Wheel. The light grew stronger, and as she crossed under the Wheel, she could hear Ixion's screams filling the Fields of Punishment.

"Alekto?" Persephone hadn't seen the Erinyes in their domain for a quarter-century, not since she and her husband had sent them to Knossos to scourge a *cultus* that feasted on those sacrificed in Asterion's lair. "Tisiphone?"

"My sisters are preparing to leave. They'll be here shortly," a lone voice said. The air stirred and bright golden wings spread as Megaera, the youngest of the Erinyes, touched the ground. She bowed low before Persephone.

"Where are they going?"

"Business above," Alekto said, circling before she alighted next to her sister. Tisiphone joined her.

"I would go," said Megaera, butting her hip into Tisiphone, "but sadly lost our game of knucklebones. Now *I* must stand at the Trivium, in case one of the damned crosses the river."

Persephone's lip twitched. "It's been a while since we've pulled anyone from above into Tartarus."

"It has," Alekto said. "But we may be returning with a very *deserving* guest."

"We'll see," Tisiphone said. She idly twisted her scourge of scorpion's tails at her side. "We *might* simply drive them to madness— haven't decided yet. Free reign was given."

365

A smile threatened the corners of Persephone's mouth. "So my husband finally *did* send you."

They exchanged quizzical looks. "Hades said nothing."

"Then *who?*"

None spoke. When the silence became too heavy, Megaera replied. "Hera."

Persephone seethed. "For Fatessake, why?"

"To torment Sthenelus, the king of Tiryns. She wanted him cursed with madness. There is one there who—"

"You're running an errand for Hera? Hera, who murdered my child?!" Persephone bared her teeth. "No. You have a new task: drag her here, and chain her beside Kronos!"

"My queen…" Alekto began carefully, "it would fling the cosmos into war. You must know that we've been called up by Hera many times before this."

She blinked, suddenly deflated. "What?"

"There was never a reason to deny her, Praxidike. Her husband rules over all the gods."

"And I rule over Tartarus. And *you*. Is your allegiance to me just words?"

"Of course not. But we cannot do as you ask. Not without violating what was arranged. Your husband—"

"*Quiet,*" Tisiphone hissed at Megaera.

"What did Hades do?"

"It is not our place to speak about it. We cannot act against her, by oath," Megaera said stiffly. "But neither are we bound by her commands," she added. "You overrule those."

"Then I forbid you from going to Tiryns. And if I hear of it…" Persephone turned and walked away through the Fields of Punishment.

"My queen," Megaera said, stepping after her. "Praxidike…"

Persephone turned, irises burning, flesh paling further, dark veins prominent under her skin. "*Get out of my sight!*"

Megaera gathered her sisters to her. All three sheathed their scourges, flying as far away from Persephone Praxidike as Tartarus would allow.

Persephone stalked past Tantalus, his shadowy form reaching, voice hoarse, desperate for the illusory grapes that dangled above him. She wondered if she should let him taste one, let a drop linger on his tongue before she tore it from his throat.

Beyond him lay the fathomless walls of the Pit stretching upward into the dark, and a slowly steepening incline, where one shade pushed a round boulder ever upward. Sisyphus's legs were grossly disfigured where she had snapped his bones all those years ago in Ephyra. As she neared, she could hear the reedy chant he had repeated since he was set to his task. "I can, she said— I'm free if I can…"

Sisyphus yelped and cowered when he caught sight of her, the stone rolling back and crushing his arm. His lightless shade lay on the rocks, his throat dry, voice cracked, moaning in agony. He would have to roll the stone up the hill with his good shoulder for the next several months. Persephone halted stiffly. There was a metallic taste behind her teeth and a high-pitched whine in her ears. One she remembered too well…

"My queen." His voice rang in her head, its owner too far away to be heard directly. It came from within— from Tartarus by way of the Key.

"No."

Kronos sighed. "To have lost so much. To those two, of all the gods…"

"I am not my husband." A charge shot over her skin, raising every hair. "If you think to tempt me when I'm vulnerable…"

"Come now," Kronos scoffed. "You must know I have more respect for you than that."

"Your mind bends only toward being released from your bonds," she said. His voice haunted her thoughts and she walked across the fields, past pits churning with the damned, closing the distance to the deepest level of the Pit. If she must endure his voice, it would be where she could see him.

"It does," he crooned. "But you know better than I that it is impossible at present."

Persephone descended to the lowest recesses, the light above her growing fainter. She felt the pressure increasing, her ears popping, her sense of time slowing. Grabbing a torch, she struck the white *magnes* and flooded the chamber with cold, colorless light, then pressed her hand into the wall, calling forth the steps to descend the last fathoms of the deepest pit. A basalt staircase ground from the walls before her, a few steps at a time, and crumbled behind her as she descended.

On the floor of the pit, she saw an enormous foot in the shadows. Briareos. She looked up at the hundred pairs of eyes glinting back at her in the paltry torchlight and nodded to him. Fifty voices, so deep they turned her stomach, rumbled through the thick air. "Say the word, Praxidike, and I will silence him. The chains can be wound tighter still."

"I know." She stared up at multitudinous eyes blinking like starlight. "But we will let him speak freely. For now."

"As you wish, Praxidike."

She walked on. Iapetos appeared first. But instead of leering at her as he had last time, he averted his eyes, his face drawn.

"I told my brothers to be silent. To honor all you've endured," Kronos said.

"How magnanimous of you." Persephone stopped in front of Kronos. The family resemblance with Aidoneus was unsettling, but she was well acquainted with both their demeanors now, and she knew the similarity ended at their regal features. She was on her guard— the last time she saw him, Kronos had given her a vision of him violating her, torturing her husband, incinerating and devouring the world above.

"Rest assured, Iapetos would not mock you, Persephone—he has nothing but sympathy for your plight. His second son, Menoetius, was lost forever. Thrown off the edge of the world, falling endlessly, even now. As near a thing to death as we can suffer. It's the ever-present threat levied against us should we attempt to escape. Another reason why I would never dare test my wiles on you now. Your wrath is limitless." His voice was smooth and deep, almost soothing. Her shoulders slackened.

Persephone clenched her jaw. Every word from his mouth was a lie. Bait. "You're protecting Iapetos from himself… along with the vanishing chance that I'll free you. He could have told me that."

"He would have." Kronos's face changed, softened. "But even among those who have lost as you have, what solace is there? Who could understand what you've endured?"

Her jaw tightened. "This path will lead you nowhere."

"You're right. I am certain you don't believe me. I don't expect you to. As I told you when we first met: you are not a simple creature."

"Then speak *truly*, Titan, or be silent."

"My son was right when he told you that vengeance against Hera would be meted out slowly. Already, she has lost the line of succession to *you*, and she doesn't even know it." He smiled and his voice grew warm. Too warm. Too much like Aidoneus. "The walls are closing around her. Your father's ill-struck oath will be fulfilled, and her world will collapse upon her. She will find herself falling and completely alone after my grandson, the rightful inheritor of the cosmos, is born."

Persephone's blood turned to ice. The room began to waver. "What…"

"One who is twice woven cannot remain your own." He savored each honeyed syllable, triumphantly repeating the words the Fates told her in the Cave of the Moirai. Kronos's eyes lit up with mirth. "Hades gave away your son's heart. To Zeus, of all creatures. He has been sown into another's womb by Hecate, to be reborn. And so Zagreus is dead. No longer yours, he is now Dimetor. He of two mothers."

Her eyes welled with tears and she shook her head.

Kronos raised his brows in mock innocence. "Surely this isn't the first you've heard of it? I recall you told me your husband is... *sworn* to tell you the truth. Did he neglect to mention this? Oh worry not, sweet one, it probably just slipped his mind."

Persephone's free hand shot out in the direction of his neck and the chains belted him against the column, their weight growing tenfold. His tongue thickened, his eyes bulging as he struggled to breathe. When she dropped her hand in exhaustion, he wheezed around rasping laughter. Without a word, she ran to the staircase, the voiceless taunting of Iapetos and the others following her.

The stairs reformed at her will and she sprinted upward, each step shaking as it cleared the wall to keep pace with her. When she reached the top, acid burned in her lungs, tears soaked her vision, and all was a blurred mass of watery red below and sallow light from above— of blood and sinews, promises, and opened pomegranates. She dropped her torch and screamed.

⁂

"Wake up." Her voice was sharp on the edges of his consciousness. The curtain was wrenched back and light poured in from the hearth fire.

"Mmhmm?"

"*Get up now!*" Persephone screamed and Aidoneus jarred from sleep. He kicked the sheets away completely, backing up against the wall. His blood raced, the hum in his ears subsiding.

370

"What is it?!" Aidon leaped from the bed and hurriedly donned his tunic. She was covered in the iron dust of the Pit. His mind raced. Someone had escaped from Tartarus… hopefully he'd prepared enough, still had time to seal off Chthonia… Persephone looked wild, intensely silent. Her hair was disheveled, her fists clenched, red rimming her puffy eyes.

Aidon pulled his belt tight, his heart drumming, his stomach churning. "Sweet one, what happened? Are you alright?"

"You broke your vow!"

He froze. "What?"

"The vow we made before our *hieros gamos!* We swore to *always* be truthful with each other! You broke it!" Her words burst out around angry sobs. "You gave Zagreus away! To Zeus! After… after you told me— that *he* was the one responsible…"

His pulse slowed, but his anger simmered. He'd told Hecate to stay silent until he had a chance to tell her. Aidoneus reined himself in and spoke calmly. Deliberately. "It was the only way to save him."

"To be born to another?" Tears traveled old paths.

"He would have died if I—"

"Who is she?"

"Who…"

"Where is my baby, Aidoneus?! Who has him?"

"Semele!" He spat the name at her and regretted it. He had to stay calm, or there would be no calming her. Aidon inhaled slowly. "He's *alive* and growing inside Semele. He will be *safe* from them because the truth of his lineage will be secret until he comes of age."

"A mortal. A mortal…" She threw her hands up, then planted them on her hips. "*Zeus's lover* is carrying our child…"

"Whom in her place? Which of the deathless women should have that power over us? To whom, if you were in my position, would you have given our child?"

"Who do you think?!"

"Persephone," he said, searching for a way to reason with her. "Hera's poison ensured that it couldn't be you. I wish it weren't true, but it would've killed him. The wards were failing and he would have died at midwinter."

"Midwinter…" She shook her head. "When you went to Tiryns. You've been… *withholding* this from me for two months…"

"*Longer*," he growled. "And I did it to protect you! Even the mention of Zagreus would send you into—"

"Oh please, I'm not that frail. I've been getting better, and you *know that*. But not quite in the way *you* wanted me to heal."

"What does that mean?"

"It means you would have told me if I was still fucking you. You wouldn't have hidden it from me."

"How can you accuse me of that? I have been nothing but respectful of you! I've had to bank my desire for you for *months*. And the very night you find out that I've… allowed myself some relief all this time— *this* is the night you choose to unleash on me! I'm sure it's *purely* coincidental."

"Don't turn this around! You decided without me for *our* son to be born as one of Zeus's bastards— to never know he's ours! When were you planning to tell me? After he was born? When I… saw some new god at Olympus who bears our likeness?"

"I was going to tell you when you were *ready*, but Hecate clearly decided for me—"

"Hecate didn't tell me."

"Who, then? Hypnos?"

"Hypnos knows too? Who else knows?! Our whole kingdom? Now I see why everyone's been avoiding me!"

"Who told you?!"

He realized he'd shouted at her when she flinched. She fought off tears and squared back her shoulders. "Your father."

Aidon retreated a step, his eyes widening. "What were you thinking?" He whispered.

"I needed to—"

"What were you thinking?!" He snarled at her. "You have no idea what you could have done!"

"Nothing happened."

"Do you remember what he did to you last time?!"

"I was perfectly fine!"

"Oh, of course, you were *perfectly* fine, Persephone! That's why you went to *fucking Tartarus* to speak with Kronos!"

She winced again, then narrowed her eyes. "I didn't go to speak to *him*. I went to send the Erinyes after Hera. Because I've had *enough* of waiting around for you to act!"

"So you only went there to instigate open war..." He spun around and paced next to the hearth, fingers raking through his hair.

"You're deflecting this again."

"Why on earth would you speak with *him* when you are so vulnerable? Have you completely lost your mind?"

"Don't you *dare* accuse me of madness, not after you handed our *child* to our enemies! Are these your sown seeds and broad justice?"

"To have our son be born? Yes. To have the line of succession pass through you, and not through Hera's children? Also, yes."

"What do I care about succession?! That won't matter for aeons. And since Zeus is busy fucking a new woman every year, I doubt he's in a rush to quit this form and become the thunderclouds!"

"It is the only language they understand. The only consequence with *real* meaning is to wrench the inheritance from
their children and give it to ours."

"This *timoria* wasn't for me; it wasn't for Zagreus, even."
She gritted her teeth and tears spilled over. "This was about
you."

"How so?"

"This was *your* male pride! Our son was just one more *thing*
taken from *you*. First the shortest lot, then me for half the year,
and now *him*. Because the Fates were never fair to poor Hades,
were they?"

"You're out of line."

"The cosmos took too much from you, and now *you* could
finally have your day."

"I wanted *our child* to be born for *your* sake! I did it because
you have wanted a child *so badly* for so long. It seems to be all
you *ever wanted*, Persephone!"

"Really. So *I* was pushing you to do something—"

"I could have been content with just you if that's what the
Fates allowed me."

"Why did you go to Orpheus alone, then? Why did we
even bother?"

"Because I wanted you to be happy! But it seems you can't
be if it's just us, can you?"

"I told you before we made our vows that it didn't matter
whether or not we had a child."

"You bring up broken vows, wife… the lies we tell ourselves and each other…" He spoke flatly. "It seems seventy-
seven years and nine times trying have borne out the real truth,
haven't they?"

She tightened her jaw. "Perhaps they have."

"And to think…" He scoffed, folding his arms. "If you
had stayed with your mother instead of going to Olympus and

playing with fire, you'd have gotten all you ever wanted out of me."

The room turned cold. Persephone's eyes swam as she searched for something, anything to say to him. Aidon bit the corner of his mouth until he tasted blood. He shouldn't have said it. He should have kept his blame silent until the world broke. Her lip quivered and she turned on her heel.

"Persephone…"

"Don't follow me."

"Sweet one…"

"Don't ever call me that!" Fire blazed in front of her.

"Wait!"

The ether wheeled shut behind her and she was gone.

19.

"PERSEPHONE?" His voice echoed around the darkened room. Their son's crib still sat at its center. Aidoneus closed the door. Nothing there but cold memories.

Two weeks had passed, and they had avoided each other long enough. She hadn't gone back to Tartarus. Alekto had made that clear. He had waited a long day at the entrance to the Elysian Fields until the sun went down and Orpheus had spotted him and warily approached. They'd spoken, and he'd learned she had not been seen entering or leaving Elysion.

Aidoneus made his way down the stairs. His last words to her lanced through him. Persephone had said enough for her part, but *that*...

Before the loss of their son, it would have been impossible not to know exactly where she was. He could feel her every footfall, knew when she fell asleep and awoke, every expression that flitted across her face, each emotion she felt. She had that same knowledge of him. She was his wife, sealed by their *hieros gamos*, queen of their domain. But for months now they had spoken little, touched but rarely, made love never; now their innate connection was severed. Like a tree felled by a storm, still verdant, unaware it was already dead.

He stopped on the landing, the great hall spread before him. Empty save for one.

"She spread her wings, Aidon," Hecate said.

"It was a mistake not to tell her."

"I doubted the wisdom in telling even you," Hecate said.

"That is *my son* you're talking about," he said, his voice a low warning.

"Zagreus was spun together by *phanes*, itself. Woven and whorled by you and by her, drawn and drafted from the Cloth of Life. He was no mere weft, but a warp that could have unraveled the great tapestry of the Fates. If I hadn't found a loom to accept his threads, then all the Weavers' work would have come undone. And if Zeus had seen the sword hidden in that shroud..."

Aidoneus glared at her.

"Your mind's river churned with storm-flood."

"I could have determined that myself."

"Persephone's eyes too were sharp enough, had we not hooded them." She looked down. "I was wrong. I would tell her my apology, but she cannot hear me."

Aidoneus leaned against the banister. "How did it come to this?"

"My warning is a year departed—"

"Warning of *which* calamity, Hecate?" He paced before her. "That the conception of our child could unravel existence? Or that losing him would destroy my marriage?"

"I see only the river, Aidoneus, not the ripples."

"And yet, if he was *not* meant to live, we would have failed at Samothrace. Had you considered that?"

"With all eyes... In the Cave of the Moirai, their words to her told the destiny of *all* your children: 'all at last aeon's end, and all to end the aeon.' Crystal and glass, as *they* said."

"Then there's nothing to fear. We will have no more children."

"So speaks the winter gust of summer breezes."

"Persephone wishes nothing more to do with me. She hasn't returned to the palace for a fortnight."

Hecate rolled her eyes. "At the first snap of a branch in a storm, you consider the forest lost."

"The forest, as you put it, is rooted on poor soil. We already sacrifice half of each year. And the other six months we have devoted ourselves to chasing the hope that we could create a family of our own. I claimed an earth goddess as my bride, naively hoping that she could find happiness with an infertile realm and husband. She bound herself to *both* not knowing the truth of it, and her love for me blinded her and convinced her that it could not be so. And with all the damage we quietly did to ourselves and each other over decades, and a loss that almost destroyed us, then yes, perhaps it is best that I let her go."

Hecate narrowed her eyes. "Your vows before me bind you to her eternally, Aidoneus. The pomegranate seeds anchor her to this realm, forever."

"The seeds make her return. She need not see my face while she's below."

"This bog has drawn you both under. Pull each other out, or you will drown, alone and together."

"I can't even *find* her, Hecate. She's not in the palace, she hasn't been seen in Elysion or even Tartarus."

Hecate bit her lips. "Persephone flew to open skies above. And she's been beyond my sight for quite some— wait, Hades!"

He was already plunging through the ether, her voice fading behind him. He rose through the crimson and silver twists and shimmers of the void, half expecting Hecate to chase him down. When she didn't, he pressed onward. The Key seared his fingers as he hurtled through the boundaries between worlds faster than he'd ever dared without the aid of his chariot. He emerged in Eleusis.

Aidoneus exhaled a white cloud and inhaled what felt like shards of ice. He bundled his himation around him and glanced around the well-lit but frigid Plutonion. The effigies of him and his wife were cloaked in saffron with wreaths of winter aconite and cypress crowning their heads. Oil lamps burned along the walls in celebration of the birth of their child.

Demeter hadn't told the mortals. But then, how could she? They'd torn Orpheus limb from limb for telling the truth. Would mortals burn down the Telesterion and Plutonion if her priests did the same?

In desperation, he reached out to Persephone, in the faint hope that she was nearby, or that some faint thread of their connection remained. Another presence loomed instead. Aidon squinted as the door opened, early morning sunlight flooding in, and an indigo-clad figure shut it tightly behind her.

"I wondered when you'd come after her."

He swallowed. In the early years of his marriage, he was certain Demeter prayed unceasingly to the Fates for this— the moment Persephone would finally see through him and leave him and Chthonia for as long as the pomegranate seeds would allow. "Demeter, I was trying to give her as much space as she needed and—"

"I know. That's why you missed her by a week."

The air left his lungs.

"Aidoneus..." She made sure the door was locked. "I know it wasn't negligence on your part."

"What did Persephone say to you?"

"That's between my daughter and me."

The cold realization that she was gone staggered him and he could only stare back at Demeter. He nodded, his throat closing. "I did it to save our son; to save her. I would have endured centuries of her anger to save her."

"During the war," Demeter said, "whenever the tides turned against us, you would throw yourself upon the front, trying to right our course single-handedly, oftentimes to no avail. When Koios set loose the demons of Echidna, they slaughtered thousands of the mortals who fought with us in a single afternoon. You sprinted to the vanguard to save the few you could, and even then you couldn't forgive yourself for what happened. Nothing Hecate said back at camp could console you."

"This isn't the war. And if you are trying to convince me that I deserve forgiveness, that's out of the question. If you knew what I said to her..."

"I know what you said." Her mouth was set in a thin line. "Quite honestly, I don't know if there is a way to remedy that. But I do know this: you must let go. Let Persephone exact her own justice."

"If true and deserved *timoria* was exacted for what they did, the war thereafter would end this world and us with it."

"She knows that Aidon," Demeter said. "But you need to trust her to do what she must, or she'll never truly heal."

He spoke low, his words just above a whisper. "Do you know where she is?"

"No."

He snorted ruefully. "I suppose I'm foolish to ask for *your* aid. Of all the idiot things I've done this winter..."

She shook her head. "If I could help you, I would. Kore's happiness is my only concern, Aidon. And with you she is..." Demeter looked at the stone floor. "She knew you'd come here first when you realized she'd left, and asked me to convey a message."

He looked at her expectantly. Demeter shook her head.

"'Do not follow', she said. 'Go home.'"

He walked away from Demeter, staring up at the statues of himself and his wife. Silence settled over the room.

"That battle… after all that needless death, some good did come of it." She drew in a breath. "One of the men you saved from the manticore that day was Iasion."

"He said as much when he arrived in my realm."

"Even if it seems like the end, like all is dead, some good may yet bloom from this."

✵   ✵   ✵

Winters in Cyrene were mild and ripe with opportunity. Though Apollo hated these new seasons, the dreary reminder of years passing, there was a bright side to the fallow months. He could sow other seeds. Ideas. Poetry. Invention. Everything that separated men from livestock and made caring for them worthwhile. The mood had been dismal on Olympus since autumn had brought news from the Underworld. Hermes hadn't spoken with him since, and rather than sit anxiously wondering what the Trickster had pieced together, he left for warmer climes.

Cyrene was awash in sunlight, bolts of vermillion cloth drying in the breeze, dyed with silphium straw, heavy with sulfurous mordant, and far more lustrous than anything dyed with madder. The bolts would soon be loaded into carts bound east for Aegyptus.

There was an unexpected scent in the air. A Deathless One was nearby— he could feel it. Olympians rarely ventured this far south. They were called different names here, seen differently, with stories as unrecognizable as their graven images. These lands put most of them ill at ease. But one of *them* was south of the city, near the great desert that marked the ends of their familiar world. It was a distinctly vulgar presence— like a common rustic god, but powerful. That alone was worth his attention. Cyrene was out of the way, thoroughly his, and if anyone thought they could cross the sea and take it from him…

The ether opened, and he cast no shadow as he left its embrace, his pathway marked by blinding sunlight since he was a child. A lone female stood in the scrub on the edge of the endless desert, cloaked in the same red cloth of Cyrene. The aura of the earth hung about her.

"Ah, Demeter! I thought it might be you. To what do I owe the pleasure?"

She was covered in two days' worth of dust. Her hand appeared from within her cloak, fingernails caked with dried dirt, as though she had crawled out of the ground itself. When she pushed back her hood, Apollo's heart dropped into his stomach.

"Persephone."

Her voice crackled. "I've waited."

"For how long? You look—"

"I'm not entirely sure…" she said distantly. "Long enough."

"You're usually with your illustrious husband in wintertime. Especially this year, since…" He couldn't glean Persephone's motives. Perhaps she'd finally realized the folly of loving a dead god. And this place was remote, away from spying eyes. Apollo placed his hand over his heart. It thudded against his palm, begging him to run, but he quelled his fear. She could have come for any number of intriguing reasons. "We've had our differences, radiant one, but your loss gave all of us the *greatest* sorrow. And you're clearly in need of my hospitality. One of my favored cities is a mere ten leagues away. I would gladly—"

"Such a small thing," she said, staring down at her hand. Her fingers opened one by one, revealing a single silphium seed. He froze.

"It is." What did she know? Hades and Zeus already had cause enough to come for him after Asklepios had been made immortal, but neither had. But compounded with *this*... if anyone knew, he would already be in chains. Apollo bit back his panic and betrayed nothing. "There's much I can show you— so many verdant things on this side of the world."

"Tell me about this one."

"It..." Apollo's mouth went dry. "You already wear its rich color. The dye from it is unmatched..."

"A red like blood. I hear that silphium can heal. Healing is one of your domains, no? You have so many. It's hard to remember them all."

"It does wonders for the melancholy humors, and..." he smiled broadly at her and raised an eyebrow. A heart that needed to be healed. "It can stir the passions."

She grinned softly at that. Maybe that was why she was here. "And it starts women's courses. When they *need* them to come."

Apollo paused, briefly breaking eye contact. "Yes. *Yes.* When necessary. A boon for womankind. Surely, your realm has received too many who have died needlessly on the birthing bed. This has saved many who knew that enduring childbirth might end them."

She held up the seed between them. "Why did my courses come, Apollo? When they weren't supposed to?"

He took a step back. "Your... I... I couldn't know, my lady. Childbirth is not among my many domains. We should get you back to Olympus. Perhaps Eileithyia could help you— or your mother, she's been there often this season, and she can look after you. You've endured so much."

"I have, haven't I?" Persephone stepped forward, the silphium seed between her thumb and forefinger. "And all for a silver lyre. To think you started this, Apollo, over a lyre."

Apollo tittered and shifted his feet. "Radiant one, you speak in riddles of mysteries. The sun shines so brightly here, even the ground wavers. You must be in shock from being out so long."

"I assure you, I am perfectly well." She shielded the seed with her own shadow and stared intently at it. "Eurydice, though... she is dead. Because of you. Orpheus, your son, is dead. Because of you."

"I didn't kill Eurydice." He retreated with every slow step she took toward him. "I wasn't anywhere near Samothrace. I know you were fond of them. For you, I would set loose a plague on those barbaric Maenads who—"

"You've already loosed it, Apollo. Hera's viper. Hera's nectar. Laced with this..." She held her other hand under the seed and it smoldered.

"What are you doing?"

"This killed my son." The silphium crackled with black flame. The fire's edges licked with orange, destroying all light that touched it, drawing his shadow and the shadow of every scrub brush and rolling hill toward it. Only a cinder remained. "Cuttings might thrive, for a time, but you will never receive honors from these seeds again."

"I don't understand."

"I destroyed its fertility." The shell broke apart, ash on the wind. The shadows grew. "One day, it will pass from the earth, as though it never were. Worry not, Apollo. Humans are resourceful. They'll find something to replace it."

"How...Why would you do such a thing?!" He advanced on her. "Insolent cunt... Your bitch mother can only shield you for so long! When Zeus hears that a lower goddess has trespassed on one of the *Dodeka*..." his voice went silent, his lips still moving. Apollo stopped when he realized no sound came forth. He touched his throat, his ears, strained to hear his own voice, screaming silently, his face red.

Persephone Praxidike stepped forward, her pupils lit with fire, the sky darkening. Apollo stumbled back, a great maw bending through the ether at his heels. A hand, immeasurable and crushing, reached up to grasp him, pinning his arms to his sides, emptying the air from his lungs as it squeezed. From below came the incessant chant... *Wanakt-ja... wanakt-ja Praxidike wanakt-ja...* And then a voice, fifty at once, as deep as the Pit, each word grinding like stone.

If he dares strike out, Praxidike, be assured I will pull him down.

"You've heard that voice before, haven't you?" Praxidike said.

Apollo looked behind him and closed his eyes. He felt tears leaking down the sides of his face. It was impossible. They wouldn't... It couldn't be allowed...

"Briareos climbed Olympus and broke your rebellion, all those aeons ago. And I am his queen."

He mouthed her name, enunciating so she could see. *Persephone, please.*

She unfurled her fingers. "You may speak."

"I thought Hera would relent for her love of children—that she couldn't make herself go through with it!"

"Lies. You're the god of prophecy. You knew *exactly* what Hera would do."

"I fall upon your mercy! Persephone... august queen... I *only* wanted Asklepios to live, and that her anger—"

"You saved your son and murdered mine. You armed Hera against me when she was at her weakest."

"Why are you sending me to Tartarus and not her?!" He turned his head, staring into the depths below. Fifty pairs of eyes narrowed when they stared back at him.

"I have yet to say you will go there, Apollo. Though you deserve it."

"Then what? Gods above... mercy. I *beg you.*"

"Gods above… What mercy would the other gods have if they all knew the truth? You've proven yourself willing to wantonly murder our children when it suits you. But since I am lesser in your eyes, surely my judgment won't be as awful as theirs." She leaned over him. "What broad justice befits *you*, God of Prophecy?"

The Destroyer of Light gripped his temples, darkness piercing deeper, burning cold. All he could see was her face, her eyes the only light, two embers as the sky blackened to starless soot, the sun gone, the earth cold and barren. His scream sounded hollow.

"You slake your lust for power on nymphs, muses, mortals. You set woman against woman with the whispers of the sister Fates."

His voice grew hoarse and everything within him burned and froze. There was no plea she would hear.

"In Eurydice's name, I curse you. Just as your poison dust, so is your inheritance. Choose your Pythia well, Apollo. Because the foretelling of mortal women is all you will ever hear again."

As her last word was uttered he fell back. Not into the Pit of Tartarus, but hard against the ground. The wind was knocked out of him. Persephone was gone. Briareos no longer caged him. He inhaled and stared up at a clear blue sky, the breeze wafting across his shoulders and legs as he tried to still his racing heart. Apollo sat up, looked around him, and felt a trickle across his lip. He wiped it away, a streak of shimmering ichor smearing his fingers. Where there had once been scrub brush, only level sands surrounded him, stretching north, far further than they ever had before.

He strained, hoping that it was all an elaborate display to scare him off from meddling with the gods below. Apollo listened for the guiding voices of the Fates, for a hint at what lay in store for him.

Only silence answered.

✳   ✳   ✳

"I remember when you first asked this of me."

"It's how we began. Only fitting that it's how we should end."

Morpheus frowned, his shadowed brow crinkling. "You have argued with her before. More *fervently* than this, I'm certain."

"That was a lover's quarrel. A misunderstanding when we knew nothing about each other. But this…" Hades's eyes closed. "I subverted the Fates so we could have the child that she desired, I lied and deceived to save her, and now we've drifted so far apart that… I suspect our entire marriage may have been built on sand. What sense is there in continuing to up-end her life?"

"Your mortal friend, the mystic, told you when you first solicited his aid that you would be asked for a sacrifice. Your son is already gone, Aidon. When he is born to that woman, he won't be yours or Persephone's."

Aidon shook his head. "Orpheus said that *ananke* would demand a sacrifice of us during the rites, of the thing most dear to us."

"You would never have made the choices you made and endured such torment if you didn't love each other."

"And now we've reached the heart of the matter. Over the greater span of time, perhaps love is not enough."

"Aidon—"

"I should have been the one to tell Persephone. Not my accursed father."

"You were trying to protect her. She was… fragile after she lost the babe. And you're not to blame for what Kronos did. He took an opportunity to hurt you both because it's all he *can* do. And Persephone shouldn't have even been in Tartarus asking my sisters to drive the cosmos to war." Morpheus sighed. "She's angry at you, yes. But—"

"She's gone, Morpheus," he said. "She left Chthonia without telling me, and has closed herself off from me utterly."

Morpheus leaned forward.

"I can't read her; I can't reach her. I searched on foot in Eleusis and Thesprotia, but never found her. I only know she was in Cyrene because Briareos told me about the *timoria* against Apollo, but when I arrived, she was gone from there also. In our realm and the world above, she is lost to me."

Morpheus nodded. "So I am your only recourse."

"I'm sorry, my friend."

"You realize what Hecate will do if your marriage ends by my hand— what my mother will do."

"I'll protect you from their wrath. Besides, it would fall tenfold upon me before they even spoke to you."

Morpheus scoffed and withdrew his left hand from the breast of his robes, his fingers gently curled over his palm, and extended it to Aidoneus. When they unfurled, a large blue-winged butterfly tapped its delicate feet up his fingers, tottering toward him. Morpheus tilted his head at him. "You know the way to my kingdom."

Aidon gave him a curt nod and the butterfly took wing, flapping silently to alight on Aidon's nose. Ink black eyes stared into him and a black tongue uncurled and tapped his brow. Its wings spread, blurring and blotting out his sight.

Aidoneus opened his eyes in the middle of an endless garden, naked, his skin unscarred by war and his father's cruelty. A pink and orange sky hung overhead, dawn and dusk circling the horizon with watery light. Faint stars dotted the moonless canopy. Thyme flowers carpeted the ground and forked into three narrow pathways. One to the Door of Horn, the second to the Door of Ivory, the third path twisting thinly over tree roots to a pond. A small island in its center supported a living throne of white elm, a vine of purple flowers winding over its highest branches, their long tendrils draped into a bower, all perfectly reflected in the still water.

There sat Morpheus on the Throne of Dreams, his appearance as unspoiled as Aidon's. Great raven wings spread above him and his hair was as lustrous and weightless as his mother's, his eyes as midnight blue as his father's— the way he had looked before Kronos's sickle had robbed him of face and flight.

"You know the choice I offer, Aidoneus. Two doors. Identical in appearance. One the door of truth, the other of falsehood."

"Truth."

"Are you certain? Your heart will be laid bare, your true desires exposed. You will have no choice. Whatever you told me about your intentions as we stood before your throne makes no difference when you stand before mine."

He raised his chin. "I understand completely."

The Lord of Dreams nodded and closed his eyes. Aidon heard the wings of the Tribe of Oneiroi at distance, their delicate flutter the only disturbance in this still kingdom. A vast swarm of blue butterflies approached, circling Morpheus, so different from their shadowy appearance in the waking world. Morpheus's gaze fell on Aidoneus again. "Find the queen."

Aidon watched the butterflies turn and swoop, encircling them. With a great beat of his wings, Morpheus rose from his seat, rippling the surface of the water as the Oneiroi swarmed closer. He landed beside Aidoneus and extended his hand. Aidon took it and through the maelstrom, his feet lifted off the ground and the Door of Horn pulled closer.

*   *   *

This was a dream. The moon was still full, but this wasn't Aegyptus.

389

Larkspur didn't grow in Aegyptus. And larkspur hadn't been seen with white flowers for a mortal generation. Not since… Persephone opened her eyes again and saw the faint outlines of green willow shoots, rushes beneath her, violets were strewn about. She was back in Hellas. It was her bower beneath the sprawling oak tree in Eleusis, long ago when she had been Kore.

"Persephone…"

She closed her eyes and tensed. His voice sounded just as it did that night. His warm hand stroking her shoulder was torture, and her heart begged her to lean back and into him. She resisted, her whispered reply veined with ice. "Why are you here?"

His hand stopped moving. "I'm sorry, wife. It was the only path left open for me to find you."

"By invading my dreams." She rolled over to face him and her breath caught. They were both as naked as when she first saw him, before her descent, before the deadly winter and the pomegranate. Before he had given away their child. She could smell the lilac strewn through her hair, just as it had been that night. "Did you think coming here, as you did when we first met, would undo all wrongs? That we could put grievances behind us and start anew?"

He stared back at her. "No."

Persephone's mouth went dry. "Then answer me: why have you come, Aidoneus?"

His eyes were unreadable. The threads that wove her to him had frayed and been severed by months of anger and complacency, and she couldn't sense his thoughts. He cupped her face with his palm. She swallowed.

"Are you here to scold me about Apollo?"

"I would never. He deserved to lose far more than you took. But you'll have to be careful, now."

A tear leaked from her eye and his thumb brushed it away. "I nearly lost control. The desert itself…"

"My fault. If I hadn't been so overly cautious with you, if I had told you the truth, you would have been able to channel your wrath at that moment instead of sapping the earth. If I had let you have your rightful vengeance. If I hadn't kept something so vital from you."

"We *did* tell each other the truth," she said, her jaw setting. "Every word we said in your room was true, wasn't it?"

"Which is why I'm here."

Persephone stared into his eyes.

"I release you."

"What do you mean?"

"The pomegranate seeds bind you to the Underworld for far less time than we arranged with your mother."

"I know."

"You'll need to return below for a few months every year, or Chthonia will pull you under, and I cannot prevent that. But you no longer need to return for my sake."

"Aidon…" Her words caught in her throat. "Are you saying that we should… dissolve our marriage?"

"I am." He let out a long breath.

"You no longer wish to be with me."

"That's not the reason, swee—" He stopped himself, swallowed his emotions, and spoke measuredly. "Persephone, for the better part of a century you've endured much for our sake. The damage we've done to each other, not just recently but over decades, might be too great for it to be laid to rest. Continuing this ritual of coming and going if little feeling remains, is unfair to you. I love you. That's why I release you."

She paused, leaden weight filling her lungs, her stomach. "I can't make a decision like this, Aidon. Not here."

"Please think on it. Take whatever time you need. When you're ready, you can tell me your choice." He leaned forward and kissed her forehead.

"Wait, Aidon—"

She felt warm wood pressed to her cheek and opened her eyes. Outside her window, sunlight touched the top of the polished limestone obelisk that stood sentry over the great city of Waset. Morpheus's shadow sat at its peak and when she looked closely, he vanished— just as he had after she first met Aidoneus in dreams. She heard a slow purring. Amenti, her hostess's most favored cat, leaped onto Persephone's settee with a curious trill and nestled beside her, kneading her belly with small feet. Her pulse slowed as she petted Amenti's soft fur.

"My lady?" A servant of the household stood at the door. "You cried out. Is something wrong?"

"It's nothing." Persephone sat up and the striped cat leaned in. She scratched under her chin. "I didn't see you last night. What is your name?"

"Sekhet, honored one," she said, eyes trained on the ground.

How much did they know about her? Persephone had heard the whispered name of *Isis* and *Goddess of the West*— *Henwt Ament*, after she arrived in the palace. She had journeyed across the burning roads to lands the Olympians avoided, afraid they might seek retribution— that she'd gone too far punishing Apollo. But Hermes had seen Persephone heading west with the traders, and he would certainly have warned her.

"You serve Lady Isetnofret?" Persephone spoke in halting Egyptian, wrapping her shawl around her shoulders. Sekhet nodded. "When she of the Two Ladies, the daughter of Sedge and Bee awakens, tell her I am grateful for her hospitality. It will one day be returned in kind."

After Sekhet left, Persephone brushed her hand down her gown. The stiff, gauzy *kalasiris* changed to her familiar wool *peplos*. She placed her crown of asphodel on her head and plucked one flower free. Amenti sat on the settee, her eyes blinking slowly at Persephone, her tail curling around her feet. When the asphodel touched the ground, a great ring of fire grew to the height of the doorway. The twisting crimson and silver light of the ether stretched before her, but she didn't know where to go.

20.

WINTER CLUNG LISTLESSLY TO THE WORLD, WAITING to end. Persephone sat in Thesprotia, at the retreat she had built in the world above for herself and Aidoneus, under the branches of the pomegranate tree he had planted. The constellation of The Hunter was high overhead. She plucked a lone crocus, cradling it in her hand. There should have been a carpet of purple blooms beneath her feet; here was but the one. She should be in Eleusis.

Yesterday would have marked her return from the Underworld. One last morning with Aidoneus before he bid her farewell, and then she would emerge in Eleusis as Karpophoros, the bringer of spring, exhausted from renewing the world, inundated with the fanfare of mortals welcoming her. Persephone's sense of time and self was broken and recast with every journey.

If she so chose, she would never have to do that again. She could stay here, drawing spring forth gradually from the frozen earth. Chthonia would call her back for three months a year, perhaps less. Aidoneus had given her the choice.

How had he so calmly considered dissolving their marriage?

In their dream last night he had been so determined… rational in his insistence, measured and emotionless with his responses. The mask had never slipped. She stood outside the ramparts he'd erected for everyone else in existence. The walls he had once torn down for her alone. Morpheus had given him a choice and he'd chosen the Door of Truth. She heard him choking back his true desires. He wanted to reconcile, but only if *she* wished to do the same.

Did she?

Perhaps Aidoneus was right. She was angry beyond measure. The scars of hurt and mistrust were deep, perhaps too great for their marriage to be salvageable. Some offenses couldn't be forgiven.

She'd still be Queen of the Underworld in her own right, and he would be its king. Their rulership could survive without their marriage. It might take years, decades— millennia even, but she was certain they could eventually learn to coexist for the few months she was below. A partnership might even develop between them. She trusted him enough to honor his word and respect her decision; he would neither render her his prisoner for those three months nor spend the rest of eternity in a vain quest to win her back.

The air was silent, absent of crickets and nightjars, or any creeping, living thing. The Pomegranate Agreement dictated that she spend six months below while the earth lay fallow. It would be dissolved along with their marriage, freeing her to spend three more months with the flowers and sun, with her loving and grateful mother. Freeing the world to thrive in longer summers. The mortals would have to reserve fewer stores for winter, needn't strategize to plant to survive, wouldn't need to cast better tools, or learn to grow hardier crops…

And wasn't that exactly what Olympus wanted? For Hades and Persephone's bonds to break? For the flame of human innovation to be snuffed out? Fearful of change, the gods had withdrawn fire from the mortals before. With the advent of the seasons, the immortals changed faster, hurtling headlong toward aeon's end.

Zeus wanted the world returned to how it was before Aidoneus had taken her. That was the reason he arranged her ill-fated introduction to Apollo when she came to Olympus— for him to seduce her and shatter her marriage, and with it the new honors that had been bestowed on Persephone and her husband as the Gods of the Earth.

Her vengeance had been just. It had been a balm, even if Aidoneus had said it was the least Apollo deserved. A month had passed since she had burned away Apollo's gift of prophecy. In place of her need to set it all right, an emptiness and hunger grew. Knowing what Aidoneus had done to let their child be born, she didn't dare turn her vengeful gaze to Hera... She could undo everything— everything Aidon had done to keep Zagreus alive. Persephone stood, staring up at the star-filled winter sky.

Her husband had brought down *timoria* in his way— strategically, coldly, methodically. He had risked open war, not only to hold Zeus to his word but to ensure that their child might live. In his place at that moment, she could never have given Zagreus up. Without Aidon, Persephone realized, Zagreus would have died. He must have known what he risked by not telling her. Of course, she would find out— he knew he might sacrifice her love for him in order to save their son...

Persephone's throat tightened. She didn't need six months to decide. Fates, she didn't need six hours. She had known, in her bones, her answer the moment he asked her to choose. She flung away the crocus and splayed her fingers toward the asphodel growing from the courtyard floor. Its anthers burst, light radiating from its center before it bloomed into a great ring of flame.

"It never troubles you that your works and deeds would be forgotten?"

"Never," Orpheus responded.

"Even your music? All you did, only to see it vanish…"

"These things have vanished before." Orpheus chuckled. "I come from warlike people, Aidon. The old city on Samothrace has been rebuilt as many times as the Tyrrhenians and Trojans have launched fire at it. I scattered *pithoi* all over the island with papyrus scrolls inside. The Fates blessed me with a prolific hand, and I'm certain that one day they will be found. But here, I have Eurydice."

"Strange that your ambitions changed so drastically once she came into your life." A crocus curiously caught his eye and he stooped to pick it, turning the flower over in his hand, wondering what drew him to it.

"Hardly. In a decade, I wrote perhaps eight and twenty hymns. Then you gave me the lyre," Orpheus said. "But it would have been useless without Eurydice. Three months, *three score* songs I wrote with her."

Aidoneus nodded and spoke quietly, contemplating the purple blossom. "I know what that's like. To have been self-reliant for so long, to have your life ordered and everything in its place, only for someone to arrive and upend everything so gloriously that you can no longer imagine how you had carried on so long without them."

Orpheus smiled gently. "You visited Persephone?"

"Yesterday, in dreams. I told her that when she is ready, she can tell me her decision. And I will accept it."

"She will come back to you."

He looked pointedly at Orpheus. "I blamed her for the loss of our son. I withdrew from her because it was easier than re-living the pain of losing him. I went behind her back and gave away our child. Those things are not easily forgiven. She bound herself to me forever when our love was new. Time and trials surely have made her reconsider."

"So it is for all, I have no doubt."

"Your lives are short. Not so much time to make grave mistakes. Maybe that's why every marriage among the deathless ones is a disaster. Not just for the *happy* couple, but all humanity. Mine included, it seems. Mortals strive for happiness with each other because they know that their end is inevitable. When you return—"

"I'm not going back."

"You'd remain in the land of the dead?"

"If it means being with Eurydice, yes."

Aidoneus shook his head. "You'd forsake *living* to stay with her forever."

"Of course." Orpheus pointed across the sea to the islands and Aidoneus followed his gaze. "You see that one? I saw fires there some nights ago. I visited them yesterday. Now that their memories are restored, the souls are building there. One day it may become a city. That was their home in life, and Paradise is what you make of it. Most will leave when they're ready, I have no doubt. New arrivals will add their visions of Paradise to compliment what was built before. And they in turn will move on once they've rested here. But their Paradise isn't mine. Mine is with her. Just as your wife's place is with you. She'll come back. Sooner than you think."

✳   ✳   ✳

"Aidon?" Persephone closed the pathway from Thesprotia and stepped out onto the terrace of their palace antechamber. Returning to Chthonia would be so much easier if she chose to do it this way every year. She glanced around the empty room and up at the ceiling, diamond-studded with the constellations of winter. "Aidon, where are you?"

Persephone waited. Silence.

She wound her way down the stairs and carefully opened the door to the throne room, pushing aside the tapestry that hid the way to their private rooms. Closing her eyes, she reached out for him but felt only her own pounding heartbeat. Their connection was fully severed. She ascended the dais, sandals tapping the marble floor, and sat on her throne, the one he had made for her. She placed a hand on the ebony arm of his chair. Persephone's vision blurred and a teardrop fell on her hand.

"Your grace?"

She gasped and sat bolt upright. Pasithea.

The girl curtsied. "If you'll pardon me, my queen, isn't to-day the second day of Spring?"

Persephone swiped her eyes with her thumb and index fin-ger. "It is."

Pasithea was dressed in a short chiton, not unlike the one Persephone used to wear when she was Kore. She nodded re-spectfully and moved to leave the throne room.

"Wait." Persephone stood. "Have you seen my husband?"

"I've just come from Elysion, and he's usually there, but I haven't seen him; no."

"It's vast— easy to miss him I'm sure," Persephone said, half to herself. "Tell me… what do you do there?"

"Nothing, my lady." Pasithea smiled. "Well, that's not en-tirely true. Most would call it idleness. My mother certainly would. I weave flowers, watch the grass, listen to the waves, and sometimes take a scroll and ink, to practice. You don't mind that I borrow a papyrus now and then?"

"No; that sounds lovely. What are you practicing?"

"How to write. Hypnos has been teaching me how to read, as well."

Persephone blinked, frowning thoughtfully. Pasithea had been denied an education on Olympus, confined to her duties and instructed only in her immortal role, just as Persephone had been a child of the fields and flowers. How little she had known, how much she had yet to learn before she had made her home with Aidoneus in the world below. Before her husband had taught her to read, to write, to fight...

"Does your husband treat you well?"

"He is kind and gentle to me, my lady. I admit I was afraid of what..." She dropped her eyes shyly, then met Persephone's gaze. "He makes no demands of me, and told me exactly why."

"And what of your desires in marriage?"

"I never sought a husband, nor a lover, man or woman." She shrugged. "So this suits me fine, I suppose. It seems we're well matched."

Persephone nodded at her and Pasithea bowed, preparing to leave.

"Where are you headed?" Persephone asked.

"His bedchamber. I find it... oddly comforting. Like him. He's not there often, but when he is, we sit and talk before we fall asleep." This time Persephone turned away, her earliest memories of Aidon coming each night to her bedchamber sneaking unbidden into her mind. She too had found unexpected comforts during those first strange days in the world below...

Pasithea suppressed a yawn. "Forgive me, I've been up for hours already. I wouldn't *ever* miss dawn on the Styx."

"I treasured watching it too when I first arrived. We would—" Her brow crinkled as she recalled all the times she'd jostled Aidon awake early after a full moon to see the wash of silver lighting Chthonia fill with the colors of dawn.

"When you reach Elysion, turn right at the white sycamore, and go down the hill. If he's there, he's usually visiting Orpheus and Eurydice. They favor the linden grove in the valley."

"Thank you." Persephone hurried out of the throne room and traversed the great hall. By the time she crossed she was jogging. She threw open the garden doors.

"Queen Persephone!" Askalaphos shouted from the foot of a tall cypress, confusion on his face. "Aren't you supposed to be above?"

Persephone ignored him and hitched her skirts above her knees. She kicked her bothersome sandals off, sending them end over end into a thicket, and ran. Tears streaked into her hairline and her heart pounded in her chest. She burst through the grove, blinking in the sudden sunlight. It was so warm here. Persephone sprinted down the hill, past the white sycamore. She hadn't set foot in Elysion since she had killed the tree...

"Aidon!" she called out. Persephone breathed hard and turned to the right, as Pasithea had said. The grass brushed against her bared calves and she peered all around her, hoping for a glimpse of him. "Aidoneus, please!"

Further downhill, the stalks grew taller. She ran onward, calling out as she went, birds scattering from the field. Two figures walking the winding path in the distance turned to look like a cloud of sparrows fluttered above her, rising and falling on the breeze and settling in another part of the meadow.

"Aidon!"

He took a step back, wide-eyed.

Orpheus smiled, then hastily covered his mouth with his hand. The hymnist bowed to her. The Lord of the Underworld stood silent, still, as she ran to them.

"Orpheus... it's good to see you again."

"And you, my queen." A smile played at the corner of his mouth as he looked from her to Aidoneus. "If you two will pardon me, I need to... see to my wife."

She nodded and he walked off into the tall grasses, glanced back with a soft grin, then wafted on the breeze, vanishing from sight.

They were alone. His face was unreadable. "Aidon..."

"Why are you here?"

"I had to speak with you."

"I didn't expect to see you for six—"

"I'm not waiting six months!"

He paled, biting his cheek as he always did to keep his face from betraying his emotions. She could tell he was preparing for the worst.

"How could you ever think I'd want to dissolve our marriage?"

Aidoneus didn't move. "You left early."

"*Yes*, I left early. I was *furious* with you!"

"You had every reason to be."

"That doesn't mean I no longer love you!"

"Persephone..." He sighed heavily. "Love isn't the question."

"Then what, Aidon?"

He inhaled. "The warning we received about the consequences of the rite. The sacrifice that would be demanded of us..."

"Yes."

"For you, it was our child." His forehead knotted. "And for me, it was you. I sacrificed *you*, unwittingly, to give our son life. You've had to give up *everything* to make our marriage work. Splitting your time between worlds. Suffering the enmity that exists between the gods above and my realm. Then my deception gave our child to another. I've put you through enough."

She nodded. "Losing Zagreus wasn't our first hardship. And it won't be our last." Her lip quivered. "His loss consumed me, Aidon. That this… *body* of mine couldn't keep him safe."

"No…" His face softened. "It was not your fault, wife. Not at all. Gods… I've never regretted saying anything as deeply as I regret my last words to you. We did *not* lose him because of you. And I tried *everything* to bring him back to you."

"Will we fall apart every time something terrible happens?"

"I don't know. Every quarrel, every hardship, we were there for each other afterward. This time—"

"I don't want children anymore."

"What?" He stared quizzically. "Why? It's what we've wanted for—"

"We?"

"Yes. Yes, Persephone, *we*. You and I. I wanted a family with you. To be the father of your children and for you to be the mother of mine."

"But if this is what happens to us, then it's not worth it. I'm done. I'm tired of tearing myself, you, our *marriage* to pieces over it!" She blinked back tears. "I'm angry with you for what you did, Aidon, but I meant what I said long ago. Whether we have children or not, it doesn't change what I feel for you. And I'm not willing to sacrifice *you* to keep trying."

He froze, absorbing her words, then cautiously moved closer to her. "Alright, no more. Never again."

"Don't you understand? When I ate those seeds, I bound myself to *you*. Because I've never wanted anything in this world more than I wanted Hades Aidoneus Chthonios. Not this kingdom, not a family, nothing but—" Aidon cut her off, his lips crashing against hers, fingers weaving into the hair at the nape of her neck, arm circling her waist. Her lips parted for him and her body crushed against his, his tongue stroking hers. When she mewled into his mouth and writhed, gripping his arm, he pulled away.

"I'm sorry." He stepped away from her and shook his head, eyes as wide as hers. She lightly touched her lips. "Persephone, forgive me, I shouldn't have done that. I—"

She vaulted at him, her arms wrapping around his shoulders, legs around his waist. Her lips silenced his voice. He stumbled and sank to his knees, still holding tightly to her, matching her kiss with equal fervor. Persephone still couldn't sense his thoughts, couldn't break through and find that rapturous exchange that had been woven during their *hieros gamos*. She broke away. Small panting breaths feathered against his cheek. "Just stop apologizing! Stop... Please... I need you..."

"Sweet one..." The endearment caught in Aidon's throat and he laid her down on the fallen grass, his lips fused to hers as he twisted out of his himation and pushed it behind him.

Persephone grasped at his arms, his muscles bunching and cording under her hands, his limbs caging her. His mouth was insistent and needy against hers. Instinctively, he settled between her legs and flexed his hips. Persephone gasped, desire flashing through her like wildfire, passion trickling like melting snow. He pulled at her earlobe with his teeth and she clawed at his shoulders, wild beneath him, desperate to be closer. Her mind was a tumult, fresh sensation searing her skin and warming her bones.

Aidon panted against her neck, drinking in her scent. He grasped fistfuls of her peplos, hoisting her skirt up to her thighs as she twisted and raised her hips, grinding against him, helping him pull it past her waist. He hissed when the scent of her arousal rose with her displaced dress and licked his lips. Aidon braced to draw down the length of her body, but she grabbed his tunic and yanked him back, face to face. "No! Just take me."

"You haven't reached ecstasy for months," he whispered. He leaned his forehead against hers, and his eyes dilated, staring directly into her. She shivered under his gaze. His warm palm slid up her thigh and cupped her vulva gently, then flattened hard against it, folds separating and slipping between his tensed fingers, heat enveloping them. His jaw set with feral intensity and the heel of his palm kneaded against her mound and she could hear the slickness even as she felt it coat his long fingers.

"I can't… It's been too long." She breathed heavily and gripped his hair, her back arching as his hand worked against her sex. She reached for his loincloth, desperate to grasp his cock and destroy his resolve, but his arm held her hips close to his and thwarted her. She twisted. "I just want you inside me."

"Stop denying yourself," he rasped into her ear as she bucked against his hand and moaned. "I'm not going to come without you, do you understand?"

She nodded and closed her eyes, surrendering as his fingers spread her apart, opening her to the prickling breeze and his soothing touch. He coaxed out her bud and brushed quick circles around it. Persephone melted and gripped his shoulders until the fibulae left red impressions on her palms. Her body tensed and slacked and his hand suddenly left the warmth of her crease to move aside his loincloth. Cool air shocked her trembling flesh and she cried out in protest.

A heavier heat replaced his fingers. His cock ground and pulsed hot against her labia, nestling into her lips from tip to root, covering him in her wetness, readying him and driving her to madness. Aidon sighed with relief, his face softening, his breath slowing, every sinew in his body gaining the measures of control she was losing. He pillowed her neck with his forearm and panted against her forehead, pressing all his weight onto one elbow, as he fed first the head, then one slow inch after another into the fiery center of her.

Half-sheathed, Aidon held and pushed against the spongy ridges with the tip of his cock while his thumb returned to her clitoris with soft, practiced strokes. Years of knowing exactly which touch would melt her guided his every move. She cried, frustrated and at the edge, pleading softly for him to fill her completely until those half-hearted words died on her lips as she was subsumed by her impending climax. The familiar coil wound taut within her, closing around the piercing weight and width of him, and straining against the finger strumming against her.

The bowstring snapped and Persephone rose to him, swallowing him deep. Her legs shook around his hips, her toes curled and her face and neck flushed. Her thighs squeezed as tightly as his hips would allow before they rose and her legs locked around his waist. Wave after clenching wave rolled along the length of him within her, and her long wail resounded through the field.

Aidon steadied, waiting as she fluttered around him. He closed his eyes, savoring each pulse of her release until she came back to him. With a heated look, he presented his soaked hand to her. His hungry gaze never left hers as he licked each of his fingers and his palm with a groan before planting his hand in the grass beside her. He surged his hips forward.

Her head tilted back and she grasped at his shoulder blades, surrounded by him, each successive thrust gliding through her, flaring the rippling walls of her channel. He thickened within her and his brow tensed, eyes boring into her, the telltale vein prominent at his temple. Her hand moved down to his flanks, squeezing, feeling each flex as he advanced and retreated. They sang wordlessly and she angled and braced against him, his lids squeezed shut, his head bucking. He rammed deep and held there, his shout lost in the breeze as his seed charged into her depths.

Arms shaking, Aidoneus collapsed against her, heart beating hard through their clothes. When his weight grew too heavy Persephone pushed against his shoulder.

"Not yet," he groaned and lifted himself fractionally. Persephone shifted under him and he leaned on his elbows, giving her space to move. They lay there, breath slowing as he stroked her cheek and her lower lip with his thumb. "Stay with me."

"I wish I could," she whispered. "More than anything."

"What day is it?"

"The day after spring."

He looked her in the eye. "Oh gods, we have to get you back to the surface! We agreed—"

"I don't care anymore. We did that out of deference to *them*, and after all they've done, I simply don't care," Persephone said. Slowly, he slipped from her. Aidoneus quickly pulled up his loincloth and smoothed down his tunic, mindful of her dress.

He lay at her side, watching the same passing cloud, and spoke softly. "I know this doesn't mend everything."

"No. It doesn't."

He sighed.

"It's a start, though," she said, her throat dry. "I need time, Aidon. Time away to heal myself, and when I return in autumn, time with you to mend what grief destroyed."

21.

P ERSEPHONE HAD RETURNED TO ELEUSIS THREE WEEKS before and with her the first faint breezes of spring. But the snow was slow to melt this year, and the sunlight streaming through the quartz ceiling of the Anaktoron did nothing to chase the pervasive chill from the room.

Demeter bundled her mantle around her shoulders and pushed her hands into the soil of a raised bed. She felt the pull of the earth coursing through her and tried to pour its warmth into the flax seedlings to help them along. They would be moved outdoors after the last frost, though it would take twice as long to plant them. The winter wheat had already been in the ground for a month, growing slowly. Demeter hoped the coarse, hearty grains would provide enough nourishment this year, here and all across Hellas.

"Perhaps she'd emerge from her room if she wasn't met with congratulations on her baby at every step. I just don't understand," Triptolemus said, digging around a patch of flax. "Why can you not tell the priesthood what really happened?"

"Because my kind doesn't have the luxury of weakness or fallibility." Demeter's brow unfurrowed and she sighed. "I'm sorry."

"*O Helioeida*, this has been… stressful for everyone." He gently stroked the white roots trailing from the base of one seed, grateful for this evidence of fertility in the soil. Triptolemus leaned back and dusted off his hands. "There's still plenty of grain in the silos from last year. But…"

"It will last. This won't happen every year, and if the Sparing Ones see fit to spare her further pain, it won't happen ever again."

"And if they don't reconcile?"

Persephone had returned days late from her journey across the known world. Hermes had told Demeter of what she'd done to Apollo, and that Zeus was the only other Olympian who knew about it— the quieter it was kept, the better for all. When Persephone had finally arrived in Eleusis, a thin trail of crocus bloomed in her wake, her expression serene. Just as she had been the night after she sent Sisyphus to the Pit.

"They'll reconcile," Demeter muttered under her breath.

"A shame these have sprouted already."

"Why? They'll be ready to plant before long."

"Because," Triptolemus said with a hungry look, "there are more *enjoyable* ways to make the ground fertile."

Demeter bit her lip. "We could always encourage their growth…"

"Look at me like that again, my lady, and you'll make something *else* grow…" He winked and she laughed, and Triptolemus planted a quick kiss on her lips. He drew her into his arms and reached into her peplos to fondle a breast. She arched against him.

Keryx knocked at the door and they flew apart, startled. His voice was muffled. "Mistress?"

"A moment!" Demeter smoothed her dress and stood. She batted his shoulder playfully and Triptolemus smiled, returning to the flax.

Keryx cracked open the Anaktoron door and cleared his throat. "I beg pardon, my lady, but your daughter has been calling for you from upstairs."

"Why can't she just come down?" Demeter frowned.

"She wouldn't let me into her room. My lady, she was crying."

Demeter nodded and left the Anaktoron, hurrying past the two thrones on the raised dais. She rounded the corner and up the stairs, coming to Persephone's closed door. There was sobbing on the other side.

"Persephone?"

"Is anyone else with you?"

"No. Triptolemus is in—"

"Good."

Demeter hesitantly opened the door and peered in, struck by the chill in the room. Persephone was curled up on her bed, facing the open window. The air smelled sour. "Are you well?"

"No… Shut the door," she whispered. "Please…"

Demeter closed it and walked to the edge of the bed. "Daughter, I know coming back here has been difficult. Especially since no one, save Triptolemus and me, knows the truth. If it would be easier for you to—"

"I'm pregnant."

"What?!"

"Please," Persephone turned, her eyes wide, her hands out in front of her. "Please *whisper*. No one can know… They can't— I can't do this again!"

Her daughter's voice choked and rasped and her eyes filled with frightened tears. Demeter pulled the kline next to her bed and leaned in close. "Are you certain?"

"I'm late," she said.

"You've been late before."

"But I haven't—" she heaved, holding her stomach, and spat on the ground.

"Oh gods, Kore…"

"Please, no one can know! No one!" Her voice cracked as she grabbed a cloth and leaned over the edge of the bed, soaking up the acrid bile. She tossed the rag into the basin where she'd emptied her stomach earlier.

Why was Persephone in such a panic? The Olympians were not to be trusted, and she rightfully feared them finding out, but… ice settled in Demeter's stomach. She poured Persephone a cup of water, not meeting her eyes. "Is Aidoneus the father?"

"How could you ask me that?!"

"I only ask so I know how best to protect you. And from whom. You were on the verge of ending your marriage the last time I spoke to either of you. Then you traveled halfway across the known world, in the company of mortals, across the domain of the Potamoi doing… Fates know what."

Persephone sighed. "Yes. He's the father."

Demeter sat back and nodded.

"I don't know how it happened. It's not possible. I went back below," she cried. "After spring, which I've never done before. I saw him in Elysion, and we… talked. It was… we still can't *hear* each other."

"Once those bonds are severed, they are not easily repaired. Sometimes they're gone forever."

Tears stung her eyes and she looked skyward. "He had visited me the night before in dreams, telling me he wished to reconcile, were it his choice; but since I was the one wronged, he said, since I'm the one dividing my time above and below, he left it up to me. So I went below and told him that we'd sacrificed enough— that I didn't want to sacrifice him, or our marriage. We vowed to not try for children ever again, and then we… well…"

"Well," Demeter said, drawing a deep breath. "It was meant to be. You might never know why or how. Sometimes, when the last hope has faded, a baby happens. Or so it's been for mortal women. Enough have prayed to me for fertility over the years... I should know."

"Mother, if anyone on Olympus finds out, who knows what they'll try? Especially after what I did to Apollo."

"I know."

"I'll be showing by late summer, and there won't be a himation thick enough to hide it," she cried. "And I can't go out and vomit all over the fields! You *know* they'll start talking. First the Eleusinians, then every nymph and god within fifty leagues!"

"I'll protect you. Your nausea will abate; trust me. And if I get nectar—"

"No. No! Not from them!"

"Calm, Persephone. Olympus has never been the sole source. The *Kabieroi* make their own ambrosia on Samothrace from honey."

"Samothrace?" She stared out the window, looking east. "Eurydice's honey..."

"And her mother before her. We don't have to leave Eleusis— they'll bring it to me." She grasped her daughter's hand. "But you *must* be seen, Persephone, and all must appear normal. We have a few short months to ensure that humanity doesn't starve. And I will *desperately* need your help with the crops if the second part of my plan is to succeed."

✳   ✳   ✳

"I'm as big as a foaling mare."

"Nonsense! You're lovely. Besides, you're so short we'd need two of you— one standing atop the other to even *reach* a mare's shoulder."

Semele playfully smacked him in the center of his chest. Zeus had spirited her away to a small villa in Nysa, the hidden garden of the gods, when she had started to show. Great blue

412

tapestries adorned every wall. Oaks shaded the villa, allowing dappled light through the heavy linen covering every window. She could hear birds, but he'd warned her against peeking outside.

Thanks to the dire threat posed by his wife, it had never occurred to Semele when she'd asked Zeus for his child that she would be endangered by other mortals. She should have known: her great ancestor Kadmos had fled Phoenicia with his pregnant sister after Zeus had seeded her with child. The Phoenicians were prepared to kill her for the sake of family honor, and Europa had barely escaped with her life. But Zeus had sworn he would protect Semele. From Hera, from King Sthenelus, from any creature above or below the earth, he'd said.

She didn't mind being whisked away from Tiryns. They were neither her family nor her people. She was little more than a captive in that city— part of a trade to keep peace with Thebes. Here she was safe in the arms of the most powerful being in the cosmos, in a land where no mortal could set foot.

She teased him again. "I don't know how you can stand to look at me now."

"You're more beautiful than ever," he rasped into her ear. "And so perfect a fit, now that you're heavy with child…"

Zeus had enjoyed making love to her since she started showing. Her body was even more responsive, more attuned to his touch. She ran her hands down the sides of her breasts and her wide belly, along her hips. "But these awful lines…"

"The silvery marks of a mother. Like ripe fruit. A fertile, beautiful *gynae*." Zeus clenched his jaw and narrowed his eyes, then smiled and the momentary storm that seemed to trouble him passed. He advanced on her, his wolflike grin liquifying her. "Come…"

"That's not been so easy these past weeks."

"Oh?" He gently tipped her back onto the bed. "Have you tried in my absence?"

She tilted her head back and laughed. "I can't even reach anymore."

"I suppose I could help with that."

Settling into the linen sheets, she watched him over the horizon of her abdomen, her popped navel a solitary hill at its zenith. Zeus's fingers were agile, his touch deft. As ever, he sought to make her pleasure his own when she reached her peak. He tapped his phallus against her swollen lips, each strike making her breath hitch. When he slid it along slick heat, she whimpered and writhed, earning a quick swat to her rear. "Zeus!"

"Yes?" He rumbled like a distant storm and she twisted under his intense gaze.

"Please..." She licked her lips. "I want all of you. Every last bit of you."

"Oh, I'll gladly finish you," he said, cocking an eyebrow, "but don't hurry me."

He slid against her sex and the weight of her pregnant belly pinned her in place, giving her no escape from his touch. Zeus reached beside her and billowed a thin sheet over her, its cool canopy descending on her like a cloud. Zeus smiled as he disappeared. She made out his shadowy outline through the linen. "What's this?"

"Maybe dulling your sense of sight will help you focus where you ought... lose control..."

Semele could answer only with a long moan. The head of his cock parted her lips and she heard him sigh, felt the glorious stretch as he filled her, ever so slowly, mindful of her condition. His caution wouldn't last long. Heat expanded within her, touching every nerve of her passage and she tensed around him, pushing back on his cock, naturally resisting his invasion. Then her entire body swooned as he reclaimed that sliver of an inch and more, bottoming out against the entrance of her womb.

She felt a sudden, rough pinch on her nipple through the sheet and cried out. He groaned as the shock tightened her around him. So this was his plan for the sheet— she couldn't see what he was going to do next. That uncertainty made her tremble and squeeze tighter still.

He would take her eventually, but Semele knew there was an instinct holding him back. As a girl, her mother's midwife had told her that laying with a man in the last weeks would urge the baby to be born. Even as her pleasure swelled, she felt tired, so heavy and unlike herself, nagged with worry that if her baby grew larger, the birth would end her... just as her stillborn brother had killed her mother. Perhaps if she made him lose himself in her it would help bring the baby forth. The child was *hemitheoi*, with divinely blessed parentage. Her cousin's twins had come early too...

Semele bore down on him and Zeus cried out, his hands tensing on her hips before he withdrew and filled her again. His voice shuddered. "What are you doing?"

She breathed through the damp sheet. "Fuck me harder."

"What?" He laughed. She gave a quick squeeze and he growled at her, then swirled his thumb against her bud. "Prim little princess... it's good you feel less inhibited under there. But you don't want me to do that. Not really."

"Yes, I do." Semele breathed harder as the pad of his thumb worked faster. "I'm small, Zeus, not fragile. I want everything you can give me."

For effect, she bore down again and his thumb ceased its rhythm. He snapped his hips and she wailed in relief, pushed back on the bed as his hips smacked against her thighs. He grunted through his teeth. "Gods, you're tight..."

"More... please, more! Let me have all of you!"

"Yes…" He placed his arm beside her shoulder to brace himself, his fingers still hovering on the apex of her mound. Her heat was excruciating, and his head light. His knees felt like they would give out any moment and his eyes squeezed shut, testicles drawing up and tightening, ready to release. He tipped his head back and as he climaxed, he sent the finishing jolt through her, a bright shock of light flaring before his closed lids and…

The room smelled acrid and sickly sweet. He opened his eyes. Semele was gone, the sheet scored black like a lightning strike. The light… the light. Fates below…

"Oh no…" Zeus stumbled away, still breathing hard, his heart drumming in his ears, looking frantically around the room. "Semele? No… no, please no…"

Semele was gone. Dead. Burned away in a flash of heat and light. *His* light. Gone, with Hades and Persephone's child within her. His damnable weakness, his lust, would end them all. He'd pushed them into war.

"Loud Thunderer."

Zeus startled and his knees finally gave out. A woman, hair red and thickly streaked with silver, crowned with selenite beads, pushed aside a tapestry near the west window. He curled forward, shielding his flaccid penis with his hands, and stared at her with wide sky-blue eyes. "Hecate, please. I can explain."

"No more sounds of thunder after lightning." She said, advancing the room. "This was foreseen."

"What?" His eyes darted around the stinking, scorched room.

"Not water and blood to herald his birth, but a flash of flame and light." She strode to the bed and peeled back the sheet. Beneath it lay an infant with dark hair, shaking, his fists balled tightly. When the cold air washed over his skin, the newborn wailed. Zeus saw his toothless gums, his face red, a film of white on his skin. The afterbirth and cord had burned away with the rest of Semele. A wine-red birthmark swirled across his left leg and licked up his side.

The child lived. Never had Zeus been so glad to see a newborn boy. As relief washed away shock and horror, he realized: he would not be the ruin of all, nor would he spend eternity imprisoned alongside his father. "How…"

"From the spark of life that lit the fires of the cosmos he was created; so was he destined to be born into the world. Thus was it my duty to witness your fornication and wait. It was Fate… the storms gathered, and the bolt would one day strike her."

"You watched us— Well." He stopped hiding his cock and folded his arms across his chest. "I suppose a sworn virgin has to find her entertainment somehow."

"Don't flatter yourself. Only the well-being of this child could compel me to see your lechery play out on Semele's hapless body."

His jaw tightened. "Is it over? Are you to give him to Persephone now?"

"Your consort killed that hope with the same poison. He is of two mothers, yet neither breast can nourish him." Zeus glanced haplessly at the dust strewn across the sheets. "This is what you will do," Hecate continued. She swaddled the baby deftly and gathered him up in her arms. He cried and shook. "Do cover yourself, Loud Thunderer. My eyes are sore enough, and you walk a long road this day."

He slunk to the kline near the door, tail between his legs, and donned his tunic. The baby's piercing wail filled the room. Time seemed to slow and he keenly felt Hecate's glare boring into his back. He laced his sandals and wound his himation over his shoulder. Still, the babe cried unceasingly. He strode back to her and she held the swaddled infant out for him. Zeus looked once at the child, then to her stern face, and took the squirming bundle in his arms. When the boy settled against him, he quieted and cooed. His eyelids drooped and finally shut. The baby's breath was uneven. How easy it would be, while he was still so fragile, to end Hades's claim to his throne…

"If you do the babe any harm, Cronides, you know he will come for you. And all the dead shall follow," Hecate said, her ever-changing eyes piercing his soul and seeing his thoughts. He should have known better.

"What would you have me do?"

"You will carry him to Crete, where sacred Amalthea's milk will nourish him."

"And leave him with the wild gods?!"

"You have forgotten that you suckled at her breast, too? The *next* to wear the crown of heaven will grow strong on the same rich milk. You will present him to them as yet another of your *hemitheoi* whelps. They will cloak him in this false raiment and care for him as one of their tribe. To the Kouretes, he will be Zeus's hidden bastard; to none will he be recognized as Zagreus, son of Aidoneus and Persephone."

The baby wriggled and a tiny hand emerged from the swaddling clothes, the fingers strong but trembling as they grasped the edge of Zeus's himation. "He can never go by the name of Zagreus again, you know…"

"What did Semele wish to call him?"

The newborn breathed peacefully, shivering still. Zeus tucked his cloak around him. "Dionysos."

✻   ✻   ✻

As a rule, Hermes preferred not to wake early. When he did so to visit the Underworld, he hated it.

Time, however, was not on his side: Elysion was vast, and he needed to find Hades before the Chthonian dusk. Aidoneus's frequent absence from the palace was unlike him, but

Hermes could guess what drew him regularly to the sun-lit paradise. He flew on, the chasms of the world below winding through sterile earth, then opening to the broad reach of the Styx, its waters darkened. Veins of flickering torchlight wound their way along the cliffs and he dove for the terrace outside the great throne room.

He found Aidoneus leaning over Minos's scroll, finger tracing words as he pored over it with the ancient founder of Crete, stopping at a single name. Hermes removed his hat and dropped to one knee, head bowed. Minos cleared his throat. "This one… by fire. Born in Thebes. She'd be Rhadamanthys's problem, but she came without coin."

"Pardoned. Let her cross. Asphodel."

"But—"

"I *said…* let her cross." He enunciated each word and stared Minos in the eye.

The judge looked at the floor. "Yes, my lord."

"If that is all," he said, rolling the scroll and handing it back to Minos. The judge nodded and retreated from the throne room. Hermes formally bowed again once they were alone. Aidoneus grimaced. "Oh, get up. This isn't Olympus. What brings you here?"

Hermes straightened, picking at the edge of his petasos. "That was Semele, wasn't it? The one who—"

"Choose your next words carefully, Psychopompos."

"Aidon, I know about it because it exists to be known. It's who I am."

"You're also an unrepentant gossip. And if you breathe a word of it to your *friend…*"

"I broke with Apollo in early winter." He shook his head. "After what Hera did, and Apollo, Semele… and now the babe, Dionysos, and his true lineage… I know. Other than official messages, I am done with Apollo. Same with everyone else on Olympus, unless they prove innocent in this. I know my father was involved, else he would have stopped it."

Aidoneus exhaled and stared at a point on the edge of the dais. "I suppose it would be foolish to think any events of this past year would have escaped your notice."

"Which is why I'm here. To apologize for my part in it." He scuffed his sandal against the floor, his brow knitting. "I should have told you that Apollo was insistent on getting the lyre back and that I suspected he knew. Though I didn't know he harbored such bottomless malice toward you and your wife. Maybe this wouldn't have…"

Aidoneus waved his hand to stop him. He descended the dais. "Hindsight is revelatory, no?"

"If I had spoken up at court, instead of protecting him, maybe none of this would have come to pass."

"No, Hermes. This was *ananke*. We all had our parts to play. I was so desperate for something, anything to give us a child that I threw caution to the wind. It nearly destroyed everything— my wife, my marriage…"

Hermes shifted on the balls of his feet. "Persephone won't see anyone. Not since Cyrene."

"While the gods above take their enmity out on each other's worshippers, our ways are different. We spare the hapless mortals our ire and spite. Persephone thought she was in danger after punishing Apollo. Not from him, but the others. I don't think he will bother us again. Surely, he realizes that if I even see the whites of his eyes… Persephone's *timoria* was inventive, but mine would be final. But that still doesn't rule out sheer stupidity on his part."

"His pride will safeguard you both. To admit that she weakened him so? Took such power away from him? Better he pretends to be his father's prophetic scion than to acknowledge Persephone's curse. I wanted to reassure her, but she will not see me. I tried going to Eleusis and Demeter almost pulled the wings off my sandals when I went looking for her."

"Can you blame her?"

"Persephone for secluding herself, or Demeter for making sure she wasn't disturbed?"

"Either." Aidoneus twisted the rings on his left hand. "It's been three months since I last heard from my wife."

"Another reason I was trying to find her. This time of year, I usually spend more time ferrying messages between you two than anything Zeus has for me."

"This has been an unusual year. I must ask you for a favor."

"Anything."

"Never speak about Dionysos. To anyone. Leave no room for accidents."

"You have my word."

"And," he hesitated, staring at the ground, "don't make any special journey there on my behalf, but if your travels take you near Crete…"

Hermes smiled at Aidoneus. "I'll look in on him from time to time."

✲   ✲   ✲

"Thank you for coming."

Hera relaxed back into the cushion of the divan. "It's been a while. I was at Kanathos for longer than I expected. And you… even after I returned… have you been traveling? This is the longest we've ever gone without one of us barging in on the other."

Hestia smiled thinly. "Yes. I thought it best to explore— to make myself scarce on Olympus. As much as I'm able."

"Bactria?"

"Not until autumn. It's doubtful their harvest will be kind to them this year. No; my travels took me past the Indus

421

again," Hestia said. She ladled hot water into a cup and handed the tisane to Hera. "That's where I found most of the ingredients for our tea today. I've been trying to unlock the secrets of a particular spice since the last time we met."

"It seems like aeons since late summer…"

"Much has happened in the interim, nay? Pasithea was married, I hear. To Hypnos."

Hera's face fell. "Yes."

"Have you heard anything from her?"

"No." She sat back and stared at her tea, then took a long sip. "Willful girl… she hasn't sent so much as a word with Hermes, yet. To her *own mother*."

"I thought you would have let her take the vows. She never seemed much interested in marriage or children." Hestia watched Hera drink. "Do you like it?"

"It's divine. A hint of sweetness. Honey?"

"No."

"Take no offense when I say this, Hestia, but no daughter of *mine* will ever be a sworn virgin." She exhaled. "Though she might as well be, considering her husband…"

"Yes… Hypnos takes as much pleasure in men as Ganymede, they say." She circled the rim of her cup with her finger. "You could always ask Persephone how Pasithea is doing. You'd become *such* good friends… so close to her last year."

Hera sputtered and almost dropped the cup. "I… we haven't spoken. Not since… We really shouldn't mention it on Olympus. Who knows what speaking about her misfortune could visit upon the rest of us?"

Hestia's face was serene. "I know you poisoned Persephone."

Hera merely sat still, holding the cup closely, as if she had frozen in place.

"There's no point in denying it, is there?"

Her eyes teared up. "I didn't… I didn't want to, wouldn't have if…"

Hera wobbled, and reached to set down her empty cup, nearly missing the table. Hestia held hers out to her side and poured its steaming contents onto the stone floor.

The queen lurched up and staggered, gripping the side of the divan to anchor herself as the room began to tilt. Her pupils were blown and she shielded her eyes from the wavering hearth light. Hera tried to form words, but her mouth had gone dry.

"Nutmeg, I've found, is delightful. Wrapped in fiery strands that must be torn away, sweet and pungent. But if you consume too much, you *see* things. Terrible things, Hera, that gnaw at your soul."

"Sister…"

She stood and advanced on Hera, drawing her veil over her head. "You came to me knowingly, directed by Apollo, playing the wounded calf. You allowed me to think you'd been ravished by your husband, Hera, so I would distill the silphium for you. It was never *intended* for you, though; it was for her. All that time you sat there… lying to me… risking every freedom I ever managed to carve out for myself in this wretched cage your lord and master created for us all."

"H-Hest—"

"You're in for a long and very unpleasant evening, Hera."

She stretched her hand out and drew the flames from the hearth toward her until they swirled and flared behind her sister. Hera shook, foam gathering at the corners of her mouth. She convulsed. Hestia pulled the ring of flames toward her, enveloping the Queen of Heaven. She'd have to find a way back through the ether by herself.

"Don't ever come to my hearth again."

22.

"ONE OBOL... ONE OBOL... ONE— AH." SEEING THE shade's rounded belly, Charon sighed. Her face and skin were shrouded by an indigo cloak. "A pity. But only one is needed for you."

Her bronze coin dropped into his waiting palm and she settled in silently with the others. The Boatman cast off.

"What will happen to me... really?" said an old man from the great city of Ilion. "Men are told all manner of things. Unlike these *autourogoi*, I've traveled far and seen much."

"Oh?" Charon scoffed. "What have you heard, wanderer?"

"There isn't a soul in Hellas or Ilion who doesn't know of this place, and few speak its name. But in Aegyptus, they say men's hearts are weighed against a feather. Those from the Indus say souls are reborn to the world in a cycle as endless as man. Longer even... that we've existed here for a *Kalpa*... a day as old as the earth itself."

Charon nodded. "You *have* traveled far..."

"You're mad." The Mycenaean next to him muttered. "Best hope they take pity on you and don't send you to Tartarus."

"Don't worry yourself about that one. He's full of knowledge and perhaps some wisdom," said Charon. "There are grains of truth there. You only have two eyes to see with, as does every mortal. And all of us, gods and immortals alike, see what we wish, no? The stories you tell about us are without number. All come here by as many paths as the gods they worship. Wouldn't their eyes see only the end they imagine or fear?"

"But…" The Mycenaean sputtered. "All our eyes are open!"

"Indeed."

He pursed his lips, unwilling to challenge the Boatman, then barked at the man from Ilion. "Look around, you fool Trojan. Where do you think we are?"

"You are home," the pregnant shade said.

Charon whipped around at the familiar voice. She pushed back her cloak, revealing blue-gray eyes and a slight smile. Persephone raised a finger to her lips. The Boatman swallowed his delight and paddled onward, grinning broadly after he'd turned away from the shades.

✳ ✳ ✳

It was nearly dusk on the Styx. For the second time today, and at least the dozenth time in the last few months, he sat down to write to Persephone. As each time before, he couldn't get his stylus to move in the right direction. Nothing in his heart reached the page except one scratched-through blot of ink after another. Again, he fed the papyrus to the brazier's flames.

A woman who committed matricide had been sent to Tartarus that morning and it had been Aidoneus's misfortune to visit the Trivium just as she arrived. The shouts and accusations the woman had leveled at him rang in his head all day— as had her screams when Megaera grasped her by the arm,

425

bound for the Phlegethon. He had escaped to Elysion to visit Orpheus and Eurydice at their home under the linden tree. Its bower of fragrant flowers and pale leaves had shaded them in the afternoon sun while they enjoyed the steady hum of bees. Eurydice had sent him on his way with a sweet honeycomb wrapped in waxed linen.

Aidoneus unwrapped the honey, broke off a small piece, and sampled it, sticky sweetness bursting from the chewy wax. He thought again of Persephone, cautious warmth washing through him, almost as if she were there. Four months had passed and not a word from her. It had taken more time than that for their marriage to fray; it could take thrice that or longer to repair it. Or, he mused, she had reconsidered, and their coupling in Elysion amounted to a farewell.

He spat the chewed wax into the hearth and poured oil over his hands to slough off the honey that stuck to his fingers. The oil made it worse, so he picked up his bronze water thief to refill the basin. Bathing would do him good, and perhaps chase any despondent thoughts from his mind. He carried it to the terrace and rinsed his hands in the freezing water, then submerged the bulb into the catchment, single-mindedly filling it. The rush of the falls filled his ears, and the sound of the door opening behind him registered belatedly. He turned to look and froze.

"Persephone!" Had he lost track of the days? "Sweet one, it's only two moons past midsummer. What are you doing—"

She threw off her thick indigo cloak. The water thief clanked to the floor, its contents gushing out and puddling on the mosaic. It could have landed in Tartarus for all he cared. Persephone placed her hand atop her rounded belly. "Aidon…"

He finally closed his mouth and stepped forward, eyes flitting between hers and her womb. "How…"

"I don't know." Her voice wavered. "All I have are guesses."

"In Elysion?"

"Yes." Her eyes filled with tears and her face contorted. "Aidoneus, I'm so sorry, I couldn't tell you, and I didn't dare cross the ether! I couldn't see *anyone*, even Hermes, for fear of Olympus finding out. *No one* knew except my mother, so she could keep me safe..."

"Of course you couldn't." He gathered her close and held her, his hand tangling in her hair. She was pregnant. He had lain with her in Elysion, and now she was with child. *Their child.* And just as suddenly as his astonishment had set in, he felt the cold alarm, the terror that had stricken him when they had crossed the Styx a year ago, the loss that had nearly destroyed them... He flinched from her, eyes flitting over every detail, any sign that something was amiss. "Your feet..."

"I walked," she said.

Aidon blinked. "From Eleusis?!"

"Had I traveled any other way, I might have been found out. The baby was growing too fast for me to hide it and... Please." She closed the distance he'd retreated. "Aidon, I need you right now. Don't shrink away from me."

His throat hurt. "But what if I... what if this place—"

"Our child began here. It will be safe here. Please... I can't go through this again. Not alone."

Aidoneus swallowed and moved closer. He touched Persephone's face, still wondering how this could be real, how she could be here. He framed her cheek and brushed back her bedraggled hair. "Do you have any inkling what it might be?"

"No. Only that I started showing so much earlier than before and it kicks and moves constantly."

Carefully he held her waist, then placed his hand over hers, resting on her womb. He closed his eyes. Aidon heard a heartbeat, quick and anxious. Hers. Then his.

Then, faint and urgent, another heartbeat. *And another.* An unfurling of light and darkness. The lands below and the blinding sunlight above. *The flame shining in the dark... the augury of the world to come...* dark hair, light hair...

His eyes opened wide and he knelt, rounding his hands over her belly. Aidon looked up at her as she stared down at him, both bewildered.

"Twin girls," he whispered.

Her gasp was sharp, nearly a laugh. "Gods, what am I going to do? I wasn't prepared for one..."

"We." He splayed his fingers across the small of her back and pressed his cheek to her womb. "Persephone, what *we will do* is welcome our daughters in five months. Together."

Aidoneus rose and she leaned into his chest. *One who is twice woven, cannot remain your own. Two, the ether bound, who shines the torch in darkness. Three, the blessed harbinger, who reaps the reaper's heart...* Her breathing slowed, her body softening and relaxing in his arms. He tilted her chin, and leaned down, his lips brushing hers. She tasted like the long paths she'd walked to return to him. Persephone wrapped her arms around his neck, drawing him to her. He bent forward, careful not to press too hard against her, and felt a rolling against his abdomen as one of their children kicked.

Their children. Their daughters. Persephone broke off the kiss, her gaze searching for what he felt. Aidon pulled her to him again, supporting her weight, tongue flicking against her lips until they opened. He held her, enjoyed her closeness, then lifted her upright. Aidon carefully framed her belly with his hands.

"We should get you washed up." His voice came out rougher than he intended.

She breathed steadily, her heart racing. "I think you dropped the water thief."

"I did." He spun around and snatched it from the floor, his bare feet splashing in the puddle, and submerged the bulb in the shallow catchment. Aidon took his wife's hand and led her back to their bedroom. "When did you know?"

"Almost immediately," she said, sitting next to the hearth. He stood beside her, warming the water thief in the fire. "Not three weeks had passed since I was with you and the nausea began. And it came on mercilessly."

"I wish I'd been there for you."

"Or that I could have told you." She smiled softly at him as he filled the basin. Steam rose and he soaked a sea sponge in the water.

"It was wise of you to conceal it. Here..." He knelt and unlaced her sandals. Dust clung to her ankles in the pattern of crossed leather straps, and the skin beneath was rubbed raw, unable to fully heal after days of walking uneven steps. He cautiously sponged away the dirt. "Does that hurt?"

"Not like I thought it would."

"They're swollen."

"That's been the story of this past month," she chuckled ruefully.

"Walking here couldn't have helped. If I had known, if we could still..." He stopped himself. There was no point in dwelling on their lost connection. Aidon tilted olive oil into his palm, warmed it between his hands, then smoothed it into her skin, doubling back wherever he had washed. She sighed, her shoulders drooping, her head leaned back. He rubbed her abraded heels carefully as the skin healed and wove his fingers between each toe, massaging the oil into her feet. "Better?"

She nodded. He wetted the sponge and took each of her hands, running it over her fingers, her palms, her forearms, then working the flesh with more oil. "It's good to be home."

He smiled at her. It struck him that he hadn't known until this moment if she'd ever call their room that again. Tears stung his eyes.

"Husband?"

"I'm glad to hear you say that." His voice shook. He wrapped his arms around her shoulders, holding her close, and kissed her on top of her head.

"We can't let anyone know I'm here."

"You're safe with me," he whispered against her scalp. "We should take care of the rest of you."

Persephone unwrapped the thin sash that held her peplos closed over her growing belly and coiled it beside her. He looked to her for approval and she nodded, allowing Aidon to pull loose the fibulae at her shoulders. "Are you too warm?" she asked.

"What?"

"You're inches from the hearth and still wearing your himation."

He grinned back at her and pulled its heavy length off his shoulders, neatly gathered the corners, and set it aside. "I suppose I was."

Aidon cleared her peplos from under her, mindful of her oil-coated feet and legs, and shook out the fabric in his hands, preparing to fold it. When he took in her naked body, he handled the cloth clumsily, unfocused.

His eyes traveled across her skin, her rounded belly and flattened navel, her heavy breasts, and darkened nipples. She swelled with life, like the small clay sculptures he'd seen on altars in the human encampments during the war— his first real exposure to the nude female form. The memory of that first sexual stirring and the sight of his wife sitting at his hearth, big with child— with *his* children— made heat pool low in his belly.

"Aidon?"

He blinked and realized that he'd been staring at her, intent and serious. Persephone shivered. In the past, she'd teased him that when he gave her that heated look, she thought he might eat her. He cleared his throat as that image played through his mind in delicious detail. "Where was I?"

"Getting warmer, I believe."

"I *was* standing quite close," he said, his voice lower. Aidon stepped in front of her, brushing the sponge across her neck and back, her thighs, then gently from her vulva to between her cheeks. She leaned forward, holding her belly, and hummed, relaxing with each pass of warm water. He caught her scent— a hint of faint flowers rising from her skin, but also ripened fruit. Pomegranate. Dates. After she sat back down, he poured more oil onto his hands and kneaded her shoulders and arms, her neck.

Persephone leaned heavily against him, eyes closed. She went limp, her breath radiating hot on his stomach through the wool as he worked days of tension from her limbs. Her closeness, her heat, her scent tempted him and his fingers twitched. Aidoneus set his mind to his task, trying not to think about the soft roundness of her abdomen, or her enlarged breasts resting atop it. He tried to ignore the pleasant caress of her fingers on the back of his legs, the sound of her tiny moans as he massaged her until she was languid, and that she was panting just above the head of his cock…

"We might accidentally get oil on your tunic."

He leaned back to look at her. Persephone's eyes were lidded but lit with familiar want. "You're exhausted, my love."

"I am, but…" She untied his leather belt with a practiced hand. "I've missed you, husband."

The belt dropped behind him, and he lifted the cloth over his head, pins and all. Her eyes trained unblinking on his loincloth, his phallus hard as iron underneath, the outline pronounced and the tip already seeping. His mouth was dry. "I've missed you too."

He poured more oil into his hands and knelt in front of her, splaying his palms on her thighs, fingers traveling glacially slow as her legs parted for him. His hands reached her hips, her vanishing waist, and rounded over her belly. He planted a kiss atop it. Her eyes closed as he tested the weight of her breasts in each hand.

"They're sensitive," she warned breathlessly.

"Too much for this?" He squeezed upward and lightly grazed her nipples with his thumbs.

"No." She exhaled sharply as the flesh beaded.

He wound his tongue around each peak, brushing its mate with his fingers, traveling one to the other as her breath grew shallow. He took his time, listening for her plaintive moans, retreating when it became too much. Aidon planted a kiss on her heart, the last one on her womb, then stroked the thatch of hair below. He gently pulled her forward.

"Oh, I don't know if I can stay upright for that."

"Just a kiss," he whispered against her inner thigh. Persephone angled backward for him and flattened her palms against the stone hearth. Aidon crouched, her thighs resting on his shoulders. He held her at the small of her back, parting her lips with his tongue, and her voice hitched. Honey and salt flooded his senses. Eventually, soft fingertips pushed at his forehead. Her limbs were weak, and there was time enough before them— nearly two months more than he'd thought. Aidon was flush with long-absent joy and a sharp hope he hadn't felt since Askalaphos had hollered at him from the Styx, fateful pomegranate in hand. He stood, her legs parted around his knees, and she reached out gingerly to touch his loincloth.

Persephone's fingers traced the descending lines over his hips and danced across the hardness beneath his loincloth. Her palm settled on the shaft and cupped the length of him through the flimsy linen, barely soothing the taut heat coursing through his veins. He untied the ribbon holding her hair and combed his fingers through the russet waves falling around her shoulders and down her back. While his hands were occupied, she unwound his loincloth from behind, deftly unraveling the finishing wrap. He doubled over when her hand encircled his freed flesh. She bent forward, her breath falling hot against the straining head, her fingers tugging on his foreskin. Tension knotted his body, pulling him away.

"Are you sure?"

"The nausea was terrible, worse than before, but it's been gone at least a month." Her eyes met his and her voice lowered to a whisper. "It's been too long, Aidoneus. Let me taste you."

Gods… He looked to the ceiling as she stroked him from root to tip. How could he deny her? Her lips drew him off balance. His fingers wove into her hair and all he could feel was the enclosing heat, the wet softness, the rasp of her tongue, her eagerness too sweet, too much, threatening to undo him… Aidoneus reluctantly wrenched himself away from Persephone and stooped, gathering her carefully into his arms. Even with their bed just three strides away, he didn't want to risk her slipping on stone and oil. He settled her on the center of the mattress and she rolled to face him. He lay next to her. "Are you more comfortable on your side?"

"I think so. My bed in the Telesterion isn't big enough for me to sleep any other way."

"You have an infuriatingly small bed," he chuckled. Aidon kissed her, pulling at her lips and tasting her, arousal mingling on their tongues. His free hand learned and mapped every new curve, winding its way to her thigh, then delving inward when she hooked her leg over his hip.

He groaned when his fingers met blossoming heat, the delicate folds of her labia parting for him, his digits slick. He meandered to the apex of her mound and circled there, strok-ing, traveling between the swollen bud and the wetness at her entrance. He strummed at her flesh until she broke off their kiss and gasped, holding him close, his cock trailing his arousal against her thigh as she cried out. She wrapped her fingers around his shaft and aligned him with her channel, begging him with half-formed words to enter her as she came.

Irrational fear slowed him but her cries urged him onward, inch by inch, enveloped by heat, the sensation of her rippling around him in ecstasy at last. He couldn't enter her fully in this position. She grasped at his flanks to drive herself down on him, angling her body to receive more. He groaned and shuddered at her heat. She closed around him, her most inti-mate embrace, the exquisite pressure already building in the head...

I'm not sure how long I can last.

Persephone met his gaze, eyes wide with surprise.

"You heard me?"

"Yes." Her eyes grew wet and she kissed him again. *I heard you, my love.*

Aidon pressed into her triumphantly, holding Persephone's face so he could see her, feel her. Slowly at first, he reached through her, sensing the tension in her limbs, then the sound of her heart, the feel of her flesh giving way and accepting his as he made another long thrust. Their consciousness poured back and forth, one into the other. He could feel the twinge of pain in her lower back as if it were his own, the way he could always feel her pleasure and pain since they first shared The Key... the touch and sensations he'd comfortably shared with her for decades came roaring back to life and the balance and pulse of the worlds above and below flowed freely between them for the first time in months. Persephone snapped her hips, trying to move closer, to have her fill of him.

I need more of you. Please...

Give me your back, he answered.

Persephone nodded and separated from him with a whimper, slowly rolling over. Aidon pulled her by the shoulder and hips against his chest and lifted her leg over his. He panted against her neck, desperately seeking reconnection, and gyrated, the head of his cock prodding until it found its way back in. A single thrust and he was seated deeply within her.

The air rushed from their lungs as he claimed his place. One arm supported her under her head and she grasped his hand for balance, their fingers interlacing. Her back bowed as his other palm traveled up her thigh to toy at her mound, fingers quaking against her bud, rushing her toward another climax as he thickened within her. His face and neck flushed, and his teeth gritted in determination as she began to flutter around him. He hastened, hips slapping wildly against her. She clenched around him again, squeezing, crying out his name, finishing him.

Aidon stilled, spine straight, his essence pouring into her, then tightened his embrace, his chin resting on her shoulder, his heart pounding against her spine. A sheen of sweat and scented oil slicked every point where his body cradled hers. Slowly, he withdrew, lowering her leg and supporting her womb, exhausted.

She sighed, content. "I love you."

"And I you, sweet one." He held her close, both breathing in unison. *Welcome home.*

✷   ✷   ✷

Persephone lounged at the end of the bed, clutching a clay cup filled with a lavender tisane, her feet and head supported by pillows. Aidon had painstakingly arranged their bed into a plush nest before leaving to see to their realm.

"Thank you for bringing me tea, Hecate. I'll miss the smell of these flowers next month when they're blooming in full."

The goddess of witchcraft, her eyes framed by crow's feet, sat on the hearth across from her, hands folded on her lap. "Few know I've returned already. My mother, my husband, Charon... and you. There's little anyone can hide from you."

Hecate nodded. "Secrets have been dark, of late. Your last descent left you submerged in isolation. I came here to learn if melancholy held you in the deep."

"No, I'm well. We're well. My spirits are lighter, in more than a few ways." She placed her palm on her belly; one of her daughters was awakening. The other would soon. "I know you can keep a secret." She narrowed her eyes. "You excel at keeping secrets. Don't you, Hecate?"

She bowed her head. "My queen..."

"Aidon told me."

"Then you know I stood where three paths branched before me. One would drown you in the abyss, one would end the world, and one hid a secret behind my lips. The Fates let me walk."

Persephone knit her brow. "How could *his* loss have snuffed out all life?"

Hecate looked to her for approval, then sat before the hearth fire. "You are gods of life and death itself. The crowns of Chthonia unbind you from mortal desires, while your Olympian brethren remain tightly bound. But that very freedom imperils the souls you watch over."

"So his thread in the cloth of life ran across ours, not alongside."

"Yes. And now that thread weaves through many and will touch far more. He has been reborn." Hecate paused a moment, trying to gauge the young queen. "May I speak of him?"

She sat up eagerly, setting her half-finished cup aside. "Please."

"When I sowed him into fertile ground, he was no longer Zagreus. He will exist eternally, but his name would be Dimetor thereafter: he of two mothers. Had you nourished him at your breast, still his grown feet would never carry him home to you."

"But Semele is dead. She died in… childbirth. How does my son still live?"

Hecate folded her hands. "During the Tyrant's terrible rule, I convened in secret with Prometheus and Metis at the old citadel of Olympus. Rhea was heavy with child again— her sixth babe, your father."

Persephone shrugged impatiently. "I've known that Kronos swallowed the Omphalos stone in Zeus's place since I was a child."

"The rock in his place, but whereto the babe? Newborn and hungry for the milk of the Deathless Ones, to sup on ambrosia and then live forever. The Kouretes, children of Ouranos and Gaia, first concocted ambrosia and guarded its most secret ingredients. They embraced him, raised him for millennia, and concealed his existence. They now look after your reborn son." Hecate looked Persephone in the eye, anticipating her next question. "His name is Dionysos Eubouleus."

"The God of Nysa," she whispered.

"It is the name Semele chose for him."

The God of Nysa… The Good Counselor… it was the name Aidon had told Orpheus to disguise his identity. "But I can have him again one day, can't I? When he's old enough."

Hecate looked down. "All at aeon's end…"

"…And all to end the aeon. I know. I've pondered their words a thousand times. But what does that mean for Dionysos?" she said, eyes brimming with tears. "That I can only see him at the end of the world?"

Hecate smiled. "No. You will lay eyes upon your son long before, and one day he will know his mother. But he will not stroll into your arms; he will walk a treacherous path, guided by none, with sorrow and hardship his regular companions. At the end of that journey will he find the truth."

One day... She could fly through the ether *now*, to Crete, where the Kouretes resided, and steal back her stolen child. Persephone wanted to call Zagreus— Dionysos, she corrected herself— her own again. To love him, to hold him, just once.

But in that direction lay madness. He was forever changed by the manner of his making, his destiny rewritten. Had Hecate told her of her baby's fate a mere fortnight after she lost him...she shuddered to consider how it might have rent her soul.

Both twins were awake within her womb now, tiny limbs stretching, fluttering. She grasped her belly and stood up, rocking, trying to soothe them back to sleep. She could pursue those thoughts no further. Her son lived, with a destiny not of her choosing, but one that would draw Dionysos back to her one day.

Hecate stood and took her hand. She pulled Persephone close, resting her head on the queen's shoulder. "Nothing can set it right. But I did all I could. I'm sorry."

"I know you did." She sniffed and pulled gently away from Hecate, still holding her hands. "And he will be a part of me until I can see him again."

"You will."

She stretched and lay back down. The dull ache from her long walk to Chthonia still lingered in her limbs, and she propped her legs on the pillow. "These two need me right now."

Hecate nodded, smiling. "Your mother will be beside you when your time comes. She, too, is tired from the journey."

"Indeed," Persephone replied, easing the strain on her lower back. "She protected me. It was her idea for me to walk here from Eleusis. She knew those roads from long ago." She stroked her belly, almost afraid to ask the truth from the Goddess of the Crossroads. "Hecate?"

"You wish to know how twin sprouts took root."

"Please."

"Each year, you and your husband sacrifice your fertility on the altar of the world above. The seeds of the eternal nourish the corporeal. But you kept those winter fruits from the altar, and spring's fertility arrived not above, but in Chthonia…"

She nodded. They hadn't coupled throughout winter. Then she'd sapped fertility from the southern Mesogeios when she confronted Apollo in Cyrene, just before returning after the first of spring… "So this can never happen again."

"All is possible. The cost remains the same; would you allow it?"

"It would make a desert of my marriage, not to mention the whole earth. Hecate, about the silphium… I shouldn't have—"

"No. You shouldn't have. Its demise wrenches the scepter from women, and delivers the choice of whether the womb bears fruit into the hard grip of *men*."

Persephone looked down. "I was furious and desperate to exact *timoria* on Apollo. I didn't think."

"None of us is perfect." Hecate smiled thinly. "Aidoneus and I proved that, wielding with two hands the very prod that drove you toward Cyrene."

One of her girls rolled over and drove a foot into Persephone's ribs, and she winced. "Speaking of unintended consequences…" Hecate petted her shoulder until the pain passed.

"Your family has borne many twins." Hecate nodded at her belly. "Have you found their names?"

"Yes. Aidoneus and I have decided. Call it superstition, but after losing Zagreus, I refuse to speak their names until they're born."

23.

"Come," he said, grasping her hand. He tried to match her cautious pace as they walked along the high bluffs beside the sea, but his quick steps betrayed his excitement.

"Do they know?" Persephone gave his hand an earnest tug, and he fell back in step alongside her.

"No. You and I agreed to tell no one," Aidoneus said with a smile.

On their anniversary, Hades and Persephone had called for a celebration, inviting those who frequented the palace to join them in the great hall. Hecate, Nyx and her children, Askalaphos and Nychtopula, Menoetes, Orphne and Clymena, and the judges. It was a merry gathering, brought to a crescendo of astonished cries when Persephone entered the hall, her womb swollen with life. The king and queen embraced each guest in turn, accepting heartfelt congratulations and well wishes.

The mood turned somber when Aidoneus reminded all of the threats to his wife and their children. One by one he extracted Stygian oaths from them: each swore not to speak of Persephone's pregnancy to anyone outside the palace walls. Pasithea took her oath especially seriously. The celebration resumed and carried on into the night, until he gently dismissed their guests, reminding them that his wife needed her rest.

Hades and Persephone did not rest right away.

He made love to her on an island in Elysion, in a cove ringed with date palms, his himation spread beneath them on the soft sand. The moonlight shone silver on their skin as he reverently knelt with his forehead pressed to her shoulder and his hand cradling the roundness of her belly. They delighted in their rekindled connection, playing with shared sensations, each weaving through the other's thoughts and emotions. All the essence of the earth above and their realm below flowed between them, sprouting irises and sweet night jasmine beneath the trees. Memories of anniversaries past floated between them, all sweetened by the knowledge that next year, and every year thereafter would be very different.

They slept there until sunrise, then bathed in the warm shallows, and now made their way back to the entrance to Paradise, crisp sea air giving way to floral breezes.

When they reached the valley, they heard a single lyre string being tuned. Aidon called out ahead. "Orpheus!"

The tuning stopped. Eurydice ran through the grass toward them. "Aidon? We haven't seen you for an age! How are—"

Persephone grinned at Eurydice, a hand resting on her womb.

Eurydice stopped in her tracks, her mouth agape. She covered it and tears filled her eyes. "Orpheus! Quit that and come here, for fatessake! Oh, gods..." She walked to Persephone, swiping away tears. "I had no idea!"

"We kept it secret," Persephone said. "I couldn't even tell Aidoneus until I arrived. I returned below early, and have been in our private rooms since late summer to avoid being seen."

Eurydice couldn't stop smiling, her eyes aglow. She approached hesitantly. "May I...?"

"Of course," Persephone said.

Eurydice reached out a timid hand and touched her belly, then gasped. "The baby's moving."

"One of them is."

"Are they twins?!"

She nodded, and Eurydice threw her arms around her. Tears came to Persephone's eyes as she remembered the day she'd met Eurydice, of them digging for roots together, and all the dolorous time she spent avoiding Elysion after reuniting Eurydice with Orpheus. "Gods, it's good to see you again. Here, and happy."

"By my counting," Orpheus called out, "it's been two months, Aidoneus... and my queen. How are you?" He padded down the path, halting when his wife stepped back from Persephone. "Gods below..."

"Yes. And there will be two more gods below by midwinter," Aidoneus said with a broad smile, eyes flecked with gold. Orpheus shook his head and embraced his friend. Aidoneus returned it, patting his back.

"How did this come to pass?"

"When I came here in the spring to find him," Persephone said, blushing. "Just... after you went to see your wife."

"So," Eurydice tittered. "It seems Orpheus presaged the making of *all* your children."

Her husband's face fell and he glanced nervously from Aidoneus to Persephone.

"Oh gods," Eurydice said, quietly. "I shouldn't have said that."

Persephone put on a smile. "Our son has been reborn, and we will see him again," she said, voice wavering. "One day."

Aidoneus nodded. "I do not doubt that."

"I'm so sorry," Eurydice said.

Aidoneus chuckled. "Orpheus *was* at the rites, so it's the truth, no? You both bore witness in some way. Come, think nothing of it, Eurydice."

Orpheus cleared his throat. "I've been constructing a lyre of shell and hide. One tuned the way I wanted it."

"Oh?"

"I thought I might add an eighth and ninth string to this one. We'll see."

"Better you're busy with that than ruining my garden." Eurydice gave him a quick kiss and they laughed.

"Thank Fates, yes," he said.

They spoke of music and Eurydice's carefully tended herbs and the arrival of the twins until midday, then said their farewells. Persephone walked slowly up the hill and came to the white sycamore. She stopped beneath its bare branches, quiet. A breeze rolled through the grass. Aidoneus stood beside her, listening to a lone bird twitter somewhere in the field.

Persephone stared out at the sea. "Aidon…"

"He *will* return to us, sweet one." He placed his hand on her shoulder. "I'm certain of it."

Persephone wiped a tear away. "I still want to go to Crete, to bring our son home, hold him in my arms. *Just once.* He must be so small right now. So helpless. There's so much we're going to miss…"

"While Dionysos is there, he is safe from Olympus. I asked Hermes to look in on him when he can manage it." He rubbed her arm. "I want him to be with us, too. But this keeps him safe until he comes of age— until he becomes the god he was meant to be."

"I could go with my mother to Crete sometime— but… the Kouretes are a world apart from the tamed fields. They're gods of the wild places. Hidden. And Dionysos wouldn't know me. I'm not really his mother anymore."

"Yes, you are," he said firmly and kissed the top of her head. "He will come to us. He will rule over everything in this world we made. From horizon to horizon."

"We don't know if that's still who he is, my love. Iris said something to me, the day he was taken from us. She couldn't have known what was about to happen. But one thing she said stood out— that children rarely fulfill the destinies we imagine for them."

"We have millennia to find out…"

She glanced up at him, her lip quivering. "What did our baby look like? Surely Hecate told you."

"He has light eyes and dark hair." His brow furrowed and he rubbed his eyelids with thumb and forefinger. "Just as we saw when we first learned you were carrying him. He has a wine-colored birthmark on his left leg…"

She leaned into him. "Thank you for saving him."

"I should have told you. You should have been beside me, Persephone— had a hand in his rebirth."

"I know," she whispered. "But he is alive, because of you."

He tipped her chin and kissed her slowly. "And one day, he will reside with us, and our family will be whole again."

✴   ✴   ✴

Numberless years had passed since she'd last journeyed here.

Demeter had told the Eleusinians she and Triptolemus would be spending the winter in Phrygia, teaching mortals how to plant for two harvests each year instead of one. It was half true. She had called up her ancient chariot and its flying serpents for Triptolemus, and it had borne him and six *choenikes* of grain toward those ragged lands. Winter blew colder this year but no one on Olympus dared to question her about it.

While Triptolemus rode for Phrygia, she had discretely stepped into the ether. She stopped at one of the last barriers between the worlds, continuing her journey on foot. She felt the vitality of the earth disappear behind her, the currents deep within the rocks changing and reversing, alien and uncomfortable.

Demeter had been nearly nine months pregnant with Persephone her last time in Chthonia. It was more orderly, now. Back then, Iapetos the Piercer had ruled the lands below in blighted chaos, the Stygian nymphs and Lampades his playthings, the Phlegethon overflowing its banks, forever staining the Cocytus red.

It was into that fragmented world that Aidoneus had pulled her, just paces ahead of their pursuer and his long spear. They had tumbled out near the Phlegethon. She remembered the spark of Aidon's bronze sword against the Piercer's spear, him shouting at her to run as he beat back Iapetos again and again. The Titan had the advantage and fought with all the brutality they'd come to expect. She'd reached safety in Nyx's company, the great Goddess of Night pulling the Helm from her head and sending it to Aidon just in time. She could almost hear their voices ringing off these cavernous walls, Zeus's chariot rumbling through the earth, then the sickening wet slice as Aidon cut off the Piercer's head and kicked his limp body past the Phlegethon's edge, and silence at last while it fell the long way to the Pit.

Demeter shuddered and pulled her indigo himation over her head, hiding from lifeless stone and long-buried memories. She stepped again into the ether, traveling the last leagues to the shores of the Styx.

The scent of the Underworld was vaguely sweet— asphodel growing in clumps, stark clear water that echoed the blue skies she had left behind, and the tinge of decay on the near shore. Slow waves sloshed against bare pebbles and the air hung thick, unmoving. Colors were muted, like a foggy winter day just after sunset.

It had grown, too. The eternal golden poplar was still there, but instead of sheer cliffs with aeons of rubble at their feet, the stone dropped sharply to a set of stairs winding from the water's edge to the palace entrance, torchlight marking hallways carved through the rock. Iapetos had no palace when he ruled the Underworld. His home was on Othrys with the others, Chthonia little more than a berm between Tartarus and the verdant world.

The waves lapped more insistently at her feet, and a boat broke through the mist clinging to the water. Charon.

"Flaxen hair is a rarity here, even among the shades."

Demeter held forth a golden obol. "What does it matter if the dead see me? They will all drink from Forgetfulness."

The Boatman pocketed her coin. "There are more creatures here than just the dead, my lady. And idle gods and nymphs are terrible gossips, no?"

"No one ever said our worlds had nothing in common." She smiled and pulled her cloak up over her head, shielding her face. "How long has it been?"

"Since I saw you last? Forty thousand years, give or take a century."

Demeter climbed into the boat.

"How did you manage to hide her condition?" Charon said, pushing off.

"Once she started to show, I would mention to anyone with ears that she was headed to Locri and Sikelia that year for the festival of Koreia. Before that, I gave her enough ambrosia during the day so she would never be sick in front of the mortals. Nights were terrible, though. She had to drink so much of the stuff to keep up appearances while the sun was up that she couldn't have any after nightfall."

Charon raised an eyebrow. "The golden elixir of Samothrace. Couldn't bring enough by sea, eh?"

"I have the loyalty of the Kabieroi. When I ask after their ambrosia, they don't question it. But too many emissaries from their island would have raised Olympian suspicions."

"Iasion's late wife was one of them, no?"

"She was."

"And on through their bloodline until Eurydice took up her mother's art. Who harvests the honey of those sacred hives now that Eurydice resides in Elysion?"

"Eurymedon of the Kabieroi had many daughters, Eurydice's mother among them. All have that sacred knowledge, and all distrust the Olympians as much as we do."

"We," Charon scoffed. "To think... had you allied yourself with us all those decades ago—"

"Aidoneus and I *both* had our foolish parts to play in that." Demeter looked him in the eye. "And I know he has told you as much."

Charon nodded. "It's unfortunate, is all."

"It was *ananke*. And your lord would agree with me."

The Boatman smiled, the expression strange on his dour face. The mists over the river were tinged warm and pink with the coming dusk, and he headed away from the palace and through the Acheron Riverlands. Asphodel stalks were replaced by wavering ghostly grasses, then twisting black reeds. The air smelled acrid as Demeter stepped off the boat, aided by its frail oarsman. The rocks sounded hollow under her sandals, and their sharp edges pricked at the sides of her feet.

"Welcome to the Cocytus. I was told to leave you here. Her request."

"But..."

The Ferryman had already pushed off the shoreline, his boat lost in dark reeds and mist, bound for the other shore and the waiting souls. Indigo-clad shades stood by the small tributaries and bends of the Cocytus, staring deeply into the water, unmoving.

One of them turned toward her and Demeter held her breath. Persephone's slate-blue eyes peered at her from beneath a hood. "Hello, Mother."

"Kore!" Demeter whispered cautiously.

Persephone panted with each slow step. Her feet were wrapped in cloth beneath the straps of her sandals. Even the heavy pleated wool wasn't enough to hide her pregnancy. Demeter wrapped her arms around her daughter, both bending far forward to make room for Persephone's belly. "It's twins. Twin girls. That's why I was showing earlier than we predicted."

"Oh, look at you." Demeter covered her mouth with one hand, sniffling.

"I've been well, Mother. Aidon dotes on me relentlessly. Honestly, it's good to finally have some time to myself." She exhaled and stretched, drawing another slow breath. Her hood fell away, revealing simply plaited hair, a bit lopsided— her husband's handiwork. "I figured a direct path straight to our antechamber would be best. The fewest eyes."

"You poor sweet girl, all the way out here," Demeter said, tears clouding her vision. Persephone smiled wearily. "How could Aidoneus allow you out this far? I could have met *him* here instead."

"That's…" She shook her head. "The necessities for traveling through this realm *together* wouldn't be to your liking, I think. Besides— he's attending to our kingdom, and I desperately needed some air. This is the only place I can get it."

"Some air." Demeter scrunched her nose. "At the Cocytus of all places… it smells like a corpse-strewn battlefield."

"Many shades end up here because of the spears wielded in their name. I chose the River of Lamentation because you would have been recognized immediately had Charon left you at the entrance to the palace." Persephone took careful steps on the rocky ground. "The Stygian nymphs and Lampades don't come here."

"Do you doubt your people that much?"

"Nyx and her children, Hecate, those residing within the palace, I trust. But those outside our walls are as fallible as anyone above," she said flatly.

Demeter frowned. She expected such distrust from Aidoneus, but it pained her how dramatically the loss of Zagreus had altered Persephone. Then again, Demeter was hardly the naive creature she had been after being disgorged by Kronos.

Persephone mapped her disapproval. "Mother, I'm not taking any risks this time."

"This entire river is a risk. Just look at it," Demeter muttered. Shades stared unceasingly into the blood-red waters. "What are they doing?"

"Remembering. Redeeming themselves." She pointed at one shade, a king with arms covered in Thracian ink. "I sat upon my throne for the first time when he was judged. Before I could speak his language. He razed a city to the ground in Dacia, took his wife unwillingly on their wedding night, but spent the rest of his life making amends to her for it. He has only a score of years left here to contemplate his sins. Once he does, I'm certain Minos will send him to—"

She stopped abruptly and her eyes widened. Demeter looked at her quizzically. "Persephone?"

"No…"

"What's wrong?"

Persephone wailed incoherently, pulling up her skirts, bunching fabric as she went. "Not again, not again, Fates, please… no!"

"Kore." Demeter put a hand calmly on her shoulder. Persephone struggled to breathe, her fingers wet. Her mother's voice was low and peaceful. "Persephone… peace, my child."

"Not again..." She wept. A warm rivulet trickled down her thigh, soaking into the dark earth. "I can't lose them!"

"Daughter, this is normal. Calm yourself. It's time to get back home."

"What is this?!"

"Your water has broken. The babies are coming."

"But they're too early!"

"Oftentimes twins come early. Just as they did for Leto." She grasped Persephone's hand and squeezed it. "You'll be alright."

Cerberus bayed in the distance. Persephone squeezed back and exhaled long and low, then extended her hand toward the ground. She hissed. "I can't concentrate. I can't take us..."

"Let me."

"No! It's too precarious without the Key. You—" She winced and gulped for air.

"Breathe."

"I can't!"

"With me." Demeter grasped her daughter's temples and stared her in the eye. "Look at me. One, two..."

"Demeter?!"

They turned in unison, looking into the mists. Hermes touched down next to them, and Demeter stood between him and her daughter, cloak spread, teeth bared. "What are you doing here?!"

"What am *I*... I heard shouting on the silent Cocytus and came to see what it was. What are *you* doing..." Hermes stared past Demeter as Persephone doubled over. His eyes went as wide as the moon, his jaw slack. "Sparing Ones, preserve us..."

"No..." Persephone croaked, sucking in another breath of air. She wept, all their secrecy undone.

"My queen, let me help you," Hermes said. "Both of you. Please."

"Don't you touch either—" Demeter threw herself at Hermes, who caught her by the arm and advanced toward Persephone.

"Demeter, you can yell at me all you want, *after* I get you both to the palace!"

Persephone howled and Hermes grasped her around the waist, and all three were off, the hollow thrash of reeds left in their wake.

24.

"I DON'T WANT ANYONE FROM THAT SHIP LINGERING at the Styx for long."

"They set out for Tanis on the new moon," Rhadamanthys said. "No one is expecting them back at Mycenae for the season. Perhaps a year."

Aeacus leaned forward. "The Egyptians will find the wreckage before winter's over. They're trading with Ugarit again and pass by Dor. Perhaps if we wait…"

"It can't take all winter, Aeacus. If they aren't properly mourned or buried by the day after next, just give them coin and let them cross."

"The day after— My lord…" Minos cleared his throat. "If I may speak, it's not customary to give this much leeway to the unburied. You haven't done so since the Great Famine. They can certainly wait. The hymnist from Samothrace who crossed last year may have softened your heart to—"

"This has nothing to do with…" Aidoneus stopped himself. "My motives in this *are* personal, Minos. Considering the queen's condition, and the secrecy we must maintain, you'd agree the Styx should be free of stray eyes, ears, and tongues, no? It's safer if those souls are in Asphodel."

Minos nodded and started gathering his scrolls, and the judges prepared to leave. As the last papyrus rolled up, Aidon felt a sinking in his chest, his breath catching. Something was wrong. He stood up. A moment later, he saw Hermes on the balcony, two indigo cloaked figures with him.

"Leave us," he said quietly to Minos. Aidon looked at Rhadamanthys and Aeacus. "Go!"

The door shut loudly behind the judges as he jogged to the terrace. "Sweet one?"

"I can't…" She breathed shallowly, slowly counting in a whisper. "One… two… three…"

"What happened?"

"Hades, I'm sorry; I know I'm not supposed to be here," Hermes blurted out, "but I heard shouting from the Cocytus— and I usually don't go there, but I was curious and—"

"Her water already broke," Demeter said, her face dead calm as she pulled back her hood. "They're coming early."

"All of you, inside," Aidoneus said, glancing around the riverlands. "That means *you*, Hermes!" He reached Persephone and held her at the small of her back, moving slowly. "Let's get you upstairs…"

Hermes stepped back, then jumped when he stepped on a calloused foot. Hecate grinned, crow's feet crinkling the corners of her eyes, silver streaking her hair. "Good evening, God of Thieves."

"Hecate, I—"

"It seems the winged sandals have grown roots, Messenger. I trust you aren't called far afield tonight?"

Hermes swallowed. "I… I'll stay as long as I'm needed."

"Long enough to still wagging tongues."

"If you require an oath of silence about this, I'll swear it," he said, following them through the break in the tapestry.

"Oh, you'll bind yourself more adamantly than *that* before this is over," Hecate said with a sly grin, her footsteps soft behind him on the narrow staircase. When they reached the top, Aidoneus dashed ahead of Persephone to throw open the doors to their private rooms.

"Another pang is coming…" She breathed, trying to steady herself.

"Hecate!" Demeter called out. "Take her other arm. Where's the bedroom?"

"That way…"

Aidon strode after them through the antechamber.

"Acolyte." Hecate planted her bony hand in the center of his chest. "This time is for women."

"No! I need to—"

Hermes stopped next to him. "I heard the same with Penelopeia. Just trust them."

"Aidon…" Persephone breathed, exhaling long and low as Demeter led her toward the bedroom. "I'll be fine."

He nodded, grasping her hand one last time before they passed the door. "What can I do?"

"Fill this," Hecate said, thrusting the water thief into his hand, "and your obligations will be fulfilled and beyond. Nyx travels this way."

Aidon scowled. He wanted to be beside her, to feel what she felt, to calm her and quell all her fears. To hold her… to quell *his* fears… ease *his* disquiet at seeing her in pain. He shook his head. This was a time for women. It had always been this way— and no doubt that was why. He dropped the bulb into the catchment and the mists above darkened.

"We're here. Hypnos has to bring Pasithea the long way."

Nyx touched one foot to the cobblestones and floated toward him, Erebus draped around her like a weightless cloak, foggy wisps trailing behind her. "How far apart are they?"

"Are who?"

"The pangs of labor," Nyx said, motioning for Aidon to hand her the water.

"I don't know," he said, his mouth dry. "Demeter and Hecate are in there with her."

Nyx traversed the room and opened the door to the sound of Demeter steadily counting. It closed quickly behind her. Aidon sighed and began pacing the antechamber. The breathy clap of black wings greeted him, and Thanatos alighted on the terrace. Hermes rushed at him. "No, no, no, what are you doing here?! At a time like this—"

"I need to be close to those who can bind me," Thanatos finished, "lest the unthinkable happen." Thanatos set his sickle down at the base of a column and flopped down, draping one arm across the rest of a divan, his wings folding. "This time we're not taking any chances. That's the arrangement. The queen knows I'm here."

"So you're just going to lounge there and not lift a finger?" Hermes said, folding his arms. The hallway door lurched open behind them.

Thanatos stretched out his legs. "What would you have Death touch, Psychopompos?"

"You could take a moment to reassure your *friend* who's soon to be a—"

"Seething Tartarus…" Hypnos swore, running into the room with Pasithea a few steps behind. "An *Olympian*?! After everything we did to keep the gods above from finding out?"

Hermes sighed. "I was delivering a wayward ghost from Thessaly and heard your queen screaming in agony at the Cocytus. *My apologies.* Anyway, I'm staying. And… cousin, you look…" Hermes smiled at Pasithea, his eyes traversing her long chiton. "Lovely! Quite sun kissed, for being down here so long."

"Well, I spend most of my time in— never mind." She glanced at the antechamber full of men, all the women already secluded in the bedroom. Pasithea started to feel ill.

"Wife," Hypnos said. "You don't have to go in there."

"I do, though." She grew short of breath. "I-I can help."

"You can. But you don't *have* to." Hypnos placed a hand on her shoulder.

"Listen, I've helped… in my own stupid way… with Eileithyia so many times—"

"And you hated it. You don't have to be here *at all* if you don't want to, nor feel guilty for—"

"I only hated the blood, and afterbirth… the screams, and…" She grasped his hand. "Please. Husband, I'll be a pile of nerves if I can't be useful in some *small* way. Early on, I think…"

Hypnos smiled. "All right. Do what pleases you."

Pasithea approached the door nervously and cracked it open. Inside, Hecate propped Persephone up while Nyx placed a fresh cool cloth on her forehead. The queen winced, gulping air.

Demeter scowled at Pasithea. "Instead of standing there, can you find us more linen? And tell Hypnos and Hermes to move a divan in here. Fates knows why there isn't a birthing chair *somewhere* in this palace…"

"What a useless thing where no blood flows," Nyx scoffed.

"I-I will get their help in a moment," Pasithea said. She looked to Persephone. "How long has it been since your first pangs?"

Persephone looked away, thinking. "This morning."

"Kore, how could you put yourself at such risk?!" her mother blurted. "Going out to the—"

"I didn't know I was in early labor!" Persephone gritted her teeth.

"Does it hurt terribly?" Pasithea pursued.

"Yes!" Tears filled her eyes. "I feel like I'm just carrying on, that it shouldn't be this bad."

"Oh, it's real; carry on all you like. I mean, you're *giving birth*. Where do you feel the pain most?"

"My back… very sharply."

"It shouldn't be so intense yet…"

"How would *you* know?" Demeter said, her voice low.

"Because my elder sister is the Goddess of Childbirth?" Pasithea shrugged her shoulders without looking at Demeter. "It's twins, yes?"

Persephone nodded.

"May I?"

When the queen nodded again, Pasithea drew back the bedsheet, exposing Persephone's swollen belly. Pasithea felt the shape of her womb, cupping a hand underneath, running her fingers up the side, tracing, gently squeezing faint outlines… Persephone tilted her head forward. "What is it?"

"The first babe is a footling breech."

Demeter and Hecate exchanged a heavy glance. The white witch spoke low. "Are you certain?"

"Here," Pasithea said, pressing against Persephone's belly. "A leg cast down to the mouth of her womb, and there's the other, tucked up right here, and her arm, the head… with the other babe crowded across the top, though her head might still descend first…"

"*Kakodaimonos…*" Demeter cursed.

"What does that mean?!" Persephone was suddenly wild-eyed.

"Ah, well, at least we know why your water broke so early."

"Are my babies in danger?!" She gripped Pasithea's forearm.

"No!" Pasithea looked her in the eye, placing a hand over hers. "No. Relax. You *must* relax, Persephone. Breathe. Another one is coming; look at me. Shh…"

Persephone met her eyes, sweat beading on her forehead.

"Just listen to my voice… Breathe," Pasithea said slowly. "And now it's ending… You're going to be fine. Your babies are fine. This happens often with twins. It will be a little more difficult, but you will get through this."

She calmed in measures, relaxing under Pasithea's gentle voice. "W-What if I got on my hands and knees as Aphrodite did?"

"Only if its head's down and its face is up— to turn it and prevent pain when it crowns. But... the backside of your baby is coming first, my lady. Maybe the leg will tuck up, but even if it doesn't, you're going to be fine." Pasithea moved the curtain aside. "The flames... focus on those when each pang comes. You'll need to reserve your strength to push."

Persephone smiled up at her, sniffling. She grasped Pasithea's hand and squeezed it. "Thank you."

"Roll her on her right side," Pasithea said to Demeter. She grinned back at Persephone. "Please excuse me..."

Pasithea felt her heart beating fast and cleared the door, her breath shallow. She blinked in the bright torchlight. Aidoneus stood up. "Is she all right?"

"My lord, it may be a while."

"You're pale," Hypnos said. "You should sit down."

"What did you see?" Aidon's brow furrowed.

She nodded, darkness starting to descend on her vision, little stars flitting at corners. "Maybe I should. But..." Pasithea heard a whine in her ears. "They need the divan in there."

"Next to me, then," Thanatos scooted to one side, patting the seat when Pasithea drew back. "I won't bite, despite my reputation."

She settled into the cool cushions. Her skin felt clammy at first, and voices started to sound muddled. Hermes and Hypnos picked up the other divan and carried it through the doors. Her heart drummed in her ears.

"Are you well?" Thanatos leaned into her vision, his face blurred.

"The firstborn… it will be a footling breech," she heard herself say and heard the door shut as Hecate banished Hypnos and Hermes from the bedroom.

"She's a what?!" Aidoneus crowded her, his form a looming mass. "What's happening to Persephone? I can *feel* something's wrong. Tell me, you *must* tell me!"

"Give her space, Aidon!" Hypnos's voice arrived from leagues away. Her arm gave out. Pasithea slumped forward and felt Hypnos catch her from behind, his hand on her forehead.

Pasithea breathed. "I'm fine."

"Like Tartarus you are…"

"That's my wife in there!"

"And this is *my* wife out here," Hypnos said. "She needs to leave these rooms. She's done enough."

"She's the only one who knows—"

"No, she's not. Persephone is well-looked after. The birth might be more difficult, and she's in pain, but she is *well*. She's *far* stronger than you're giving her credit, Aidoneus, and she's being attended by three of the most powerful women in the cosmos!"

Aidoneus backed away, his shoulders dropping. "Forgive me, Pasithea."

She sat up. "My lord, of course. Fates, when Aphrodite was laboring, Ares almost tore the door off its hinges to get to her."

Aidon's mouth quirked into a grin. "Then I suppose this is all part of it, no?"

"It always is," she said. "You're doing fine. I think I need to lay down, though. Or vomit."

"I'll take you home," Hypnos said. He pointed at Hermes and Thanatos. "Until I return, you two *watch him*."

✵ ✵ ✵

Persephone exhaled again. The pain was stronger this time. She hissed, straining to take in another breath. There was only mounting pain, fighting for every breath, for hours upon hours. Night had long since fallen, and she half expected to see dawn flooding the Styx every time the door opened. She just wanted to sleep.

Every woman who has ever given birth does so alone. No matter who's in the room, or wipes your sweat, or changes the linens.

Though her mother was here with her, she knew now—Demeter had been right. She'd never felt so alone. Aidon was outside, but she hadn't spoken to him through their bond. Neither had he reached out to her, hadn't peppered her with questions, as she half expected him to do. He was respecting her time, and no doubt it would alarm him to know how much pain she was in. Judging from the yelling she'd heard outside the room when Pasithea had told him the birth would be difficult, he was already anxious enough.

The divan loomed at the far end of the room. A makeshift birthing chair. She wanted to run, from this room, from her body itself, to feel grass and soil under her bare feet at a full sprint...

"I need to walk."

"Are you sure?" Hecate said.

"My side hurts again."

Demeter helped pull her feet over the edge of the bed and she stood up shakily, took a turn around the hearth fire, and sat on the other side of the mattress. Her mother rubbed her shoulder. "Is it just labor pain, or—"

"I don't know. They're sharper. My hips feel like they're about to crack like an egg."

Demeter nodded. "Lie back. I need to check."

"Again?"

"Persephone, it's getting close. It's closer than you think."

She lay back and Demeter felt along with two fingers. Hecate leaned down to see.

"It's descending. She's open, but not nearly enough." Persephone looked away. It was as if the lower half of her were detached, belonged to someone else, except she was the one feeling all the pain. She reeled back from Demeter, kicking her leg and twisting to the side.

"Just stop touching me! I don't even want to *look* at anyone in this fucking room!" She pounded her fist into the mattress and sobbed anew. "I know you're trying to help, I don't mean it, but…"

"Kore, I said far worse to Cyane when I was preparing to push *you* out." Demeter smiled as she wiped her hand clean.

"Did *she* ever leave?"

"For a few long minutes to give me some air. Yes."

"Was there anyone else?"

Demeter tried not to make eye contact with Hecate. "No. No one else was there."

"There could have been." Hecate's face fell. "Demeter…"

Demeter shook her head. "None could be spared. It was the final day of the war."

"My child, I should have come once Typhoeus was buried, but we hadn't spoken for a month. Not since the pact. I was—"

"It was aeons ago, *hiereia*," she said, her eyes watery.

Persephone half-listened to their voices, watching the flames of the hearth as Pasithea had advised, but the pain was one rolling wave after another, battering her, pulling her under, each deeper than the last. She gritted her teeth and groaned until she thought they'd break.

"Persephone, I'm sorry. I know it's difficult, but you *must* rest."

"How can I rest?" She moaned as another spasm ended and tried to breathe deep as a new one began. "It's so much worse than before— than just minutes ago… Why…"

"Because within the hour," Nyx said, "you'll have to do the hardest part."

✲   ✲   ✲

He stood at the edge of the terrace, darkness stretching across the reaches of the Styx. Thanatos and Hypnos dozed on opposite sides of the divan. Light would touch the river before long. "Have you ever seen dawn here?"

"A few times," Hermes replied. He leaned against the palace wall, watching the water. "I don't often come to the riverside at dawn when I'm in your kingdom. It's… disorienting for me."

"You understand that we're not holding you captive, Hermes."

"I do. It's… it's good. It's given me some time to think."

"And I thank you for staying, as it's given me time to *not* think." Aidon heaved a pointed sigh. He could feel her, her pain radiating outward from their room in steady waves. "Was it ever like this for you?"

"When Penelopeia had Nomios, I arrived just in time to be shooed out of her home by her sisters. Of course, I did as they bade. She and I don't have the… connection you and your wife share."

"Even when I try not to, I can feel her." He exhaled hard. "The pain's grown worse. She's scared."

"Is it that strong between the two of you?" Aidoneus nodded in reply. Hermes raised his eyebrows and looked back out to the river. "Others who had a *hieros gamos*, this faded over time. Disappeared, eventually. My father and his wife… it lasted for a time but at great cost to them both."

"A great cost… For a time after we lost—" He stiffened, pain constricting his stomach, his lungs.

Aidon, I need you…

Cold washed over him. She hadn't said a word to him all night. "She's calling for me."

"My lord, you really ought to stay out here."

Please…

"It shouldn't be this way," Aidon muttered, traversing the room.

Husband, I can't do this alone…

"It should, especially now!" Hermes said. "She doesn't need the distraction. I know you're tempted, that you love her, but—"

"Damn what everyone says. She needs me there!" He shut his eyes, listening. *The pain, I can't… they're moving me to the divan.* "It's time."

"She is strong enough on her own!"

He glared at the Messenger. "We both have too many scars from the last time I was forced to leave her alone and in distress. I'm *not* doing it again!"

Hermes stood off, saying nothing. The commotion roused Hypnos, who rubbed his eyes. Ignoring his sleepy protests, Aidon loomed toward the door and pushed it open.

"Persephone?"

"Aidon, the baby… S-she's coming, but…"

"You can't be in here!" Demeter snapped.

"Demeter, she *called* to me to come in, her voice as clear as you can hear mine. And when she calls, I answer."

"Fine," she said, winding her hair into a chignon. "If you want to be useful, these sheets are all used, and we need more cushioning."

He unfurled his himation and draped it over the divan and onto the floor, folding it over.

"You know that will end up covered in afterbirth."

"I could not care less." He approached Persephone, a short sleeping chiton draped from her shoulders.

"I need to stand. Mother, everyone… out. Please. For a moment."

Nyx smiled faintly and ushered Hecate and Demeter through the door.

Aidoneus held Persephone through another wave of pain. Words eluded her, only a mewl escaping into his shoulder. He swayed with her and rubbed her back. When her shoulders slumped in relief, he tilted her chin up and looked in the eyes, wiping a tear away. Even amid all the pain, she had never looked so singularly beautiful to him. Aidon brushed his lips across hers and she returned his kiss, relaxing against his body, letting him hold and support her. She breathed out, long and low, and shut her eyes, her head tilting onto his chest.

"I wish I could take this pain away from you."

"You can't," she said softly. "This only ends one way."

"I know. Soon."

"What time is it?"

"Nearly dawn. You've been laboring here since yesterday afternoon."

"It feels longer." Her breath caught around another strong contraction. She tried to distract herself. "Did you sleep at all?"

"No."

"Can you kiss me again?"

"Of course." He smiled and hauled her up, her hand framing his face, her lips hungry for him as they rocked together. She sighed, content, then felt a drop and her legs nearly gave out under her. Aidon held her close and she gasped, crying out. "Sweet one?"

"Oh Fates!"

The door flew open and Demeter rushed back in. "Kore?"

"It feels like fire!"

"It's time," Hecate said. "Nyx is warding against trespassing eyes and ears. So when the pushing starts, you may howl as if moon above might hear."

Aidon pulled Persephone to the divan, sitting beside her. He looked up at Demeter, wide-eyed. "Tell me what to do."

"Shelter her hand in yours," Hecate said.

"No; let her lean back against your arm." Demeter threw her mantle off and girded her peplos under her legs and around her waist. She scoffed lightly as she crouched on the edges of Aidon's himation before Persephone. "Fates below, using a man for a birthing chair…"

Persephone winced a smile and sighed, shaking her head, then tensed. "Oh gods, it's coming…"

"You'll never feel worse pain in your *life*, but that pain will push the baby out," Demeter said. "Gather your strength. Now, Persephone!"

She squeezed her fingers between Aidon's so hard his knuckles turned white. "You can do this…"

Persephone groaned long and low, then gasped in air. "Nothing… nothing happened."

"It may not, the first few times." Demeter got up and grabbed an amphora, striding to the door. "Hermes! Fill this to the brim with hot water. You have that here, yes?"

"He knows where," Aidon called after her.

"The first few…" Persephone shook her head and tried to breathe. "The first few *pushes*… how many…"

"When my aunt birthed Artemis, the ninth hour marked her final push."

"Nine hours?!"

"Don't frighten her, Hecate, you *know* Hera purposefully delayed Leto's twins." Demeter met Hermes at the door and poured the amphora of warm water into a basin.

"All the more reason to keep our children safe from the Olympians," Aidoneus said. He glared at Hermes, who was loitering by the door. "Shut it now!"

"Push, Persephone."

Her face reddened and she bore down hard, then released. The next time, she collapsed against Aidoneus's shoulder, breathing lightly. Demeter handed him a cloth and he wiped her brow. "I can't... Our babies... If anything happens, I'm sorry. What the Fates said to you—"

"Persephone, stop; they're well. Here," he whispered back. He took her hand and placed it on her belly. "You hear their hearts? They'll come."

"I see a heel," Demeter said from below. "Pasithea was right. But you can do this. I've delivered—" She stopped herself and thinned her lips. "When Leuce had her child, it was a breech birth."

Persephone swallowed. Why was the birth of her twins so complicated, so extraordinarily painful? Was this punishment? Were the Fates conspiring to exact vengeance for Minthe, in the very room where she had reduced the nymph to ash? "I can't do this..."

"Just get through the next one," Aidon whispered. Persephone sat up and breathed, feeling the world contracting with her, and bore down, her cry filling the room.

"Almost!" Demeter said. "But this angle is impossible..."

"What more can I hope to do?" She sobbed, her body wracked and aching, trying to steer through and focus.

"Rise and the earth will pull them down," Hecate said. "If you let it."

"Then let's ease their way." Aidoneus kept a steadying hand on her back as he stepped onto the divan and crouched behind Persephone. He grasped her under her arms. Sweat dotted her forehead, and Hecate wiped it away with a warm cloth. Aidon leaned close to her ear. "Sweet one..."

She turned to him, her breath shallow, her eyes puffy.

"My love," he said, "you are the strongest person I've ever known, even when you feel weak. Now breathe. With me."

She grimaced through the first breath, but matched him and gathered herself by the second. "It's coming again."

Aidoneus hauled her up from beneath her arms until she squatted, supported solely by him. "*Push!*"

She clenched her teeth and veins in her neck and forehead stood prominent. Her arms shook in his hands, but he braced himself. Persephone shouted, determined.

"A foot! Hecate, help me! Aidon, hold her fast!" Demeter gently worked the other foot from the mouth of her womb, then the arms, and finally eased the head free. Persephone felt a great release and slumped forward, eyes closed, finally able to draw a full breath.

"Set me down…" she rasped.

Aidon lowered her carefully to the divan, and both breathed hard and stared at the tiny being in Demeter's arms. It lay limp, pale arms dangling. Aidon felt his heart stop. He clutched Persephone's hand, the room silent.

Demeter rubbed the baby's back. There was a cough, then a watery cry, then another. Demeter carried her to the hearth and Hecate set to work, tying off the cord and gently cleaning the afterbirth with a warm cloth. She wailed with a small strong voice, her tiny legs kicking, wisps of dark hair framing her scrunched face.

"Melinoe," Aidoneus said, his voice hitching.

"She's crowning," Demeter said, a happy tear slipping down her cheek. "The other one turned the right way— I can see her head. Daughter, you're almost there."

Aidoneus knelt behind her and she leaned into him and bore down once, and rested. She took five even breaths before she felt it begin and pushed with all her might. Persephone cried out and felt the head. She gasped, hearing Demeter's voice distantly, and rocked forward as her mother lifted the child to see her, pale hair nearly invisible, mouth open and wailing. Persephone slumped back happily onto Aidon's chest. "It's Makaria."

He listened to the voices of his children, tiny squalls ringing through the room, and watched Hecate clean and tend to Makaria now that Melinoe was swaddled.

"I'll take care of the rest." Demeter fetched the basin and sponged Persephone's legs. "Just look at your beautiful children. You'll need to push again, lighter this time." Persephone felt a few brief pangs, barely noticed amidst the bustle in the room and calm, euphoric warmth enveloping her. Her mother carried the basin of afterbirth away, forearms stained red, and dropped its contents into the cleansing Phlegethon flames of the hearth. Aidon's himation followed, dimming the light as blood smoldered and sputtered, burning away.

Aidoneus rose first, his heart pounding, and leaned his wife against him as they walked to the bed. Persephone winced as he tucked her in and tended to her, pinning up her hair where it had come loose. As he lay her head back on the piled pillows, she gave him an exhausted smile.

"Are you ready to meet them?" Hecate carried Melinoe to Persephone first and laid the swaddled infant next to her. "Best to feed them one at a time."

"Where is your ambrosia?" Demeter called out, scanning the room. She held Makaria in one arm, the babe fussing enthusiastically.

"The *pyxis* by the door," Aidon barked back from his seat on the floor beside the bed. "Why?"

"Tradition." Demeter brought Aidoneus his daughter and handed him the jar. "Among the gods, the father gives a child her first taste of ambrosia, alongside their mother's milk."

He nodded and dabbed his finger in the ambrosia. Melinoe stirred and Persephone pulled the pin out of her chiton, then held her breast. He coated her nipple in its thick sweetness and she drew Melinoe closer. The babe started pulling her lips in to suck at her mother's nipple, and Persephone awkwardly gave its fullness to her daughter. "Am I doing it right?"

Hecate smiled. "You'll learn together. It will feel as natural as walking, soon enough."

Demeter handed Makaria to Aidoneus, and she wiggled an arm loose from the swaddle. He reached to tuck it back in, but she caught his finger, pulling at it with her fist, a perfect little hand clutching his smallest digit, refusing to let go. Persephone watched from the bed, relaxing on her side, floating and blissful as Melinoe drank her first meal. "Aidon, you're a father."

A tear rolled down his face. He tipped his head on the edge of the mattress and breathed steadily, Makaria wriggling in his arms. Melinoe unlatched and he handed Persephone their youngest, then gilded her other nipple with ambrosia. Once Makaria was settled at her mother's breast, he took Melinoe and held her, watching her. She yawned, her eyes closed, and her face softened as she fell into an exhausted sleep. "Good morning, little one. You had me and your mother worried for a moment."

"It won't be the last time…" Hecate said. Her brow wrinkled before she masked it with a smile.

Persephone lifted her breast from Makaria's mouth as the baby drifted to sleep, quiet and content. She gathered the infant and placed her alongside her sister in the woolen basket Aidoneus had fashioned for the middle of their bed. Persephone pinned up her peplos and pulled a blanket over her, her teeth chattering. Aidoneus retrieved his cleansed himation from the hearth and shook it out, then tucked its warm folds around his wife and children. His family.

A knock sounded at the door, and the hinges creaked. Hypnos peered in. "I didn't want to enter during all the commotion. From the sound of it..."

"Is Pasithea with you?" Persephone smiled warmly.

"She wishes to come in if you'll have her."

"Of course," Persephone said. "Tell Hermes and your brother they're welcome too."

Dawn flooded through the doorway, outstripping the hearth fire, the antechamber outside filled with light from the Styx. Thanatos cautiously stepped into the room, and Hermes darted around Nyx's sons, his hand over his mouth as he stared at the twin girls. "They're beautiful."

Pasithea's eyes flitted around the room and came to rest on the twins. "I'm so sorry you had to learn how difficult it would be from *me*, of all women."

"No," Persephone said. "I don't know what I would have done if you hadn't helped me relax."

"Well, my lady, if you don't mind," she tittered, "I don't much care to do so again."

"I know what you mean." She leaned around. "Thanatos, please. You can come in."

"If it's all the same, my queen, I think I'll stay outside."

"There's no danger," Persephone insisted but was caught by Hecate's worried face.

"None from within." She looked pointedly upward.

Persephone darkened. "What are we to do? How can I possibly keep them safe— keep their lives a secret— when I have to go above in only three months?"

Aidon shook his head. "I don't know."

Demeter exhaled. "This first year will be difficult. It will be awful for you, Persephone, but you can return here in an instant. For a time, you must exist in both worlds."

"Deme," Aidoneus said, "I will call upon every god of every wellspring and cavern, the fields of Enna, every vassal I have in the world above, to assist you in this year's planting and harvest. I swear it."

"We'll never be able to take our daughters above, will we?" Persephone said. "They'll never know their… their brother."

"There may be ways and places," Thanatos said from the door. "Once they're grown. But until then, what's to keep the tongues of the *Dodekatheon* from wagging?"

Demeter seethed. "I would *never* betray—"

"I didn't mean *you*," Thanatos said, his eyes narrowing at Hermes.

"Oh, I wager I won't be able to either," Hermes said, "not after today."

Hecate grinned and folded her arms. "The Styx will witness your oath to conceal all you know?"

"No."

Hypnos's wings tensed, ready to give chase if the God of Thieves were to fly for Olympus and herald Melinoe and Makaria's birth. But the Messenger merely nodded and produced a half pomegranate from the folds of his *chlamys*, its ruby seeds glimmering in the morning light. All eyes were trained on it. It was from the entrance to Elysion— the fruit of the Underworld.

"Hermes, wait…" Persephone said.

He plucked a single seed. "I had something more binding in mind."

"Messenger—"

"I know too much, Hecate. About the twins, about Dionysos. I've seen enough, this year and for so many years past. Too many broken oaths, too much needless cruelty."

"Hermes." Aidoneus stood and walked quickly toward him. "If you wish to prove your fealty, you *do not* have to do this. The bond is irreversible!"

"I know I don't have to, my lord." Hermes smiled, stopping him in his tracks. He bowed to Hades and Persephone and placed the single seed on his tongue, then swallowed it whole. "But I want to."

This tale continues in THE INEFFABLE SEEDS.

Acknowledgements

It's been six years to the day since I published DESTROYER OF LIGHT. And much has happened professionally and personally in that time, bringing with it all life's highs and lows. For those who kept the fire burning since I first wrote RECEIVER OF MANY, who sent me notes, emails, and sent cards and letters of encouragement as I wrote THE GOOD COUNSELOR, I have you to thank for this novel. Without you, we wouldn't be making this trip back to Chthonia.

To my author and artist friends who have loved and mentored me through this whole process: Addison, Asphodelon, Elaine, Eris, Kat, Linda, Li, M.M., Molly, and so many others in our community, I thank you from the bottom of my heart for your constancy, your support, your encouragement through the years. You remind me why I do this.

My eternal gratitude to Juliana Delsante who provided Ancient Greek translations for select words and phrases throughout THE GOOD COUNSELOR and patiently went back and forth with me about words and the exact meaning I was trying to convey.

To Ben and Ivy for your love and friendship and for being there for me through all of this, whether you're near or far. And to Elizabeth for editing the second round and being there with me through many rounds of laughter and tears.

To Morgan, who designs my beautiful, thoroughly lickable covers, and who is an even better friend. And of course, I want to thank my husband Robert who tirelessly edited and proofed this novel as our boy grew from a bump to an infant to a toddler to a child who draws books of his own. And finally, I want to thank William, who I love more than all the world and everything in it.

About the Author

Rachel Alexander has been a resident of California all her life and finished her first novel, a work of speculative fiction at age 16. She wrote the highly-acclaimed novels RECEIVER OF MANY in 2015, and DESTROYER OF LIGHT in 2016. When not writing, Rachel can be found sewing corsets, overstocking her spice cabinet, and petting chickens. She lives in the San Francisco Bay Area with her wonderful husband/editor and their son.